The Scheme of Things

Brian Hennigan was born and raised in
Scotland, although his business career spans
many industries and countries. His fiction
and drama have been broadcast on BBC Radio
Four and BBC Radio Scotland, and his first
novel, *Patrick Robertson – A Tale of Adventure*,
was published by Jonathan Cape and is
currently being adapted for film with David
Mackenzie as Director.

The Scheme of Things

Brian Hennigan

First published in Great Britain in 2005 by Polygon,
an imprint of Birlinn Ltd

West Newington House
10 Newington Road
Edinburgh
EH9 1QS

www.birlinn.co.uk

The publishers gratefully acknowledge subsidy from

towards the publication of this volume

British Library Cataloguing-in-Publication Data
A catalogue record for this book is available on request from the British
Library

Design by Peter Dyer

Typeset by Palimpsest Book Production, Polmont, Stirlingshire
Printed and bound by Thomson Litho, East Kilbride, Scotland.

for Margaret Hennigan

one

When Pommy Freiberg closed his eyes the world turned more slowly on its axis. Each morning the Chief Executive Officer of Belston Corporation enjoyed the jolt of speed as he woke and focused on the large ceiling-mounted clock above his bed. When up and about, Pommy achieved the same pleasant feeling of acceleration by shutting his eyes for short periods, often while subordinates addressed him. This unnerved his employees, particularly as he often changed the direction of his gaze while his eyes were shut. Pommy's senior staff called this "the switcheroo". Pommy knew this because he bugged their offices, bathrooms and company cars.

There was a vibration in his trouser pocket and Pommy leaned forward, switching off the silent timer he used to gauge the passage of meetings. He had considered using a normal, beeping stopwatch but chose instead to generate the reputation that Pommy Freiberg was a man who could measure ten minutes with digital precision in his head.

Eyes still closed, Pommy made out the oh-so-measured tones of Richard Weathervane, rigorously tanned London head of Omniview Consultants.

'As we all know, companies develop organic-like processes for dealing with their operations. Many of these processes are unarticulated and unspecified. They are part of the collective corporate management brain mechanism, if you will.'

Pommy used such presentations as opportunities to hamster sleep. Good managers always hamster sleep when they can. A rested mind was so much less prone to distraction.

Pommy readied his timer for re-activation, then, on an

internal count of three, he opened his eyes. Whoosh! Weathervane stood directly ahead, lean tennis-playing hands wide apart in mid-sentence. Along the length of the table a whirr of adjustments took place as both management teams took on board Pommy's emergence from hibernation. Papers were pushed, pens uncapped, intelligent faces pulled, as everyone tried to look mission-minded. 'I see,' announced Pommy, closing his eyes again as the consultants got ready for the final push. Click.

Every two years Belston Corporation made a point of calling in the consultants. This was not because Pommy appreciated their advice.

'Who the fuck wants an "independent view"?' he had raged on the way to the Omniview presentation. 'What we need is more "dependent" views, from people who are in here, doing the fucking business. Not some fucking jargoneer whose main concern is his own company's invoice.'

Nick Durning had scribbled this down in the notepad he kept for Pommy's words. One of Nick's duties was to capture such wisdom so that it might be formalised and made part of the management practice of the whole Belston Corporation, from the depleting rainforests of Brazil to the deepening mines of Nigeria and the privatised steelworks of Poland. Belston Corporation. Mostly unknown outside those in the know and largely ignored by those in it, left to "plod along and deliver the fucking basics". Which is exactly how Pommy liked it. Don't want the fucking public eye. Public eye leads to nothing but lack of focus. Need to keep fucking eye on the things that mattered. Pommy smirked at the public consumption of all the facts and figures about each successive "new" industry – and he had seen so many such industries. Because Pommy knew that every such industry could always be boiled down to something tangible, hard and preferably rare.

'Take fucking tantalum,' as Pommy was fond of pointing out. All those "e-mail-female fuckers" like nothing better than to slope around with their "hand-wank hard-drives" telling everyone about what's on the horizon. 'What matters is what you can't see – not what you and every other fucker can!' Pommy would snap. Tantalum is one such significantly invisible material. Essential for the mobile technology sector, tantalum – sourced from the ore columbite-tantalite – is found in 'Belston's backyard': West Africa. Pommy's supply-chain domination of the mineral product meant that 'we grow with the neo-fuckers but without the fucking pain of the public eye.' The cost of fostering ongoing insurrection in various emergent African democracies was a cross made of balsa as far as Pommy's Calvary was concerned, rendered almost weightless by his PR-atheism.

Pommy had, though, caved in on consultants, a strategic concession he had felt compelled to offer. This did not stop him hating every one of the parasitic fuckers.

'It stands to reason,' Pommy continued as he and Durning marched, he more regularly than the younger man, down the corridor, 'Whoever is paying your wage bill is the person you care most about. Don't give me all that fucking nonsense about "customer needs". When you look at your pay slip you don't think about "customer fucking needs". You think about your fucking employer.'

Pommy's hatred of consultants did not stop him getting them in, though. Pommy remembered that the first time he ever heard the word "consultant" was as part of the phrase "beauty consultant". This was how he saw them still.

'Beauty consultants for the fucking City Boys,' he muttered, waiting for Durning to catch him up. The older man glanced down at Durning's feet, averting his gaze as he caught the air of resentment from his junior companion. Good man, Pommy thought, never mentions the leg. Others would. Leg, leg, leg all day. Not Durning. Solid, despite leg.

'Fucking consultants. Beauty consultants for the City Boys'.

They were off again, Nick taking that little bit longer to reach "Raging Speed".

3

'Get them in now and then. Short, back and fucking sides. Everything fine. No questions asked.'

Whenever the consultants appeared, Pommy made sure that one or two of the City Boys were in on it; let the word get around. Made sure they understood the basis of having consultants in though – "precautionary maintenance" – "always looking for extra value" – that sort of thing.

'Let them see we're being . . .' and here he swallowed, '. . . pro-active in our approach.'

Pommy despised the word and the culture that made it.

'"Pro-active"! What exactly does than mean? Tell me,' he had enquired of one of his first-ever consultants, a man who had used the word so often that Pommy suspected that he was on a royalty deal.

'What is the difference between me "actively" wanting to go to the toilet, and me "pro-actively" wanting to go to the toilet? Do I dance about a bit more? Make a map to where the toilet is? Is that it?'

Yet Pommy managed to contain his dislike of this and other terms when the situation demanded.

'Best to use one or two new words when you're dealing with City Boys. That way they know you're doing your fucking bit.'

Durning nodded, writing.

'No point standing out. City Boys don't like to see people dragging . . . slowing things up. Like to know you're part of the modern fucking civilised world.'

Concessions had to be made. Let them know you're in touch. Get the consultants in every now and then. Show the world that you're not complacent. Show the world you're not afraid of being examined. Have them write a report or something. Make sure everyone hears about the "radical shake-up of fundamental business". Watch share price shift about a bit. Get on with the real job.

Need to beware of own people "going native" though. That had happened too. Over the years a couple of Pommy's people had gone native with the consultants, rendering themselves useless in the process.

'Like having someone from fucking Mars on the team,' Pommy bellowed, blasting through the double doors of the Board Room. Durning caught one door with his right foot, toeing the heavy mahogany sheet back with muscular ease. The waiting group of senior managers and consultants turned in time to catch this precision flip. One of them went 'Ooh!'.

'Ready?' Pommy asked, sitting down at the end of the long oak table. As the assembled group tidied themselves into position, Pommy swivelled round in his chair and beckoned to Nick, now standing, notepad ready, by the door.

'Right, who is talking?' Pommy asked.

'Omniview Consulting. Richard Weathervane,' Durning answered, 'You screened them personally.'

Pommy shook his head and shrugged, 'Fine.'

Durning turned to leave and with the briefest scowl Pommy told him to wait. Against the now silent room, Pommy considered Durning for a moment. Good man. Need more in the same mould. Must get him out there and active a bit fucking more. Yes. Got a particular task in mind for Durning. Tell him later.

Then the Chairman, Chief Executive and Managing Director of the megalithic Belston Corporation swung back to the waiting group, leaving Durning to head for the double doors with no hint of rebuff.

'Let's go,' Pommy commanded, staring down the middle of the table, invisibly switching his timer on. Richard Weathervane stood up, Pommy closed his eyes and the world slowed down.

For two hours Pommy slumped lifelessly in his seat as – one by dreary one – the consultants took their turn at the screen. All knew that he was not sleeping. Every now and then a question would be barked out, interrupting their carefully honed business-school flow.

Pommy winced at the sound of someone spilling coffee on

the carpet. A pause descended and moves were made to clean up. 'Leave it. Keep going,' Pommy commanded.

Carpets can be replaced, time can't be. Cheaper to keep going. Not that the whole consultancy exercise wasn't costing enough already. Still, less expensive than the alternative. Alternative? City Boys ask you to get the consultants in. And "ask" means "tell". City Boys always looking to catch you out; to make some suggestion you hadn't thought of. Most such dumb ideas Pommy could work with, but not the fucking consultants. When the City Boys want the consultants in, you're in real trouble. Double-screw situation. First, you have to pay for the consultants. Second, they aren't really working for you. City Boys make sure that they get to hear directly. Consultant's wet dream. Fucking MBA chumps get the feeling of power and before you know it you're part of the problem.

Pommy had been in such situations early on. The first time – a troubled insurance company, pre-Belston – Pommy had watched the cars arrive at 8 a.m. on the Monday, having never seen, let alone met a consultant before. Unknown species back then. Pommy did the instinctive thing – panicked. When his turn came to "have a word" with the consultants he was defensive, evasive, difficult . . . an immature arsehole. Might as well have painted a fucking target on my forehead. They could smell fear like sharks. Show fear for your job and they'd fucking have you.

Pommy had been out as soon as the report was in. Nevertheless he had learned.

'Best to learn a lot at the fucking start of the struggle,' he had explained to Durning one day.

Several years later, Pommy was wiser. The carpet manufacturer of which Pommy was Sales Director, one of many, many Belston subsidiaries, had been discovered to have irregularities in the books.

'Fucking worst place for them. If you're going to have irregularities make sure they don't appear in the fucking books.'

The consultants duly arrived. Pommy was Mr Hospitable.

Showed them around, charming. Opened all the files, a friendly Labrador. Meanwhile advised Marketing Director not to co-operate. Told him that consultants would use all information received against him. Best to say nothing. Three months later Pommy was Sales AND Marketing Director.

'They can smell fear; I fucking swear it.'

For this reason Pommy always insisted on one particular piece of information from whichever consultants Belston was using. Not that he cared which. Pommy couldn't even recall how this Omniview lot had been selected.

'All the fucking same, like newsagents. Might stack the news-papers on the shelves in a different way. End of the day, no one cares. As long as the City Boys see you going into the newsagents, they don't care which one.'

The information Pommy insisted on was the names of those five people in the company who seemed most fearful for their jobs, with the very most fearful at the top of the list. Once the consultants' report was in, and word of its arrival rocketed around the company with a speed Pommy knew to be unrivalled by any formal means of communication, there wasn't much need to do anything else. Simply call in the Fearful Five one by one and see what they had to say. Having them in Pommy's office with the report sitting unopened on the desk was usually enough. Most offered up some sins and asked for a move, either out or down.

'Bit of self-maintenance,' Pommy called it, 'Popular in fuck-ing China. Get people to confess things without asking. Doesn't matter about details. Or truth. Fucking good incentive for everyone else.'

Good for City Boys too. They always liked to see people being made to walk the plank. Nothing better than a good bit of walking the plank. Showed things were happening. That they were being pro-active.

Pommy shivered in his seat at the horrible word. He sat forward and opened his eyes. Everyone in the room was look-ing at him. Pommy noticed the phrase "Strategic Conclusion" on the screen. He stood up and began his well-worn conclusion.

'Well, Ladies and Gentlemen, I can't say that all of that was entirely comfortable listening. Indeed some of it was downright disturbing.'

Always better to let them think that they had been somehow provocative.

'It's vitally important that we know these things though . . .,' pausing picture-perfect next to the neatly bound report, picking it up ponderously, as if actually weighing it.

'You will appreciate that there is a lot that we need to take on board here . . .'

Then Pommy started, as he noticed the bulky sight of Andrew Midgely standing next to the light switch. How long had he been there? Didn't even hear the fucking door.

'So . . . ' Pommy continued, as he began a sleek saunter towards his Company Secretary. Midgely raising his stubby arm as if in Roman salutation.

'So, we will need a little time to give adequate thought to your findings, before progressing to the next stage.'

Pommy felt the air change as the consultants heard their favourite phrase: "the next stage". Fucking leeches, he thought. Happy nevertheless that everyone was distracted, Pommy plucked a folded piece of paper – little more than a stamp really – from Midgely's paw-like palm.

As self-congratulations and talk of "hard work ahead" flowed along the table, Pommy had time to flash open the tiny note. In Midgely's unjoined, lower-case script was one word: *argentina*.

two

Nick Durning sat down at his desk, pleased with who he was. Nick Durning, Business Analysis Director for the mighty Belston Corporation. More importantly, he knew he was a Pommy Freiberg favourite, one of the few known trustees of Pommy's wishes, even if Pommy himself had never said any such thing. But other people knew too. Where Nick walked, Pommy's blessing walked with him, like a rabid dog on a lead.

Rubbing his left leg, Nick began flicking through the notes he had taken that morning. Pommy hated electronic devices. 'Get it on paper. Black and fucking white.' Blue and white if need be, but on paper. Nick transcribed the notes in fifteen minutes and then they were on their way to the next stage in the ceaseless process of integrating every gesture, phrase or tick of Pommy Freiberg's into the management systems of the enormous, the legendary, the still there and still expanding Belston Corporation.

Belston Corporation without a "the". There was no "the". Absolutely there was no "the". Pommy said so.

'We're not fucking "a" this or fucking "the" anything. We are fucking Belston Corporation.'

Nick had witnessed this volley being launched at innumerable presentations. If the presenter was a supplier, that was the end of it.

'Can't get our fucking name right, might as well fuck off.'

If the presenter were an insider, then all there would wince at the sight of a career walking into a propeller blade.

The use of "the" had given Nick his first toehold. Sitting in a presentation to new employees, Nick had listened as a middle-management personnel official welcomed them to "the Belston Corporation".

'Isn't it just, "Belston Corporation"?' Nick had asked.

'Fucking right it is,' a voice thundered from the back of the room and, as the middle-management personnel official contemplated a position elsewhere, Nick felt the glow of approval warming the back of his neck.

Belston Corporation: the business conglomerate on which the sun never set. On six continents, in 118 countries, you could walk into a Belston office somewhere, as Pommy often did unannounced. Nick had been there, on occasion, accompanying Pommy. Nick would not need to see the end of the world when it came; he had seen it already on the faces in the offices that Pommy had walked into.

Belston Corporation was a far-from-extinct dinosaur, a mammoth criss-crossing of industries and technologies which had defied so many harbingers of doom and "the end is nigh" Square Mile soothsayers that even they had stopped wondering about it. Property development, tin extraction, dye manufacture, franchise ownership (automotive mostly, and mostly on the Indian subcontinent), petrochemical distribution, agrochemical production, flooring manufacture, aerospace parts.

'What do we make?' Pommy would ask at any of the intake class of trainees which he always, always found time for, 'What do we make? Fucking profit. That's what we make. Don't fucking forget it.'

While others referred to it as a "last of its kind" or an "institutional anachronism", Pommy Freiberg knew exactly what it was; one of the few existing businesses that showed how one man could make all the difference. That man was him. Pommy knew that he was that decisive rarity, a commanding force within a public company that drove it through the application of sheer willpower.

In five years of saying the right thing – and that was never "yes" – Nick had become part of Belston's inner process, reporting directly to Pommy. This latest task, the literary distillation of his leader's ways and means of doing things, was one of Nick's proudest responsibilities, giving him noise-free reception of Pommy's ruminations.

Nick's capturing of these original thoughts was only the first part of the process; the unambiguous meaning, raw and straight. In authorising what was ultimately a highly diluted version of his thoughts, Pommy acknowledged that the raw truth would prove too strong for most. After Nick there was a strategic framing of the thoughts by a couple of business academics, and then a copywriter would render them nicely. After which it was back to Pommy for red-penning before the process repeated.

Looking up from his notes, Nick caught a side view of Andrew Midgely wafting past his door. This made Nick pause. Midgely was an unearthly figure, never ordinarily abroad in the daylight corridors, a confidential whisperer in Pommy's ear, his title of Company Secretary having long ago been changed, internally, to "Company Secretive". Although his fat, heaving frame seemed unsuited to the task, whenever issues of devilish importance appeared, Midgely would emerge from the corporate shadows bearing small, handwritten notes that Pommy would take, read, and rip up. Even seeing Midgely on the move was enough to cause speculation. The possibility that he might just be going to the bathroom seemed altogether preposterous. Nick waited for his unease to pass, then returned to the notes in front of him.

Yes! The message had come from Jenny, Pommy's secretary. 'Mr Freiberg has asked that you sort out Two Lips.' Nick thrust his way along the corridor. Two Lips had been rumbling on for months. If Pommy thought that Nick was up to sorting out Two Lips, then this was of significance. Nick would be handling, not just analysing. He would be involved. Yes!

Considering, commenting, suggesting and revising. That was how Nick had become Business Analysis Director, all the time knowing that this was not business itself. Business itself meant doing it. Business after all, is not a verb. "Do" is the verb of business. Everything else is words. Nick had done the words but not the doing. He was not in business yet. Two Lips would put him in business.

Pivoting round another desk, Nick glanced up at the idle, stationary figures around him, at their desks, by the machines, talking, standing. None of them moving, not like him.

Nick was right that no one was moving like him. The way he was moving was part of the reason no one else was moving. They were all watching, using the reflections from screens, or glass partitions; watching after he'd passed, or before he caught their eyes.

Few things amused the troops more than Nick's galloping slalom through their desks. 'Scoot! Scoot! Scoot!' the mocking whispers went, as Nick launched himself after whatever corporate stick Pommy had just flung. And though no one said it, they were all glad about the limp. 'Serves him right the ambitious little shit', the unmistakable tracer fire his every journey drew. If pressed, some few might indeed have been of the opinion that his leg had shrunk over time in response to his ceaseless crawling endeavour.

Nick himself had had occasional doubts that he was popular. But that was as far as it went. He did not know, for instance, that people imitated his lengthy speech patterns, mouthed 'Good Boy' as he approached. Nick did not know that he was a source of bitter amusement.

The instance when Nick had got home from work one night to discover that – for what must have been most of the day – he had been wearing a yellow Post-it sticker on the back of his jacket, with the description, "Scooter!" laser-printed on it had, at the time, troubled him. An investigation of the company's stationery supplier's catalogue had confirmed that this was not one of the numerous witty pre-printed Post-its available. Somebody had made this one especially, crafting it with care to ensure that the word fitted the pad perfectly. The completion of the design and printing element followed by the attachment to his suit of the resulting sticker must have been observed, if not plotted, by many rather than one.

Scooter. Standing in the all-seeing fluorescence of his kitchen, dabbing at the residue of stickiness left in the dark night blue of the jacket's back, Nick could only think of a puppet character from a children's' television show, and he knew that he looked nothing like that. It was all part of office life, Nick supposed, and tried to give it no more thought.

16th, 17th, 18th floor.

'All I am saying is that if, you know, we keep building taller and taller places to live and work in, then it stand to reason that one day human beings will grow, or evolve wings. It's obvious.'

Nick tried not to hear the debate between two clerks about the potential for human flight. Instead he thought about Two Lips. He had the file in his briefcase as back-up.

'Will we need runways, or just be able to take off, you know, like bumble bees?'

The lift doors opened and Nick was out.

'Henrietta Kilpatrick?'

'Third door on the left.'

Nice and curt, Nick thought. Some of his colleagues seemed to prefer chatting to conveying information. Nodding gratitude, Nick counted his way along the corridor. One, two . . . .

'Do you hear me? I think you don't. I think that maybe there must be something wrong with this connection. Hello? Yes, hello? You can hear me? I don't think you can. I don't think you can be hearing me correctly judging by the content of your speech.'

This female voice held Nick mesmerised at the third door.

'Let me refer you, no, direct you, to the letter of the twenty-fourth with my name at the bottom of it. The conditions are clear. The conditions are so very clear. So very clear that if you hold the letter up to the window of your once-designer office I will be able to read the conditions from here. That is how

13

clear the conditions are. Would you like me to do that? Because I think that you are having . . . difficulties.'

Until one hour before, Nick had never heard of Henrietta Kilpatrick. That was when he had got the message to sort things out with her on the Two Lips trademark dispute. Pommy had asked Nick to deal with this personally. Pommy through Jenny, that is. That was whom the note was from. This must be part of Pommy's development plan for Nick.

'Watch the details, Durning,' he had told Nick while scrutinising the December office accounts for a minor printing offshoot in Lyons.

'If people know that the details might be looked at then they will be that little bit more careful.'

At which point Pommy seemed to circle an entry entirely at random before writing, 'Explain this,' and dropping the paper in his OUT tray.

'And that little bit more careful is where we succeed over all the other fuckers.'

Nick had nodded and Pommy looking up regarded him for a moment before standing.

'Bit too much of the "up-here" stuff with you, Durning,' Pommy said, tapping Nick lightly on the forehead with his index finger, 'Need to get you a bit more fucking active. Fucking development or something.'

Nick hung at the door, enjoying this new phase in his development.

'So. Call me this afternoon once you've had time to give it better thought.'

A long, weary breath out. Nick rapped twice and walked in.

'Hello,' he smiled, extending his hand to the slender woman behind the compact, organised desk, 'Nick Durning'. She took his hand and gave it a tug, leaving it hanging where she found it.

'Hi, Henrietta Kilpatrick,' she said, sitting back down while Nick pulled his hand in.

'Nice to meet you, Henrietta.'

'Well, shall we get to business?' she said, pulling a black file from the top drawer.

The Two Lips trademark dispute concerned the registration of a motif. Market Research at Jenkins Clinical, Belston's Consumer Health subsidiary – something Pommy had picked up for a bit of fattening prior to selling it on – had thrown up the opportunity for a range of textured lip gels targeted at the 25–36 age-band. An external design agency had developed the name "Two Lips", together with an appropriate logo – a pair of lurid lips side by side.

A notification of intention to register the logo, placed in the appropriate trademark journal, had prompted a fierce response from Humble Imprints, a small, privately-owned company. Humble Imprints had ownership of a similar logo – no teeth showing – which they used for a collection of sexy stationery. With the Belston side adamant that the name and logo were exactly what was required, some probing was now needed to determine how far Humble Imprints could be pushed. Nick knew all this from the file. The task with Henrietta, Nick had realised while walking over, was to identify the next appropriate move in this respect.

'The Humble registration covers paper products and stuff, including – let me see precisely – "Items of personal use", Henrietta semi-lectured, pointing to a photocopied page.

'I see,' said Nick, looking up for more information.

'I figure ten people – twelve tops – work at Humble Imprints. Not big at all. Small,' Henrietta said, almost to herself.

Nick took this on board then asked,

'Do you think they are familiar with this sort of dispute?'

Henrietta snorted happily.

'Good point,' she murmured, 'They have no idea how much time and material, resources and . . . stuff they could find themselves using up.'

Nick thought about another question but Henrietta didn't stop.

'Their MD only got wind of the trademark issue from some lawyer friend – Family not Corporate – who happened to see the journal entry somewhere. I think he thinks we, sorry, you, are going to make him an offer.'

'What type of offer?' Nick fired out.

'You know. They'll grant you an exemption in return for some cash. That sort of thing.'

Nick didn't have a question ready.

'Their turnover,' Henrietta continued, fingering through the file, '. . . is . . . around . . . 500,000.'

And she pushed a piece of paper over to Nick, who just managed to focus on it and say, 'I see,' before . . .

'Exactly. 500,000. Nothing. They aren't going to get into litigation with a turnover of 500,000.'

'Definitely not,' Nick announced.

'Nevertheless, if they did . . . I believe that the court would not be unsympathetic to their claim,' Henrietta concluded.

'Trouble,' Nick said, trying to make it both question and answer.

'Exactly,' said Henrietta, marshalling the various sheets of paper back towards her and into the file, 'Let's face it, they've got some dumb family lawyer friend who has heard too much about the enormous amounts that logos are worth. They are a small company, negligible turnover, working all sorts of dedicated, small-business hours. They probably make deliveries in their own cars. I think we should make them forget us. Start to draw them into the cesspool of legal dialogue. Send them the type of enquiring letter that their Child Custody chum can't answer. Let them see how much one reply from one cheap corporate dummy will cost. Then start to lay it on with the petty questions. Give them a demonstration of how many bite-sized chunks we can take out of their bank account with every little exchange. Make them see how much easier it would be for them – not us – to walk away and forget the whole thing.'

'That sounds like a sound strategy,' Nick pronounced.

'Great,' said Henrietta, closing the file, 'Lunch time.'

*

16

'How was this marinaded?'

As "marinaded" hit the waiter firmly in the face, Nick became uncomfortably aware of his erection. That Nick was not good or comfortable with women did not really bother him. That was just the way it had always been, it seemed. He wasn't really sure why and preferred not to give it much thought, especially when there was so much else in life to get excited about. Pommy had once advised him to do something about it, on the grounds that it was important to display virility: 'City Boys like it, even if they're City Girls, if you see what I mean. Like to see virility. Lets them know you've got what it fucking takes.' At this point Pommy had pressed a small piece of paper into Nick's hand. On it was a telephone number. 'Give it a go,' Pommy urged, adding, 'Two at a time isn't a problem for this lot, you know.' Nick never called, not even for one.

It would perhaps have annoyed him to know that Henrietta's sexuality was the cause of vexation for many men she met. A magazine analysis of her power might have stated that she was blessed with being slim yet well-proportioned, using clothes to suggest a bountiful harvest. The hair was worn long; the fingernails a juicy red. But such measures could not alone account for how someone with a self-proclaimed 'run-of-the-mill' face could affect men, and women, so deeply. No, it was her manner that sealed it and for that she was indebted to an old college friend, Elspeth.

'Always have about you the suggestion of a loaded gun,' Elspeth had explained on the way to a dance one evening.

'Men love guns. Women with guns turn men on in a way that no special, new mascara ever will. It's a matter of mixing sex, menace and authority.'

At this point Elspeth stopped, shifting her stance slightly, widening her lips to reveal the keenest sliver of teeth. This pose, she explained, was how she did it.

'How you do it is up to you. But always think, "I've got a gun!"'

This was credible advice. Elspeth was a large girl who could look threatening even when reading a book, yet was seldom without male company. From then on, Henrietta worked to perfect her own "loaded gun" demeanour.

Elspeth herself was killed on her first visit to New York, shot down in a bank, while waiting to exchange currency, by a nervous security guard who was convinced that "the big girl" was up to no good.

'I will check,' said the waiter, taking with him both plates of guinea fowl.

'I can't stand over-herbed marinade,' Henrietta snapped.

'No. Me neither. Nothing worse. May I?'

Nick poured the claret then excused himself. Seconds later he was sitting in one of the toilet cubicles, slapping his face, trying to get a hold on the situation. Henrietta thought about poor Elspeth while she waited, and not at all about Nick or the hasty arrangement of his visit.

"Please come to Pommy's office on your return – Jenny."

Nick considered the handwritten note lodged under his keyboard. Pommy would want a de-briefing on Two Lips. For a moment Nick continued to scroll through the e-mails on his screen. He had other, more time-stricken projects to get on with. While Two Lips was important, it was not by any means URGENT. Nick had a file for URGENT.

Yet long ago Nick had learned from Pommy the importance of "dancing to the beat of the top bongo player".

'Only fucking idiots look at what's best for the company,' Pommy had explained as the two had looked over the atrium and down at the newly-installed coffee area.

'Deal with what the top bongo player wants. Once you've dealt with whatever fucking nitwit thing they've fixated on, then you're free to get on with the stuff that matters.'

As Nick strode through Commercial a few heads looked up, but not many. So very quiet, Nick thought. He did not know that the approaching sound of his ever-so-slightly irregular foot-step was all that his co-workers needed to assume postures that made it clear that they were keeping themselves to themselves. Still, it was indeed quiet, even allowing for the tell-tale tattoo of his tread.

Malcolm Campbell waved from across the room; a short, tick-tock movement that Nick felt compelled to return, in the manner of a chum. This wasn't the sort of thing Nick enjoyed, any more than communal coffee breaks or office sweepstakes. Come the Derby each year the clipboard would appear and everyone would sign up for a horse, with humour being taken from the matching of horse names to workers. Nick hated it. There was always one horse named "Legless" or "Shorty" or "Mr Footsure" and no-one ever suggested Nick take that one, despite it being the most obvious connection to make. So one year Nick had asked for it. The horse was called "Sir Limpalot" and Nick said, 'I suppose I should take "Sir Limpalot"'. Then he had laughed long and hard and alone. Before he knew it everyone had wandered back to their desks, even Malcolm, whom Nick had once caught doing a limpy impression of some-one, presumably Nick. But it wasn't for any of this that Nick hated speaking around the office. What he hated was the clear message that most of the people in the company were only doing this for a job. 'It's a job', 'Have to do something', 'Fill the pension up and that'll be me.' How could they be so disin-terested?

Nick hated it. But went along with it. No point in not. Comply with the trivial and don't make a fuss. Maybe even put some effort in now and then. Nick even volunteered to play Santa Claus, aided by the realisation that, with a big false bushy beard and moustache obscuring his mouth entirely, it was pos-sible to get through the whole dismal Christmas evening with-out having to force a smile. Amidst the slapped thighs and mistletoe japery Nick's face relaxed and he was able to pass the time with little discomfort.

So Nick waved back to Malcolm, a restrained, precise move,

19

accompanied by a composed smile. Having been so acknowledged, Malcolm re-immersed himself in a discussion at a nearby desk. Nick noticed how the two men and one woman of no importance burst into laughter soon after Malcolm joined them. Malcolm was, Nick knew, the office funny person. With Malcolm negotiated, Nick checked his course for Pommy's office.

Nick was always earlier than early for a meeting in Pommy's office and not because of his boss's complete intolerance of anything late. No, Nick liked to have time to play around. Had anyone ever happened to come into the large, barely-furnished room during those minutes of padding, they might have found Nick lounging against walls, sitting on the floor, even trying Pommy's chair. All part of Nick's acclimatisation strategy. While most employees looked like mice who felt that a trap might be near, for Nick Pommy's office had become a place where contemplation was both possible and fruitful. Thanks to his policy of making himself feel comfortable there, Nick had mastered the ability to think deeply and quickly on his feet in front of Pommy.

No Jenny, Nick thought, walking past her empty desk and chair. Then he put his hand on the handle of the door, knocked twice and walked with bright confidence into Pommy's office, where Andrew Midgely was holding a scone. Both men shot a different glance at it.

'Pommy can't make it. Business,' Midgely announced, keeping the scone motionless in front of him.

Nick looked to the scone. No Pommy, but Midgely, with scone. Nick raised his left arm and considered his wristwatch, eager for something to mask his surprise.

'Business,' he said, nodding his head knowledgeably with considered approval.

Looking up Nick saw that the scone was gone, replaced by a brilliant white envelope. There was the hint of a downbite from Midgely. Then silence. Then a swallow.

'Pommy can't make it,' Midgely repeated softly.

'Business,' Nick said, now shaking his head sagely in understanding.

'He asked me to give you this.'

Midgely moved forward, presenting Nick with the envelope as he passed.

'And he says "thanks".'

Strange, Nick thought. He felt himself floating. Which he was, more or less, supported at the armpits by two men wearing dark suits and non-conversational expressions.

Nick managed 'What?' as this trio moved from Pommy's office. He caught a side view of Midgely as the company secretary did an about-turn and whirled back into the office he had just left. Nick twisted to try and see more or even speak but instead found himself already entering Commercial. Doing so, his longer leg skimming the ground, Nick was punched by a vision of Malcolm pretending to be Nick on a skateboard. *Scooter.*

'No,' Nick gasped, 'No, no!'

But it was too late and they knew he was coming. Of course they had known. How wouldn't they? The complete silence, which he had not recognised on the way to Pommy's office, began to change. Now he knew it was the silence of knowledge. Somehow, somehow, somehow, someone had known what was going to happen and that one had become many and then all. In a way that no technology could ever mimic, the spread of gossip had occurred in the few seconds it required for total dissemination. They had known. Then he heard the growl; a low, rumble of voices which rose and rose all around him. Spinning his head about, his body still moving at speed with voluntary submission, Nick was amazed at how many people there were. Far more than when he passed through when? Two minutes ago? Half the building seemed to have crammed in. People were standing on chairs at the back of the room. Someone was levering themselves up using the coffee machine. Nick whirled his head back and forth, desperate for something, somebody, *Pommy* . . .

Propped against the water-cooler was Malcolm Campbell,

laughing with someone Nick thought he knew from Logistics.

'I already waved goodbye to you, didn't I?' Malcolm announced, collapsing with mirth at his own repartee. He had known. They all had known. As the end of the room approached, the speed seemed to intensify and Nick felt himself in a tunnel of faces and voices, comments pecking at his wake.

'Maybe we can get a decent Santa this year. You know, ONE THAT SMILES!'

Ha, ha, ha . . .

'Scoot, scoot, scoot . . .'

Ho, ho, ho . . .

'You can talk to yourself all alone now.'

Hee, hee, hee . . .

Nick's office swished by, door closed, three figures visible inside, emptying drawers, cabinets, cupboards. . .

'My off . . . ice . . .,' Nick sighed, gulping air, the lift doors closing behind him. A distant cheer, as of voices in celebration.

About five minutes after walking into Pommy's office, Nick was standing outside the almighty front doors of Belston Corporation, still holding, he noticed, the brilliant white envelope in front of him. He looked down at it and felt a sharp pain, as a hand reached round and gave his nose a savage pinch. There was a flash and a voice, 'Got it!'

Then there were no hands holding him and Nick found that he had to steady himself. He realised that his two escorts were still there on either side of him. Breathing deeply, he turned around and looked up at the silent flat wall of smoked glass. He caught a long row of faces falling back from the gleaming windows. Nick felt something being deposited at his feet. The two escorts were now staring at him through the glass doors, hands by their sides. Straightening his tie, smoothing down his suit jacket, Nick picked up his briefcase and limped off down the street into a hell of unknown provenance.

three

'Why would someone call our son a "fudgepacker" in the first place?' Jonathan Greenmeadow asked, still hovering between bemusement and confusion.

'We have to tell him something, don't you think?'

Alison stirred the coffees. She hadn't known what to say to Samuel at first.

'No, you're not, no, you're not,' was her hushed comfort, eventually. There had been other days of upset but always over stolen toys, lost books or not-being-pickeds. Of these, the not-being-pickeds were the more difficult to resolve. Each time it happened, and sport was not Samuel's strongest suite, it required the efforts of both Alison and Jonathan to build their son up to his usual boisterous shape.

'We picked you, didn't we?' she would croon, as he lay curled up on his bed, pillow to face. Jonathan would then explain the concept of jealousy; how other boys and girls didn't like the fact that Samuel was so much more talented than they and that this was their way of exacting revenge. Today was different though.

'It's just some strange words, Samuel. Stupid people say them for no reason. They just want to hurt you. Because you can do things they can't,' Jonathan said ever so slowly, hand resting on his son's back through the duvet.

'They were all shouting it, Daddy. Even the girls.'

'How did it start, Sam?' Alison said, coming in from Kimberley's room.

'Albert Hunnicliffe ... he ... he ... said that he had seen people like me on the television with his mum and dad.'

23

'Uh huh?' Jonathan, wanting more.

'He said everyone knew I was a fudgepacker.'

'Samuel, what is a fudgepacker?' Alison, matter-of-fact, hoping he had no answer.

'Someone who takes it up the bum.'

'Takes what, Samuel?' Jonathan, so in-control.

Samuel turned his red face to his parents then rejoined the pillow.

'I don't know, I don't know,' said the little, muffled voice.

From downstairs came the sound of the kitchen being cleared.

'Everything will be fine tomorrow. Don't you worry now.'

Samuel sniffled. Alison left her son's room, tidying the odd thing up as she went, watching his breathing through the covers. Samuel knew that if he called she would be right back. Alison felt proud of his hand waving goodnight as she pulled the door to. Her little soldier.

Once in the living room she and Jonathan talked again about what Samuel had said. Did he really not know or was he hiding his knowledge, thinking that the knowledge alone was in some way bad?

Later Alison scanned Jonathan's newspaper while he watched a documentary on emerging new species. There were two cereal coupons, which Alison tore out with satisfaction. In so doing her eyes caught the top of the paper; Wednesday. Her stomach lurched. Tomorrow would be Thursday. Again.

Thubada Thubada Thubada THUB . . .Thubaba Thubada Thubada THUB. Alison looked out of the corner of her eye and caught sight of the pile of shopping coupons on the bookshelf. With any luck there might be one for coffee in today's paper. *Thubada Thubada Thubada THUB.* Thursday mornings were – generally – good for beverage coupons. They must have worked it out; the approaching weekend or something. She didn't know for sure. Nor did she know or care why her husband had decided that Thursday mornings were to be "Spontaneous Sex" times.

These sessions had been going on for the last month.

Alison presumed it was because of some article Jonathan had read in one of his men's magazines. That would certainly fit. For almost a year now he had been trialling any number of relationship schemes, all of which had the potential – the editorials claimed – of keeping the fire burning in some way. So they had had "sexy lingerie", "non-consummated foreplay" and "baths". Of these it was the baths that Alison had found least unpleasant, as it saved her having to shower the next morning. Yet given the aim of these various exercises, she still could not say that any identifiable fire was being serviced.

Alison would nevertheless have been happy to continue in similar vein. Spontaneous Sex however was not in a similar vein. Alison's strongest objection was that it was always in the morning. The weekly ordeal of waking up to find her husband's indelicate fingers wriggling like hungry pups inside her was bad enough. But the sex that followed – with Jonathan maintaining a magazine-prescribed *Thubada Thubada Thubada THUB* rhythm – was grim. And of all the words she could think of to describe sex – wild, passionate, rough, reckless – none struck Alison as being as bad as 'grim'. Grim Sex.

Had Jonathan not initiated his Spontaneous Sex regime, Alison would most probably have continued to bob along in the same current of indifferent contentedness that supports most marriages. But now a vista of Grim Sex stretched toward the horizon, like one of those never-ending deserts you see in documentaries and Alison was not sure she could bear the lonely trek across such fruitless land. It was as if the occasional banging of her scalp against the headboard that accompanied the final *THUB* had awoken her. But what it had awoken her from or to she was as yet unable to recognise.

Two thoughts alone kept her in the bed, stopped Alison slapping Jonathan's puppies away. Firstly, Samuel and Kimberley asleep along the corridor. Secondly, the fact that Jonathan was at least trying. Alison reasoned that for this alone she should put up with his unwelcome stimulations. Besides, this was surely just one more men's-magazine activity; another month, another suggestion and it would be over. Yet it had become impossible to deny a voice deep inside her, in places where Jonathan's well-meaning, chubby fingers never reached, which asked what was she doing here, enduring this calendar of dreariness? Wasn't this just like being a prostitute? No, it was worse. At least prostitutes, she reflected, were living their own lives, making their own choices. Alison felt she was stuck in a life bereft of choice.

So each Thursday morning Alison made the effort to moan and writhe, moan so very softly, for the sake of her children, her husband, their marriage and for the lives she would never lead.

Alison had married with less care than she had used in choosing the bathroom tiles in their first house. As it had been for many, her spouse was someone she had known at university. At the time it had been a matter of love, youth and a world without boundaries. She and Jonathan had been going out for three years, nearly fifteen percent of her existence; fifty percent of her adult sex life. They had met at the Geography Society Christmas Party. The fact that neither of them had studied geography was as close as their personal history got to having an edge. After a night of drunken shagging they had started going out. By graduation the question had been asked and answered, in parallel with a number of their friends. It felt as natural – and in retrospect as exciting – as walking along the street.

They toyed with the idea of going round the world. Everyone seemed to do it. Alison went so far as to buy a guidebook that showed all the routes that might be taken. She annotated all the places she wanted to go. Jonathan smiled and was enthusiastic but did not get beyond looking at rucksacks in catalogues. Having dug a deep hole of debt during his studies he was eager to get back on level terms.

'The world will still be there in two or three years,' he assured her as they agreed to postpone any voyage. Besides, wouldn't it be more fun going round the world with some cash in the bank?

Jonathan was taken on as a graduate trainee by a thriving construction firm. His engineering degree was – he confided to any who asked – 'Almost immaterial. That's not what it's about.'

'What they really look for,' he would explain, 'Is the type of person who can think for themselves, you know . . .,' and he would stop talking and mime someone coming out of a box and looking around. His vice-captainship of the university second rugby team and an interest in environmental conservation had mattered too, of course.

Alison was proud that she was marrying someone who could think outside the box, even if it meant she would have to put off going around the world.

Alison went into publishing, where she discovered that a degree in English was of but conversational relevance. After bumping around a few departments she settled in Historical Fiction, where she swallowed her offence at 12th-century knights who said things like 'I'm gonna kick your butt' in favour of a trouble-free life peddling "accessible realisations".

'People would never read anything at all about history other- wise,' her Oxford-doctorate Editorial Director would incant with time-served regularity, as if by saying this often enough he could expunge the stigmata of "sell-out" that marked his palms and gave him a moist, unconvincing handshake.

'Is that with underlay?'

Alison blinked.

'Is that with or without underlay?'

A scrawny man in a bizarrely green suit was questioning her. Alison looked at him then snapped out, 'With underlay,' her voice disappearing into the vast, muffling space that was "Karpet Kingdom". Kimberley swung on her hand, eyes agog at the rolls of colour all around. Alison picked her up and walked after the scrawny man and his untied shoelace.

At the till Kimberley stared with wonder at the man as he completed the delivery note. Yes, they could take away the old carpet. Yes, there would be a charge for this. No, he couldn't give her an exact time: morning or afternoon only.

Kimberley seemed in a state of awe, saliva dribbling out of her mouth as she strained to take in the magnificence of the green suit. For a child it was not bizarre or cheap or affordable – it was revelatory. Alison had by now figured out why the suit was so strange to her eye: it was about two years out of fashion, more or less the worst possible gap. Any longer and it might have been retro, any shorter and it might still have sneaked "in". Nothing is so discomfiting as a fashion that is just, and only just, "out".

While Kimberley basked in the suit's radiance, Alison felt the damp cloak of retail depression coming down on her. This was also a recent development, probably beginning around the same time as Spontaneous Sex. Karpet Kingdom was exactly the type of place that brought the cloak down. The realisation that for the people working there this building defined their existence. That each of them – she had seen other badly-suited assistants scurrying around – might well spend most of their waking hours here or thinking about here or talking about here filled Alison with horror. That they went so far as to seek out affordable suits so that they might look the part was painful. For the man crouched over the till in front of her, with his suit and his shoes and his worn collar and streaky hair, working in this shop was his life. Every day would be defined by what happened in Karpet Kingdom. Trouble with barcodes, new stock, lost keys . . . everything. The four corners of this scabby warehouse were the four corners of his world. And it mattered to him deeply each time there was a staff meeting and he didn't get to crack a joke, each time someone else got a great customer, every cup of coffee "just how you like your women Bob – warm and sticky". Every single piece of gossip; every single "Sorry, I used the last staple".

Forget all that nonsense about how big the universe is, Alison

28

thought as the man tried to get her telephone number to fit the available box. Take a look around and see how small most worlds are! As this vision became total, Alison would try to pull herself out, take it easy, get a grip. She would hold onto something a little bit tighter, tell herself to laugh or smile. Which she always managed to do, thus avoiding the imagined manic conclusion when she would grab Bob, or whoever, around the shoulders and beg them, beseech them, order them to flee the Karpet Kingdom and run out into the blue and green yonder, there to enjoy the rest of their lives. They could fly kites, chase lovers, jump streams, and climb mountains. For fuck's sake, they could go round the world!

Home lives are quality lives. Alison didn't know where she had picked this up but it had the feel of the Internet. The idea that by staying and working in one place, and not having to travel to work, your life would be so much better. She herself worked part time from home now doing freelance editorial work for her previous company. After Samuel, the first born, she had returned to the offices but the arrival of Kimberley had brought so many logistical complications that the end was never in serious doubt. Jonathan had taken paternity leave for Samuel but Kimberley 'and not because she's a girl' was less pressing. Besides, too many projects were at critical stages to warrant such absences. 'It's what pays for all this after all,' Jonathan had gesticulated, wine glass in hand on the back garden patio of the new family home in their commuter town. The same town Alison had grown up in.

Alison agreed with Jonathan. She was happy. The birth of Kimberley, her own little girl, was the most exciting day of her life. Looking down on the puzzled, sleeping face in her arms Alison had never known such deep contentment.

"Listen, everyone is dying . . ."

Alison had almost finished blue-penning the third chapter of *Black Rat Posse*, a piece of rubbish centred round the bubonic plague that had killed one quarter of London's population in 1665.

"No way dude. It's only rat fever, you know. Just chill."

Since resuming work for the publishing house Alison had found it even more unrewarding. Moron fodder, she thought. That so much moron fodder was produced did not bother her. It was the fact that she was involved in its production.

In the hallway the clock struck two. Time to wake Kimberley, get some shopping in, pick up Samuel. Alison put down the manuscript and looked out of the window.

The coupons weren't there. Sitting in front of her, being bagged even as she raked through her handbag was a feast of shopping. Nearly every item had a matching coupon sitting at home. That very morning, had she not sat at the kitchen table with her gridded wipe-clean shopping board? Almost every square on the chessboard pattern was covered by a coupon. Only cheese and chicken – always chicken! – had proven resistant to discounting. The tokens had been piled to one side afterwards, next to the post. Where, Alison now pictured, they still sat. How could she have done this?

Kimberley thrust both hands into the gaping handbag, eager to see what her mother was looking at. Alison slapped the small hands away, 'Not now Kimbo!'

Kimberley recoiled. One hour previously, as her hair received a gentle brush, her face a caring wipe, she had been Princess Kimberley; Princess Kimberley of Snugglebunny. Now she wasn't even allowed to look in the handbag. This was surely some sort of mistake. Without hesitation she pushed her hands back inside the bag. Smack! A firm, severe smack on the hand. Princess Kimberley's wail rose from the shopping trolley and became a cloud over the checkouts. Other shoppers covered their heads and hurried away. Alison's frantic search of her bag and pockets continued. She had forgotten the coupons!

Samuel careered out of the school gates as if on fire, his legs hammering the ground with the wasteful might that only children can afford. Flinging himself past Alison and into the rear of the car, he sank down to the floor, trying desperately to hide his tears. Alison looked down at him, sighed, and got into the car. As she pulled out, waving to so many other parents, her son's sobbing seeped under the seat. Then Kimberley, sensing that the emotional focus had moved from her, joined in. Alison continued waving. Then, suddenly, she braked and with firm anger reversed the car back into its space. Getting out of the car, Alison scanned the swarm of faces, running, milling, playing.

Standing at the school gate was a group of boys from Samuel's class. Taller than the rest, his back to her, Alison recognised the wiry form of Albert Hunnicliffe. She had seen him before at the school nativity play, an arrogant, stupid Wise Man who made himself sick by drinking the frankincense. Alison walked up and tapped him on the shoulder. The boys around him gaped in wonder then fell away as a parent entered their fold. Albert whirled round, expecting the prank of another child. His mouth opened and stayed that way.

'Albert, what did you call my son?'

Albert's face trembled with shock.

'Samuel!' Alison urged, 'Samuel! What did you call him?'

Alison crouched down to address him face to face. Yet now he seemed to smile, perhaps in embarrassment, yes, a distinct smile. He pushed his hands deep into his pockets, swivelling at the hips.

'What did you call him, Albert?'

Albert's supporting cast had disappeared, shuffling backwards into anonymity.

'Albert, can you hear me?'

His smile twitched but remained. Alison leaned forward so that their noses touched for an instant.

'Albert, if you call Samuel any bad name ever again I will break both of your arms.'

These last words were a low, rumble through Albert's head.

31

Alison realised that she had raised her arms as if to take hold of him. Dropping her hands, she stood up. Around her the last children were being herded into cars. Looking down she saw that a puddle of urine had formed at Albert's feet. She smiled at him and strode back to the car.

'Stop! You! Stop right there!'

Alison knew she was the "you". She took hold of the car door-handle then looked over her shoulder. Puffing after her was a dumpy woman in a coat of vague colour, dragging an immobile Albert.

'What did you do? What did you say to Albert? How dare you?'

The dumpy woman planted herself about two arms' lengths from Alison. By now, few other parents or children remained.

'You must be Albert's mother,' Alison said.

'Yes, I am Albert's mother. And I want to know who the –'

'Mrs Hunnicliffe, do you know what a fudgepacker is? Do you?' Alison cut in, stepping forward.

'Of course you do. Because the other night you sat with your seven-year-old child and allowed him to watch a programme about fudgepackers.'

Mrs Hunnicliffe was still, while behind her Albert wriggled and twisted to be away.

'You did, didn't you? Is that the type of programme you think is suitable for seven-year-olds? Is that the type of language you think is appropriate?'

'How does that entitle you to speak to my – ' Mrs Hunnicliffe spat out, recovering breath.

'Because I do not like my son being called a fudgepacker. I do not like being forced into explaining to my son before the appropriate time what sex is all about.'

'That still gives you no –'

'So I'm going to tell you what I told your son and I want you to listen,' Alison stepped into the face of an alarmed Mrs Hunnicliffe.

'If my son is called any more bad names by your son, I will

break both Albert's arms and then I will break your arms too. Is that clear you fat, stupid cunt?'

Mrs Hunnicliffe jumped, then started to back off, face like a slapped cat. Alison moved with her a few feet and stopped. Then Mrs Hunnicliffe turned and fled, pushing Albert before her. Reaching her small, red car, she fumbled with the keys, before bundling Albert into the passenger seat.

'Who the hell do you think you are? Who the *hell* do you think are?' she hollered, voice trembling. Then she was in the car, starting the engine and stalling it twice.

Alison raced to the back door of her estate. Yanking the back up she delved with precision into the grocery bags and came out with a tin of alphabet spaghetti. As Mrs Hunnicliffe's car eased onto the road, Alison hurled the tin with all her strength. In an exact arc it landed square on the Hunnicliffe rear windscreen, smashing through it. The car braked sharply then, with smoke burning from its wheels, it sped off down the street. Alison looked round at the empty street before closing the rear door and getting back into the car. Samuel peered over the seat at her, his face confused and thrilled.

'Sorry,' Alison said, manoeuvring away, 'It'll have to be beans tonight.'

It began to rain and she flipped the wipers on. That was better.

four

Sitting at the dressing table the colour of the duvet appeared no different than it had done from the window. Initially inconceivable, it was now absolutely clear to Pommy that he was looking at plain old Sky Blue and not Orphan Blue as he had agreed – 'the slightest wash of colour, as the proud boy considers the faded uniform of his father, lost at sea.'

Pommy paced back and forth between window and dressing table, throwing livid glances at the bedspread, cursing himself for having gone on holiday and left the redecoration entirely in the hands of Martha. Fine; Martha was the Interior Designer, fine. But when it comes to execution 'it always pays to be on fucking hand', just to make absolutely, personally sure. How many times had he told people that? Why else had he insisted on hiding in the cupboard when Midgely had done the business on Durning? He was never going to leap out and join in, of course not. Not the right thing to do. No fucking need for that. But Midgely knew he was there and that made all the difference. Everything had happened exactly as he had wanted it to. No more, no fucking less.

Pommy prowled the room, eager for another perspective. Opening the door briefly he boomed, 'Stepladder!' then slammed it shut and sat down on the bed.

Pommy knew he had only his misplaced optimism to blame. You return from what was barely a week in assorted African nations to discover that your precious designer has – and there can be no other word for it – compromised. Somebody has fucking compromised! And who would have to bear the consequences? He would. Once again somebody has compromised on his behalf, leaving him to tidy things up. If it wasn't lawyers with their "under the circumstances" or Financial Directors with their "within the parameters", it was Interior Designers with their – let me guess – "entirely in keeping with the conceptual palette". Did these people think that he was a fucking fool? They always shook their heads when he asked them. So why did they fucking do it? With no sign of any stepladders, Pommy stepped up onto the dressing table chair and then the dressing table. God damn it, that was Sky Blue! Well, not this time, not this time she doesn't. Pommy marched over to the door and threw it open.

'Wilson!'

No answer.

'Wilson! Where are you?'

'Yes, sir?'

From a marbled distance came the clip-clip of well-heeled feet.

'Wilson!' Why should he be calm?

'Yes, sir?' closer now.

Pommy could picture the butler at the bottom of the stairs, smoothing over what was left of his oily hair.

'Wilson, get Martha on the telephone or something. I want her over here immediately. *Not* after croissants, *not* on the way to the tennis club: immediately! Got that?'

There was a pause, then the hesitant voice of a man asking a question against his better judgement, 'Sir, . . . Mr Freiberg, it is Sunday and . . . '

Pommy pounced,

'I know it's fucking Sunday! Do you think I don't know the days of the week? Is that it? I know it's Sunday. I don't care if it's fucking Christmas Day, May Day or her fucking birthday. Christ, the money I pay her she can probably afford to have two birthdays like the fucking Queen! Just get her round her now!'

Wilson waited a dignified second,

'Very good, sir!'

35

Wilson listened for the door closing above him and then started back towards the kitchen. There was a telephone there and he'd better get breakfast underway too. Then the door flew open again.

'And once you've done that,' Pommy's voice seemed to shrink the house, 'Come up and get this fucking whore out of here. My fucking wife will be back this morning and you know she hates meeting them.'

The door closed again and there was the muffled sound of someone objecting to being called a whore, followed by Pommy's brusque 'Be quiet!'

Wilson's already bleak Sunday turned bleaker. Mr Freiberg refused to allow any of his personal cars to be used for taking the whores home, on the grounds that his wife might detect their perfume. The butler was obliged to use his own Ford Mondeo, a car that had traversed its way down the Freiberg offspring before landing inelegantly with Wilson. It moved with reluctance, groaning with each change of gear as if remembering every champagne-fuelled handbrake turn it had been forced to perform. Wilson had nightmares of the car breaking down somewhere remote and having nothing but a tired prostitute to survive with. Still, best get on.

The larger-than-practical front door groaned open. Pommy smiled, more or less with satisfaction, knowing that Wilson had returned from taking – what was her name? Madeleine? Madrigal? – home. It was only this difficulty with names that prevented Pommy from ordering two whores as often as he wanted to. An experiment with name badges had rather annoyingly failed and he found they didn't much like numbers either. Been a while since the last pair though, he chastised himself as the door closed with a portentous thud. Pommy had demanded specifically a "portentous thud" noise for the front door. That way, when it closed behind them, people would know that something dramatic had happened. That they had arrived at, indeed were within, Pommy Freiberg's personal domain. Oh yes, the door was his idea, not that of some suck-faced, bottled-water swigging designer.

Pommy continued with his breakfast. Hmm. This kipper was excellent. Wilson was a good find. Ex-army of course. Always knew their kippers. Good for you too, kippers. People had been eating them for thousands of years. Part of earth's heritage and all that. Full of values. Yes, a very moral fish, the kipper. Hmm. That would be a nice theme for the forthcoming International Management Conference he'd been asked to address.

Pommy got up and made a note on the kitchen whiteboard – 'Lot of good thinking done over food, Martha; need have somewhere to write it down when you think of it' – and remembered the Sunday papers. He gave Midgely a call.

'Anything in about Argentina?' Pommy asked over Midgely's hello.

'Not a thing. The Durning move must have nipped it in the bud.'

Pommy's company secretary was one of the few people not intimidated by him. That Durning had been another. He respected that. Still, Durning had to go. Needs must.

'Fine,' Pommy ended the call. No point in all those good-byes and stuff anymore. Pity really. Everything moved so rapidly these days. Particularly information. There was practically no time now between you yourself getting the information on some development and the fucking analysts getting it. Before you know it they're on the line demanding forecasts, strategy implications, bottom and top lines . . . Which was why you needed to beat them at their own game. Make the information. Don't wait for other people to fill the demand. Make it yourself. Bastards. He knew about information. Don't need spin doctors for that. Fucking greetings card salesmen.

'I'm in here, Wilson!'

Wilson entered the conservatory, where Pommy now sat on a bamboo recliner next to the fish pond.

'What the devil kept you?' Pommy asked, looking to his naked wrist and a tanned Rolex outline. Wilson had the shaken appearance of a man who had "gone though the jungle side-ways", as Pommy was fond of saying whenever someone looked in any way out of sorts. 'Might have to let you get some R&R,' was a common follow-up, meaning that Pommy might well dispense with your services.

Pommy had never been in the army, had no connection with it whatsoever, but knew that things that sounded military in spirit always made people sit up that bit straighter. Wilson gathered himself. While his worst nightmare of being marooned with only a call girl for company had not come off, it had turned out that there was something worse.

'Sir, while I was transporting young Ms. . .,' Wilson searched for the correct exotically untrue name.

'The whore,' Pommy prompted.

'While I was escorting the young Ms Whore home, we had an inconvenient occurrence.'

Pommy closed his eyes. Everything slowed. He opened them, ready for the tale.

'An accident, you mean, Wilson?'

'We were involved with another vehicle while negotiating the crossroads along from the big supermarket,' Wilson fired out, continuing at speed, 'although, thankfully, no-one was injured and it was merely a matter of exchanging insurance notes with the driver of the van.'

'Whose fault was it? Not yours I . . . presume,' Pommy hesitated over the choice of verb. He had been about to use "hope" before realising that "presume" would allow him a greater depth of anger should his suspicions prove correct.

'Oh no, sir,' Wilson announced. 'No, he went into the back of me. Of that there is no doubt.'

Pommy grimaced and fixed Wilson with a frozen stare to see if he might flinch. The butler remained impassive.

'Mmh . . . well, then . . . you're OK, I . . . hope?' Pommy said, reaching for the piranha food, mindful to keep Wilson on side.

'Fine, sir,' replied the butler, a swift smoothing of his hair indicating that all was once more in a state of order.

'Good,' said Pommy, dropping to his knees and staring deeply into the pond. Where was Big Pommy? Little Pommy was there. But no Big Pommy. 'Right then, Wilson, best get everything tied down for Mrs Freiberg's return,' eyes still searching the depths.

'Of course, sir,' Wilson said, heading for the door.

'Wilson!'

The butler lurched to a halt, 'Sir?'

'Nice kippers.'

Pommy was right in his suspicions about the accident. Wilson, impatient to get onto the main road, had made a sharp pull-out at the junction, leaving an approaching van little chance to slow down. It had skidded trying to do so and hit the Ford in its rear left-hand corner. Wilson's young lady passenger, until then enjoying the radio, had begun cursing the butler without pause, an assault soon joined by the driver of the van battering with menace on Wilson's side window. The matter was resolved upon appearance of the Wilson-summoned police, who made it safe for him to get out of the car. At which point there had been an unhappy exchanging of insurance details, just as Wilson had said. There really wasn't any need to tax Mr Freiberg with those in-between bits though.

Wilson turned into the kitchen and looked at the large words on the whiteboard – "Explore Virtuous Kipper". Well, that could wait until he'd had a cup of tea.

five

'Genevieve Marsden, Emergency Line.' The entire train carriage stopped talking as Genevieve's sharp tones burst along the compartment. Even those on other mobile telephones hushed their voices to hear. It was one thing to listen to details of what someone had for dinner the previous night, or which film they saw, or who they snogged; it was quite another to encounter a real emergency, a doctor or something. Since most people on their telephones were only engaged in telling other people on their telephones where they were, Genevieve's emergency was worth hanging up for. And this was a Sunday! Anyone having an emergency on a Sunday had to mean business.

'Where is this, then?'

The small, round man sitting opposite Genevieve tried badly to pretend that he wasn't straining every sinew to hear the other end of the conversation.

'And a rough group size?' Genevieve asked with reflective calm, snapping open her crocodile-skin notebook, drawing a margin line in thick red felt-tip pen down the side of one sheet. Into this she wrote, "Who", "Where", "When", "Why", "How".

'Exact time?'

A frown, more scribbling in the notebook.

'Ostensible and actual reason?'

'What does "ostensible" mean?' a man at the far end of the carriage asked his wife, who shushed him and leaned forward to hear better. The small, round man stopped all pretence and sat with open-faced curiosity. Genevieve caught his naked interest reflected in the window.

'And what has been achieved so far?' A knowing "guessed as much" smile.

'Right, leave that with me. You'll hear from us tomorrow afternoon. Goodbye. Oh, and . . .' this latter piece in a contrasting tone of total care, '. . . please rest assured that everything will be so much more than fine.'

Genevieve rang off with one finger, made some more notes, and then regarded the small, round man opposite. She inclined herself towards him with conspiracy, beckoning with her little finger. He shimmied to the edge of his seat.

'Has that helped to fill some of the vacuum that is your life?' Genevieve asked politely. At first a look of incomprehension, then of indignation crossed his pudgy face. He jumped back, wrapping himself in a newspaper with all speed.

Why oh why did they ever drop the First-Class service on this line? Genevieve thought, still watching her companion as he sought to establish a barrier of newsprint. You never used to have to see, let alone deal with, people like this. Look at him, with those "genuine leather upper" shoes, carrying his own groceries, counting the pennies. It was people like this man who caused Genevieve so much needless hassle.

Of course, this was her husband's entire fault. Yes, it had been she driving the car, but it had been his useless lawyer who didn't get her off. All that nonsense from the judge too: 'Never in this court's experience' and 'unprecedented disregard for the lives of others'. All for being a bit under the influence. Not even a crash – just asleep behind the wheel, in a ditch.

Then to ice the cake Pommy had refused to get her a chauffeur for the six months. Said that that would be seen as 'rewarding a criminal'. Not the type of thing a FTSE 100 CEO can be seen to condone. How the hell was she supposed to run London's most exclusive, most prestigious event company (and definitely not the biggest) using public transport? Bastard. He'd pay. That Wilson had better be there to pick her up when the train arrived. It was bad enough having to go back every second weekend or so.

More than most though, Genevieve knew the importance of maintaining a meaningful charade. Keeps the questions away, lets the flow go.

Besides they never really saw each other, even when beneath the same expansive gabled roof. The presence of hard corridor floors throughout facilitated an early warning system for both of them. Most of the rooms had two doors and it was easier to pick up one's stuff and shuffle out than to sit and endure those few terrible seconds of inconclusive bitterness which was the norm for Pommy and Genevieve when near one another. An amazement that reproduction had ever occurred was one of the few perceptions they now shared.

Genevieve faced the window, taking in the passing pastoral scenery with an equanimity bordering on contempt. Better get on to the Rutherford job. Stuffing the red emergency phone back into her handbag, Genevieve pulled out the standard-issue phone that her staff were required to have with them, fully charged, at all times, 'even when you're on the job'. Genevieve alone had a line reserved for emergency calls from her staff for when her own standard-issue was turned off, and more importantly for those special turnkey clients whose continued, visible patronage (Genevieve preferred the term "dependence") was her primary marketing tool.

'Charlotte, its me. Stop shagging whomever it is and get a piece of paper. There's a top job you have to get onto pronto.'

Genevieve smirked, thinking of Charlotte – in effect her only permanent "staff" – crawling around the bedroom for both something to write on and with. Fat chance there'd be anyone else there, but why not let the girl pretend?

Genevieve made a point of only employing ugly organisers, those who wouldn't be falling victim to otherworldly propositions at any point in the critical path up to completion of an event. Initially she'd gone the obvious route – lots of leggy ex-P.R. stuck-up blondes, the type that would have the male clients drooling. These had proven to be good only for trying to worm their lower-middle class way upwards, ready to squander every resource on making sure their own pictures were on the society pages, taking care always to be hanging about when the most eligible men were around. No, stick with the Dependable Uglies. They never let you down. Fear the limelight, in fact.

Genevieve heard Charlotte's heavy breath on the line again.

'Listening? Good. The Rutherfords have forgotten about some shindig they'd promised to hold in aid of Save The ... Save The ... some sort of animal anyway; four legs I think. Thing is, it's only three months away and they've arrived back from somewhere in a wild panic. Probably too much tagliatelle, ha, ha! Get into the usual venues and then do an audit of the theme ones. And please, *not* the Natural History Museum. Everyone from Dunhill to Domestos has been there. Try to think of something special - it *is* the Rutherfords. About 500 they reckon. Nothing has happened yet apart form a few rash dinner party promises, so we've got a more-or-less clean canvas. Right, off you go. Call me this afternoon. Bye.'

Genevieve and her staff had Sunday numbers for all the major contacts. Every venue knew as well as she did that a Genevieve Marsden party could herald a deluge of wannabe bookings, as every soap star, television cook and television presenter sought to classify themselves through association. Genevieve was unimaginably proud of this term, "classify", and almost as proud of its corollary, "declassify". The Natural History Museum had undergone extensive declassification, as had most celebrity-chef restaurants. Some places, the private room at The Ivy came to mind, still had a certain aura. But the whole thing was getting out of hand. Soon there wouldn't be a decent venue in town that hadn't been contaminated by a public renewal of wedding vows by some inconsequential daytime never-be.

The train slid jerkily alongside the platform, rousing Genevieve from her wrathful daydream. For the small, round, humiliated man opposite her the journey could not end quickly enough. He opened the door, cautiously extending one foot, touching it on and off the platform, trying to establish a firm grip and only succeeding in getting himself more agitated.

Genevieve stood directly behind him. And he could feel it. As the carriages juddered to a halt, she caught his trailing foot as he leaped from the door, sending him sprawling across the concourse. Genevieve then dismounted, walking with disgust through the scattered value-brand packets and tins.

'You shouldn't open the door before the train has stopped, you know,' she informed the prostrate figure as a station attendant walked morosely up to help. Now, where was Wilson?

six

Nick considered again the photograph of himself looking like a parrot. Not a normal parrot; an angry parrot – one that had been kicked off its perch or something. It was ten days since his dismissal. Since then a lawyer had been engaged, who had explained to Nick that the contents of the brilliant white envelope were perfectly in order. That is to say, that Nick's position – and therefore Nick – had been made redundant. There was no mention of any wrongdoing. Indeed, there was nothing but thanks. Midgely's thanks. Not a word from Pommy.

A six-month pay-off had been given; more than Nick was legally entitled to.

'Its always worth checking,' the lawyer smiled, as Nick stood up to leave. Worth it for you, Nick thought. Repeated calls were made to Pommy, all of which went unreturned. Nick was no longer referred to by his first name. He was Mr Durning. Pommy's secretary Jenny was as formal and distant with him as he had heard her be with any unsolicited calls from people nobody wanted to talk to: 'I'll see he gets the message'.

Two letters had been written. The first, to Pommy, was a considered piece of Nick Durning prose – the type of writing which Pommy had so admired – thanking Pommy for the opportunities that Nick had had and wishing him and the company well for the future. There was no hint of bitterness, only gratitude. Everything that Nick did not feel. The second letter, also to Pommy, was nothing but a scrawled "Why?" in brazen, black letters across a piece of A4 which Nick discovered he had written upon waking up the morning after two bottles of wine.

Nick had not imagined that anything could hurt like this in

the adult world. And now a photograph of him being ejected from the building had somehow appeared in the "Career Moves" section of *Commerce News*.

That first day Nick had arrived home and gone around not knowing he was in a state of shock. This involved being obscenely good-natured with a local grocer, with whom he engaged in small talk about football before sweeping along the shelves and filling a wire basket to overflow with interesting-looking foodstuffs.

In later days the shopkeeper would remark to himself how strange it had been. That this busy, busy man, whom he had seen so often walking with crisp purpose past the shop, had unexpectedly turned up one day, laden himself with several bags of provisions, chosen almost at random, and then discussed in depth the relative merits of the defences of most of the teams in the league, a subject on which the man was entirely unin-formed. That but one week later when the same man had entered the shop, looking somewhat altered of mind, he had stared at the shopkeeper blankly when asked for his thoughts on the previous night's big match, and then backed out of the shop, clutching nothing but a tin of hot chocolate. In due course the shopkeeper put it down to the man being another one-off small-talker, not a professional like himself.

Nick sat at home on his sofa. He did not have a favourite seat, although he was aware of such things existing. They were often mentioned at work – 'Ex-work. Get it right, Nick!' – particularly with regard to what people were looking forward to on their return home. For an afternoon Nick experimented with the two armchairs in his lounge until realising that he could never imagine finding anything stimulating enough about any of his furniture for it to become "favourite". He could just as readily imagine having a favourite fork.

He called another lawyer, a specialist. The first one had been a specialist too, but this second one was a specialist in bigger type. Being an even bigger specialist meant that this lawyer could dispense wisdom more directly. 'You're fucked with Belston,' was his verdict. Time passed. Nick felt it swimming outside his window like a giant sea monster, waiting to devour him.

It was an almost pristine waiting room. It was the "almost" that showed the truth of the situation. Pristine – that was fine, ambitious. Messy, disorganised – that could mean active or busy; dynamic even. But an almost pristine waiting room indicated a perfunctory interest in the people who sat in it and nothing more. They needed somewhere to sit and that was that. Nick pictured Janice, the receptionist, dealing with it in only the sparest of moments.

There is no better indication of one's place in the world than the amount of time you spend waiting on other people. Unattractive people on begrudged second dates, the unemployed at a bank, anybody selling anything. Nick could feel himself slipping into the category of someone whose time was infinitely expendable. This was his seventh recruitment agency in three days.

He had been waiting thirty-five minutes, which meant they were twenty-five minutes late in seeing him. Nobody had kept him waiting in a long time. Now there was no implicit danger of him "taking his business elsewhere". He had no "business" and "elsewhere" was another room like this.

At each agency the tone of pleasant disinterest was the same. In effect his interview was over before it started. Jones Williams Kennedy Executive Search would go over his curriculum vitae, listen to his story – asking enough questions to be polite – before explaining that there was "nothing on our books right now" but that they had a "pro-active client approach" and hoped to contact him again soon to discuss "appropriate opportunities". Indeed, the only difference between one agency and the next was their choice of buzzword to describe their unique, identical approaches. "Inplacement", "Position Acquisition", "Management Matching" – Nick now had a new section in his mental thesaurus, all for the same activity of phoning up a bunch of companies and asking 'What jobs have you got going?'

Jones Williams Kennedy Recruitment Specialists would be no different. And, just like all the others, they would know his name and parrot face from *Commerce News*. Because every day these people scanned every industry publication to discover who was moving up, down, in and out. One agency even had the piece on Nick stuck to their notice board, with a Post-it reading, "Squawk! Watch out for this guy".

His two interviewers at Jones Williams Kennedy could barely contain their excitement at having him in the office, smirking to each other, heads bowed, even passing a conspiratorial note at one point. In the recruitment industry Nick's abrupt removal had quickly become the new best example of how not to leave a company. After his three score and ten minutes were up (nobody ever complains of being shabbily treated if you give them more than an hour of your time) Nick was escorted to the frosted glass door by Heather, while Marcus waved goodbye from the front desk.

'We'll talk soon,' Heather said.

The morning's thin drizzle was continuing on and, having left his umbrella under the interview table, Nick was forced to take the lift back up to retrieve it, arriving just in time to catch Heather bawling down the phone, as Janice buckled with laughter, 'You'll never guess who I just had in! Yeah, Squawk! You too? Snap! Who's a Pretty Polly?'

'Ha har, me hearties!' screeched Janice, looking up to see who was in the doorway.

The next morning there was an envelope, franked from Belston Corporation. Inside was a letter from Jenny, thanking Nick on Pommy's behalf for his letter and wishing him well. Nick tucked this into his jacket pocket as he left, although this time he had no agencies to see.

He sat among the bustle all that day, moving from coffee bar to coffee bar. Around seven o'clock he found himself in that most solitary of positions – the last customer in an about-to-close coffee bar. It was his sixteenth of the day. The foreign students behind the counter had become increasingly jolly as their witching hour approached. Eventually Nick tired of their dishcloth-slapping merriment and left. He came out and entered, without joining, the flow of the evening.

As the sky swelled into a thunder-dark ocean, the city prowled and rippled, yearning for satisfaction, escape, passion. The buildings searched the sky, seeking some heavenly anchor. And the people, let loose at last, marauded the streets, making light of the old predicaments, anxious for new ones. From these eternal patterns Nick was marooned. A coarse wind swept around him, wrapping his isolation with the dusk of the multitude.

seven

"'Nobody was hurt,'" Jonathan repeated, with a gentle lilt he had intended to parody Alison's verdict on the tin of alphabet spaghetti episode. In the week since then their suburban existence had been through a whirlwind of enquiry and speculation. The headmaster had taken control, desperate to deflate and ultimately hide any ugly event which could affect reputation or ranking or future funding. 'Everything is reputation, everything is reputation,' he whispered down the line to a shame-soaked Jonathan. Alison's absolute lack of guilt barred her as a point of contact.

By a small grace of God, the headmaster had explained, Mrs Hunnicliffe was driving a car that was uninsured and untaxed and had therefore been unwilling to make an official police report. The conversation between Alison and Mrs Hunnicliffe was a matter of hearsay. Or rather, it was treated as one. Alison was quite happy to repeat what she had said to anyone who cared to ask. Nevertheless a deal – 'for the sake of our children, for goodness' sake' – had been brokered by Jonathan. Alison would not drop off or collect the children from school for one month. She would send a note of apology to Mrs Hunnicliffe. Jonathan chose not to mention the note of apology. He wrote it himself and got someone from work to sign it in a female way.

Alison's smug grin on the way to the see the doctor – 'I know I don't require medication' – had barely dimmed over the following days. Two days later, when Samuel presented her proudly with a "PsychoMummy" crayon drawing, she had pinned it above the fireplace. Samuel himself was now strolling about the playground with a retinue of followers, his aura of invincibility a glowing tribute to Alison's "decisiveness", as she explained to Jonathan. The term "PsychoMummy" came, Jonathan learned with dismay, from the staff room.

'Half the kids are terrified to go near him,' he pointed out over a mug of late-night coffee.

'So what?' Alison retorted, 'Who wants to associate with the offspring of people like that anyway?'

'This isn't decaffeinated, is it?' he asked accusingly, holding his mug out as if it was the murder weapon. His wife looked at him blankly.

'For God's sake, Alison; it's after nine-thirty, you know,' he muttered sharply, marching into the kitchen. Alison smiled. Not only was hers not decaffeinated, it was mostly vodka. This was not the start of some plunge into suburban alcoholism. It was because tomorrow was *Thubada* Thursday and it was the only way she knew to avoid thinking about it in advance.

As it turned out Alison and Jonathan were united in appreciation of two rare experiences that Thursday morning. Most women can only imagine how a man would look if he was told that he was no good in bed. And most men can only guess how they might feel. It had been one *Thubada* too many for Alison, although the headache she had from half a bottle of vodka must have contributed to the occasion.

She could remember thinking, 'Will this never end?' but it was only when Jonathan said 'Pardon?' that she realised she must have said it aloud. Without waiting for her answer he had rolled off her and the bed and into the bathroom, leaving Alison exposed, prostrate, in a state of shocked akimbo. What had she done?

The front door had closed smartly while she was still in the kitchen dealing with Samuel and Kimberly's breakfasts. By then she had had some coffee and vodka and, feeling emboldened, was glad about what had happened. Already Thursday seemed a brand new day. To live in dread of sexual intercourse with your husband was no way to go through life, she said to herself,

51

as the children's cereal bowls crackled with sugary delight. Ordinarily it would have been Jonathan's turn to drop Samuel at school, but Alison recognised that some form of punishment was required, and given how good she felt about the crime, she was happy to take it.

'Just look at them, won't you?' Jonathan pleaded through the bathroom door. Alison sat on the rim of the bath and watched as first one magazine, and then another appeared under the bottom of the door. A bright cover promised that there were "25 Ways To Keep Your Marriage Hot! Hot! Hot!". She picked up one of them and started to flip through it, unsure whether or not there would be any coupons.

The publications were back on the floor under the ceiling-mounted halogen spotlights long before ear-to-door Jonathan had padded downstairs and the sounds of his favourite documentary of recent years – 'It's the first such award given to a Mongolian' – became audible through the house's lifeless night. It seemed silly to sit there doing nothing so, having pushed the magazines back under the door, Alison shampooed and conditioned her hair. When eventually she came out into a dark house to get something to eat, the magazines were gone.

The next morning, after six motionless hours spent lying next to each other like a pair of mummified pharaohs, Jonathan and Alison put on a show of normality for the children, Jonathan straying once too often into the kind of abnormally ebullient jollity that even children find unnerving. As they loaded up the car, Samuel tapped his father lightly on his arm,

'Is everything OK, Daddy? You and Mummy seem strange.'

Jonathan stopped, momentarily frozen in the headlights of a Sam's preternaturally astute question.

'Everything's fine, Samuel. Everything's fine,' he smiled, wrapping an arm round his son.

'Mummy and I have . . . both been working very hard and . . . we need to relax a bit. That's all. Just relax a bit.'

eight

The seats were the same. The carpet was the same. The view was the same. Nick shivered, his eyes wandering over the living room that time, but not he, had forgotten.

'Here you are, son,' said his mother, handing him coffee in a dimly-remembered mug, then sitting down, perching, on the edge of her seat, ready to pounce on his next requirement. His father stood at the window, looking out. Nick wished now that he had arrived unexpectedly. As it was he had telephoned ahead, allowed them a full day to get everything ready.

Nick had walked into a full-blown montage of things he liked. Certain biscuits, a particular duvet cover, even some films circled from the television schedules.

Funnily enough, he found telling them the news easier than expected. The initial conversation was all over in a matter of minutes. How everything had been going well (they knew that); how quickly he was progressing (they knew that); how "strategic disagreements" had started to occur (they didn't know that, shook their heads convincingly). Making his explanation, Nick sensed their incredulity that anyone could disagree with him over anything to do with business. Their son was, after all, an acknowledged expert on business. When it came to business there was little he did not know. Had he not sat as a teenager and given marks out of ten to company reports on the financial pages? Hadn't he been able, aged fifteen, to explain each twist and turn of any company's activities, while his parents listened diligently, achieving the kind of temporary understanding that occurs when anyone knowledgeable and passionate has a willing but ill-equipped audience. Ten minutes later they were never any the wiser, but they knew that knowledge had occurred. No, if someone disagreed with their son about business there could be no doubt who was in the wrong. This attitude can be witnessed in courtrooms the world over on a day-to-day basis, as parents refuse to believe that their child could have done such and such a deed. Nick supped at the spookily familiar mug. What other things lay unburied?

'So, you're looking for a new job then?' his mother asked as tentatively as possible. It was this tentativeness that set Nick off. He looked up briefly and sighed deeply, leaving his mother in no doubt that she had transgressed.

'You'll want time to think,' his father said from the window.

Nick nodded, slowly. What was he doing here? For the thousandth time since getting off the train barely one hour before the question hammered his mind. It had all been instinctual. He had simply packed a small suitcase and left his flat. On the phone the previous night he had been vague with his parents, 'Just coming home for a bit.' He had, briefly, considered going travelling, going so far as to download a list of airline ticket prices to a roster of trendy, non-democratic destinations.

'Travel does broaden the mind you know,' Nick remembered his father's advice when he had explained that he had no intention of taking a year out after university. Nick remembered asking his father caustically, 'So where have you been?', and his father's hurt exit from the kitchen. And Pommy's off-the-cuff observation one day,

'Travel? Of course it broadens the mind. So does getting run over by a steamroller. Show me a broadened mind and I'll show you an unfocused one. Bit of sun is a good thing, now and then, mind you.'

No, Nick did not want or need his mind broadening, not now. He knew it was too late for that. So he had come home. For all that Nick wondered what he was doing there, he knew that he had nowhere else to go. No matter which way he looked at it, he was alone.

'I have no people,' he had found himself thinking repeatedly as the mild countryside that fringes London swished by. So home it was, to the gallery of achievements where he now felt so at odds. He had never been so discomfitingly aware of just how much of his life was captured, framed and on display. From nursery school to his first appearance as a "New Face" in the Belston internal magazine, every stage of his development seemed to have found a place somewhere in their house. It is one thing to know of a museum of your life; it is quite another to find yourself living in it. Museums were not for living things. So here he was: just another artefact that the curators were pleased to have acquired.

After another half-hour of sitting, Nick did what everyone does when they go back to their parent's house. He went for a walk. And he had no more an explanation for why he did that than he did for the cutting he carried in his jacket pocket. The same cutting that his father had in his bedside drawer, of Nick looking like an angry parrot.

He wandered into town, a near two-mile walk from his parents' suburban detachment. Once there he ambled in and out of shops, looking without thinking, taking in without responding. Pausing outside a recently stocked fashion window, he had never felt so irrelevant.

Lying in bed that night, the pillows so familiar that their comfort was upsetting, Nick once more went through what he could do. He considered again the phrase "start your own business". It held no draw for him. Thinking it over, he could no more see himself starting his own business than becoming a dentist. 'I am a company man,' he murmured softly, over and over again, as the first tides of bitter, unrestful sleep washed over him, 'It is who I am.' Yet with each repetition he felt the pain of this statement. What is a company man without a company? What is a company man that no company wants?

He woke up with the words "Bottle of Rum" banging inside his head. Distracted, it took a breakfast of eerily enjoyable tastes from the past – his mother hovering nervously in the kitchen doorway, relishing his recognition – before he was able to let go of the words and the sense of anger he felt building.

'Thanks Mum,' he mustered, 'that was great.'

Her face beamed with renewal. Then he got on his jacket and said he was going for a walk. His mother wanted to object. It was raining. It was cold. It was her son. Mr Durning held her back.

'Let him go,' he urged his wife, as they watched their son toddle down the garden path, 'He just needs to relax a bit, you'll see.'

nine

Pommy Freiberg was not a man to relax. Relaxation implied a lessening of attitude, a dropping of one's guard. His last-but-one doctor had tried to get him to relax, sending him to several of Europe's best health farms or retreats. It was at one of these, in Belgium, outside Maastricht, that Pommy experienced his only major health scare. Rousing himself one afternoon from a non-specific thought, he realised with horror that he had been in a state of unawareness, or as others might call it, relaxation. Shocked beyond comprehension, he suffered a heart attack there and then in the thalassotherapy pool, having to be rescued by a recovering alcoholic and a retired football commentator. Immediately on recovery – he insisted on a quick one – Pommy fired his doctor and managed to find one who recognised, or was at least willing to understand, that "without pressure there is no life". Nevertheless, even Pommy had pressure he could have done without. Some things are meant to be if not exactly easy ("Beware the easy!"), then certainly clear-cut, even, on occasion, simple.

Argentina, for example. Argentina was supposed to have been a "win-win situation". Everyone had agreed. Apart from anything else, Pommy enjoyed working with the Argentinians.

'Good people. Know their beef. Wine, too. Beef and wine.'

It was a simple property deal, nothing particularly clever either. No leasebacks, or rent-to-buys or, thousand-year mortgages. All done in cash, old-style.

'Only beef involved is at the table'.

Unlike Uruguay, which had been a near-disaster saved only

by a windfall deal involving the Russian mafia, a fast-food chain and several flags of convenience. Oh no, Argentina was all above board.

'So why wouldn't we tell the fucking analysts about it?' Pommy had said to Andrew Midgely at the time. Let them know what's cooking. Build up the share-price. Give us a bit more ammo. Maybe start talking about some "aggressive market-share building"; give some weedy competitors the takeover blues for a while. Makes them take their eye off the ball. You nip in and score. Crowd goes wild. That sort of thing.

Pommy even went out to "the Argentine" himself. Took a few City Boys along. Let them see what we're up to. Give them some beef and wine. They like that sort of thing. Don't do enough of it, according to fucking expensive corporate communications people. 'That fucking showed them,' Pommy murmured to himself on the jet back.

Spent three hours going round the site, checking the plans. Let them meet some men in hard hats. The City Boys always like meeting the hard hats. Get to put one on too. Big thrill. Explained to all that he, Pommy, had personally approved the proposal. Then, after apologies from the architect – 'tied up in New York' (don't want that fat dreamer ruining the day with all sorts of vision stuff) – it was off to the ranch to play at cowboys. Let the boys chase a steer, wear cowboy hats. Get their pictures taken. Have a barbecue. Beef and wine. Then off home the next day. Wave goodbye at the airport. Tell them you're staying out for a few days to supervise things. Get next flight home incognito. Be sure to send them souvenir baseball hats. Just to make sure. 'Can't get enough souvenir fucking hats, the City Boys.' Pommy explained to Midgely.

Then something came up. Legal documents from a bygone age. Something to do with "the General". Property rights appeared to have gone "a bit funny" at some point (Legal Department words). It seems, Mr Freiberg, that the people we were dealing with didn't own the land they sold us. Not all of it anyway. Not for all time. Legal Department assume heads-down position; 'running around like donkeys in a thunder storm, the fucking lot of you.' No sense of discipline.

'Get it fucking sorted,' Pommy had told them straight, 'And do it in person, on the ground. Fucking get out there!'

Needed to disguise that too! Whole crew flying via Madrid and the camouflage of some make-believe condominium deal. Lots of panic e-mails from Buenos Aires. Eventually Pommy had to fly back out to the Argentine too. Quiet hotel. Wanted to bang heads together but half the heads not there. Argentines all vamoosed. Like Bermuda Triangle. Whiff of Uruguay everywhere.

Time to head for cover, re-trench, and start some disinformation. Private briefing with City Boys. One to one. Tell them straight. Need to re-evaluate the Argentine. It's a man's world, property. No place for shilly-shallying. New calculations show that its better to off-load investment now, take minor short-term loss. Original investment schedule over-optimistic. Pleased to announce re-allocation of funds to major development in Rio. Need to get them out there pronto to see "the fundamentals". Legal Department already out there arranging the fundamentals. Hats in production. All hunky-dory, almost. Sacrificial lamb required. City Boys need to see blood. 'Make sure they don't think we think they're fucking idiots – even if they are'.

First law of scapegoating: you can't make someone who knows the truth the scapegoat. Once fired they've got nothing to lose and can soon be off and blabbing to whoever cares to listen, and there will *always* be someone who cares to listen, and then you're fucked. Before you know it you're worse off than you were. No, keep those who know firmly within the circle.

Second law of scapegoating blame someone plausible.

'There is no point in bringing out a stable boy when everyone's expecting the jockey'.

If someone good – senior, respected – takes the fall then it will be believed. Knocking someone's halo off is one of the City Boys' favourite sports. You can even get something out of it. Show the boys you're clean, thorough, and ruthless. Particularly ruthless.

Only language they understand. Bastards. Pity it had to be Durning. Solid worker, Durning. Exceptional mind. Not an action man, but God he could explain things, see right into the heart of the matter. Big brain. Name vaguely familiar known to City Boys. They would understand. Young man, eager to progress, hasty investigation, over-optimistic initial evaluation. Don't want to ruin him though. Young man. Out he goes, into the wilderness. No need to publicly crucify a young man. Show the humane side of ruthless. Ruthless but humane. Get Midgely to make fucking arrangements. But must personally approve. Don't want a repeat of Kennedy situation; man hanging out of window, begging for pension clause. Needs to be simple, swift, safe. Get some sort of picture taken. Let picture tell the story. Put it somewhere the City Boys will see. That will be that. Business as usual. Tickets for Rio coming round by courier. Looking forward to seeing you at the carnival. All that rubbish. Signed personally. Pity about Durning. All for the City Boys. Bastards.

ten

'Those aren't the right palm trees. Take them back.'

Genevieve placed the cool side of the sparkling mineral water bottle to her forehead, 'Charlotte!'

Genevieve suspected that her testiness had been brought on by the impending meeting with the Rutherfords. She sighed wearily at the prospect. From across the room the bulky form of Charlotte emerged lugubriously from a montage of plastic tropical fruits. Genevieve knew better than to question her best assistant about the palm trees. There would be a good explanation. Charlotte was one of the few who understood the need for not deviating one jot from what had been agreed with the client, regardless of what was practical or available. She was the best Dependable Ugly Genevieve had ever had and whatever change had been made to the palm tree specification would undoubtedly have been done for a reason. Charlotte understood the point extremely well.

'It is,' Genevieve would tell Team Genevieve newcomers, 'absolutely the client's prerogative, indeed, their right, to make an absolute mess of their event exactly as they want to. We advise them, of course. We guide them, of course. We explain what we think works and doesn't work, of course. When we have done all that then it is up to the client to decide what they want. And that is exactly what we give them, appropriately costed, of course.'

To this end Genevieve would always sit down with each client, be it corporate or private, titled or plain, and go through each item for the entire occasion, at the end extracting from the client a signature, and herself promising to deliver exactly what has been agreed. Inevitably, the client would regret one or two of the choices made, which was why Genevieve always focused on the two or three most likely items to need "redefining" so that, apparently at some immense effort, she was always able to step in with a save-the-day as the final countdown began. Thus, the light in which she was perceived as the premier event planner was ever more intensified.

Some clients, particularly corporate clients, inevitably fell by the wayside. The blandishments of rivals, her so-called rivals, would always, she told team members, 'divert those not totally committed to quality'. That choice was theirs to make. Occasionally she would make it for them. It always made a good story for the industry rag that Genevieve Marsden had dropped another client on the grounds of 'not sharing her commitment to excellence in depth'. In so doing Genevieve had built up a portfolio of clients that was select, complimentary and rewarding.

'If you want a cheap affair go get a budgie,' was the much-circulated apocryphal advice she gave one would-be customer who queried a wine selection too many. Clients paid for her 'absolute consideration'. From the thickness of the card (the size, shape, colour and type font being other variables) to the stitching of the cloth napkins, nothing was beyond discussion, sampling, testing. A series of stories formed part of the delicate web that captured clients' imaginations. A prawn pulled from a buffet selection on the grounds of its 'anguished expression'. Two hat-check girls at a Chelsea restaurant replaced because 'their demeanour is incompatible with the pudding.'

And all this, for what? So that a client could relax and rest easy, knowing that nobody would question their event once people knew that Genevieve Marsden was behind it. Peace of mind. In a world where risk had become the byword to success, providing a safe haven for the risk-takers was how Genevieve had built her expensive church.

*

'Do you call that a Windsor knot?' Genevieve's opening remark to Pommy had stunned him in a manner that few had ever been able to. At an autumnal party for one of the lesser royals and their new range of aristocratic thermal underwear, she had spotted him in the company of one of her erstwhile lovers. Engaging the latter in a spot of sickening best-chums banter, Genevieve had gained the introduction she sought and then hit Pommy about his tie. At that time Pommy had been careless, almost haphazard about his dress sense. This was not exactly the same Pommy, of course. This was a younger, sparkier man, less rigid in his ideas, more willing to listen, determined to learn. Being the unfinished product did not matter. Dress did not matter. It was a peripheral, at best a distraction. So long as one turned up looking and acting like a businessman, everything would be fine. People who looked like they'd spent more time selecting their clothing for a meeting than preparing their positions could not be taken seriously. Three grey suits, some shirts and a couple of ties were all you needed. Anything more was bordering on fashion.

That afternoon had transformed everything. Nobody had ever tackled him on his appearance before. Besides, he had always considered his Windsor knot to be a particularly fine one. Genevieve led him round the party, pointing out the character failings of many of those there.

'Because Pommy, believe you me, each of these sartorial indiscretions is a pointer to some greater flaw within the person.' And there they were, for all to see.

'Backs of shoes unpolished. A clear lack of depth. All show and no substance.'

'Large, garish cufflinks. Insecure about status. Likely to do something to impress rather than concentrate on what is really necessary.'

'Suit inappropriate thickness for weather. Unwillingness to adapt. Might end up squandering resources on a point of principle.'

'Collar a size too small. The type of person who would rather endure the pain of deception than face up to truth. Untrustworthy.' This latter of Pommy's Chief Accountant, who was 'released by mutual agreement to pursue other challenges' that same afternoon.

With each revelation Pommy had felt a layer of his own comfort stripped off. The change began the next day, starting with a lunchtime shopping trip with Genevieve, who became his lover shortly after that first fitting for a bespoke suit.

Now Pommy had the appearance of the man for whom the word "groomed" might have been created. It was always a plain blue single-breasted suit, with either a white, blue or pink shirt, and a yellow tie. Yet it was not always the same suit, shirt or tie. Each season he and his tailoring advisor would spend one day touring the shops, selecting five or six particular blue suits, to be matched with appropriate ranges of that season's shirts, topped off with a handful of yellow-based ties. Thus, while he was never cutting-edge, he was always of the moment. He adored that latter phrase.

A final, private audit of the purchases and outfits by the fashion editor of one of the glossy magazines confirmed the selection, and Pommy's automatic inclusion in that publication's annual "12 Business Men Who Wear It Well" feature.

'Serve the ego and it'll serve you,' Pommy would crack, in faux self-deprecation.

Within nine months Genevieve and Pommy were married, with the immediate effect that she was dropped from her role as Dress Consultant. Pommy felt it inappropriate once they became a couple to have her advising him on such matters, confiding to his lawyer that in the event of a divorce, the last thing he would want detailed in court was the extent to which Genevieve was the backbone of his wardrobe.

'Don't intend to find myself out of millions on account of a few bits of fucking cloth, do I?'

So he muddied the waters, obscuring her initial involvement altogether. As his wife she accompanied him everywhere, the accomplished Lady to his dashing Knight. But both of them knew the roles that they would eventually play.

Pommy's reputation as an addict of the flesh had never worried Genevieve. Nor had she been of the mind, as so many women mistakenly are when it comes to remorseless bed sharks, that she would be the one to change him; make him behave. Rather, she had recognised from the outset that he possessed the right social and financial fundamentals, in a generally acceptable form, to be a good husband and father. Genevieve had sufficient experience in men to see all this, and was wise enough to her own needs to know what mattered and what didn't.

Pommy had been only too happy to help her set up her own company.

'Excellent idea. Get some extra money coming in,' was his dinner-table banter on the subject.

'Good. Keep her occupied,' was his private thought, staring into the dressing table mirror. By this time, a full five years into the marriage, Pommy's hands and wallet had become increasingly receptive to the call of the wild. His small apartment in Marylebone had resumed its intense schedule of cavorting and cleaning, while the occasional run on champagne created stock problems and sackings at the 24-hour grocer downstairs.

In the country, Genevieve tucked in the children and planned her release.

Some twenty years later equilibrium was in place. Both Pommy and Genevieve now maintained separate London apartments; he off Bond Street, she, more expansively, near The Angel, Islington. At weekends they might meet back at the family home in Berkshire.

By now Pommy was heavily into paying for sex. It suited him.

'No time for the three-course shilly-shally of shall-we-shan't-we,' was his locker room chat, 'Better to get a few decent suppliers you can rely on, whatever the weather.'

Genevieve enjoyed the company of two or three men, one of whom was inevitably some chum of Pommy's.

'Marriage is, after all, a social arrangement,' Genevieve would confide to various intimate female friends, often themselves spoiling for a bit of release.

'As soon as one recognises that marriage is all about the roof over your head, and that's the social roof mind you, then you're free to enjoy the great outdoors.'

And she would laugh uproariously, while inside her the little girl of true love squirmed, twisted and suffocated.

The Rutherfords were one of the most prized customers on the circuit. Everything they ever wanted to do was of a quality threshold few others ever approached. And they held at least two, sometimes three, do's every year. Others would try to anticipate the likely dates so as not to clash. Yet inevitably there would be a number of events whose own theme would be usurped by an irrevocable air of "All Those Not Good Enough to Be at the Rutherfords". One year the Romanian Orphan Karaoke Ball had become a scene of misery of operatic stature, as room after room revealed groups of elegant men and women in dinner suits and gowns gnashing their teeth behind the song sheets. The sound of 'It's My Party and I'll Cry If I Want To' was too much for one of the organizers. Getting up on stage to begin the Bucharest Hospital Raffle she finished the half-bottle of vodka she had been carrying since arrival, shouting 'We are all Romanian Orphans now!' into the microphone before being grappled into the wings by two imported traditional musicians.

If you clashed with the Rutherfords you might as well face it: yours would be a gathering of self-doubt and bad temper and nothing you might say or do could alter the genetic coding on that one. It was here that Genevieve's role as a power broker came into its own. For most projects she was engaged at a sufficiently early stage that she was in a position to advise on the final date chosen. At any rate she would always know the crucial "when" significantly before the wider audience. Genevieve's "advice" was therefore much sought after so as to avoid a head-on collision with a real attendance-draining bash by the likes of the Rutherfords.

People would sidle up to her at drinks parties, trying ever so slightly to gain an inkling of what was cooking. Genevieve had an off-pat, amusing line for such unofficial enquiries; 'You know me darling, it's all or nothing,' and the pair would laugh off the incident. But the message was clear. Until engaged – expensively engaged – not one sparkle of intelligence would bless your happening.

'And we want something different. You know, special.'

'Yes, special.'

For all that the Rutherfords were one of the most desirable customers, it was not because of their ability to articulate what they required. Genevieve put down her pen and pad. How many times had she heard those words?

'Something different. Special'.

Occasionally she had, with lesser clients – those one-splash-wonders who would be talking about their feeble little party for decades to come – come very close to letting them know what she thought. Letting them hear her insight on who they were – or more precisely, weren't – and would never be.

All Genevieve's experience in the events business told her that people who wanted "Something different. Special" usually ended up prancing around in End of Empire Indian costumes, or leering pathetically behind black and white masks. She wondered which it would be this time. While she was waiting, politely making sure that this was as good as the brief would get, Genevieve scrawled "usual face-painting" in her book. Regardless of theme the face-painting was almost standard. The provision of a magician to go round the tables wasn't even worth writing down as a "special" anymore. It was no more special than using cutlery, despite what some of her "cutting-edge" corporate clients seemed to think.

Genevieve became aware that Johnny Rutherford was speaking again.

'. . . too much, you know, not this time. We were at an Indian bash the other week, which was fun. But this time it has to be something really different.'

'You know, special,' Ginny Rutherford butted in excitedly, slapping her more than adequate thighs with excitement.

'Well, why don't you . . . ,' Genevieve started to prepare the ground for a suggestion of a "special" black and white mask ball.

'No. Wait! Wait! I've got it!' Johnny exclaimed, before pausing with much drama. Beside him Ginny gripped her knees in anticipation.

'Why don't we,' he began slowly, deep-voiced and serious, 'Why don't we have . . . something to do with animals?'

Ginny clapped her hands in exultation, 'Oh, what fun!' she cried.

'It's in aid of Save The . . . you know, anyway!' Johnny blurted.

'Yes! Yes!' agreed Ginny.

They both looked to Genevieve for confirmation that they had indeed hit upon the greatest idea of all time.

'Right,' Genevieve said with spontaneous enthusiasm, 'Animals it is then.'

'Yippee!' Johnny and Ginny exclaimed together, as Genevieve wrote "animals again" in her book.

'What are you thinking of in terms of venue, Genevieve?' Johnny asked with unexpected pointedness. Genevieve felt herself snap almost too visibly into an answer,

'We're looking into that right now, Johnny. There are a lot of possibilities and for this one I would prefer to get it absolutely spot-on.'

'Great. I agree,' Johnny said, smoothing down his trousers.

'And can we have face-painting?' asked Ginny, officiously.

'Oh, yes, and a magician?' Johnny piped in.

Tick. Tick.

That afternoon Genevieve was back in her office, with Charlotte sitting opposite her, "RUTHERFORD" file in her lap.

'So what do we have then?'

Genevieve surveyed Charlotte's list of "Unavailables".

Charlotte looked at her apologetically, 'Well, there's the OXO Tower, if we book today they say; The Design Museum . . .'

Genevieve groaned.

'The Law Society, the London Underground Museum, or . . .,'

Genevieve looked up apprehensively.

'There's the Natural History Museum,' Charlotte spluttered out.

Genevieve's head hit the desk with a solid thump.

'And which of these are remotely connected with animals, Charlotte?' she asked, her face buried in a pile of animal-shaped balloon samples that had been couriered over.

'Mm, well I suppose the Natural History . . .'

'Stop!' Genevieve looked up, eyes bulging, 'I think we all know that we are not going to the Natural History Museum. Was London Zoo absolutely booked, I mean, every single area?'

Charlotte consulted her notes.

'The reptile house has a fashion show. There's a launch for a new Japanese rubber-based toy in the visitor centre, and two ex-stars of rival soap operas are renewing some aspect of their lives in the monkey house.'

Genevieve breathed deeply. Was there no decent place that wasn't up for the cheapest of shags? Oh for the joy of a virgin venue. The phone rang. Genevieve indicated with a troubled wave of the hand for Charlotte to get it.

'Hello, Genevieve Marsden Associates . . .'

Genevieve winced. Genevieve always winced on hearing her company name, knowing full well that adding "Associates" to your own name as good as told the world that it was you, your dog, a telephone and any recent graduate who happened to be walking by. For all the talk of Team Genevieve, and there was much, in down times this basically meant herself and Charlotte.

'Oh, I'll see if she's free, and whom may I say is calling?'

Genevieve shook her head angrily, as Charlotte pressed Hold.

'Genevieve,' she whispered, 'It's Mr Rutherford.'

In a flash Genevieve had the phone, nearly breaking Charlotte's finger as she beat her to punching out the Hold button.

'Genevieve Marsden. Hello, Johnny, how are you?'

Charlotte watched as her boss's face went through a number of unfamiliar contortions.

'Well, Johnny, I'm not sure I'd recommend that necessarily. Well, hmm, don't you think that we should maybe think . . . no . . . OK . . . fine then . . . .. Well, I'll wait to hear from you on it then. No, I'm sure it'll be fine, eh, and fun, yes, fun. Bye.'

Charlotte looked up from her pad. Genevieve was staring at the ceiling with an expression that suggested the soul of a woman about to be called to the other side.

'That,' Genevieve said sharply, pointing to the telephone, 'was Johnny Rutherford.'

Together they stared at the offending telephone.

'Johnny,' Genevieve continued emotionally, 'has decided that the preparations for this party, and the party itself, are to be filmed for a docudrama programme.'

Charlotte bit her lip. This, she knew, was terrible news. One of their so-called rivals, Party Poppers, had featured in a docudrama a few months back. The cameras had caught the Account Manager describing his customers as "the type who would've made it off the Titanic, only with less style or shame".

Genevieve looked at her assistant with undeniable concern.

'OK, Charlotte, time to buckle ourselves up, girl. This is going to be a tough ride.'

eleven

Alison stopped on the corner, panting, Samuel smiling, laughing, enjoying the race, Kimberly, squirming in her arms, begging to be let down.

'Please sweetheart, be quiet, for Mummy,' Alison whispered softly, shifting her daughter's weight onto the other arm. Then they were off again as the lights changed, dashing past startled pedestrians in pursuit of the half-recognised walk of someone Alison had last seen when she was thirteen. It did not seem that long to Alison. It did not seem like sixteen years ago that she had last seen Nick Durning.

Half an hour earlier Alison had come to and found herself looking at a list of flight-only prices in a travel agent's window. Tokyo. Sydney. Mexico City. Lima. Everything was so cheap. For the cost of a wardrobe for just one of her children, Alison could be on her way somewhere exotic or profound, maybe both. Samuel swayed determinedly on her arm, pulling her left side down. Phuket, Jo'burg, Nairobi. Any of these would be good.

'Mummy!'

One of the children was calling. She didn't know which. Alison pulled herself away from the window. Kimberley. It was Kimberley.

'Toos!' her daughter said, pointing at her feet.

Alison smiled unhappily. Getting the children's footwear was Jonathan's responsibility, one of the little demarcations they had worked out early on. Alison hated shopping for shoes, even for herself. All such arrangements seemed to have fallen off the edge of late, Alison realised. Samuel tugged at her arm again.

'Toos!' Kimberley called more indignantly. Oh be quiet, Alison thought, I'm alive too.

Then they were standing in front of a window display of children's footwear, a grinning fat cat being the recurring motif of the expensive arrangement. Alison crouched down to her children's height, where Kimberley was pressed fast against the glass as if staring deep down into the depths of the ocean. Wearily, Alison felt Samuel's familiar tug on her sleeve. She turned to scold.

'Try to think of someone else for a chan– .'

Clippety clop. Clippety clop. Clippety clop. Not possible. It must be someone else. Gone, anyway. Back to the window. No, it was just the same instinctive gut wrench that she always felt on seeing anybody with an impaired walk. Once, watching *Treasure Island* with Samuel, she had sat with her eyes closed for most of the film, begging the Golden Age of Movie-Making actors to be gone. And now looking at the designer fun of the children's shoes, she knew for sure who was walking away from her down the street, the limp neither humbling nor despairing. Grabbing Kimberley round the waist she had hauled her daughter to her chest, before snatching Samuel's hand and informing him that they were going to have a competition about who would be first to the traffic lights. For the length of the run she knew she could be wrong. It could be anyone. Why would he be here?

She knew he was a "bright spark" at some big conglomerate. Lindsay, passing through, had told her this over coffee one Saturday afternoon.

'You'll never guess about the limp guy – Nick – remember him?'

At the mention of him Alison's stomach had ridden abruptly upwards, upsetting in the intensity of movement, forcing her to pause before a tentative, 'Yes.'

Lindsay's husband's industry journal, *M&A Yearbook* or something, had a picture of him, standing next to the "grand fromage top honcho", as Lindsay put it, trying to sound clever and jokey.

Pushed, Lindsay was unable to recall anything else – the name of the company, the location; anything.

Now, standing on the street corner, pulse racing, Alison knew why Lindsay was incapable of remembering anything, capable of no great thought whatsoever. Lindsay had married a full year before Alison. She had three children and had never really worked in her life. Alison could see Lindsay's brain now, worn smooth by years of inconsequential anxieties, rotten through inaction. No wonder she drove an automatic. Alison hit the other side of the crossing at a run, Kimberley now wailing profusely despite Alison's constant 'Sssh! Sssh!'

Where had he gone? There was no sign of him on either side, this limping man who probably wasn't Nick. She ducked into the nearest shop, a bookshop on two floors: no sign. Next door, a bank: no sign. Next to that, a woman's lingerie shop. She paused and got hold of herself. Red-faced, breathless, as a gleeful Samuel ran amok through a valley of bras, and Kimberley sucked in enough air to power a wail through to Christmas, Alison looked at the bemused faces of two customers, waiting to pay at the till. 'Where to now?' she wondered.

'I'm sorry, sir, but the library is closing now.'

Nick looked up from his magazine. He wasn't even sure what it was. He had by now read every current issue kept by the library and was working his way through the back boxes. If pressed on the contents he would have come up with *Household Appliance Surveys, 10 Things Every Woman Should Know About Men* and *How We Can Predict Earthquakes – A Radical New Theory*.

The library was where he came when the shops shut. Nick was always the last to leave the bright reading room. Had this been the British Museum or some other impressive edifice from the age of empire, sitting in the reading room, the basic act of reading, might have appeared scholarly, dignified, even in some way grand. But the modern libraries that service modern towns do not have that aura to bestow. Modern, functional buildings lack entirely the obtuse glory of an empire's heritage. Bright interiors, with plastic seats and public service tables cast a slur on all those who enter, making them small, sad, seedy.

Nick had embraced this bleaching anonymity. No one disturbed him. Indeed, quite the opposite – they stayed away. Most people do not know the feeling of being stayed away from, never hear the tell-tale avoiding stumble round a chair nearby, catch the hurried, curious glance up from a book. Nick did and he was not surprised. He knew that he was a person best not met. Badly shaved, his clothes put together with the indifference known only to those who know they will not be talking to anyone that day, his eyes were the final warning sign. Distracted even while reading, they betrayed a mind racing with something too close to horror.

Nights were passed at home with his parents. No one said anything. They had toast and coffee, sometimes cocoa, while watching television. His parents tried to guess what Nick would like to see but there was little evidence of a preference beyond "anything". Mrs Durning felt that he seemed to brighten slightly with "naturey stuff". The Discovery Channel was often on. Mr Durning read thrillers. Mrs Durning read the paper, especially the obituaries.

During the days Nick wandered the streets of schoolboy memory. Individual shops had changed but the formula was the same. There was no mistaking the small-town smell. Still, he was eager for distraction. Words came back to him from a research report: "Retail is the primary form of entertainment for most of our population." Go with the flow, he thought, wandering up and down the aisles. By most afternoons he had lunched stodgily somewhere garish, considered the vague charms of identikit individual clothing, and smirked at the claims of any number of wholesome cosmetic products.

Nick had to spend most of his time out of the house. At home, the numerous reminders of his former position compounded the discomfort of familiar foods. The diligently framed photographs of him at various moments in his career were shards of glass waiting to be stood on. There he was, company New Boy, shaking hands with Pommy Freiberg. In the hall, an article on printed on pink paper, in which he was quoted on the future of international trade. His life seemed to ooze out of every nook and cranny. There was no space for him to think here.

And he knew that all this time somewhere far away his true world was rumbling on without him. Elsewhere, not here, business was being conducted. In his sleep he could hear it, like the convergence of oceans, the glorious turbulence of the market. Walking the streets he knew that he was entirely outside that world, removed from its undisciplined adventures, the endless concatenation of desires that powered the cavalcade. He was not even swimming in the wake. It was all around him and yet Nick was not in it. He had been left behind, an idiot on the beach, staring out to sea in contemplation of something he thought he had understood. Marooned, abandoned, lost. Home for cocoa.

twelve

'Right – let's have the next one in.'

Fifteen seconds later a smiley-faced accountant called Jimmy Scofield entered Pommy's office. Pommy rose from behind his desk and greeted Scofield with an authoritative handshake. Then he sat and indicated genially for the accountant to do the same. Pommy looked at the two piles of personal reports on his desk. Cautiously, as if dealing with an unexploded bomb, he lifted the top report from the left stack and brought it towards him. He looked at Jimmy then placed the report in front of himself and laid open the hard manila cover.

'Jimmy,' he said, after a moment of deliberation, 'Tell me about that Brussels warehouse.'

In that single moment of consideration, Jimmy Scofield, and all those who had gone before him that morning, felt the search-light of Pommy's scrutiny playing over their world. This was an impromptu "Remember This?" session. Pommy had profound belief in these sessions. Having had a constructive series of interviews already that morning with the Fearful Five from the Omniview management consultancy report (one pack-aged off, two moved sideways, two off to "consider what they really want out of life"), Pommy was in good spirits. Indeed, thirty minutes later Pommy had still been in the mood for cross-examination and had asked Midgely to put down whatever he was doing and arrange a "Remember This?" session.

These were relatively quickly done. A cross-section selection of employees, typically eight or so, was made. Eight, Pommy had been advised, gave a 95% statistical likelihood that every-one in the building would know at least one of them. With seven, it dropped down to 75%. Confusingly for Pommy, the number had to increase to sixteen to get a figure of 100%. Nevertheless, Pommy was happy with eight.

A quick trawl was made through their Employee Development Record; failure to complete same was a sackable offence for any of their direct managers. From these records two or three items of less than adequate performance were taken out, together with one of sound or above-average performance. The list might be taken back as far as three years, where applicable. Pommy would then go through the list, asking the individual for their recollections on the subjects.

'Accountability – that's what this is about. Don't mind fucking empowerment. Empowerment is good – get the package moving. But must be accountable – whose name is on the fucking package? Let people know that those at the top will see even the smallest deed. Make them feel the fucking focus.'

In this way all employees were aware that floating above any decision or indecision, action or inaction they might take, there was the hand of Pommy, searching for stones to turn over.

'Make them think: what would Pommy do?' Pommy had told Nick Durning before one such session. It wasn't all reprimand, though. Far from it.

'No point kicking the fucking dog all the time. Got to give it a bone now and then.'

Pommy would always finish off each "Remember This?" interview with the one good item from the employee's list.

'Let them out on a high. Let them know that although I'm fucking watching them, I'm also their fucking friend. Hell, I don't want them to fail. I want them to fucking succeed.'

Pommy would always offer his warmest congratulations on the deed well done upon completion of the story, sending the employee back to their station on a cloud of well-endowed euphoria.

'But at the back of their mind, they can feel the focus. And it's the focus that makes the fuckers fulfil.'

'Well, Mr Freiberg, the warehouse in Brussels, just outside

Brussels actually, was part of a deal we inherited from the Hoofstrat takeover. At first it appeared to be . . .'

Pommy sat keen-eyed, the fingertips of both index fingers touching his nose in classic "Church Hands" pose. Yet in truth his attention was elsewhere. It was outside his office door, contemplating Jenny, his secretary. Jenny, who Pommy had hired deliberately because of her efficiency, demeanour and near sexlessness. In one of those occasional periods of self-knowledge which Pommy disliked but which, he knew, must have saved him from innumerable, unfortunate incidents, he had made a decision to not have temptation so close at hand.

'Spoils the concentration. Work is work and play is play. Start mixing the two and fuck knows where you might end up. Work and play don't mix – like oil and water. Separately, both can be a lot of fun. Nice bit of oil here. Nice bit of water there. Together – fucking mess.'

He remembered saying as much to Nick Durning one day, shortly after they'd passed the desk of a particularly attractive female supervisor. He'd even gone so far as slipping Durning the exclusive telephone number he used for obtaining prostitutes, advising that 'There are some things that are better home-delivered.'

Yet, in those quiet moments, such as when an employee was talking to him directly, he often found his mind wandering in pursuit of a merger of the two, and it was always the efficient, sexless Jenny who got him started.

'. . . but I've, sorry, *we've*, learned our lesson from this episode, not least about Belgian tenancy laws, and are more prepared for any future such occurrences.'

Pommy considered Jimmy Scofield's nervous smile.

'Mmh. Let's hope you're right Jimmy. Now, this Bradford depot – bit of a triumph, no?'

Five minutes later Pommy was clapping a much-relieved Jimmy on the back as he left the office. He looked over at the tidy Jenny.

'Jenny, could you possibly arrange a sandwich or something for me? For lunch?

Poor Jenny, Pommy thought.

'Many thanks,' he said.

Pommy walked out onto the main floor, and over to the water cooler, from where he took a full plastic cup back to his office. He seldom drank this daily dose but knew the importance of being seen as one of those CEOs who uses the water cooler. Bit of City Boy appeasement. God, how word travelled nowadays.

All in all Pommy was feeling good, the direct and unmistakable result of having a Fearful Five followed by a "Remember This?" Above all, such things filled him with a feeling of paternal governance that he knew was the key to being a good CEO.

From his coffee table Pommy picked up that day's crisp, unread copy of the *Financial Times*, glanced briefly at the front page, then threw it with weighted precision across the room, where it dropped dead into the centre of his black plastic wastepaper bin. Then he strode to the window and looked down. Yes, things were looking good. Now.

thirteen

One of Genevieve's first actions was to team up. It is customary, expected even, for small service-providers like Genevieve's to lie about how many people work for them directly. Nobody is impressed with a staff of two. So everyone else whom the two staff members meet, talk to or exfoliate with regularly are roped in for reference to as colleagues. At major presentations, the two staff members will refer to all the colleagues who will be helping them out, indeed, who are already, "Considering The Options", often pro-actively. Mention may also be made of a "Network of Contacts". These are all the people who the staff members have worked with in the past and who they enjoy seeing again from time to time. These associates can quickly become specialists, although it is generally better not to refer to them as gurus. Gurus cost serious money and any mention of one will send most clients running for their original budgets. This would be a mistake. One of the prime goals of all service-providers is to keep their clients away from original budgets. The idea is to proceed along an incremental path of attractive "value-adding" options, until a significant difference has been obtained on the original budget. If all goes well, the client won't care too much about this. If it goes badly, well, the client did approve the additional measures.

Genevieve knew she needed to team up quickly. The Rutherford event was going to be a biggie even before the docudrama people came on board.

'Charlotte, we need to go through the Rolodex!'

Charlotte lumbered over to Genevieve's desk, taking her position with the notepad. Then they began. Over the course of an hour they telephoned around all of the preferred people, until a hard core of three had been obtained; Jill Prestwick, Olly Hampton and TipTop McGee. This would be the top layer, the senior triumvirate beneath which the subsequent layers would be installed, all the way down to the Greeters and Pointers. In addition to the senior trio, Genevieve knew she immediately needed a couple of Runners. Runners were the mainstay of the business. Generally speaking these were graduates making a start in the industry and/or the stupid offspring of rich friends eager to get them doing something. The problem with the former was that, if they were any good, they never hung around for more than one job, and if they weren't any good, you didn't want them anyway. The stupid offspring were never any good, and as often as not disappeared to India or Australia once they'd had their fill of prole-mundanity. What this meant was that there was a constant need for runners, vacancies filled in the main by the steady inflow of CVs from people desperate to get into the industry.

'Who do we have then?' Genevieve asked. Charlotte flicked through the brown file.

'Only four just now,' she said glumly.

'Four?' Genevieve exclaimed, indignant at this insult to her desirability.

'Well, it is holiday time. Most of the students will be going round the world or something.'

Genevieve sniffed, 'I suppose you're right. Let's have a look then. Usual pile of shit I presume.'

Charlotte handed the file over, still looking down.

The state of the curricula vitae Genevieve received never failed to amaze her. Many seemed to regard spell-check as some form of ungodly machination best not meddled with. Others felt that their résumé was an opportunity to discuss how badly the world had treated them. Of these four, two fell into the spell-check fold; one had forgotten to put any address or contact number. The other looked OK.

'Right,' Genevieve barked, handing the files back to Charlotte, 'Get this one in.'

fourteen

'I think that Joe and Philippa have been great, don't you?'

The car turned out of her parents' driveway and onto the main road, the windscreen wipers already taking most of Alison's attention. Jonathan was being steady at the wheel. It had been his idea to telephone Joe and Philippa who had in turn telephoned Alison and suggested that the children might enjoy a few days in the country, 'You know, give you and Jonathan some time to yourself, you know.'

And although her father hadn't said "to sort things out", the intent was clear. This suited Alison fine. The children were proving increasingly bad-tempered on her shop-and-search missions.

Since that first suspected encounter not a day had gone by when she had not dragged them straight from school to the centre of town for a comprehensive wander through the main shopping area. For two hours or so she would rove randomly through the stores, not caring that she had spent most of the day there already, having abandoned her editing work entirely. Jonathan had called in sick for her – 'personal, eh, family matters' – once he realised that her editing work had ceased entirely. Now, freed from both publishing and offspring, Alison had the whole day to spend looking.

When she was not looking she endured the torments of self-questioning: what if it hadn't been him? What if he's gone already? What if he doesn't remember you? These were all disturbing questions. Searching kept them at bay. So each day she continued the hunt, never ceasing to believe, never allowing a pause long enough for doubt to gain a foothold.

On the first day without children Jonathan had insisted on going with her, despite Alison's repeated, angry insistence that 'I just want to go shopping.' They had walked together, but not as a couple, for four long hours. Jonathan occasionally tried to hold hands. He could tell she was looking for something, but what? He imagined some lost memento of childhood, picturing Citizen Kane and the sledge *Rosebud*. As a result he had insisted that they go into the largest toy shop in the county, where he spent an hour wafting various perennials – US dolls, Danish building bricks, small plastic ponies – in front of his wife's indifferent face, looking for that spark that might signal a connection.

'I thought I saw something with the frisbee,' he confided in a late-night phone call, 'Were catching games a big thing with her?' sending Joe and Philippa into a fury of forced memory retrieval.

Had she been pushed, forced to explain her behaviour, Alison would probably not have mentioned love as her motivation. Certainly not first love. Nothing had happened between her and Nick; there had been no exchange of letters, let alone kisses.

And when people talk of the first true love it is always of the requited kind.

"There is no love like the first love" refers to those innocent passions that overwhelm two people when they are, incredulously, confronted with the existence of someone who thinks more of them than they do of themselves. The desire to rediscover such first love is the source of most divorce. Yet there is another, more potent, force, one level beyond, a gulf of power apart. That first affection, the first *lust* is never baptised as love, never acknowledged as such. It is at best an infatuation, more commonly, a crush, a fancy, in short, a form of joke. Its might is seldom realised in recollection. Most people never have occasion to revisit it, other than in terms of how funny it all was. So it is dismissed. But in those first feelings lurks passion of the strongest kind, undiminished by experience or reflection, untainted by mutuality; fiery, unruly passion. This is why, for the most part, it is best to avoid its regeneration. We are meant to grow wiser. A smothering blanket of wisdom is applied to any resurgence of such wholly primitive desire. For the most part this wisdom grips, grows like moss over the humanity beneath. Yet on occasion, when the bland overlaps of life are stretched or ripped by unnatural movements, a slight trickle breaks through and, left unchecked, can soon become a torrent of longing which knows no reasonable barrier.

'Its better with the TV off, isn't it?' Jonathan said, pleased with his latest improvement of the norm. They were sitting in a motionless living room, wearing their new slippers, hers a fluffy "tart's pair", his a couple of cross-eyed puppies which squeaked when you walked. Both pairs bought – 'Hey, why not?' – on Jonathan's jovial insistence.

Two and a half hours before this he had begun a barrage of upbeat conversation topics: this year's summer holiday; why don't we get a dog? let's build a conservatory! Soon enough though he had exhausted this and there was nowhere to turn but themselves.

'I really don't know how I can help, Alison,' Jonathan had started, 'Perhaps if we both . . .' His suggestion was cut short by the sound of the television going on. Two hours later neither of them had changed position. When, eventually, Jonathan got up to turn the television off, he had barely sat down, barely got out his first observation, when Alison announced she was going to bed.

As she fell asleep that night, Alison could make out the voice of her husband in the study, talking on the phone. 'Yes, well, these things take time. She seems a bit better. No, I'll call you tomorrow.'

'Tomorrow,' Alison thought, 'Down to the shops,' and was asleep before her husband joined her.

fifteen

'This is as good a place to start as any,' Nick decided, ambling into a US clothing chain that sold no clothes made in or even near the US. The day before he had spent the morning in an ice-cream speciality shop, trying to understand the determining factors in flavour descriptions, while most of the afternoon had been passed in contemplation of the various ingredients in a yoghurt-based beauty products shop. The retail environment was, he found, most helpful as a source of distraction.

Nick passed silently through the men's self-coloured tops, before stopping at the jackets. Melting Green. Rumbling Brown. Dagger Grey. Why? There was a tap on his shoulder. A bright, smiley sales girl was asking him if he wanted to try anything on. Nick thought for a moment.

'OK,' he said, mirroring her breezy friendliness, 'And what, typically, would someone wear in accompaniment to this?' he asked gently, holding up the Dagger Grey jacket.

'Well, people like these pale cords right now. It's a nice set actually,' she said, pleased with her ability to recall the training-day phrase, handing Nick a pair of the cords, gesturing towards the fitting room.

'And we'd be happy to take them in for you, to get the right fit.'

Nick nodded and went in. He never knew how to handle clothing people who referred to his leg. Did they say that to everyone? Looking at himself in the mirror, he was not convinced that the outfit was, in fact, a set. He stood, with his back to the mirror, head looking over his shoulder at the view from behind. Then jumped as someone burst into his fitting cubicle.

'Hello!' said a dark-haired female standing next to him, gulping air. Nick knew not to fear. There was an assistant outside.

'Hello,' he said quietly, 'I'm afraid this room is being used. Why don't you try the next one along?'

'It's you I've been looking for,' she announced.

Nick didn't know what to do now.

'It's me: Alison.' she said. 'You're Nick.' Pause.

'Remember?' she asked. Nick looked at her again and remembered.

The empty school corridors of a sunny lunchtime. Fatty Boy is closing and Nick does not want to go down the toilet again. 'Come on, you,' Nick urges his left leg, looking for that little bit more, that little bit more that can never come. Behind him, steps in the corridor. Clear, even steps. Tappity-tap-tap on scratched vinyl tiles. Maybe they won't catch him this time. Then they are closer, no longer the flat slap of the heaviest feet; now the random splatter of schoolboy shoes hammering along. Nick hurls himself through another swing door, his shoulder already numb from the previous three.

'We can see you, Pegleg!'

'Thar she blows, me hearties!'

Nick turns, catching a slice of Fatty Boy's leer as the door swings shut. Ten minutes to the end of lunch. Ten minutes to avoid the flush. Intersection. Doors on both sides and dead ahead. Nick thump-kicks the right-hand door, leaving it flapping as he speeds off in the opposite direction, aglee with cunning. They'd see the door movement and think he'd gone that way. Don't let up though; keep going. He glances down at his shorter leg, feeling the camaraderie of having got through this together. Not long now. Can't go back to the library. The canteen is always dangerous. Maybe the gym. Or the basement. Even *they* might be wary of going into the janitor's basement. Nick pivots on his longer leg and launches himself down the stairs.

'Land ahoy!'

Nick is hanging, held at the top of the stairs, arms and legs thrashing in mid-air trying to burrow down into the off-yellow belly of the school. With a whoosh he's yanked backwards, landing stunned and breathless amidst the braying laughter.

'Even pirates aren't allowed down there, Captain Nicky!'

'Looking for hidden treasure, no doubt.'

'You'll walk the plank for that!'

The floor sweeps past underneath as Nick hurtles along the empty hallway, carried like a battering ram. Bang! His head rattles as the group go through a set of doors. Then the echo changes, becomes airy, quiet, and clinical. The toilets. Clang! The metal cubicle door smashes against the wall and even though he knows its coming Nick is still shocked to find himself vertical and going down.

'Into the waves with you, pirate!'

Only enough time for a single scream before the water rushes in. Up and down he goes, the steady plunging rhythm a tribute to the power of malicious teamwork.

'Oh I do like to be beside the seaside!' the boys sing as Nick gasps. Abruptly he is falling, his body clattering to the ground as the school bell signals for peace and Geography. Panting, wet and weary, he gets up and limps over to the hot-air machine.

None of this is as bad as the drive to Martin's Mobility Centre. Nick sits in the back and goes along with his parents' deceit, as they pretend to have just happened to find themselves driving this way.

'Oh, look, we're near Martin's,' his father says with astonishment, although Nick has seen him hunched over the wheel, peering around for the right turn a moment before.

'You need some new shoes, don't you Nicky?' Nick's mother smiles into her son's reddening face.

One and five eighths of an inch. That's all it takes. A two-fingered salute of nature from one leg to the other. After the first-ever toilet dousing, Nick had complained to the teachers, discovering only that he would be hunted down later for retribution. It is better to endure and forget. If he was either big or muscular some resistance might be possible. Nick was neither tall nor broad nor strong. Endurance is all he has to offer. Resisting the visit to Martin's is equally futile. No amount of tears will extinguish his parents' best intentions.

Martin's Mobility Centre has a section dedicated to abnormal footwear. "The Latest Fashions," as a shabby black and white window poster rubs it in. On Saturdays the store is awash with unevenly balanced children. Nick wanders into an annexe while his parents are comparing tan suede boots. At first he thinks he's in a kitchen. It certainly looks like a normal kitchen, nicer even. Everything spick and span. Nick is far, far in before he notices the display behind him, set into the wall.

"GripFast Handi-Openers" the signage reads, above an assortment of tools created to help people open bottles and jars. Beneath one of the implements is a series of pictures showing a man with strangely wizened arms taking the top off of a tin of brand-obscure tomato soup with unrestrained delight. No man has ever looked happier, more complete, opening a can of soup.

Nick finds his parents and tells them that he wants to leave and never come back to Martin's Mobility Centre. He refuses to try on any of the shoes they offered.

'I don't need them,' he explains, sitting back on his ankles, defying his father to try and force the shoes onto him.

'They're trendy,' his Mother pleads.

'Then you can wear them,' Nick says, his bright eyes raging defiance.

But he wears them. He is made to. They all stood round him: the assistant, his mother and father, with uncomfortable satisfied smiles as they looked at the newly symmetrical young boy with tears rolling down his face.

Oliver Durning was a self-employed bookbinder for whom finances were a misery. His wife, Justine, worked part-time at the second-biggest supermarket. The kitchen shelves and freezer bent with ill-matched discounted foodstuffs. Dinner might be spaghetti and duck breasts or ripe avocados stuffed with tinned meatballs. Much later, their son would be persistently dismayed by the lack of imagination in so many of the highbrow restaurants he took business lunches in.

Nick always felt his life proper started in the unlikely environment of the Winter Olympics. His father won a family package to attend the opening ceremony. It was one of but a few trips abroad. For months before Nick crammed up on the history of the games and the events involved. Waiting in the departure lounge, his father quizzed him on who had won what, and how fast they had been. Nick refused to have anything to do with any sport involving matters of judgement. It had to be the fastest, highest, longest, strongest.

'But, Nick, the ice-skaters are so beautiful to watch,' his mother said after Nick dismissed all such activities as "prancing".

'Listen, Mother: trees are beautiful and so are some rocks. Do you want to have them at the Olympics? It's speed-skating or nothing.'

So while Mr and Mrs Durning sat happily through all the rounds of the ice-dancing, Nick wandered the streets in and around the Olympic village. He enjoyed the intense anonymity of being somewhere so packed with people that no-one can even look down, let alone see his feet. Wandering, he realised that he was smiling to himself, caught up in the cheer of the sparkling night air. All around him bright signs beamed greetings while costumed characters proffered twirling plastic souvenirs.

Standing in the central square, surrounded by throngs of over-logoed fun-makers, the world was revealed to Nick in all its glory. Everywhere he looked there was a company name. The entire town had been built on sponsorship. It seemed to Nick that these companies – photographic, car rental, computing – *were* the Olympics. Take away their names and what would be left? Nick stood deep into the night, sustained by hot dogs and Coca-Cola. It was like a homecoming. While other teenage boys bustled around him intent on filling their bodies with beer, Nick sucked down the ice-cold taste of corporate power, knowing that this is what it was all about.

'It's not natural.'

His mother's voice; hissed, carried up the stairs. Nick lay still under his duvet, a soft breeze fluttering the homemade curtains.

'For goodness' sake, Justine, would you rather it was pornography or . . . or drugs?'

His father, tired, chair-weary, just wanting to watch the late-night television news.

Nick had been hearing this conversation, or a version of it, for two weeks. Things kicked off when they got back from the Olympics, although had his parents been more attentive they might have noticed the evidence accumulating before then. Nick had spent his remaining hours at the winter resort building up a collection of corporate trophies, give-aways mostly. Spiral paper hats, luminous badges, clickety-click pens, padded seat warmers – each displaying a marque showing them to be a gift from an Official Sponsor. Rather than wear or use these items, Nick hid them away, wanting to retain their pristine condition. Some had been easier to get than others. For the most part, Official Sponsor people seemed happy, flattered even, when Nick came soliciting. He had even got a tie from this guy, Kevin, at the enormous stand of the official supplier of automobiles – Kevin's very own tie that he himself had been wearing. The man's chubby companion had wheezily insisted, 'Give the kid the tie Kevin!' Nick had had to promise to make his first car one of theirs, a promise he had been happy to make in exchange for the length of shiny polyester.

He had his mother wash and iron the tie back into mint condition and it now took pride of place in his company box, which he kept under the bed. The same company box that caused his mother so much distress when she had found Nick playing with its contents. Going to the bathroom in the early hours – Justine suspected the asparagus risotto – she had noticed a faint light coming from her son's room and, imagining him having fallen asleep while reading, had eased the door open. Nick sat on the floor in the middle of a circle of marketing paraphernalia, his slender torch anointing each item in clockwise order, his breath heavy in the still of the night. At each artefact he paused and his mouth opened wordlessly, paying some kind of respect.

'Nick?' she had asked after several long, disbelieving seconds. At which point he had simply turned off the torch and frozen in position. 'You should be in bed,' his mother said eventually, before closing the door and fleeing downstairs. Later, when she checked, he was sound asleep, the box tucked tidily under the bed again.

Now, as his mother's unbridled concerns once more wafted through the crack under the door, Nick sensed an urgency previously missing. Delicately he stepped out of bed, and tucked his head down against the doorframe.

'I think we should take the box away.'

'Justine, leave the boy alone. It's not like he's masturbating into it or anything.'

'Oh, that's right! Trust you to try to make a joke of it. He's your son too. It's not right.'

'Fine. I'll speak to him. So leave it for now. Please.'

'I want that box gone!'

'OK. We'll get the box. Now can I please . . .?'

Nick tiptoed back to bed, more alert than he had been in some time. The issue of the box was crucial to him and something needed to be done. But more important still was the discovery of someone else's intentions. He knew what they were going to do. He held the upper hand now. Whatever else might happen, a bright new aspect of the world had been opened to him.

'Look at this!'

Nick crouched beneath the back kitchen window. He had ostentatiously gone out some twenty minutes after dinner. From the bushes behind the back garden he had watched his parents exchanging words, before his father, with a truculent dropping of the newspaper, had climbed the stairs to Nick's room. Nick scurried forward, waiting for him to return with the box.

'Oh my God!' – his mother.

They were looking at the magazines. That lunchtime, Nick had arranged a trade at school for some pornographic magazines: old, battered ones, the page corners thin and cracked with turning. These had been placed in the bottom of the company box.

'Well, how about that? Turns out he's normal after all,' his father's satisfaction masking the relief of not having to talk to his son.

'I've never seen those before,' said his mother, both hurt and pleased. All is quiet.

'Don't look at them!' and the sound of magazines being snatched from his father's grasp, then a laugh.

'We can stop worrying now, Justine?' a smug, accusatory tone.

'I'll put it back,' his mother, slight and unsure, and then her steps running upstairs. Nick smiled. As did his parents later, secure in the liberal conceit that their son was not only "normal" but also, thank God – but not out loud – heterosexual.

Studying the profiles of most of the Fortune 500 CEOs, it became clear that early academic promise was unnecessary. Indeed, there was almost a pattern of under-achievement. Most of them were simply "bright", a level of faint praise easily reached. So Nick had made sure that he got the right grades. For the rest of the time he concerned himself with the school clubs. These were important for two reasons. Firstly, Nick knew that extra-curricular activity figured highly in the selection criteria of the better universities. Secondly, he was eager to start learning about organisations and people.

Neither the Chess Club nor the Poetry Society offered much in the way of interaction. Indeed, the majority of clubs proved poor, simply serving as further justification for his growing belief that people are easily satisfied. The League of Young Entrepreneurs was the most disappointing. After his second visit to the lacklustre gathering, Nick realised that he should have seen the omens. For one, the school officially sanctioned the club. As often as not one of the two economics teachers would trundle in at some point, offering pithy advice on the students' projects. They patted people on the back. Talked about "real initiative" repeatedly. Gave their charges the full wealth of their own business experience. Nick could not understand why anyone listened to them. Surely if they knew anything about economics they'd be out in the real world, not standing in front of a bunch of children?

The Social Justice Group seemed better; a "grown-up" club of teenagers dedicated to "examining and debating the major political and social issues of our times". The central figures could be seen dotted round the schoolyard between classes, reading proper newspapers with intent. Importantly the group had a structure: a President, a Treasurer and a Secretary. For his first few meetings, Nick sat at the back, watching and listening, with thickly disguised disdain. From the start it was clear that his enchantment with all things corporate was not shared. Not that Nick said anything about this. He was content to listen and learn. Most days the group simply sat around a classroom after school bitching about particular teachers or the like. Still, it was more "grown-up" than the rest.

Nick never said much, not for the first few meetings. Instead he listened while the strident types battled it out with the pushy types, working out what the alliances and personal relationships were within the group. Nick wrote this all down in a separate jotter. Between meetings he would plot graphs detailing individual performance ratings, seating diagrams and assorted analyses of dispositions and preferences. Each debate or argument or tantrum was broken down, considered and mapped out.

A typical, recurring idea for a "Day of Action" was to picket one of the fast-food chains, to expose "third world exploitation", "low-wage enslavement" or "animal mistreatment". Nick watched as this and most other ideas would pop up, fizz around and then be lost in the tangential stream of personal observations and whimsy that always came to dominate the teenagers' meetings. For all that there was a President, Secretary and Treasurer, Nick knew they needed some form of true leadership. And he thought he knew now how this could be achieved.

Nick sat hunched over his jotter, hands on his forehead. He was sure he understood everything there was to understand. Just one more time then, he thought, lowering a digit finger to begin re-tracing his thoughts on paper. There was a whoosh and Nick found himself staring at a blank desk.

'You've been looking at that same page for ages.'

A curly-haired girl stood above Nick, holding the jotter between pincered fingers.

Nick swiped at it but the girl yanked it further aloft

'Ah – ah – ah!' she chided.

Others in the library turned round. Nick looked round at their disapproving faces then turned back to find the girl now sitting opposite him. She began flicking through his writings. Nick knew who she was – Alison Critchley, part of one of the lesser cliques from the Social Justice Group.

'How is he?' she whispered, pointing at biography of Andrew Carnegie at Nick's right-hand.

'He's fine,' Nick whispered.

'What are you going to do about all this then?' Alison asked.

'What do you mean?' Nick said, reaching out for the jotter.

Alison tugged it just enough away from him.

'All this is fine,' she said, flipping pages back and forth, 'But what are you going to DO?'

Nick made another swipe for the jotter. Alison tut-tutted, and kept reading.

'Some of this is very good indeed,' she said, smiling at him.

Nick slumped back into his seat. Alison kept reading.

Five days later there was an elaborate, magnificently planned coup at the Social Justice Group meeting. Before then Alison and Nick had conducted an intense but informal "getting to know you" campaign, accompanied by the planting of pieces of incendiary tittle-tattle and caustic gossip. On the day itself the inevitable warfare that erupted was allowed to roll on for as long as it took for most to become fraught and exhausted, and Nick to be proposed as a new peace-bringing President. Alison would wait before becoming Secretary (too obvious).

Over a few compact weeks filled with nothing but themselves Nick and Alison consolidated and planned and managed. They would make the right things happen.

Nick had gone to his chemistry class early. He had told himself it was to read over last lesson's notes before the methodical Mrs Kendrick arrived. But his sense of purpose betrayed him once he was there, as he headed straight for Alison's desk, sitting down in her seat with great reverence, throat suddenly dry with anticipation. Then he slowly lowered his head onto the wood, arms embracing the sides, his cheek pressed flat against the grain. This had been going on in various classrooms for over a week. By doing so he was sure that he could feel her presence, an aura of something inexplicably good.

Approaching footsteps rang an alarm and Nick got up for his own seat. Rising, he caught sight of some delicately scratched letters in the varnish, barely visible but which he was sure had not been there two days previously. Bending down into the light, the words became clearer: ALISON LOVES LONG JOHN SILVER!

Over the next week Nick noticed other scrawled lines. There were scratchings on most of Alison's desks. PEGLEG WANTS INTO YOUR PANTS was one; HOPE HE'S NOT ALL LIMP another. Disturbingly, they were not the work of the same hand, although all looked feminine. Someone, Alison presumably (hopefully), seemed to have made an attempt to distort or erase the letters, which made him feel proud and humble. But he thought it best not to mention these messages during their times together.

Such time as this was did not actually amount to much. Mostly they talked about what the Social Justice Group was going to do. There was little that Alison did not want them to do. Insurrection and revolution is easy when you're young. No more difficult than saying how many houses you want. So in between Geography and Physics, or at lunchbreak, Nick and Alison plotted the downfall of everything, although it was Nick who did all of the scurrying around for facts and figures on who to hit where and when and how. Alison was content to listen to his schedules. It was the potential that excited Nick: the thought that every now and then he might brush against her. Once or twice they held hands, Nick making sure his was lowermost to hide the sweat running off his palms.

The sound of a chant disturbed him. Nick was sitting in an empty classroom composing a poem for Alison, although he realised that it would most likely end up as a poem 'to' Alison, joining the numerous others to her that had never been handed over and now sat in his Company Box. Nick folded the poem away and tidied up the volumes of poetry around him. His work in verse was generally a convoluted amalgamation of the more emotive lines from Tennyson, Auden and Shakespeare. As he stood by the door, the voices grew louder. Peering out through the crack in the door he caught the figure of Alison, pursued by a group of five or six other girls.

'Alison! Alison!' one of them was shouting, 'Who's this?' and the questioner's voice changed to that of a rough-tongued sailor, 'Ha har, me hearties! Yo ho ho and a copy of *Business Week*!' Nasty laughter boomed up the corridor. Nick gingerly opened the door. The gang were now running down a side-corridor, shrieking with joy.

'Alison! Wait! Tell us about the long and short of it!'

Alison didn't go to the next day's Social Justice Group meeting. Nick and she had prepared case studies (pros and cons) of three South American countries that were to form the basis for a debate on which should be targeted for protest letters. In the event Nick, morose and tetchy, had to deliver both sides of the argument. His ill humour turned to indifference and, after two hours of lacklustre discussion, the meeting closed with no further action being agreed.

Alison was found, eventually. She was standing with her back to him in the gym, talking with a group of girls, most of who were sitting on the ground. He approached firmly, slowing slightly as one of the group tapped Alison with her shoe and said something, causing Alison to tense visibly. Nick recognised one or two of them from the corridor chase.

'Alison?' he asked softly, suddenly aware of his own lack of presence.

She half-turned, looking at him with one eye, not wishing to look at all.

'Alison, I was expecting you at the Social Justice Group'.

A snigger came from one of the girls on the ground. No one said anything.

'Alison, I . . .'

'I'm not coming to that any more. It's boring,' Alison said quickly, turning back to the group. Several of them now had hands over mouths, pushing back what would have been wild guffaws of mirth.

'Oh,' Nick said, wishing for his own disappearance.

'Oh.' An imitation from within the group, then another, then another. Suddenly all around was the sound of staccato 'Oh's, then a headlong collapse into uncontrollable laughter.

Nick turned and walked off, a volley of 'Ha har, me hearties' hitting the solid wood door as he closed it gently behind him.

Nick looked at the woman in the cubicle and remembered. He remembered Alison standing with her back to him as he tried desperately to control himself. He remembered crying himself to sleep, his mother waiting by the door. He remembered insisting on a transfer to another school, refusing to say why. He remembered not speaking to another girl for six months, and then only to be polite. He remembered forcing himself even

deeper into his schoolwork, bludgeoning the hurt with reading, reading and reading. But he did not remember, could not
connect with, this easy-to-maintain pageboy haircut; this full-
faced young mother in a "fun" bright blue and red parka with
jeans and Nike baseball boots.

'Yes,' Nick said, 'I remember.'

'Are you going to buy that then?' Alison asked, nodding at
his clothes. 'You should – it suits you.' For no reason he could
identify, Nick hobbled over to the counter and bought the outfit.

sixteen

Thubada thubada thubada THUB. Alison squealed, her body arching, soaring in delight. Jonathan grinned, every muscle in his twice-a-week, semi-toned body tense as he maintained the rhythm. God damn it! That magazine had been right after all! All this time it must have been building in her mind like . . . like . . . (Jonathan struggled to get his mind to find a good analogy) like . . . water building behind a dam. Yes, that was it. Alison reached up, pulling him to her. Here comes the flood! Jonathan couldn't remember when it had been this good. When they were younger, students, that had been great, of course, feasting on each other like guests long denied the banquet. But this! This was like proper raunchy Adult Sex, the kind that film actors, models and celebrities must have all the time.

Jonathan had hardly been able to believe it when Alison had come home last night from her shopping trip, strode into the living room and announced – just as a particularly interesting programme on seahorses was starting – 'I would like you to come to bed with me right now!'

Her husband had actually been concerned at her prolonged absence, even calling Joe and Philippa: 'She might do anything in her state of mind.'

He had managed a quick follow-up call: 'Everything's fine – all home safe and sound,' as Alison had marched up the stairs, throwing off her clothes. Now, lying there afterwards, both sweaty and still, he asked her why she had been so late.

'Thursday. Late-night shopping.'

So that was it. Thursday. Her clock had clearly clicked onto the Thursday position and known what was missing. God above.

The magazine never mentioned anything about that possibility. 'Would you like something to drink?' he asked, adding, 'baby,' as quickly as he could.

'Water, please, with ice.' her croaked reply.

Jonathan kissed her on the forehead then padded downstairs to the kitchen, collected two glasses of iced water and then sneaked into his office – 'Just a cupboard really,' – where he snapped on the computer and wrote an e-mail to the magazine. Apart from anything else, they always offered a posh pen for the best letter published each month and he had noticed how it was generally letters that referred to previous articles that won. They always allowed you to be "Name and Address Supplied" for sex stuff anyway. Jonathan felt himself redden as he re-lived it all on paper. He wondered how graphic they would allow him to be. There was a noise behind him and he quickly pressed SEND, clearing the screen. A hand reached over his shoulder and lifted one of the glasses of water. There was a prolonged slurp, then an icy hand stroking the back of his neck. 'Come on you,' his wife whispered, gently caressing his ear with her lips, 'I want more'. Alison needed as much torrid distraction as possible.

After leaving the clothes shop they had gone for a coffee at the mall Food Court. Initially jaunty after his purchase, Nick had become uneasy once outside the shop, wanting to be away. When Alison would not let this happen, insisting that they have a coffee – 'so you can tell me what's been happening' – Nick felt even more down. Once settled though he was pleased that Alison asked a series of questions that he could answer "Yes" or "No". This was familiar enough to be comfortable. It was so basic. If you want real answers, never ask questions that can be answered "Yes" or "No". It's not, "Will this plan achieve our targets?" but "Where are the vulnerabilities in this plan?" If need be, "What other plans have been considered?"

Still, Alison continued.

'Is everything going well?'

'Yes.'

'Do you still see anyone from school?'

'No.'

'Do people still make fun of your limp?'

'Uh . . . No.'

Nick looked up, shocked. He couldn't even recall the last time someone had mentioned it directly. Alison's smile – he could dimly remember the attraction now – threw him further. He found himself being more open than before, though still withholding on his current worthless status. 'Visiting my parents,' was as close as he got.

Nick listened to a tale of crushing dullness. The finishing of school, the college years, the wacky student exploits which would serve as sole examples of an offbeat existence for the rest of her life. Marriage to a fellow student; the flag in the sand-castle that proclaimed, 'Going to university was the most exciting time of my life'. Then the inconsequential job, breeding, and a house-based existence, the lack of going round the world.

'A load of shit, basically.'

Nick caught himself. Surely he hadn't said that. Alison looked at him. He hadn't; she had. For the second time in forty-five minutes Nick found himself pleasantly surprised by something she had said.

They agreed to meet again the next day for lunch. The Food Court suited them both fine. They were just two old school friends who happened to have run into each other. They shook hands when they parted. As Alison watched Nick limp away, brown paper shopping bags with string handles held sternly at his side, she knew more than ever that things would have to change.

Yet while Alison went home that night and used Jonathan for distraction, Nick was able only to watch television with his parents. His mother sat next to him, gleefully taking up one leg of the trousers. In this respect her excitement on seeing shopping bags had been profound. Happy in her task, she left Nick alone, apart from a nine o'clock trip to the kitchen for "those biscuits you like", meaning those he had done when he was fifteen. Nick barely took in most of what passed before his eyes that night. Alison had awakened a sense of what he needed, although he was still unclear as to exactly what that was. For the first time he felt that the involvement of another person might be a benefit.

Nick became aware of the soft narrator's voice from the television,

'And the group of seahorses, realising the danger to one of their number, huddle around the young adult to provide comfort, warmth and a sense of security.' Yes, that was it.

seventeen

Jonathan was late for work, gloriously late. Even at midday, sitting down to lunch with Jake, his loins still ached from the pounding they have received that very morning – that very morning! By then he was unable to control what he believed to be his newfound knowledge. He told Jake over a second dessert ('Need the energy!')

'I just can't believe it. It's like she's on drugs or something,' he whispered to the salivating Jake, himself returned from a weekend of 'It's your turn to watch the kids,' 'This garden is a mess' and 'No more for me thanks, I'd best get back anyway.'

Jake had had many problems with his wife, particularly after the second child when he'd sent her back to the hospital for "tightening" on the grounds that she'd "lost a bit of grip". It soon became clear that it was more than a bit of delicate sewing that would be required to bring some sparkle back into their bedroom. Now, like so many men in the office, Jake's sex life took place between the hours of 8:45 and 6:15, featuring him and various colleagues, secretaries, temps and assistants in desktop fantasies. No-one knew about this though. It was Jake's secret. Complete and satisfying though his fantasy life was, the thought of something better at home was extremely attractive. He got Jonathan to outline the programme again. Only the day seemed an unnecessary barrier. Why did he have to wait until Thursday? What was wrong with starting tomorrow?

'Listen, Jake,' Jonathan explained with the air of a master, 'It's best not to meddle with these things. Stick with the programme that works. Thursdays are Spontaneous Sex days and that's all there is to it.'

Jake deferred to his wisdom. Thursday was only a couple of days away.

eighteen

The Food Court was busy, filled with mothers, grandmothers and pushchairs. Pre-school children shot around the tables like pinballs. Nick considered the options, recognising that he and Alison were still at that point where food choices and menus were the testing grounds for communication.

'There's a lot of "Not Quite" food retailers here . . .,' he said, surveying the array of non-brand fast food outlets with their imitative colour palettes, 'Apparently we can protect the environment with a cheeseburger at this café with a name derived from nature.'

Alison smiled. Her joy at simply being there was complete. Nick noticed that she did not have the vapid, young-mother look of yesterday. That is to say, she had actually spent less time on her appearance, sparing the dutiful make-up and the part-of-a-clan clothing. She looked younger, livelier. More attractive. Sexual. It was easier to see the girl he had known.

'A cheeseburger would be nice,' Alison said, smiling at Nick, taking in his new outfit, 'I told you it suits you.'

The whole story took a disarmingly short time. Most people's lives would. Intricacies are less important than attention spans; stories are compacted depending upon how much time you think the other person has. Although in this case Nick simply did not wish to dwell. He explained how he had changed school, gone to university, got a job, did well, and had been unexpectedly sacked.

But Alison was interested. She probed and, by-and-by, the details and emotion fell out, until the full extent of Nick's descent was clear. He had done very well at university, although with no discernible remnants other than his degree. At Belston he had shone from the moment his first report hit the screen. Unless he was lying, and she did not feel he was, there was no reason why he would suddenly be considered dispensable. She felt the intense anger of seeing somebody unreasonably diminished. Nick morosely surveyed his almost-empty plate, exhausted by the telling, yet also light-headed and relieved for having done so.

'You know,' he said, looking up, 'For most of my life I have tried not to be The Limp Guy. And I've succeeded. I'm now The Angry Parrot guy.'

He impaled the last chip. 'All gone,' he said softly. Not yet, thought Alison, not yet.

"I'll go under if you don't come over . . ."

The lush, studio-elongated harmonies of a manufactured band swooshed around the vast music shop. At the counter, two teenage schoolgirls pawed at the manufactured band's calendar, eager in particular for the brunette singer, naked (February), while a third read and re-read, lips moving, the back of the *For The Fans* concert book.

"I just can't deal with your sex appeal."

Brunette singer, solo, addressed the camera on the monitors overhead.

"How can I ignore these feelings I feel?"

Nick and Alison had been watching the scene for several minutes, largely because Nick wanted to.

'I wonder if there's an order to their purchases,' Nick thought out loud, 'Presumably the CD comes first, then the video, then – what? The bag, or the T-shirt, or maybe the baseball cap? What do you think?'

Alison looked puzzled, 'How should I know?'

'You're not that much older,' Nick said.

'I'm twice as old,' she replied, moving off down Pop/Rock M–R.

'People's minds never age as much as "twice" once they're

thirteen or so,' Nick said, considering the different nose sizes of an ageing American pop idol.

'Look at this,' he said, holding up a Greatest Hits, 'Only in music shops do you find this type of thing mixed in with fashion products for kids,' pointing up to one of the non-brunette manufactured band members taking his T-shirt off in slow-mo.

'What about bookshops? They serve all tastes,' Alison said, taking the disc, reading the track listing.

'Not fashion, really,' Nick said absent-mindedly, watching one of the schoolgirls slip a pencil case into her bag.

'Oh Mandy,' Alison replied, and led Nick by the hand to the escalator.

Having met at nine-thirty for a non-brand coffee, they had wandered the mall for most of the morning, Alison playing with the distance between them. Nick, she thought, seemed much more relaxed, content almost. She was right.

After learning about seahorses, Nick had engaged in conversation with his parents, let them know he was thinking about things, conspicuously enjoyed his mother's "special" meal, watched some more television without feeling awkward, gone to bed, slept, woken up eager to go the mall. All this, he knew, was good.

As for Alison, after their disproportionately passionate sex, she and Jonathan had watched one of his very favourite documentaries, then she had cooked spaghetti and they had had more sex, until her husband had to say 'No more.' Then Alison had said that tomorrow, Saturday, he could play golf, as she wanted to go shopping. She lay awake until three thinking of Nick and faraway places.

The two had already passed a couple of shoe shops before Nick paused in front paused in front of a shop offering Gentleman's Footwear, clearly expensive, its "ye olde wood" design jarring splendidly with the surrounding functional MDF. Alison had talked quickly as they passed the other shoe shops, seeking to distract Nick from their difficult products. He now tugged her back into the outlet's warm yellow light. They stared through the window in silence at the array of fine footwear. After a few minutes Nick went in, visiting each display, stopping at a pair of black brogues. Nick asked the assistant – Amanda, Senior Foot Fitter" – for a pair, '8½, I think,' while Alison took a seat in the middle of a row of handsome wooden chairs. Nick brought a footstool over, sat down next to her and took his shoes off. Amanda returned and took up position astride the footstool, pleased to see that the gentleman's feet were ready and waiting. She offered the shoes to him with a polite 'Sir?' exactly as the manual said – "As a waiter might present a bottle of wine." Nick nodded and Amanda began to place Nick's feet in the shoes. As the second shoe was slipped on, Amanda became aware that the woman had moved nearer to the gentleman and seemed to have taken his hand in her own, and that they were now staring into each other's eyes. Amanda kept her eyes down, unable to recall a training manual recommendation for such an occurrence, instead fixing her concentration on completing a firm, "but not stifling" knot in each lace. This completed, she looked up at the couple, clearing her throat. Nick looked back at her.

'Why don't you have a wander about in them for a minute, sir? Check the fit. There's a mirror over there, sir.'

Amanda then retired to her cash till, "to observe without pressuring".

Nick stood and moved slightly from foot to foot, before Alison reached up and pulled him slightly, beckoning for him to sit down again. He sat, placing his feet back on the foot-stool. Abruptly, Alison released her grip on him and moved over to the footstool, sitting astride it, still looking into Nick's face. Gently, she lifted Nick's foot out of first the right, and then the left shoe, caressing each one lovingly as she did so, their eyes locked, their breathing became short. Alison bent over slightly, sealing Nick's feet in a cocoon of hair and flesh. Then she was back beside him, their fingers entwining. There was a cough. Amanda was standing over them, looking down expectantly.

The woman broke off and looked up at her, 'He'll take them.'

Amanda nodded and began to remove the shoes for packaging, despite knowing full well that she really should have made the gentleman have a good walk round first, even out into the mall perhaps. Surveys had shown that the more you get the customer to move around, the less likely they were to return the shoes later.

Nick and Alison ascended gracefully to the second floor and then walked without words among Classical – Jazz – Country and Western, each section opening by heavy automatic door, each door ushering in a new world of music. In Country and Western, as a pained voice began to explain how he was "a lineman for the county", they realised that they had come as far as they could in that shop. There was nowhere else to go. Nick turned and took Alison's other hand, which she was already holding out.

"I need you more than want you. And I want you for all time."

As these words thronged the air, Nick and Alison's lips came together in a union neither of them had ever dreamed would happen, nor could now live without dreaming of. In one tender moment they tricked the fates and a desire of primal power was reborn and engulfed them.

nineteen

Jake avoided Jonathan at Thursday lunchtime. Jonathan tracked him down after work.

'Well?' he leered, as Jake put his briefcase in the back of his estate, next to the child seat. 'Well?' Jake mimicked sarcastically. Jonathan became concerned, 'What happened? Is everything OK?'

'No everything is not OK! Helen isn't talking to me.'

'Didn't you follow the programme?' Jonathan stammered.

'Yes I followed the programme!' Jake spat back, lowering his voice as two colleagues passed, 'It's because of the programme that she's not talking to me. She says she thought she was being assaulted, slapped me, told me to get off.'

'Oh,' Jonathan said.

'Thanks very much,' Jake said, getting into the car. Jonathan ran round to his window, rapped on it hard. Jake buzzed it down a couple of inches.

'Now Jake, listen, please. Give it time. Believe me it works,' Jonathan said earnestly. Jake glared at him, gunned the engine, said, 'Goodnight,' tersely and turned out of his space.

'Jake! Listen! Stick with the programme!' Jonathan called as Jake speeded up out of the car park. The two colleagues watched in silence, then continued on their way.

twenty

They did not see each other on Sunday. Although the mall was open, Alison had to accompany Jonathan to her parents to retrieve the children. This did nothing to improve her mood. Alison was already uptight. She had been waiting for Jonathan when he came back from his golf on the Saturday evening, but he had professed exhaustion and hidden in his study for most of the night, only coming out when he thought she had safely gone to sleep. He was wrong. Then, reminding her that they had to get up early for the children, he lay on his front, clutching the pillow lest she try to turn him over. Alison was awake until dawn, the light heralding an unwelcome day when she knew she would not see Nick. Only then did she drift off, her mind seeking to avoid such a thing altogether.

'And how are things?'

This was the fourth time that her mother had tried to extract the same information from her. Alison had stonewalled through 'Everything OK?', 'Did you enjoy the little break?' and a questioning 'You look well,' with the same non-committal 'Mmm'. Fully rested she might have played along a bit. As it was the sight of Jonathan chumming it up with her own parents served only to make her feel less connected to them all. Eager to stop the gentle queries, she took Samuel and Kimberley for a walk, allowing Jonathan time to make the right noises.

The drive home felt terminal. The children's joy at being with Mummy and Daddy again – 'Granny smells funny' – was a jolting reminder to Alison that this was her life. Jonathan could be ignored or re-cast; Samuel and Kimberley were nothing less than an insatiable beast, eating every minute of her existence. She wondered, almost out loud, why they didn't arrange a rota, so that she had no free time whatsoever. No matter what happened, no matter how big a house they lived in, how much Jonathan earned, how clever and inventive household appliances became, these children would consume her life. She could hear them gnawing away at it in the back seat.

'Stop the car!' she shouted. Jonathan slowed abruptly without stopping.

'What is it?' he asked, looking from her to the road and back.

'Just stop the fucking car!'

The car stopped. Alison got out. She leaned in.

'I'm going to walk back.'

'Don't be ridiculous, it's miles!' Jonathan said, trying to sound calm, one eye on the children.

'I'll see you later,' Alison closed the door and set off. Jonathan drove alongside her, talking through the sunroof, trying to get her back in. Eventually she stopped replying and he reluctantly drove off.

'Mummy has to pick some flowers,' was all that he could come up with, as his wife disappeared in the rear-view mirror.

Nick went to the shopping mall on his own. Even without Alison it still had some of the magic of their joint presence. In particular, the Country and Western section had a transcendental air that he was happy to breathe in for hours. Amanda, senior foot fitter, noticed the gentleman from the other day wandering around the displays and feared the worst. Then she noticed he was wearing the shoes he had bought. So he couldn't be bringing them back.

'Can I be of any assistance?' she asked with prerequisite antiquated charm.

'No, thanks,' the gentleman said politely, 'I'm just . . .' and then he was gone. Funny, she remembered him as having more of a limp. Nick spent the rest of the day going round the various travel agents, turning up at his parents' house with two plastic bags filled with brochures, which he pored over deep into the night.

twenty-one

The rain washed down for four days, bleaching the town of what little colour it had. Alison stalked the hours like a wild dog, seeking anything with which to kill time. Samuel, initially receptive of this unending attention, eventually tired of his mother's demand for activities and games. He wanted to be left alone sometimes, to live out the worlds only he could see. It was no good if you had to explain it to Mummy as you went along. She and Nick had not arranged to meet on Monday. He had said that he would call in the morning. Which he did to say that they could not meet until Thursday – there were things he had to think about.

"Things he had to think about."

The phrase preyed on Alison's mind. She did not know or care that Jonathan began to think that maybe he had done a bit too much of the Spontaneous Sex. Since arriving back on Sunday evening, clothes heavy with water, Alison seemed to switch between being happy and truculent. She took to staring out the window for hours on end, the word "dull" flashing, a neon grey sign, above the streets. A sign that nobody else could see.

'Are you sure you don't want anything?' Nick had ordered a Full Health Breakfast.

'The coffee is fine,' Alison said, adding, 'I'll get us somewhere to sit,' and disappearing into the tables of the environmental café. He sat down opposite her and took a sip from his orange juice. She ignored her coffee and they were silent for minutes, content to be at the centre of a tense universe. Nick looked at her, then opened his mouth to speak.

'Wherever you're going I'm coming with you.'

Her matter of fact tones cut through Nick's reflective air. He paused, smiling, continuing,

'Alison. I have things that I have to do. And after those things are done, I have no idea what I am going to do.'

Alison's hand had stretched out to take his as he spoke.

'I don't care,' she said softly, stroking the back of his hand.

Nick looked at her in admiration. 'You have no idea where this might take us,' he said, smiling.

'What could be worse than a life like this?' Alison asked, not looking around her, shivering in recollection of Jonathan's fingers.

As the shopping mall began to fill up, they were themselves beautifully alone in contemplation of their lustrous, unknown future.

Half an hour later, as they walked hand in hand through the car park, looking every inch the happily married shopping couple, childless but planning, Alison turned to Nick, pulling him close. They kissed delicately, with a briefness of touch too erotic to be that of a Mr and Mrs. 'What is it we have to do?' she asked, her barely audible voice emphasising the depth of her commitment. Nick looked at her, seized with the wonder of total trust. 'Travel and revenge,' he said. And their laughter burst up to the sky.

twenty-two

Jonathan came home at 7.00 p.m. He'd phoned in the afternoon, saying he was going to be a bit later than usual, and not to worry about getting any food ready.

'As a matter of fact, I'll bring a Chinese back,' adding, 'That's the food – not a person.'

Strangely, the house was dark. His first thought was that they had all gone shopping. But then there was the car, Alison's compact hatchback, parked in front of the twin garage. Paused in neutral on the driveway, Jonathan pondered the seemingly incompatible issues of the car's presence and the darkened house. Then he clicked, said, 'I see,' to himself.

It was one of those games. On a couple of previous occasions Samuel had insisted that everybody hid when Daddy came home. They would all jump out when Jonathan, with a level of extreme melodrama that tested his acting ability, broke down at the kitchen table, wailing, 'We love you, Daddy! We love you, Daddy!' Sometimes they would hit him with pillows too.

Psyching himself into the role, Jonathan opened the door breezily, with a cartoon shout of, 'Hi, everyone! I'm home!' adding 'Daddy's here!' as he set down the Chinese on the hall table. He thought he heard a snigger upstairs, and, with exceptionally heavy feet, worked his way up to the children's bedrooms. 'Isn't this place quiet?' his voice echoed round "Samuel's HQ", as the crayoned door sign declared, the edges of the poster fluttering lightly.

'Where is everyone?' Jonathan demanded with loud incredulity, pushing Kimberley's door open, the purple dinosaur mobile spinning madly in the rush of air. And their room, Alison and his, as tidy as ever.

'I think there's nobody here!' Jonathan cried, trudging despondently down the stairs, wondering if they would be in the hall or the kitchen cupboard. He picked up the takeaway and moved it through to the kitchen, banging into a chair as he did so. God, it was dark. He sat down.

'I'm all alone. Everyone has left me! Nobody loves me,' he wailed into the night. Then silence. He waited for the rush. The silence continued, seemed to intensify. 'Doesn't anybody love me?' he roared, giving them that extra bit of tittering-in-the-dark mileage. But there was no response, no sudden burst from a cupboard. Jonathan stood up and walked back to the hall cupboard, pulling it open with a loud 'Aha!' The vacuum cleaner, a brush, refuse sacks, countless odds and ends. He moved back to the kitchen, intent on the cupboard. Then he saw it on the sideboard, next to the kettle ('I always have a coffee when I come in, Officer'): a folded note, with no name on it. Jonathan picked it up, the house becoming darker.

Nick had insisted on the note. Alison had simply wanted to leave.

'Without a note, they'll think something untoward, illegal. With a note you're an uneventful disillusioned wife!'

Alison had nodded.

The note read: "Jonathan – I have left you. The children are at my parents. Please do not try to follow or find me. I will not be coming back. This is nothing personal, just one of those things. I do not want any part of the house, but I hope you will understand that I have taken money from our joint account, in lieu of a settlement, for new clothes and things. With best wishes, Alison.'

It was all Nick's composition, apart from the "nothing personal" and "best wishes", which Alison decided at the last minute she wanted to put in, 'Don't ask why.' She picked Samuel up as usual from school, and then drove both Kimberley and him to her parents. They had already been telephoned and

117

asked if they wouldn't mind looking after the children for another night, 'Jonathan and I would like a wee bit more time together.' In the boot of the car already was a minimal selection of clothing – underwear mostly – toiletries and a large, empty suitcase.

Joe and Philippa would get their own note in the post the next morning. It started "By now Jonathan will have been in touch and you will know the main points . . ." concluding with her heartfelt thanks for all that they had ever done for her and reminding them that, as their daughter, she loved them with all her heart but that they "must understand that people have to do what is right for them", which is what she was now doing. Nick explained that it was important to remind them that she was their daughter, in the light of Jonathan's apparent closeness to them. 'Keeping them on your side of the fence is absolutely necessary'.

Every penny of the joint account had been cleared out apart from what Alison reasoned Jonathan would need until that month's pay came through. Her own account she left untouched.

'Don't take any clothes, just in case the police look into it. They're far more likely to arrive at an accurate description if they can describe what's been taken. You never know, Jonathan might even hire someone,' had been Nick's counsel and the mention of new clothes in the note underlined the uselessness of issuing a "She is thought to be wearing" profile. Alison liked the idea of some wholesale jettisoning anyway.

Nick had also suggested the meeting with a lawyer. Nothing grand, one of the local practitioners. Alison asked an Alistair Hampshire to act for her, in her absence, outlining what she was doing, 'leaving my husband', and agreeing a small retainer to cover any likely matters arising. One specific duty was for Hampshire to notify Jonathan in writing the next day that she had indeed left him and that any enquiries should be dealt with through his offices.

Leaving the children she found oddly simple. For whatever

reason Alison felt no need for note or gesture with them. She knew they were in safe hands. This was not about them, she thought, not really.

'Hello . . . eh . . . Nice to meet you, Alison,' Mrs Durning said, bashfully rubbing her hands together. Mr Durning stood behind her, uneasily smiling.

'Hello,' Alison said, confidently, 'Thanks for having me to stay.'

'That's all right, dear. Nick doesn't have his friends over often enough, that's what we always say,' his mother said, effortlessly joining the here and now with her son's teenage years, as if but a day separated them. Mr Durning's uneasy smile continued.

Nick had asked, as a matter of notification, if one of his friends could use the spare room for a couple of days. She was having "some trouble at home" – no details – and there was even a possibility that she might come with Nick on the extended holiday that he had told them about the other evening. They both, but particularly Mrs Durning, took the depth of this sudden involvement in their son's life as an unalloyed blessing. So long the watchers, at times uncomprehending, of his hectic business life, here was their opportunity to be of use, to do something.

'We're all he's got,' Mr Durning had said to his wife late one night when Nick had gone to bed, as they once more went over how they would always be there for him.

Alison had not been happy about the arrangement. She had envisaged many things, perhaps a celebratory stay in London (she had looked up all sorts of hotels for that sort of thing), with a meal somewhere appropriate. Then a night of uncapped boozing into the small hours around Soho. All these things and more. Nick, however, had been firm. Feet on the ground, initially. Although their combined resources – the pooling of his savings, shares, and redundancy pay with her money – created a tidy pool, Nick was clear that it would disappear faster than either of them wished.

'Let's be safe, keep things in perspective,' he had urged her, as they had held hands in a shop that sold little but dough-nuts, 'This is the beginning. That must be our excitement for the meantime. Besides, we'll be off soon, and that will be more than enough of a change. Hotels could bring recognition. There'll be plenty of time for that sort of stuff later.'

Alison managed a laugh at her own fantasy start. Nick was right. Everything that had happened already and was about to happen was excitement enough. And other things would follow, of that she, they, were sure. So she agreed to stay with his parents, and both of them understood that this meant they would not be sleeping together. Not that it mattered. They were together.

twenty-three

'The idea is to provide a rough and tumble insight into what it means to be the working rich in today's Britain.'

'And who is the central focus of the programme?' Genevieve asked with care, exchanging glances with the shadowy figure of Charlotte, sitting with her notepad away from the main group of three at the desk. Steve Geroldi and Spiggy Thomlinson were the director and producer respectively of *Top Flight*, the docudrama that the Rutherfords were to feature in.

'We prefer to have a series of characters, rather than just the one,' Spiggy said, with a degree of earnestness that indicated that she felt that the programme would prove to be a landmark of broadcasting. From her previous media dealings Genevieve was aware that the degree of gravity with which programme makers treated any project was inversely proportional to its puerility.

'We never know who will turn out to have star value, be it in their character or their storyline,' Steve added, bushbaby eyes wandering the room.

'Who have you identified so far?' Genevieve asked, somewhat reluctantly, instinctively fearful of the possible answers.

The set-up was already the worst possible scenario. The Rutherfords' youngest daughter, Stephanie, had put the whole thing in progress through a friend of a friend, all in order that Stephanie might get her desired first step into media.

Getting into the media was the stated objective of a good number of the offspring of Genevieve's private clients. It had the right combination of glamour, jargon and money to attract young people who, were it not for their wealthy parents, would be borderline shop assistants. She herself was occasionally called upon to give a first step into PR for one of her clients' dense juveniles.

For themselves, Pommy and Genevieve had reached an explicit agreement some years back that it was better to keep their offspring travelling than to allow them to come back home. Travelling was relatively cheap compared to setting someone up in business, and less painful than asking for favours from various contacts.

'Little bit of cash just to keep them on the road,' Pommy had said, 'Not too much though. Enough to maintain body and soul. They can write a fucking diary or something.'

So far only Justin, their eldest, had forced his way back to the roost, after some five years on the road during which time he had lost the small finger on one of hand – neither parent could remember which – and his faith in Christianity. Justin had managed to stay home for about three weeks before Pommy orchestrated an African traineeship of unspecified duration.

'Well,' said Spiggy, 'So far we have Dan Rutherford, the eldest boy, who is just back from rural India and . . .'

'. . . has plans for his own juice bar,' Genevieve concluded unenthusiastically.

'. . . has plans for his own juice bar,' Spiggy confirmed, reading from her notes.

Of course, not all offspring wanted to get into media. The rest divided between some form of innovation in catering and something to do with information technology. George Freiberg was well ahead, mentally at any rate, with plans for his own barter-based café cooperative. Like most of the other offspring, his plans were indulged to a non-damaging degree because 'quite frankly the lad is fucking useless', as Pommy had stated to Genevieve after another plea for money. The last such discussion had ended with Pommy making any further sums conditional on George going off for 'a year or three' to do the proper research.

'Right,' said Steve, 'So, we'll be following Dan in his development work and in his socialising in the run-up to the big night itself.'

'Who else?' Genevieve asked, still nervous.

'There's Ginny Rutherford herself. She's key obviously. We can tell she cares a lot about . . . things,' Spiggy said carefully.

Genevieve knew what she meant. Ginny was as easily distracted as a puppy and liable to get immersed in areas of such inconsequence that Genevieve had considered fitting her with blinkers for their last event.

'And?' Genevieve prompted.

'Well,' Spiggy said thoughtfully, 'There's Charlie Dunsworthy – Stephanie's boyfriend.'

Of course, how could he refuse?

'Techno man,' said Steve, nodding, happy, 'Good vibrant overtones, you know.'

Genevieve smiled to accommodate Steve's attitude, effortlessly hiding her disappointment that Charlie, one of her occasional shags, would now be off the agenda for a while.

'And then,' Spiggy said quietly, 'There's the event organisers themselves,' and she opened her hands and looked around her, smiling widely.

'Meaning that you wish to follow me around for the duration,' Genevieve said with as good nature as she could muster.

'No, actually,' Spiggy said smartly, cosying up to the desk, 'We were rather hoping for one of your junior colleagues,' and she swivelled her eyes in Charlotte's direction.

'Charlotte?' Genevieve said with a yelp.

'Yeh, Charlotte!' Steve said with loud enthusiasm. They all turned to look at Genevieve's assistant, lolling behind them in her chair with all the grace of an over-ripe mango.

'Yes, Charlotte,' Spiggy said, turning back to Genevieve, adding the bullet through the forehead with, 'Johnny and Ginny said it would be absolutely fine.'

'Oh . . . did . . . well, then . . . that's . . . fine . . . then. Great,' Genevieve said softly, staring blankly at the desk top, her ears filling with the distant sound of a horse having bolted.

'So is it going out live or not?' Genevieve asked.

'It's going to be "as live",' Spiggy said excitedly.

The conversation had been going back and forth on this point for several minutes already. 'Is that live or not?' Genevieve asked, trying not to lose her patience.

'It's *perceived* to be live. The viewing audience will feel that they're right there – in on the action,' said Steve seriously, catching on that Genevieve was less than caught up in their enthusiasm.

'But it's not *actually* live, is it?' Genevieve, hardening her tone.

'Well, it's *as live*,' Spiggy responded, hardening with her.

Genevieve sighed and had to resist putting her head in her hands. Think of the client. New tack.

'And will we be able to see any footage before it is broadcast?' she asked, smiling, positive.

'No,' Spiggy and Steve together.

'I see,' said Genevieve. She made a note on her pad: "speak johnny – filming parameters". Then she looked over at Charlotte's gloomy outline, scribbling like fury on her yellow legal pad, legacy of the American crime thrillers Genevieve had found her reading in quiet moments.

'And the focus from our side will be on . . . here?' she indicated with a slight wave of her hands the world in which they sat.

'Basically, yes. Obviously you'll feature,' Spiggy said, in such a way as to imply that that must be Genevieve's major concern.

'But,' the producer continued, 'the primary storyline will rest with Charlotte and her work and life.'

'Her life?' Genevieve asked, genuinely incredulous at the thought.

'Oh, yes!' Steve bounced up in his seat, 'Her life! You need to have that 3D effect or the viewer questions the authenticity of the character.'

'Where will you find this . . . life?' Genevieve asked, puzzled.

'Oh, you know, the usual places. Homes, shopping, relationships,' Steve reeled off nonchalantly.

'And work,' Spiggy said, topping it off.

'Gosh, Charlotte, you're going to be quite the little star, aren't you?' Genevieve observed to no one in particular. Charlotte, alerted to her name being used, looked up absently, a dog disturbed from its dinner, and then resumed her notes.

twenty-four

Eighteen minutes to ten. That was the time that had been agreed. And it was almost twenty to now. Pommy glanced at his watch again, sighed. He always made appointments for precise, seemingly obtuse times.

'If you say ten o'clock every fucker saunters in at five past. Say ten to ten and its like holding up a fucking board that says TEN,' he had told Durning as they rode in the lift one day to a 3.37 p.m. meeting with a team of auditors.

'But make it somewhat removed from the norm and everyone perks up a bit. Fuckers spend most of the day thinking, "Why 3.37? Why not 3.45 or four?" And making them think about that means that they make sure they are there for 3.37. Fucking sad, really. Still, whatever makes the fuckers appear.'

Pommy stood by the window in his apartment. Nineteen minutes to ten. He sipped at his martini. Perfect – bite without fire. A taxi rounded the corner and proceeded at door-number-reading speed down the quiet street. Pommy stepped back quickly from the window. Never pays to let the fuckers know you're waiting. The cab stopped below and Pommy leaned out slightly, in time to catch the coat-tails of a figure scampering up the steps of the building. Pommy surveyed the street once more and then went and sat down by the fire, placing his glass on a side table and picking up the remote control, with which he let Haydn (or was it fucking Brahms?) fade in over the room. Load of soggy bollocks anyway. From the hallway came the sound of the door opening and closing, then a female voice.

'What a day I've had!' Henrietta Kilpatrick burst into the

room, throwing a large leather bag down by the door. She headed straight for the drinks cabinet, where she made herself a large vodka and tonic. Pommy sat. He found Henrietta's utter disregard for his elevated status quite bewitching. She was now staring out of the window, in much the same way he had been. With self-conscious good grace Pommy raised himself and walked over, circling her waist with his arm, joining her in contemplation of the glistening streets.

'It's good to see you again,' Pommy purred in his best older man rumble.

That's what they want – the older man rumble. Don't want you running around the tennis court getting all huffy and puffy pretending you're their age. If they want someone their age they can get them, generally. Let the young bloods do all that fun stuff. Fun. Don't come to you for fun. Come to you for statesmanlike maturity, unyielding mass of experience, jungle survivor. That sort of thing. Not fun. Fuck fun.

Henrietta shifted the balance of her feet so that she nestled into Pommy, her rainy hair brushing against his cheek.

'What's happened to Nick Durning?'

The question was as unexpected as it was perplexing.

'Don't know. Why?' Pommy replied, letting the sounds resonate out from his chest so that Henrietta would feel the vibrations as much as hear the words. She trembled accordingly and nuzzled closer. Pommy smiled.

'It's just that, I had to finish off the Two Lips Agreement today, and I thought of him, that's all.'

She pulled away and went to the drinks cabinet, abruptly marooning Pommy at the window in a state of mild agitation. This was a sex-based relationship and he could feel the gentle lapping of more substantial, less worthy, waters at his toes. Still, no point being fucking King Canute, standing here getting wet, he thought. Best to walk up the beach a bit, sit somewhere else. With this thought he turned from the window and went across to where Henrietta was staring pensively into her brimming glass.

Strictly speaking, having an affair with Henrietta was outside Pommy's parameters of safe affairs. She was, after all, business; a young, doing-well-enough lawyer from one of Belston Corporation's large group of supplier law firms. There was, nevertheless, something about her, an attitude that Pommy could not quite place. All he could say with any certainty was that he found she had an amazingly erotic presence. Good thing for a woman to have too, an erotic presence. Much better than a sexual presence. Sexual presence can be good or bad. Some women have about them a sort of repulsive sexuality: all body and no attitude. Henrietta was erotic though. Something about her. Couldn't quite say what. Pommy moved closely in next to her.

'These things happen in business, darling. You know how it is.'

He stroked her chin gently and she looked up at him. Then moved her head slightly, in tiny demurral, and Pommy suffered a frisson of misgiving as she began to speak again.

'It hardly seems fair . . .'

The rest of her words became a blur of noise because Pommy knew what was coming. He had known the word "fair" was coming. In every discussion involving the non-committed, and there were plenty of them around, that word always floated to the surface eventually. And the non-committed were only too eager to grasp at it, filled as it was with a sufficiently high-minded air to keep them bobbing around for hours of self-satisfying shilly-shallying. "Fair." Of *course* business wasn't fucking fair. Business wasn't meant to be fair. That was society's job. Society had laws, courts, police, jails; everything that was required to make sure that things were fair. Business was not about fucking fair. Business was about things like profit, success, and power.

'I know what you mean, dear,' Pommy said through skilfully ungritted teeth. He pulled Henrietta closer to him. He regretted having had to use Henrietta in the dismissal of Durning, but at the time it was the only plausible way to get him out of the office without suspicion. Move fast, that's the key. 'But Henrietta, you're in business yourself, you know how these things can be. Action of a certain kind was required. Nobody enjoys doing these things.'

Pommy did not lie when he said this. He did not enjoy doing these things. Such actions were neither enjoyable nor unenjoyable – they simply were. Good job she didn't know the full story though. And a good job her career was strongly intertwined with maintaining the Belston account. Still, she had done the job; kept Durning away for a few hours while things were arranged.

'Nobody enjoys doing these things,' Pommy repeated, now more softly, almost sad.

'Mmh . . . I suppose so,' Henrietta said, not yet convinced but with enough of a change of tone for Pommy to know he should seal the subject now. He turned his own body slightly and, gently stroking Henrietta's head around, he kissed her manfully on the lips, withdrawing before she might think him one-track minded, a simple rule that Pommy was always careful to observe on the first kiss of any evening. Then he lifted both their drinks and, with a slight toss of the head and a world-weary smile, indicated for her to follow him back to the window. Always have a vista to hand when talking to women about something emotional. They stood together looking out at the mass of buildings that filled every inch of the view.

'Look out across the rooftops, Henri. They go on forever. Beneath every one of those rooftops is a building and within that building will be several rooms and in each and every one of those rooms will be many different worlds.'

Pommy handed her the drink and softly touched the back of her neck. What a lot more work this was than whores. Need to keep in practice though.

'Just because young Nick has been thrown out of one world does not mean that he has been thrown out of them all. He is a young man. Clever, insightful – perhaps a tad over analytical

– but brilliant in some ways. He'll pop up in some other world and things will work themselves out.'

Henrietta's body was relaxed now and Pommy knew that the situation was drawing to a close.

'And remember, Henri,' he said slowly, tenderly, pacing his words, bringing her into his confidence, making her feel a part of his world and its concerns, 'Sometimes these things are necessary in . . .'

Henrietta turned and kissed him, her lips cutting off whatever might have been about to come. Pommy set down their glasses and they embraced completely. He felt the thrill of pulling the younger woman closer to him, her wonderful body pressing into him. In time, and not too much time Pommy realised, he would have to let her go too. For the moment though he could close his eyes and enjoy the pleasure of her. Yet for whatever reason, Pommy found that he had his eyes open and that he was staring out across the rooftops, as if searching for some sign. It was odd. So despite the feel of Henrietta tight and warm against him, the stronger awareness was of the reassuring coldness of his heart and it filled him with joy.

twenty-five

Several hours and worlds away, Nick and Alison were having breakfast. They preferred to eat out rather than at home with Mr and Mrs Durning. The latter couple evinced conspicuous understanding on this point. No shopping mall food court had ever contained such bounty. The happy young couple talked and talked about travel. For both of them it seemed an obvious thing to do. Alison was desperate to move, to keep going, while Nick knew that it was what people in their situation should do: escape and celebrate. It would give Alison strength, help make her his, and he knew that it would be good for him. Having been cast overboard it was impossible not to feel a measure of pride; he had not only learned how to swim but had found a current to carry him closer to landfall.

Over two days they stood around bookstores and travel agents, considering options, fine-tuning ideas. Together they enjoyed the excitement of a safe-enough world. They were young, clever and mutually besotted and no atlas was big enough. The further afield they could plan the greater their love would be, as if each mile covered was a bid in an auction of passion. Nick had one overarching consideration, which was to visit places that were current. For as far as his heart might take him, he could not dispense with the need for a rationale altogether. Yes, he wanted to go round the world with Alison; yes, he wanted to do this just to make her happy. But he could not dispense with his own needs altogether. Meaning was required in some form.

Nick's method was to start with the country and then select the areas within it that were relevant. Some seemed obvious to

Alison, others less so. While "France – Paris" was as understandable as "USA – New York", she was less sure of "USA – Las Vegas". 'Entertainment,' was Nick's thoughtful reply.

'What about "USA – Minneapolis?"' she asked, unaware of a single fact about a city which sounded very familiar. 'Big shopping mall – world's biggest, I think,' Nick said, as if conferring with himself, 'Either way it's a non East or West coast consumer experience. Put down L.A., by the way.'

'Are we going to enjoy ourselves?' Alison asked at one point, suddenly apprehensive about a round-the-world management survey.

'Of course we are!' Nick said, writing down "Mongolia – Ulan Bator" in his notebook, 'And as we enjoy we will take in, learn, soak up, discover.'

'And we'll be together,' Alison said, encroaching into his personal space, causing some shoppers to look away and others to steady themselves for the forthcoming intimacy.

'Yes, we'll be together,' Nick said tenderly, and they kissed against a backdrop of a million unknown places.

There was no time to get all the inoculations that were recommended. So they got the obvious ones – yellow fever, typhoid, tetanus, hepatitis A and B – and agreed to get the others as and where necessary, on the road.

'Where exactly are you going?' the doctor asked.

'Everywhere,' they replied in unison.

At a swish tent shop they bought two World Trek medical kits. Together with underwear, that was all they packed in two no-nonsense carry-on bags.

Nick and Alison were booked onto the 9.30 to Brussels. Waterloo was stiff with business people, school groups and students of all nationalities. The couple delighted in the air of so much broken English, feeling their own language made them in some way chosen. Alison in particular was beside herself with happiness. It made her shudder to think of her life barely one month ago. Now, part of an international throng, she felt that something was truly, truly happening for her for the first time in a long, bleak period and the fact of not knowing exactly where it might all end simply added to the thrill. And although Nick tried to contain his excitement, even his own analysis of the situation could not break free from the sense of something fantastic. But it was Alison who was most affected, almost laughing with fright at the wonder of it all. Look at her! She was going round the world!

Unknown to either of them, walking along the platform was Lawrence Dexter, who had at one time worked with Alison's husband Jonathan. Lawrence was returning from a conference in Antwerp. He remarked to himself how similar the woman getting onto the train was to Jonathan's wife, what's-her-name? They had met at some company do or other, along with endless other partners, spouses, preferred descriptors, none of whom had particularly stuck in his mind. But Jonathan's wife had, principally because he fancied her. And there she was now, or someone very like her, getting onto the train with a man with a limp. How strange. He had half a mind to move over for a closer look, before he was distracted by a couple of good-looking breasts coming towards him. Not a bad face either.

twenty-six

If you want to place a curse on someone, drop out of his or her life with no explanation. Obviously the degree to which this affects them will depend on their relationship with you. A shop-keeper will simply think you have moved away, an ex-work colleague that, well, people don't always keep in touch, do they? For most of our adult lives we let people fade and disappear, their ghostly forms returning through the prompt of a certain colour, scent or word. But if you abruptly disappear on some-one who cares about you in any way, then your disappearance will cause more pain than any act you might otherwise have visited upon them. It is a negation, a rubbing out, of every second they ever spent being with you, thinking about you, doing something for you. You are throwing part of their exis-tence on the fire, leaving them less than whole; a spent piece of a person.

That is what Jonathan was on his way to becoming from the moment that he opened the note in the kitchen. He sat, absolutely not believing what it said, for an hour. Then he phoned Joe and Philippa, before going round there to pick up the children. As he drove he told himself to be calm, that this would simply be a stage, that everything would work out. It would be OK when he spoke to Alison, he was sure. Jonathan maintained this outlook over the next forty-eight hours, even when the lawyer's letter from Alistair Hampshire confirmed a degree of cunning and planning on his wife's part which he would never have imagined her capable of.

'Well, we've got her details now.'

The police were polite but uninterested. Jonathan had, of

course, contacted them, but once they'd examined the various letters they were in no doubt that this was 'not a police matter, sir'.

'I appreciate that, Sergeant, but I'm concerned about her state of mind. Even her parents will confirm this.'

Sergeant Beattie leaned into Jonathan across the table, taking his time with the question that he knew would get Jonathan out of the station.

'If you don't mind me asking, sir . . .'

Jonathan leaned in too.

'Was everything all right on the home front, if you know what I mean?'

In the brief pause before Jonathan said, 'Yes. Of course,' Sergeant Beattie's chair had already started to move back. Two minutes later, having thanked Beattie for his time, Jonathan sat blank-faced, trounced, behind the wheel of his car.

'There he goes, poor devil,' Sergeant Beattie observed to WPC Finlay, as they both peered through the Venetian blind, 'Still, I'm sure her side of the story would make an interesting comparison.'

They both turned round to deal with the woman whose dog was missing.

A short drive and some perfunctory office greetings later, Jonathan sat dumbfounded, looking at the screen. Having logged on, he had immediately been struck by the number of e-mails waiting for him. Since being off on three days leave – family matters – everybody in the company seemed to have messaged him. Something must have come up on one of his projects. He looked down the list, trying to see who the most important person was and thus to whom he should reply first.

It struck Jonathan, halfway through, that none of the correspondents had given a subject title, which normally indicated that the note was of a personal nature. Surely they didn't all want to play badminton with him? He randomly clicked on one message.

Steve Kingsley, Logistics: Hey, Jonny Boy – what's the story on Spontaneous Sex? Jake says it worked wonders. Let me know sometime soon.

Then another: *Kevin Moodie, Sales – S.Europe: Spontaneous Sex sounds the business. Can we have a word sometime? Cheers.*

And another: *Derek Ward, Distribution: Listen, I need to talk with you urgently. Have spoken to Jake. Please call.*

With fresh, frightened eyes Jonathan scrolled down the list of messages pending. Nearly every married male employee was there.

twenty-seven

At that very moment Genevieve Marsden was looking at her Cast List for the Rutherfords' "Keepers and Beasts" party. The theme, with "animal" as its basic ingredient, had been enthusiastically agreed by the Rutherfords after a presentation which, Genevieve felt, was one of her best.

'It gives your guests the opportunity to either cater to their more base, animalistic urges,' *snigger, snigger,* 'or to opt for the civilising strictures of a human guise which is entirely in keeping with the bestial environment.'

'Will everyone understand, do you think?' – Johnny Rutherford, serious.

'Does this mean I can be a big monkey?' – Ginny Rutherford, euphoric.

'I would propose that we issue some minor guidance for those attending. Given that we want a balanced ratio of Keepers to Beasts, I would propose that only one of each party of, say, six be a designated Keeper. This will of course require a bit more groundwork on our part –' *nod to Charlotte* '– but will not necessitate a dramatic cost in that respect.'

At this point, exactly as rehearsed, Charlotte shuffled forward, clutching her bundle of notes. Ordinarily Genevieve would not allow her to say anything, but Spiggy had asked for Charlotte's role to be "focused up".

'We don't want to change it,' the producer had made clear, 'Just, make it more real.'

'Yeh, real,' Steve chucked in.

Genevieve's assistant did not look up as she read. Charlotte's voice rose from the pit of her body like the dead ascending, filling the room with a low drone that caused Ginny to rub her shoulders as if chilled.

'At the present time we are still ascertaining the viability of the short list of venues although we are certain to arrive at a satisfactory selection in keeping with the appropriate criteria we would prefer to consult with you at a later date on our findings thank you.'

Charlotte sat down. The Rutherfords blinked, looked at each other. Johnny Rutherford cleared his throat. 'Thank you, eh, Charlotte.'

'Genevieve?' Ginny asked abruptly. 'Do we know where we're going to hold it yet?' Genevieve gripped the side of her chair politely.

'Not yet, Ginny, but we will very soon,' she said calmly.

Genevieve did feel confident of this, although she suspected that it would require a bit of sacrificial discomfort on her part. The important point was that the client had, once again, implicitly accepted their report and the crucial phrase "appropriate criteria". It was vital for the client to let this phrase slip by unexamined. Once the venue had been selected, the criteria by which it had been arrived at could be decided upon. Going the other way round could get you into all sorts of trouble, as Genevieve remembered from her early days in the business. Always explain the rationale behind the final choice, not the rationale behind the search. If necessary, throw in a huge list of possibilities, consideration of which will tax even the most demanding of clients.

'I know we're still looking Genevieve, but would it be possible just to get a feel for where you think we might end up?' Johnny asked, sensing his wife's undiminished concern.

Genevieve smiled and nodded to Charlotte, who stepped forward with a large A4 bound folder labelled "Keepers and Beasts – Greater London Venue Options".

twenty-eight

They had a halo. It was apparent to all who saw them. For most people, such an aura of well-being is never to be had. If one were to set out to look for this phenomenon, as likely a place as any to find it would be at a wedding, or rather, in the wedding photographs. Occasionally, on turning over the thick card of the album, one photograph of the bride and groom will glow with inordinate happiness. In that single moment when the camera flashed the completeness of the couple was total; no thoughts, cares or worries can be mapped on their faces other than the joy of their absolute unification. And likely as not such a moment will never be repeated in either of their lifetimes. A murderous regime of advanced living soon takes its toll on the happy couple and bit by bit the corona fades.

Yet very occasionally one may, while waiting to cross a road, or enjoying a beer in a nondescript bar, witness a pairing of people whose implicit delight in being with each other burns through the dismal everyday world. The warmth of their lives lights up your own, briefly, before it is gone and your hopeful heart must dismiss the apparition.

So it was with Nick and Alison on their journey. The halo appeared as the train reached the coast, shortly after Alison leaned over and picked a piece of fluff out of Nick's hair, her hand coming to rest gently upon his as he gazed out over the land. Nick's index finger pulled itself out from under Alison's touch and nestled on top of her own. They smiled without looking at each other, knowing that the other was smiling too, knowing that this was special, and the train swooped into the darkness and under the sea.

Brussels is not the most exotic location to begin with. It is a small city. Outside of the historic centre – and doesn't everywhere these days have a historic centre? – it becomes harshly new, lacking either charm or style. But for Nick and Alison it was foreign and that was enough. For there is no time like that first time you are a couple in a foreign place. Neither of them would ever think of Brussels as lacking in anything, because it was filled with them. They sat around the cobbled squares and wandered aimlessly up and down the tiny streets. In a few short hours they shook off with exhilarating speed the rude intervening years they had been apart, drowning the unrealised misery of those days in a flood of unadulterated tourism.

That first night, in a restaurant on the long bowstring lane of eateries that leads from the central square to the plush shopping streets, Nick became suddenly colder, as if afflicted by a sharp breeze. Alison intuitively pulled her jacket sleeve down with her fingers, before realising that there was no wind to cause such a feeling. Then she reached over and took both his hands in hers.

'What is it? Are you OK?'

Nick nodded, although clearly still unsettled.

'It's amazing,' he said eventually, his voice quiet with shock.

'I might have gone through my entire life without ever thinking of you again, let alone seeing or being with you. It just hit me, that's all.'

He was right and Alison knew it, felt the fear of having her own life continuing as it had been, saw it stretching out to the grave, and gripped Nick's hands tighter. From then they would on occasion feel the need to hold each other, as a view to a parallel life appeared in the mind's eye, prompted by some apparently innocent item or word.

In Amsterdam the next day they buzzed around the canals in a long motor launch, high on marijuana cookies which made Nick sleepy and both of them giggle as they stumbled round the famous painter museum, the seventeenth young couple that day. It did not matter. They loved doing the young-couple things. They loved putting on clogs for photographs, holding over-sized Edam cheeses to their mouths, running in and out of the sex shops embarrassed and thrilled to the hilt. They were Super Young Couple, and this was a parade of their pairing. And it went on and on in a rush of travel. Down to Maastricht. The definition of quaint. The site of a historic treaty. Nice beer. Rotterdam. God, why did we bother? Munich. This is better. Beer halls, tradition, wide, ambulatory streets, a sense of the greatness of life. Vienna. Grandeur, eloquence, a history of empires. And on and on.

And all the time, chasing them, hurrying them along, were the unbroken storm clouds of their previous lives. They each noticed independently that moving made things better, covered up the cracks of light from the other world. The more the fears appeared, the greater the impetus to move, to be distracted. Movement creates its own momentary world, wherein nothing can be fixed long enough for it to become a hazard. By moving without thinking, by revelling in their travel, Nick and Alison were able to eliminate for the most part any wayward look over the shoulder, any frightening vision of what might have been. Movement was the key and both knew that when the movement stopped, as stop it must, there would be a reckoning to be had. Until that time they would pack their bags haphazardly, kiss impulsively in the busiest of streets and make love before dinner. Yet with each day that passed the gathering clouds in their minds would grow darker and loom nearer, and had it not been for the speed of their flight, might have vanished Nick and Alison from the face of the earth. Prague enchanted them, Warsaw upset them and Moscow surprised them. Careering down to Italy they tumbled through Rome, Florence and Milan with the abandon only lovers in Italy can achieve. Then they were moving around and up through Spain, clubbing in Barcelona, art galleries and heat in Madrid, oranges and opera in Seville.

*

On the flight from Lisbon to Marseilles, Nick looked out over the clouds while Alison plunged into sleep. As the aircraft engines reduced their thrust, Nick felt their immense power, flattening the air. He looked around the aircraft interior, at the crumple-suited businessmen, the overdone tourists, the anonymous readers. Alison's hand climbed up and came to rest on his, fingers forcing themselves together. At that point Nick began to know two things: a recovery of self, and a feeling that they would not go on from Paris. From Paris they had intended to leave Europe for Asia, first stop Beijing. But now Nick could feel the beginning of a desire to return, and a readiness to do so. He placed his hand over Alison's and her eyes briefly opened, meeting his then closing in such a way as to communicate in the briefest exchange all the faith and love in the world. When Nick looked out of the window again, he saw the glory of the sun on the clouds, and felt the crowning strength of knowing how close he had come to destruction.

And one week later, Nick and Alison ambled back to their budget hotel from the pipes outide museum. Both were quiet, speaking little although in no way uncomfortable or out of sorts. Once back in their room, they showered together and made love. Then, as they lay peacefully, flicking through the TV channels and drinking sparkling wine, they happened upon a business bulletin. Seven weeks after they had set out to see the world, their travelling came to an end.

twenty-nine

'Lawson Fucking Jennings!'

The name boomed along the corridor outside Pommy's office. Midgely hastily closed the door. The building was already on fire with rumours – that a price had been agreed; that Pommy was taking early retirement; that lawyers had been spotted on the tenth floor – without the CEO fattening the pig with his frank language.

'Lawson Fucking Jennings!'

Pommy thumped the desk again, sending a photo of his yacht *Schadenfreude* to the floor. Midgely picked it up. A knock at the door was followed quickly by the entrance of Humphreys, McClintock and Barne. Why wasn't it Barnes, like everyone else? Pommy thought. They assembled together on the other side of the desk, facing Pommy.

'Don't all stand like that – look like fucking penguins,' Pommy muttered with sufficient venom for them all to attempt a random dispersion around the room. The telephone rang. Everyone looked at it. Midgely stepped gingerly forward and picked it up.

'I thought Mr Freiberg said that no calls were to be . . .'

He paused, a look of mild shock registering, 'Oh'. Midgely looked to Pommy,

'It's Lawson Jennings,' Midgely said, holding out the receiver to his boss, 'For you.'

'What a surprise, Midgely. I would've thought he might wish to speak to you!' Pommy snapped, snatching the telephone. 'Of course it's for fucking me. Right, put the fucker through,' he said calmly down the telephone, before sitting behind the desk,

143

indicating for his people to gather round. Then Pommy leaned forward, replacing the handset, switching the telephone to speaker, so that the whole room could hear both sides of the conversation. With one finger he gestured first to the reverential audience and then to the telephone, in a manner that carried an unmistakable meaning of 'Listen very carefully and say nothing.'

'Hello?' said an uncertain voice.

Lawson's quiet tone caused Pommy to close his eyes in despair, its sheer reasonableness piercing his soul like a silvery harpoon.

'Hello?'

Pommy leaned slowly forward. 'Pommy Freiberg,' he said firmly.

'Ah . . .hi there . . . it's Lawson Jennings here, Pommy . . . I'm glad I managed to get . . .'

'"Mr Freiberg" will do fine, Mr Jennings.'

'Well, that's fine Mr Freiberg, although every calls me Lawson,' Jennings said with undiminished sincerity.

'I'm sure they do,' Pommy said, looking at his lieutenants' faces, hoping they realised that they were getting a great lesson.

'OK. Well, Mr Freiberg, I'll keep this short. By the way, is something wrong with this phone? You sound rather strange.'

'Nothing's wrong, Mr Jennings. You're on speakerphone. I've got some people in.'

'OK. Mmh, I've got some people in too,' and there was an awkward pause before, 'but I'm not on speakerphone.'

Pommy said nothing.

'Do you think you could pick the phone up for a minute, Mr Freiberg? I'd like to keep this call . . . more personal. Speakerphones are a bit impersonal, I find. In general.'

'Mr Jennings, the speakerphone stays. It will save me having to relay any of your . . . point, later. Speakerphones are useful that way.'

'OK. Well, I'm sure you've seen the gist of our offer by now. It's a good one and you know it. And that's no disrespect to your time at the helm, by the way. Nevertheless . . .'

'Mr Jennings, do you have anything of substance to add to your company's earlier statement?'

'No. But in due course we will of course be issuing . . .'

'Yes, I'm sure. And in the meantime you may wish to buy yourself a funnel.'

There was a pause. Pommy noticed with disgust that all of his deputies were perspiring heavily.

'Pardon me? A funnel did you say?' Jennings' curiosity filled the void.

'Yes, to help you shove all the statements you're about to issue up your arse.'

Pommy grabbed the telephone, now whispering, 'You see all the fun you deny your people when you don't use the speakerphone, Mr Jennings.'

Pommy placed the receiver sharply down.

'Right, that's over with. No point in encouraging the fucker or he'll be on the phone every minute of the fucking day. Is our statement ready yet Midgely?'

'Baxter's on his way with it now,' Midgely said, taking out his mobile.

'Fine. It had better be punching with every penny of what we overpay the underfed fucker.'

Pommy stood up, rounded the desk and went to stand by the window, looking down at the mid-morning traffic.

'City Boys love a takeover.' he said reflectively, 'Darwinian stuff. Bastards.'

And with that he turned and waved with both hands for his team to depart the office, as if shooing away a pack of hounds.

thirty

"Changing the Meaning of Resource Management."

It was not the stuff of Oscar Wilde, Lawson thought, but it would communicate what was necessary. That he, Lawson Jennings, was going to bring enlightenment to Belston Corporation. At this very moment the troops of enlightenment were being mobilised. Each and every department in his empire was being briefed by the Communications Team on what the takeover was about; how it would be good for everyone at Exodus; how they would help lead the way in a revolution in people's lives.

At the conclusion of each presentation, a video of Lawson was played, where he re-iterated the main points, initially walking down a street in everyday Britain. As he passed, well-cast ordinary people would stop to listen to his words, then abandon their tasks and follow him. The backdrop then morphed through a series of the countries and cities where Belston Corporation had operations, and in each Lawson achieved a spectacular level of recognition and understanding from the bystanders he met. At the end, as the final words of "Taking control for people" rolled with matey earnestness from Lawson's lips, the camera panned back to reveal the entire street swathed in the Exodus corporate colours of lilac and white, banners waving wildly like a football crowd, as the steady *thump-thump clap* of a rock anthem shook the audience.

Football crowds. It was so simple. Watch how people will voluntarily excite themselves into group frenzy and copy it, use it. All this was part of Lawson's "Dynamic Involvement" policy for how people should feel within his company. If you want people to behave like a team, then act like a team. In two days time he would have a proselytising army of 16,400 people who would spend a substantial part of their social lives talking up his bid for Belston Corporation. This was "Popular Corporatism" at its best, a phrase coined for Lawson when he had appeared on the cover of the leading weekly business publication. Subsequent press packs from Lawson's HQ omitted the sub-headline: *New Hope or New Hype?*

Yet there could be no doubt that Lawson was at the vanguard of whatever modern business was about. The loyalty he obtained from his employees – he preferred the term "comrades" – was unrivalled and unquestionable.

'If you can't convince the people you work with, how can you possibly expect to convince anyone else?' he had enthused at conferences the world over. Where most organisations treated internal communications as a necessary evil, for Lawson they were "the engine that drives our vision".

Every month there was a new T-shirt with a vital message back and front. Every week there was a personal broadcast to all employees' desks from Lawson. And at the close of every working day employees would notify the General Communications Staff of what they felt had been achieved that day, the General Communications Staff in turn piecing together a tight, one-hundred-word, no-adverbs, statement-based, seven-sentence paragraph, which would serve as the upbeat update that was waiting for every employee when they switched on their PCs the next day.

"Changing the Meaning of Resource Management".

Yes, they would get the point. Why? Because they had got every previous message, from "Changing the Meaning of Personal Finance", to "Changing the Meaning of Mortgage Advice".

'Is Exodus ready?' Jennings asked, handing the pamphlet back to Faith Barclay, his Personal Strategy Chief.

'Yes,' she said, 'In the basement car park. Fully merchandised and ready to roll. Comrades are getting into position outside The Stock Exchange.'

'Let's roll,' said Jennings. And they laughed. As he and Faith swept through the building, a tumultuous applause rose and fell with their passing, with Jennings saluting proudly each wave of appreciation. He smiled all the way down to the basement. This was what he did best and everyone who worked with him knew it.

The basement lift doors opened. There she was: Exodus, the original ice-cream van from which Lawson Jennings had built the global brand. For any major corporate launch or event Exodus would be dusted down and wheeled out, with Lawson Jennings at the helm, dispensing information and ice cream with equanimity. Exodus, the trusty Transit that had been in the carnival in Rio, the St.Patrick's Day parade in Boston, May Day in Tiananmen Square. Exodus, the happy little chugger that started it all.

Driving out from the basement, buffered front and rear by cheery-looking Land Rovers, Jennings was deep in thought about music. Although there was no doubt that the traditional rock anthem always worked, still he hankered after something more vibrant or upbeat. But nothing could match the triumphalism of rock music in the fervent enthusiasm stakes. Still, he thought, there must be something more, *comradely*. Yes, comradely. He'd ask the Communications Team to consider this.

Thirty minutes after leaving Exodus Central, after weaving a deliberately circuitous, conspicuous route around The City, Exodus was parked outside the London Stock Exchange in time for close of play. As the van played an upbeat seventies medley, forty comrades in lilac and white sweatshirts were pamphleting, while Lawson and Faith dealt with the ice-cream cones and members of the press competed for the best wacky picture. Corporate communications didn't come more serious than this.

Nick watched this display on TV in the hotel room, wondering what Pommy would be thinking of it all. He imagined his ex-boss's indignation, having often heard him excoriate people like Jennings, with their "magician's hat management" and "shareholder hypnotizing".

'Its all a fucking con,' Freiberg had said one afternoon, after witnessing a similar display over the launch of a combination dating service and pension plan for single parents, 'Fucking snake charmer. All the goons fall for it. Fuckers.'

'Alison, I think we need to go back,' Nick said quietly, as two analysts debated the merits of the bid, 'I know we had planned to do more. But I think this is something that we need to be there for. I just know it. This is it.'

Nick shifted his position and laid his head across her breasts, the placatory thump of her heart mingling with the unexpected, exciting on-screen story. Alison stroked his hair gently.

'Do you think this can be something you, we, can use. You know, for revenge?' she asked, so careful with her words, her voice calm, no hint of anger at the prospect of their travels ending.

'Yes, yes I do,' Nick, said, 'Although right now I'm not sure how. But I know that there must be a way.'

'And what happens once it's done?' Alison asked, this time more pointedly.

'When it's done,' Nick said, thoughtfully, stretching the words, never having given it any consideration before now, 'when it's done . . .we . . . get on with our lives.'

Nick could feel Alison mulling this over.

'We do need to go back eventually,' he said, breaking one of Pommy's rules of never filling a silence, 'We can't travel all our lives.'

'I know,' Alison said pensively, then, 'OK, we'll go back. Get it over with.'

Nick sat up, turning round to kiss her.

'Whatever we do, we will do it properly, won't we?' Alison asked, pushing him mildly back.

'Yes, of course we will,' Nick said smiling.

'I don't want this,' and she gestured at the television, 'to continue. We have to finish it once and move on.'

Nick kissed her again and she pushed him playfully down.

'We've not finished going round the world yet. This is only a break,' she said sternly, and Nick was unsure whether this was playful or not.

'Yes, of course,' he said. Kiss. An unexpected sound of music broke their embrace. The pair turned and watched Lawson Jennings and a number of good-looking team comrades lead a group of brokers on a conga dance to the ice-cream tingle of something jaunty from the seventies.

Later, much later, long after the television had been extinguished, they lay together in the dark, both aware of the impending unknown.

'This is the first time I've been away,' Nick said, 'You know, for such a long time.'

'Is there anything you've been missing?' Alison asked.

'No, not really. Maybe . . . no, nothing. How about you?'

Alison pulled the sheets up over them and hugged him tightly.

'Not much, really. Maybe one or two things.'

'Well, we'll have to do something about that too,' Nick said, and they drifted off to sleep in the comfort of their love.

thirty-one

Jonathan sat in the waiting room office, reading a year-old copy of a classic sports car magazine. He did not particularly like cars, had never owned a sports car and could not see what was "Classic" about many of the designs featured. "Old" seemed just as appropriate. Nevertheless at that moment the magazine was serving its purpose well – to take the waiting patient's mind off the here and now; to deliberately force them into a recently bygone age where all the predicted trends or developments will have either come to pass (allowing the patient a degree of comfort) or failed (allowing the patient a degree of smugness). Either disposition is more desirable for a consultation, as the patient is likely to be more positive. At all cost magazines that show the rich and famous at play should be avoided. Studies have shown that such publications, in a waiting-room context, induce unhelpful states of self-doubt, misery and/or failure. Most people think that the selection of magazines in a doctor's waiting room is a random one but they are wrong, particularly in private health care.

Jonathan's fingers flicked through one story of restoration glory after another, his eyes numbly taking in each tale. Generally the story worked towards a similar photograph, of a jolly looking man standing next to the polished bonnet of a sports car. The same words – "lovingly", "hand-crafted", "years of searching" – seemed to seep from every paragraph. Pictures showed hands caressing "near-virgin" carburettors, "delicately re-spun" crankshafts, "tenderly oiled" leather seats. Always, always there was the mention of "service histories". Immaculate log books dating back forty and fifty years seemed to contain every turn in the road, every litre of fuel. Jonathan looked up from the page, his eye wandering over the medical practice's bleak car park. What would the service history of his marriage look like? And then he was falling again, back into the dark hole that had woken him three or four times every night for weeks now. The hole into which he now willingly jumped each time, pursued by the wheezing laughter of his workmates, as they ran after him demanding advice on Spontaneous Sex.

'Mr Greenmeadow?'

Jonathan looked up to see a bald, bespectacled man looking down at him. Dr Portrush introduced himself and asked Jonathan to follow him into his consultation room.

'We're using Dr Rennie's room today,' he confided, as if he and Jonathan were now companions on a bold adventure. It had been Jonathan's boss's idea that he visit the doctor. He insisted on it, to tell the truth, after the canteen incident.

There had been little sign of any change at first. Jonathan had played along, conspicuously enjoying the office banter about his bedroom prowess. He had hoped to ride it out, to keep everything watertight until Alison's return. But then a telephone message about picking up the children from Joe and Philippa had gone astray, skipping from desk to desk around his department until finally claimed by a colleague who knew that Alison always picked the children up, who was able to realise that Alison had not been on the telephone for some time herself; no "as you're passing the newsagent" requests or jokey "take-away taxi" demands. The colleague saw the implicit mournfulness in Jonathan's eyes as he read the message, caught him glancing over to her as he wondered who might have understood the implications, and the pretence was all over and the pretending had begun. Everyone pretending that nothing had changed, pretending that there had never been any banter about the bedroom, pretending that Jonathan was absolutely fine and for goodness sake let's not get involved.

Jonathan could sense the lingering laughter. Each lunchtime in the in-house cafeteria was an ordeal. Everyone knew and no one said anything. God how they must be laughing. Jonathan, King of the Bed (a title confirmed by several e-mails, including one from his boss), now revealed as a – what? At best he was a fool who thought his marriage and sex life had never been better. At worst he was a charlatan, trying to lure his colleagues to destruction on the same rocks where his own life had been clearly holed below the water line. These comments floated around and beside him as he moved through the building. And in an open-plan office, there is nowhere to hide. Standing up from his workstation, he would catch the groups of three or four whispering heads bobbing down into their own plastic dens, engaged in acts of rumour too sensitive for any medium but the tongue. At the water dispenser, bodies scattered as he approached. Even the photocopier, once the waterhole at which he took jovial sustenance with his fellow workers, be they accountant, programmer or salesman, was now a miserable area where he was left to silent, solitary duplication.

Most men are not built to withstand such pressures. Their defences are still bestial, designed for the one-to-one battle, not a creeping morass of gossip and innuendo. The first fissure appeared when Jonathan was collecting his lunchtime dessert. It was a Wednesday and he always allowed himself a midweek slice of apple pie, a concession to indulgent behaviour that often gave him indigestion, and quite rightly he felt. Yvonne, the "I'm Your Trainee", was staring at him. Jonathan stared back, feeling his eyes harden.

'Would you like more custard or are you fine?' Yvonne's voice dimly in his head.

'Of course I'm fine. I'm bloody fine!' Jonathan's voice cracked through the room, extinguishing all chatter.

Yvonne looked at him in terror, her eyes welling with tears, before she turned and ran through to the kitchen, the double doors swinging to a close behind her. Jonathan looked down at his bowl. He already had custard. Why was he still holding the bowl out for more? Why had Yvonne run away? Then there was a hand on his shoulder.

'So take a few days off. Check in with the doctor. Let us know how things are, you know.'

His boss, Roger Williamson, repeated the same message using five or six different wordings, as if trying to create a fog to mask his own embarrassment. He alone had sent three different e-mails regarding Jonathan's sexual expertise. The Human Resources Manager who sat next to Roger, smiling occasionally with studied reassurance, said next to nothing.

'We know things have been . . . tough,' Roger smiled, desperate to be anywhere else. Jonathan smiled back, sealing the deal, granting Roger absolution. All this and more came out for Doctor Portrush, which was far more than he wanted or needed. He had a busy schedule that day and was keen not to get dragged into anything that required more than ten minutes and a standard prescription.

'Have you considered a marriage counsellor?' Dr Portrush asked, as much to stem the tide as out of any concern. Jonathan sank back into his seat. Yes, he had tried a marriage counsellor. ('I'm sorry, Mr Greenmeadow, but there needs to be two of you.' The patronising tone still stung in his mind.)

'Mr Greenmeadow, I'm going to prescribe a mild sedative. I think . . .'

'Doctor, I don't want a mild sedative. I want my wife back. That's what's wrong! That's what I need. Not drugs, doctor, not drugs. My wife . . . our family. That's what I need!'

Jonathan was standing now, shouting at Dr Portrush, who, having been there before, said nothing for a moment, allowing Jonathan to come to a halt himself.

'Mr Greenmeadow, please sit down.'

Jonathan blinked and collected himself, then sat as Dr Greenmeadow quickly wrote *Intense latent hostility* in the file.

'Mr Greenmeadow, until such time as you are able to say more clearly what type of help you require from me, there is not much I can do, I'm afraid.'

Clutching the rolled-up car magazine, Jonathan, eventually, went home. For hours he sat on the stairs. He had already telephoned Joe and Philippa to tell them he'd be late. That morning's post had brought nothing, and there were no messages on the answerphone. His constantly charged mobile had not played "Rule Britannia" in days. Abruptly he put his hand through the banister and lifted the handset to his ears, checked for the dialling tone, then replaced it. Then Jonathan reached down to his feet and picked up the car magazine, re-reading the same articles he had first found in the waiting room.

On this second look he found something more. At first he was unaware, like a child with an unknown puzzle. Then gradually he became conscious of what he was looking at. The headline read *MG Owners Rally – Brighton*. Row after row of mediocre-quality photographs told the same story, of happy times at the wheel of an MG sports car. The majority were red, but racing greens, blacks, navy blues and yellow made the line-up along the promenade at Brighton beach more colourful. Despite the indifferent-looking seaside weather, everyone was clearly delighted, no *thrilled*, to be there. And there were couples everywhere. Every car contained two happy people, content and at one with the world, encased in their MG sports car. There did not seem to be any class system either. Old MGs rubbed shoulders with new MGs, the sleek with the traditional, the accessorised with the basic. And all the people, the couples, seemed overwhelmingly happy, smiling, laughing, raising MG mugs to the camera, and holding down their caps in the open-top parade.

Jonathan seemed to feel himself became part of the procession, driving along, waving to the passers-by, his scarf fluttering behind him. There, by his side, was Alison, adjusting her headscarf, checking the seal on the thermos flask, loading her own camera. In that instant Jonathan saw what he must do. He must not sit waiting for Alison to come back; he must go and find her, explain; bring her back! And now he could see what he needed to accomplish this task. Without wasting any more time, Jonathan threw down the magazine and raced out to the newsagents.

thirty-two

The first shot showed a dark blue duvet with white fleur-de-lis.

'God, *not* the fleur-de-lis,' said Genevieve, distraught. Then Charlotte's head, rising, wide-eyed from beneath it, like a forgotten creature of the deep. A hand reached out, grabbed the ringing alarm clock and retreated back under cover, where the ringing abruptly ceased. Next, Charlotte eating breakfast. Orange juice and bran flakes. Just as instructed.

'Good girl,' Genevieve said, thankful that some of her efforts were paying off, although she could not help but think what a drain on resources this television work was proving. Genevieve had decided that it would be less trouble in the long run to coach Charlotte through every aspect of her on-screen presentation; that it would be better to avoid complaints from the Rutherfords rather than deal with them. There was even a degree of accommodation from the programme makers in this respect, a bit of give and take, so to speak. Despite the supposedly "live" nature of the programme, Steve was not above asking for certain deeds to be repeated for the camera, 'To fully capture the essence, you know.' In return Genevieve had been assured that best interests of all would be considered when editing.

More troubling though was the venue. Genevieve was feeling the pain of creating the fog of there being no problem whatsoever. 'Something different, special': the words disrupted her every waking moment like a next-door neighbour learning to play the trumpet. Charlotte had been sent out on numerous reconnaissance missions for venues that Genevieve knew they had no intention or wish to use, simply so the programme would have something to film. What they must not see was Genevieve's inner worry: 'Where on earth are we going to do it?' Even more so, they must be unaware of the heavy, lurking suspicion as to how the situation would ultimately be resolved.

Genevieve realised that she'd missed some of the interview with Ginny Rutherford, but didn't particularly care. She was not responsible for her nitwit noises. She sat up straight though as Charlotte came back into view, buying a paper, and furthermore the right paper. Good girl. Then on the underground to work, being repelled from getting on board two successive crowded trains, saying 'Sorry' to camera on each occasion. Shouldn't acknowledge camera. Genevieve made a note to speak to her on this. Now above ground, bustling, head down, through the morning rush, sidling into a sandwich shop for two sticky toffee flapjacks. Smiling conspiratorially at the camera. Genevieve winced. Still, not bad for the first programme.

The narrative then moved around some of the other characters. Dan Rutherford standing in the kitchen with a variety of strange fruit and a juice extractor. Charlie Dunsworthy getting up, having a shower and then talking loudly about something to do with global technologies while walking along the street at breakneck speed. Genevieve turned down the sound for most of this. It would be enough to say – with extreme enthusiasm of course – that she had watched it. Jonny and Ginny weren't capable of forming any of the piercing questions that might elicit that she had done so with no enthusiasm whatsoever.

Now Charlotte, again. Sound up. Charlotte speaking to someone off-camera, presumably Spiggy.

'I suppose I like, eh, organising things, for people . . . organising things for people, yes. Giving them what they want is very satisfying.'

Charlotte scanning the phone book for florists. 'Our clients tend to be discerning, quality-first type people.'

Excellent, well remembered.

'I suppose if the poor or, you know, worthless people, need things organised they have to do it themselves. Which must be quite stressful.'

Bugger.

thirty-three

To look back over one's life and see what one has been is to experience a form of hell. Perhaps that is what hell is. We are lucky that, in life, this vantage point is only offered to the few. Most of us flit from experience to experience without once being troubled by a sight of the whole, awful narrative. Nick had been blessed with the shock of review. And it wasn't over yet. Nor would it be until he had resolved his inexplicable departure. For most of his life he had worked hard on understanding things, in constructing a web of explicability with which he could work the world. It had failed him. He had failed. But now he had Alison and he knew what to do. He would go back to London and gain resolution. He would understand what had happened and he would not rest until he had.

Nick turned his face away from the window and considered again the newspaper report. The same information went round and round, appearing in different media and in different order but always the same information. This account added nothing to what he already knew.

City analysts had reacted favourably to the takeover news, the market finishing 80 points up on an otherwise dull day. The offer was a good one; half cash, half shares. More important still was the source: Lawson Jennings, a true golden boy, the current poster face of happy capitalism. A man who, despite raking in many hundreds of millions of pounds profit each year, was able to put it all over with such panache that he always appeared to be doing the world a favour by being in business. Lawson Jennings, the man who, starting with an ice-cream van outside Students' Unions, had built up a media and service conglomerate, servicing the whimsical interests of "youth" and "youth" wannabes through a network of radio, television and Internet stations that encompassed every permutation of broadcasting, narrowcasting, browsing, grazing, snacking and biting that was technologically possible. All done under the Lawson Jennings catchall slogan of "dynamic inclusivity".

"Changing the Meaning of Ownership", was the byline on regular corporate communications bulletins. The rest of the text, couched in quasi-socialist rhetoric, always focused on Lawson's personal involvement in each individual initiative, no matter how small. Rumour had it that the campaigns of Mao Zedong and the Cultural Revolution had been studied and dissected. It would not have been surprising; "cross-fertilisation" was very much a Lawson activity. In student banking he had introduced the concept of "Money Friends" – 'Who wants to speak to a manager?' – who took meetings in the pub and held drunken beach barbecues in the summer. Lawson Jennings. A raving capitalist who had succeeded in getting the public to think that he didn't really want their money.

Nick turned and turned all of this over in his mind, wondering how he might use it to his advantage. Where and how could he hit Pommy? What could he do that would in some way make Pommy feel what he had felt? What was there that would provide Pommy with the same humiliation? This much Nick knew: he wanted to see it happen. Watching on a screen would not be enough. Nick flinched as he remembered the hands holding him and the flash and the parrot photo. Whatever he thought of, Nick wanted to see Pommy's face in the flesh when it happened. But what? He enjoyed feeling his mind "do the churn" as Pommy himself had called it when asking Nick to consider matters of import. But the churn was not throwing out any quick results. He half-turned to Alison, but she was dead to the world, eyes closed as if in solid sleep, and Nick turned back to the window.

But Alison was not asleep; she was daydreaming with conviction, her mind as far removed from business as it could be. In part it was flying over the Gobi Desert, driving through the Nazca Plains, jumping naked into the South China Sea. For the moment she could live without all of this. She knew it would come. Sights would be seen and exotic pleasures would be had. She would go back to London with Nick and she would help him finish the business with Pommy. And Nick was right – there were one or two things that she missed. Those too would be secured. Until then, she preferred to close her eyes and surge along on what would come after.

thirty-four

'Obviously, I mean she had to go.'

Steve looked at Genevieve, with an expression that suggested his entire future in broadcasting had just been erased.

'Genevieve ..,' he said, breathless with shock. 'Charlotte is one of our stars. The first broadcast went down really well.'

'That is beside the point,' Genevieve said, standing up to assert her authority. 'This is my business. It is one thing for staff to talk about the poor; it's quite another for them to refer to them in public.'

'But . . . the reviews . . . they were . . .,' Steve stumbled.

'Excellent. I know. I saw them,' Genevieve continued for him. The reviews had singled Charlotte out as being 'a real find'. They praised her 'brazen honesty'. One critic went so far as to suggest that 'it is the rare and occasional discovery of people like Charlotte that keeps the docudrama format from collapsing into a morass of soggy ordinariness.'

Genevieve had known that this would mean trouble. Nevertheless her mind was made up as soon as she had watched and re-watched the broadcast. Too many of her corporate clients made products that were sold to poor people. They would surely be livid. And she could hardly imagine Jonny and Ginny wishing to be associated with such behaviour. Their social strand always likes to make much of their chumminess with the salt of the earth. No, better to weather a mild storm over the sacking than face several bread and butter clients walking out the door.

She had telephoned Charlotte at home at about ten o'clock

that very night and told her not to come in for work the next day. Charlotte seemed to be expecting it. Her answer had been a dull 'OK', as if Genevieve had asked her to make some coffee. Obviously, the sudden departure of a key person placed Genevieve in a bit of a spot but this was not something she was unfamiliar with. Over fifteen years she had built up enough experience of last-minute panics, blow-ups and situations to feel confident of her ability to deal with anything. The important thing was to maintain momentum. In due course another Dependable Ugly would come along. They were a rare and valuable breed, but not by any means facing extinction.

'You're hired. Can you start immediately?' Genevieve said, picking up the phone while addressing Polly, or was it Penny, who nodded her head vigorously. Not ugly by any means but, Genevieve thought, capable enough of providing assistance through the current project.

'Genevieve, it's Johnny'.

Unfazed, Genevieve asked him to hold while she agreed that Polly/Penny would start tomorrow at nine sharp.

'Yes, Johnny, how are things?'

'Not great, Genevieve, not great.'

Daughter Stephanie had called home in tears and told them about Charlotte. Spiggy had told Stephanie that with the cast down to four, Stephanie's own supporting administrative role was now surplus to requirement. Clever bitch, thought Genevieve. Ginny had apparently, been adamant that, 'It's Genevieve's business, fair and square,' but that didn't help Stephanie.

'We need Charlotte back, Genevieve, and that's that,' Johnny said, matter-of-factly.

Genevieve considered her position. There had not been any calls of complaint from corporate clients, as yet. Indeed, two had actually phoned and left messages of congratulation on the programme. In their voices, Genevieve had detected the telltale tones of someone basking in the thrill of association: 'Yes, she's the girl we sometimes deal with!'

'Genevieve?' Johnny's voice, more strident than she was used to, brought Genevieve back from her considerations.

'Yes, Johnny. Well, now that I think about it, it might be a good idea to keep her on board for the duration of the current project . . . your party, that is. I can deal with any outstanding disciplinary problems after then. How does that sound?'

It sounded "more like it" to Johnny, who asked Genevieve to let Spiggy know everything was as before. Genevieve agreed. Where some might have balked at the amount of pride to be swallowed, Genevieve was inured to such discomfort. The happiness of the client was a sufficient painkiller for such troubles. But the telephone call to Charlotte came before the call to Spiggy. Genevieve knew that it was important that her assistant did not know that there had been pressure from elsewhere that she be brought back. Above all, she must have no idea that she was in any way important. Nothing worse than underlings who think they're important.

'Charlotte, it's me,' Genevieve said smartly and, not waiting for any reply, 'Look, I've been giving it some thought and, under the circumstances, I think I should give you a second chance. We'll review everything after the Rutherfords' party is over. Until then we'll continue as before.'

There was no response, just the sound of a big body breathing.

'Charlotte?'

Down the line came a heavy 'OK' and then silence.

'Good. See you tomorrow then.'

Genevieve then called Spiggy, opting not for the mobile but the office. That way she could tell Johnny she had called but been unable to get hold of Spiggy. Sure enough Genevieve got an answerphone at Flaming Llama Productions.

'Spiggy, this is Genevieve Marsden. I thought I'd let you know that I've decided to keep Charlotte on for the moment. Thanks.' 'For what?' she thought, bringing the phone down.

One minute later Genevieve's hand had still not moved from the telephone. The minor dispute with Johnny had set off certain alarm bells. It was time to get the venue sorted out, regardless of how unpleasant it might be to do so.

thirty-five

'Courageous – audacious, dauntless, intrepid.' Pommy's finger inched its way along the thesaurus page.

'Intrepid,' said Barne, looking up from the *Dictionary of Modern Quotations*, 'That's good. Sounds like "interesting" combined with "rapid"'

Pommy eyed him suspiciously. It was not unknown for subordinates to suggest things that might make their boss look stupid. On the way up Pommy had done so himself on several occasions. Many years ago Sir Michael Jeffreys at the Belston plastics subsidiary had been advised to assent to a Polish deal which Pommy knew had "a dark belly", leaving him to step into the breach on sir Michael's enforced departure. Pommy remembered the TV pictures of screaming Jeffreys children as Fraud Squad detectives manhandled their protesting father into a police van.

No, best treat subordinate advice with caution. Pommy looked back to the book without saying anything. He didn't actually want their fucking advice anyway. Their job was to listen and react – be an audience.

Overnight the takeover bid had wiped out most aspects of normal life at Belston Corporation. For Pommy, this was most immediate in terms of his speech at some management conference he had agreed to give months before. What was going to be a bit of self-indulgent, good-natured boasting now had to be something much, much more. The speech would be widely reported. Many, if not all, of his peers might be there.

'The fox knows many things, but the hedgehog knows one big thing.' McClintock's voice broke through the intense silence.

166

'What the fuck does that mean?' Pommy asked, 'You're supposed to be finding inspirational quotations for the most important speech of my life. Fucking fuckwit.'

McClintock paused, unsure whether to reply or not. 'It's by Archilochus, a Greek . . .'

'I don't care if he was a Greek philosopher, lobster, or Minister of Transport. I am not going to be mentioning hedge-hogs.'

'In Shakespeare's time,' said Barne without looking up, 'they were called hedge*pigs*, which I've always preferred.'

Pommy wiped his hand over his forehead. They would all be there. And, even if not physically in the hall, the City Boys would be listening to every word. No, this had to be a great speech, something that would cause Lawson Jennings a degree of hesitation, uncertainty. Something that would at the very least give Pommy more time to mount a proper defence.

'That is the key. Uncertainty, doubt, hesitation.' Pommy had explained to his three underlings at the start of the current speech brainstorming session, 'Uncertainty. It reeks like rotten flesh to financial institutions. They can't stand it. Better admit to being wrong decisively than right, more or less.'

Durning had written that down from one of his mentoring sessions hadn't he? Yes, the important thing was to take a clear position. Use the speech to clarify why his captaincy of Belston Corporation would prove the most rewarding for shareholders. Pommy chuckled to himself, causing his subordinates to exchange glances. Yes, he was the issue now. Him, Peter "Pommy" Freiberg. Now was not a time to shirk from the battle. Now was the time to act with destiny. Yes, act with destiny. Destiny. How the fuck would this bunch help with that? That Durning would have been useful right now.

'Right, what else have you lot come up with?' Pommy asked, banging his tome down.

Humphreys looked up excitedly,

'To be what we are, and to become what we are capable of becoming, is the only end in life.'

Pommy paused, uncertain. 'Mmh ... fuck said that?' he asked, too weary to bother with the 'who' of it.

'Robert Louis Stevenson,' Humphreys replied, pleased that he might have found favour.

'Stevenson. One of those eighteenth-century Jocks, right?' Pommy asked slowly.

'He wrote *Jekyll and Hyde*, eh, *Treasure Island*, eh, *Travels on a Donkey*,' Barne volunteered.

Pommy shot him a glance, muttered 'Fucking brilliant. A jock on a donkey,' before returning to his own volume.

Then the telephone rang. Everyone sat up. No calls whatsoever were being permitted.

'Anyone calls – tell them we're in a war situation', had been the instructions. Pommy picked up the telephone, ready to deliver an assault.

'Pommy Freiberg speaking.'

There was a brief pause.

'Oh, hello dear,' Pommy continued, his eyes rising to the ceiling like those of a dying fish.

Humphreys, McClintock and Barne picked up their pads and slunk out of the room, avoiding Pommy's glance.

'Well, as you might appreciate things are pretty hectic here right now, darling,' Pommy said quietly. Like many, for Pommy the habit of ending each sentence to his wife with a term of endearment had increased as the passion in their relationship diminished. Now it was almost every sentence, and occasionally at the beginning too.

'I know that I am a director of your company, sweetness, but that was merely an ... arrangement. It was not intended to be a working involvement. As you well know, my ... honey.'

'Listen to me, Pommy,' Genevieve's voice boomed out of the earpiece. 'Very little in my life grieves me as much as having to ask you for a favour. Having to be under the same roof from time to time is enough to fill my cup to overflowing. But I need this and I expect you to come through with the goods.'

Pommy winced. In truth, part of him enjoyed the fact that

168

no man on the planet would dare speak to him like this. Besides, being married to Genevieve had borne, and continued to bear, its rewards. She was an excellent, nay, unparalleled hostess. Her connections, even if mostly acquired through her business, afforded Pommy many an agreeable platform on which to meet certain people. The children had fared well by her hand – it could not be her fault that they had turned out to be people who 'if they didn't speak nonsense wouldn't speak any fucking sense.'

Pommy had always known he would have to marry. It was the right thing for someone with his ambitions. 'People always trust fucking family men,' Pommy had urged Durning one day, 'Don't fucking ask why. Most of the worst kind are family men. Some sort of ruse we all have to go along with. Bastards.'

That Genevieve and Pommy remained together was not down to any sense of duty on either part. They had drifted into a state of equilibrium, where his whoring (she knew) and her occasional fucks (he didn't care) seemed as much part of the successfully balanced relationship as the remembrance of birthdays and anniversaries.

'A good marriage is like a ship you pilot through society's waters,' Genevieve, drunk, had told a female friend when questioned on their relationship. 'It's not about love or anything like that. Look at the whole package. That's what more women should do. No need to dump the car because you don't like the road. It'll still get you to work. A bicycle without a saddle is still a bicycle.'

Her own freelance sexual relationships had not started until Pommy revealed his own inability to sleep with her any longer: 'I'm sorry, dear, but you just don't give me erections when I see you naked.'

Since then she had embraced all the freedom to play that a marriage can bring if treated correctly. And occasionally, when required, Pommy could get things she couldn't.

'Do you hear me, Pommy?'

Pommy sighed, 'Yes, I hear you. Let me see what I can do.'

When he put the phone down Humphreys, McClintock and Barne shuffled back in, pretending nothing had happened, chattering lines of Shakespeare back and forth. Listening to their mealy-mouthed recitations was enough to make Pommy remind himself not to use Shakespeare. During the speeches of others he had noticed how major business leaders had shrunk in size when called upon to do justice to such words. 'Don't step outside your arena,' he thought, getting up and going to the window.

'Right, this is no time for fucking around. What was the name of that chap – Kenwright? Kendrick?'

'Bill Kendrick?' suggested Humphreys.

'That's it, Bill Kendrick. Speech fiend. That's what we need here. Someone who knows what they're fucking doing. Give shape to my thoughts. Tell Jenny to get hold of him. Wasting my time with you. Not that you've anything better to fucking do.'

In the space of a few hours, once the takeover bid had been announced, all real business had ground down to a crawl. Nobody wanted to talk to anyone from Belston Corporation. Takeovers reeked of uncertainty.

'Like trying to do business with Never-Never Land,' Pommy had noted sagely. 'And nobody likes to do that. Except the French. Fucking dreamers.'

No potential business partner wanted to start a development with someone who might not be there in a few weeks time. Nobody wanted to lend to, or borrow from, someone who could vanish overnight. Nobody wanted to sign any major supply deals with somebody who might not be there to take delivery. Nobody wanted to buy from somebody who might not be there to deliver. In short the takeover bid had put Belston Corporation into a state of minimal consciousness. Only the sound of curricula vitae being polished up could be heard above the air-conditioning. Pommy watched his team trudge back to their all-too-static desks, and then reached for the telephone.

'Jenny, before you get Bill Kendrick, get me Lionel Partridge. He's the Zoo man, isn't he?'

thirty-six

Jonathan closed his eyes and inhaled, the rich, earthy smell of polished leather filling his soul. He leaned his body slowly forward, listening to the gentle creasing of the seat. Then back again. Then forward again. Then back again. Opening his eyes Jonathan

considered his hands, exactly ten to two, on the burnished wooden steering wheel, then, without looking down, he moved the matching gear stick through the positions: 1,2,3,4,5, reverse.

'Lovely,' he whispered, now repeating the procedure with his eyes closed. Getting out of the car, he walked round to the passenger door and held it open, bowing slightly, smiling.

'After you, sweetheart'. Then he ran round and got back in the driver's seat.

'And in the summer . . .,' he shouted gleefully, undoing the clips, jumping back out and folding the roof neatly under a plastic cover, '. . . ta ra!'

'You can drive if you want, you know, eventually. Need to get the insurance fixed first, of course. Get it through the MG Owners' Club actually, which makes it almost as cheap as your little run-around.'

Then he was out again, strolling casually to the front, one finger skimming along the bonnet. He stood back, admiring his purchase.

'Love Red actually. Do you like it?' he asked with a wave of the hand.

Inside the house, the telephone rang. Jonathan opened the garage door onto a dark street and ran in through the kitchen door, stumbling over the step in the dark.

'Hello, The Meadowfield Residence,' he said brightly, then 'Oh hello, my little soldier,' sounding disappointed.

'No, of course, I'm pleased to hear your voice. It's just that I thought it might be Mummy, you know, phoning from her special trip.'

Between them, Jonathan, Joe and Philippa had worked up a story about Mummy's Special Trip, which was to see some Very Important People about a Big Secret. And no, it had nothing to do with PsychoMummy (stop saying that anyway).

'So how was school then? Oh that's good. I can't wait to see that. What is Mummy wearing? And what am I wearing?'

Samuel took Jonathan through his day before letting Kimberley have a word.

'Time for bye-byes, Kimbo. I'll see you tomorrow for a story. Is Granny there? Or Grandpa?'

Jonathan confirmed that he had heard nothing and that neither had they. He hadn't told them about the MG yet, feeling somehow uncomfortable when the need for an explanation struck him. Instead he had simply said he needed a bit time to do things around the house, and that, if they could keep the children until tomorrow, and run them to school, it would be very much appreciated.

'No, everything's fine otherwise,' he said, feeling the inappropriateness of 'otherwise'.

'I'll see you tomorrow then. Yes, about six or just after.'

He put the phone down and stood momentarily still in the dark kitchen, no sound coming in from the street. He picked up the phone, listened, then put it down again and went back to the garage.

'A handy size of boot,' he said jauntily, walking round and opening it with a flourish.

'Room for a picnic hamper and not much else!' jokey but nervous, clearing his throat.

'Back seats really a formality. Have to leave the kids behind. Whey hey,' almost silent.

Jonathan walked to the front and looked down on the gleaming car, dropped to his haunches and collapsed in tears. Had anyone been there they might just have been able to make out the word 'Why?'

thirty-seven

'Why don't we just kill him?'

It was the second time Alison had said this. Nick was still stunned from the first time. Then he had checked for some form of grin or wink that would negate the matter-of-fact delivery. But there was none, only Alison looking round the patisserie, with the crumbs from a *pain au chocolat* dotting her lips.

'We can't kill Pommy Freiberg,' Nick said, sipping his coffee, amazed to find himself lowering his voice so that the world did not know he was ruling out murder as an option in his life.

'Well, what then?' Alison said, with a degree of confrontation.

'I need to think about that. Sorry, we need to think about that,' he corrected himself.

'Thinking doesn't get much done. We need to do something positive,' Alison said, stirring her coffee. 'There is nothing I am not willing to do. Nothing,' she affirmed, ripping the top off a sachet of brown sugar.

Nick looked at her. He found her straightforward decisiveness almost bewildering at times, like being in the presence of something truly alien.

'Apart from anything else I think killing him would be . . . insufficient.' He paused and Alison could again feel the hollowness, the desolation in his voice.

'One thing I know. I want to be there when it happens. I want to see his face and feel his loss,' Nick seethed, before fading out.

'Nick, I know this. You know this. But we've known it for long enough. Let's do something,' insisted Alison.

Nick said nothing.

'You know what I think?' Alison said, stirring her coffee absently, 'I think you're scared.'

Nick looked up, incredulous.

'I am not scared Alison, I just don't know what we can do yet.'

'But even if you did, Nick, would you have the nerve to do it?'

'Yes, of that I am sure.'

'Well, I'm not. I am not sure.' Alison was smiling, and smiling in a way that made it impossible for Nick not to smile too, despite the terseness of their exchange.

'What is it now?' he asked, 'Are you going to suggest we kill him again?'

'No, but we need to kill something.'

'I beg your pardon?'

'We need to kill something,' Alison was urging, 'As a sort of exercise. To get you ready to do the real thing.'

'And what would you suggest we kill?' Nick asked quietly.

Alison bent over and grabbed his left leg.

thirty-eight

'And this is where most of the big reptiles are kept.'

Genevieve had, of course, been here several times before, notably for a radio quiz show's 100th episode party; three new, exciting potato snack launches and one of last year's best politician awards ('deliciously ironic' said every single newspaper report). Still, Genevieve looked around with what she hoped was an expression of admiration. In recent months she had often found 'admiration' supplanted by 'indifference', much to the annoyance of a couple of her one-night stands.

'Most impressive, Mr Partridge,' she said, making sure her words lacked any ambiguity.

'Can we see the monkey house now?'

'Oh yes, of course, and do call me Lionel.'

In arranging her visit Genevieve had asked that, for overall impression purposes, she be shown round every area, and not just the reptile house, which Pommy had agreed with Partridge would be available for his wife and the Rutherfords.

'You know how it is, Lionel. Raising funds is a matter of stringing together a few passes on the field. This party is an important pass, more of a free kick actually,' Pommy had lied, 'I need it to happen so that certain people will feel obliged when the time comes.'

'Well, I suppose I might be able to let the reptile house go,' Lionel had conceded, visualising the comparative upset that would result from cancelling either of the other two bookings for that night. 'Let me get back to you on this.'

'Excellent, reptile house it is then. My wife will be in touch,' Pommy had said, ringing off. No point in waiting for zoo man to get back to him. Result in fucking bag. Tell the fucking wife.

'You've got the reptile house,' he said sharply, before ringing off on her and picking up on Bill Kendrick, the speech fiend.

Arriving at Partridge's office, Genevieve had explained that seeing most of the zoo's facilities would allow her 'a greater scale of understanding towards facilitating our event.'

This said while standing very close to Partridge so that he would feel included in the 'our'. They had met once or twice but only in passing. Pommy's intervention had made Lionel Partridge decide to finalise this particular matter himself. Pommy Freiberg was one corporate supporter you didn't want to have on your case.

The monkey house was exactly as Genevieve remembered it. It was ideal though. As was the reptile house. As was everything.

'Well, Lionel, I think we are going to have an excellent party,' she said, positioning herself close to him as they looked at a couple of orang-utans fighting over a rubber tire. Lionel nodded.

'We can put the bar over there, next to the gibbons,' she said pensively. Lionel started.

'Eh, I'm sorry, eh Genevieve, but I had agreed with Mr Freiberg that you would have the reptile house,' he said, his discomfort increasing as Genevieve's face collapsed into well-rehearsed angry disappointment at his words. But her response, when it came, was decidedly more strident and not without menace.

'But Lionel, Pommy specifically told me I could have my pick of the place. And I want it all.'

Lionel looked at her, the crush of painful options all around him. Genevieve knew what he was thinking. He would have to give her the monkey house, and everything else. Either that or call Pommy back. In some respects she felt sorry for him. Genevieve had, after all, been in a similar situation many times

177

before. She knew all the terrible, hopeless thoughts that would be running through his head. She could also picture the ire of the other event organisers when they were abruptly cancelled. 'Poor Lionel,' she thought, 'Lucky me.' As the zoo chief's short-term life entered a state of entropy, she guided his unnaturally widened eyes back towards the playful orang-utans.

'Isn't it amazing,' she said, her voice full of childish wonder, 'They look so ... so ... *human.*'

thirty-nine

A placid Pommy walked towards the platform. Midway, just as the polite applause seemed to be peaking, he turned his head to the conference, and gave a slight, firm nod, and then continued to walk, possibly even more slowly, to the platform. In that slight, firm nod, that gentle indication of absolute calm on his part, Pommy connected with the crowd, let them know he knew the score.

Before that nod it is fair to say that there had been nervousness, apprehension, even fear in the air. Fear that the old man would not be able to produce the goods, might not be up for the challenge. Fear that, with the world watching, one of their number would stumble. Above all, fear that they would be embarrassed, that this would not be a performance that they could point to and say that they were part of.

In that single, firm nod, beamed to the back of the hall from two huge screens either side of the stage, Pommy assured them that all was well. From the back of the hall began a clapping which rolled towards the front of the audience, becoming in its travels a resounding clamour of war. This was a rare feast. A major city figure, a true gladiator in his field, caught in the midst of a hostile takeover, forced to account for himself before an audience of his peers. The roar was not just for Pommy. It was for everything they lived for. Each and every one of them saw on that stage what they hoped to become one day – a titan of their world about to do battle with another.

Business, to be truthful, is not often exciting. It can be interesting, educational, stimulating. But not, for the most part, exciting. Customers are difficult, orders are delayed, projections revised. There is a lot of waiting. Waiting for decisions, replies and results. No day is complete without dull tasks, dull meetings, dull reports, and above all, dull people. Nobody enters business wanting this life. Nobody enters the world of business for the sake of the average business day. Nobody wants to be "going over things one more time, for the benefit of all concerned"; to be "taking stock of our position"; to be "consolidating market share in line with available resources". Certainly nobody in this hall.

When they saw Pommy walk with defiant slowness across to the lectern they felt again that free-flowing rush of energy which was what they so yearned for and yet only dimly recognised. This was why they were in business. Yes, this! To be tested against the best in open competition, to engage with whomever stepped up. In short, to fight. When Pommy reached out and laid one hand on the lectern, he accepted the challenge for all of them. He was their destiny proclaimed. They cheered, clapped, and stamped their feet for the entire world to hear, and when they howled it was for the immaculate glory of their dreams and the fiery, raw glory of the market.

Pommy stood, motionless, the speech already unwinding onto the sheet glass prompter below the lectern. Although he had enjoyed the reception, he recognised it for what it was: adulation of the spectacle rather than adulation of the man. He knew that wild applause did not mean he was among friends.

'Half of the fuckers hate me,' he thought, listening to the tumult. The silence of the combat arena descended. Pommy waited, and waited.

'*And make them wait*,' Kendrick had said. Together they had watched tapes of Hitler at the Nazi rallies, as he stood, almost uninterested, while the vast crowds waited, almost begged, to be addressed.

'*They need to feel your contempt. Crowds respect that*,' Kendrick said, as they pored over some of the more scowling portraits of Napoleon.

'*Survey them sceptically as if inspecting them. Don't catch anybody's eye, or acknowledge any greeting. No touching of caps on the platform.*' In newsreel General Patton addressed U.S. troops in France.

'*When you begin, don't bother with all that "Ladies and Gentlemen" stuff. They know why they're there. They know who you are. They want to hear the message.*' Now the image was the Pope, Christmas Day Mass, St. Peter's Square, The Vatican.

'What about the joke beginning?' Pommy had asked ruefully, 'Everyone seems to have one nowadays. Don't like it myself. Not a fucking comedian.'

Kendrick frowned, wrinkling his nose in contemplation.

'Yes, I know what you mean. Unfortunately, the joke at the start is now such a well-established practice that to not do so alters the plan from the point of view of the audience. They'll be waiting for the joke. Best to get the joke out of the way.'

Pommy grimaced.

'*It doesn't actually have to be a funny joke,*' Kendrick continued, '*Just so long as it has the cadence of a joke.*'

'Ca-dence?' Pommy said, as if rehearsing a foreign word.

'Just so long as it sounds like a joke. That way they recognise it as your joke and you're free to get on with the message,' Kendrick explained politely.

'Hmm . . .,' Pommy said, looking at Kendrick unsympathetically. 'God knows how many thousands of pounds this fucker is being paid to get me to tell not-funny jokes,' he thought. Still, top man.

'Also,' Kendrick went on, keen to get two disagreeable bits of advice out of the way, 'It would be best to mention Lawson Jennings early. Let them know you know they know, et cetera. That way, again, you get the issue out of the way and can proceed with the message. You can come back to Jennings later if you want.'

Pommy nodded. Joke plus Jennings. Get to the issue. He gripped the lectern with both hands and leaned slightly into it. As Kendrick had predicted, the audience, to a man and testosterone-driven woman, leaned slightly forward too.

'I ran into Lawson Jennings on the way over here,' Pommy's strong-but-not-too-loud voice broke like a calming wave over the delegates. That very morning Kendrick had set up an identical sound system in an empty warehouse of similar size to the auditorium to allow Pommy to 'acclimatise the delivery for the prevailing environment.' They had been there since six a.m.

'I ran into Lawson Jennings on the way over here. Or rather, I would have done if he hadn't made it across the road in time.'

Roar! Humour mixed with the smell of blood! The conference hooted and bayed. This was even more than they had expected. Explicit, naked hatred. Pommy now held up his hand to control the response. Kendrick had advised against this but Pommy knew differently.

'*Have an image in your mind,*' Kendrick had told him, '*Be that image. Become what you wish to appear to the audience.*' Together they had poured through a fat, oversized book, full of powerful images. Most conceivable analogies were represented: lions chasing zebras, mountaineers claiming a peak, eagles soaring high.

'What's this?' Pommy asked at one.

'It's a monkey peeling a banana,' Kendrick said meekly.

'I can fucking see that. I know a monkey. Don't need to be taught monkeys. Or bananas. What does it represent, that's what I want to know,' Pommy scolded him, turning the page around to try and see some deeper meaning.

'Possibly . . .,' Kendrick ventured, 'Possibly, it represents "Delicate Exploration" or perhaps "Fastidious Discovery". Look at the monkey's quizzical expression,' the speech fiend urged.

'Who would want to picture themselves like that?' Pommy said, sharply tapping the monkey's face with his forefinger.

'Hmm . . . yes, perhaps a scientist engaged in research,' Kendrick said, eager to move on.

'Jenny, come in here please,' Pommy commanded. His secretary gently entered. Pommy handed her the open book.

'Jenny, take this photograph over to Human Resources. Tell them to select three other images and then to run all four through our fertiliser research people in Germany. Ask the boffins which of the four they identify with. I want to know if anyone picks the monkey,' Pommy said, maintaining eye contact with Kendrick.

'Won't have any fucking monkeys in this operation,' he continued, 'Bad for morale, monkeys.'

Gradually the pair had begun a discussion of the merits of various historical figures and then into history itself, before arriving at Pommy's suggestion of the American entry into World War Two.

'How so?' asked Kendrick, nervous.

'Simple. Didn't want to get involved. Eager to stay at home, mind the farm. Along comes Japan. Pearl Harbour. America. Sleeping giant. Had to enter then. Sleeping giant. Gave them what for. End of story. Me: sleeping giant. Jennings: Japan. End of story,' Pommy concluded, sitting back and folding his arms.

'So, you're going to think of yourself as America responding to the Japanese attack on Pearl Harbour?' Kendrick asked slowly, closing his own eyes in attempted visualisation.

'Just said so, didn't I?' Pommy said, regarding the reclining Kendrick with suspicious scepticism.

Pommy began slowly, a gradual rumble which some in the hall had to strain themselves to hear. What followed was a straightforward case of picture drawing, taking them all through the operations of Belston Corporation. There was nothing grand, no tub-thumping, merely a slow, methodical portrait of the business. As such it contained a simple poetry of form for the delegates. They were entranced by the lack of gimmickry, the absence of buzzwords. In Pommy's voice they recognised the rare, elusive sound of the artisan businessman, who knows each facet of his operations, is able to dissect and explain every area of his company with a familiarity unknown to most. Each division was dealt with. Property. Investment. Mining. Petrochemicals. Finance. No area was too small to merit some apparently crucial detail and it was here that the audience recognised the hand of the master.

'The Milan shopping mall, complete with off-grey anthracite, not scuffable marble, floors will open next June . . . Both of the Taiwanese joint ventures are up and running now, including the fishing operation which we had always expected would prove tricky to initiate. . .With these newer carbon-tip drills, we expect to be in profit on this field six months ahead of schedule.'

All of this flowed like the most golden honey into the ears of the delegates, yet at the same time the lack of attack after such an inspirational opening worried some. That could not be it, surely? These few tapped their neighbours, made puzzled faces, glanced at their watches. They strained to examine Pommy for signs of fight. Where is the fight? And as they looked, one or two began to make out something of the military in him, something naval, and powerful. Then and only then were they able to recognise this elegiac opening for what it undoubtedly was: the calm waters through which Pommy would (surely!) plough his battleship. Yes! Again, they tapped their neighbours, but this time to nod sanguinely, to smile knowingly, and to flash their eyes wide in anticipation.

'In essence, Belston Corporation is in good shape. Indeed, it has never been in better,' Pommy said gracefully, softly drawing the line under the description he had given.

And they were right. Pommy had created his own calm waters.

'Try,' Kendrick had advised with as much tact as he could muster, '*try to avoid the prolonged attack. People react better to what is perceived as a scalpel-like insightful hit, than the rat-tat-tat-tat machine gun or the boom-boom howitzer.*'

For these noises Kendrick improvised a Zorro-like Z thrust for the scalpel, followed by a left to right spraying machine gun and both arms punching out simultaneously from his chest for the howitzer.

'I thought crowds like boom-boom things. Fireworks and the like; they're pretty boom-boom aren't they?' Pommy noted.

'Yes, but that is in the context of all-out entertainment, isn't it?' Kendrick replied, forcing his voice down at the end in an attempt to avoid sounding patronising. Pommy considered him again. Maybe he was working for someone else, had been "got at".

'I still think they'll want a bit of boom-boom, don't you?'

Kendrick smiled encouragingly. 'Oh yes, no doubt. If we plan it right, they'll definitely want boom-boom. We have to make sure that we don't deafen them with too much, that's all. *It's important to keep control as we build.*'

Pommy sized him up and down, blew out through his nose, 'Right. Boom-boom it is then.'

'Yes, it has never been in better shape. But you all know me well enough to know that that is not and never will be good enough for me.'

Around the hall, nudged elbows preceded mouthing of the phrase 'Here we go'.

'In the fifteen years that I have been on the bridge at Belston Corporation, we have never grown less than 16% year on year. We have never done anything other than increase our dividend to shareholders, whose enrichment let me remind you is the sole purpose of our company's existence. There is a basic reason behind this successful record. And I think you all know what it is.'

'*At some stage you must flatter the audience, make them feel as smart and successful as you are, part of the same elite club,*' Kendrick said, bringing his hands together in an embrace.

'But they're not. Fucking useless most of them,' Pommy said, visibly appalled at the thought.

'*Perhaps, but we must remember our purpose in the hall for that one day Mr Frei-berg,*' Kendrick said, only just veering up and away from a reprimand with his last syllable.

'Hmm. Very well,' Pommy said, 'Bastards.'

'The simple fact of the matter is that we know our business better than most. We understand each and every transaction, in a way that many, more "modern" corporations do not. Mr

Jennings has been very busy recently with his conjuring tricks. In particular he has been conjuring phrases, producing them like rabbits out of a hat. We are, apparently, in need of "liberation". Liberation from what, Mr Jennings, liberation from what?'

Pommy maintained a steady rhythm, carefully rehearsed with Kendrick.

'*Don't start galloping simply because you can see the finish line,*' the consultant had urged, time and again.

'Is it liberation from profits unrivalled in most of our active sectors? Is it liberation from the clearly defined strategies that have allowed our share price to reach an all-time high, and this before Mr Jennings' unwelcome chicanery? Or is it that Mr Jennings wants to liberate us from the very things that have made this company a worldwide force?'

Wait a bit. Then get the machine gun out.

'Liberation from clear objectives. Liberation from no-nonsense management. And above all, liberation from discipline. Discipline,' Pommy whispered, as if to a child, 'a bath in which I suspect Mr Jennings has not taken a dip for quite some time.'

And now the tone was menacing and personal, no sense of a joke.

'Belston Corporation operates for the most part in what I like to, indeed have to, call the hard world. It is not the world of the airy-fairy service. The plans we make are, for the most part, concerned with the hard, sometimes cruel, world of primary resource development. We make hard things happen.'

A slow, laboured rat-tat-tat-tat.

'Get things out of the ground. Build things.' and

Each "thing" was now a Boom!

'Transport things and first and foremost exploit things. We exploit things.'

And again, softer this time, more thoughtful,

'We exploit things.'

'*Exploit,*' Kendrick had explained, getting excited, '*is a*

186

powerful, beautiful, dirty word which will turn this audience on because of its wanton vulgarity.'

He was right. Pommy sensed this arousal from the podium. He eyed the hall imperiously.

'And we deliver. And we are able to deliver because we do not suffer from . . . distractions.' This was spat out, something putrid, vile.

'Distractions,' now mumbled, as if painful to say, rolled round in the mouth like something bitter.

'Distractions of style.'

Boom!

'Distractions of mood.'

Boom!

'Distractions of design. Distractions of ambience. Distract-ions of non-profit generating, effete, dilly-dallying inconse-quential buzz word bunk. And you all know what I mean.'

But it wasn't a *what* it was a *who*, and the who was writ large over Pommy's deep accusatory glare at the audience. They shrank in their seats, feeling the guilt of association with Lawson Jennings.

'Do you think for one moment that Belston Corporation would be able to maintain its ruthless profit generation drive without me at the helm? Do you, or anyone you know, imag-ine that I or my management team are in some way separable from the success of Belston Corporation?'

The hall was quiet now, humble in self-consideration, each member of the audience lost in trying to recall what they really thought before the speech started.

'I know that there are already some who have signed up for the change. You like the idea of change. But there's a big differ-ence between a change of scenery and a change of manage-ment. I'll tell you that straight. Those who jump on board that swish new tub swanning gaily around the harbour, hoping perhaps to see the New World, may well find themselves going round and round on a ship of fools.'

Pommy looked out as his warning wafted down and over the

crowd like a cloud of smoke. Then he gathered himself without taking his eyes off them and, with a brief acknowledgement with his hand, departed the lectern. Silence. Then they realised it was over. They had been dismissed, and they loved it. As the audience came out of its entranced stupor, people rose to their feet and began to clap. Each individual clap set off another like a string of firecrackers until the entire arena was engulfed in a crash of applause, through which could be dimly heard a wild, vagabond assortment of cheers and whoops. They knew that they had perhaps witnessed the last of a breed, the last of a certain type of corporate tiger. This was Mario Lanza at La Scala, Frank Sinatra at The Sands. Reverence stoked the fires of appreciation long after Pommy had departed the stage.

The reaction to the speech was overwhelmingly positive. Afterwards, those that had been there could be heard talking about it on the underground, in cabs, at restaurant tables. But reaction and result are two different things. Most people did not hear the speech. Most heard or read bits or, worst still, summaries. Summaries that gutted every nuance, melting down each gleaming sword into a single leaden lump, encapsulating the whole affair in terms of a "robust defence". A robust defence was entirely predictable; Pommy's reputation alone guaranteed that. So was there anything of note? No, not really. The share price stayed the same and so did most of the opinions. Time for a change. Breath of fresh air. Pommy himself was entirely unfazed by the lack of result from the speech. Indeed, he had written it off before he cleared the platform. The simple message of the speech was this: I'm here; I'm around; don't forget about me. That accomplished, he turned his attention to the next phase of the battle.

forty

Where would you begin if you were looking for someone who had disappeared on you? First of all you would look at their habits. Where do they like going? What do they like doing? How do they like to spend their time? You would make a list of all these things and then you would visit every place at the right time and then at the wrong time and then at various, random times, making a nuisance of yourself to the people who worked there. Jonathan lost count of the times in this period when he found himself saying, 'Sorry, yes, I just thought, maybe . . .'

At least he had the car. The MG. He considered giving it a name but decided that doing so on his own would be to add another infringement to the list of those which had undoubtedly chased Alison away in the first place. No, the car would remain nameless until her return. Names were something to do together.

'Let's try for an H now, Samuel.'

Jonathan watched his son's face fold in puzzlement.

'You remember H, don't you?'

Samuel began to re-arrange his fish fingers, allowing Jonathan a moment to eat some of his own dinner. From the living room came the sound of Kimberley laughing at something on television. Jonathan undid his tie. For the sake of the children he was still dressing for work. They did not need to know that he didn't go there. They especially didn't need to know that he had no idea where Mummy was. Jonathan took Samuel to school and Kimberley to her playgroup and then over to Joe and Philippa while he continued the search before

189

collecting them in the evening, sometimes having dinner there, sometimes not.

Joe and Philippa. He would have been flattened without them. His own parents had both died when Jonathan was sixteen. An elder sister had got him started at university and then married a nice vet and moved to Wisconsin. Alison and he had always meant to visit but there had never been time, and then the children came along, like children do, inconvenient and demanding. They'd go next summer, when everything was settled again. No, Joe and Philippa were top people. They had been a bit funny the other day when they first saw the MG. Philippa in particular seemed unimpressed. Later though, as he sat with the children and a coffee after dinner, he heard Joe's voice from the kitchen.

'Poor chap needs something to keep his spirits up.'

'But a sports car. Isn't that a bit . . . childish?'

'If it keeps him going then it probably doesn't matter.'

'Well, I suppose . . .'

They both came in smiling and Philippa handed round the biscuits.

Everything seemed to be fine now. Joe had even taken the car out for a drive. Maybe, Jonathan thought, he would buy them one as a reward when Alison was back. Looking up, he realised that Samuel was holding up his plate for him to see. A misshaped H of fish fingers slid down the plate and onto the table, trailing baked beans and cut up pieces of toast in its wake.

'Samuel,' Jonathan said, 'Go and get a cloth.'

forty-one

Nick sauntered into the astoundingly bright light of the unfamiliar chain newsagents, his limp almost invisible, the merest hint of the dejected drag and scuff of but one month before. He wandered conspicuously around for ten minutes, considering the range of men's magazines, before moving on and picking up a copy of thick fashion title with a free comb stuck to the cover. Nick then got into a discussion with the shop assistant about whether or not the issue dated with that month on the cover was actually the one for last month. Neither of them knew for sure. He bought it anyway, along with an evening paper, which he rolled up and stuffed into his jacket pocket, next to a ball of Blu-TacK and a length of string. Cheerily, he left. Alison was waiting in the car and together they drove at no great speed to a junction about four hundred yards along, having established a good reason to be in the area at this time of night; this shop was one of the few 24-hour outlets in town.

'There are always, always witnesses. People you don't notice or expect. Read any court trial and there they are. People on their own with big eyes and no reason to be there,' Nick explained to Alison, 'Plan for witnesses and you're safe.'

At the junction they turned sharply left without indicating, having checked that no other vehicle or pedestrian was ahead or behind them. Then they drove about two hundred yards down to a quiet, non-residential street and turned left again, stopping about twenty yards on, the car hidden in the shadow of an anonymous warehouse.

Nick got out of the car and looked around. Alison was right: no-one was likely to "happen by" here at this time of night.

Still, he hesitated. 'Go on. Do it!' Alison whisper-urged, lips barely moving. Moving quietly, from the car boot Nick removed an old duffle bag, now heavy, that he had found in his parents' cupboards, put on a pair of gloves and walked along the darkened street and round a corner into a back lane. There he put on a black balaclava and climbed over a gate signposted "No Parking – Deliveries – In Constant Use".

Having dropped down onto the ground, Nick got directly onto his hands and knees and moved to the back of the premises. Once there he took something wrapped in a black polythene bin-liner from inside the duffle bag and placed it close to the door. From the bag he removed a packet of tinfoil. Unrolling a sizable sheet, he placed it under the bin-liner, folding the sides up to create a wide channel that led to the bottom of the door. He gently lifted the bin liner and tinfoil together, laying the duffle bag flat underneath the spot where the black bag sat, creating a gentle slope all the way to the sliver of a crack between the bottom of the door and the floor. Then he got up on his knees, taking the Blu-Tack, string and the newspaper from his overcoat pocket. He fluffed the paper up into a loose bundle and tied it together, leaving a long tail of string. Taking the Blu-Tack, he attached the end of the string to the door, about two feet above the tinfoil sheet. He then took out a lighter and lit the end of the newspaper, making sure it caught. From his pocket he took a small cross-headed screwdriver and viciously stabbed the front of the polythene bag at its base. Petrol began seeping out, down towards the door, then under it. Nick got on his hands and knees and quickly moved back to the gate, climbed over and was gone.

Had there been a surveillance camera – which there was not – it would have observed someone trying to avoid it by crawling low, rather than someone walking with a limp. It would also have been more difficult to judge that person's height and, more importantly, there would be no shoe impressions to trace.

Sitting, sweating heavily, in the passenger seat as Alison drove off, he exhaled and inhaled deeply. Not a trace of petrol. They drove confidently back to the all-night newsagent ('Forgot some milk.'), then to an all-night petrol station, where they filled up, just in case any lingering smell had attached itself to Nick. Then home, passing the burning shell of Martin's Mobility Centre. They slowed to watch. The firemen seemed resigned to the building's demise, laying down a cover of water to prevent it spreading but not aggressively tackling the blaze. That it was arson would be in doubt. That it was Nick and Alison would never be known

For three nights running, they had telephoned a hoax fire call to the premises using a different public phone box each night. Nick had remembered a public safety commercial about how important a few seconds could be when dealing with a fire, and decided that making the fire crew just that little bit tardy in attitude would gain an extra margin of time for the forces of destruction. The sight of the naked flames tearing through the roof made Nick's heart beat faster with delight. Alison was right: doing something felt good. In the demise of the shop he could see a path; in the smoke he could smell the discharge of power, feel its tender, warm embrace through the car window. Convinced of the way ahead, he snatched one last look at the fiery consumption of the building, before Alison accelerated and pulled them away into the night.

forty-two

A sashay. There was no doubt in Genevieve's mind. She knew a sashay when she saw one. And Charlotte had definitely just sashayed up to the front of the room to deliver her presentation. Not a full-on hip-swinging belly dance move, but with her bulk it didn't need to be. Merely the slightest swaying of the hips; a slow, sensuous pendulum movement, with each return paused at the upswing, to create an unmistakable sashay. Where the hell did she get these ideas?

Genevieve knew the answer all too well. That television programme. Charlotte was well on her way to becoming a mini-celebrity. The changes were there for all to see. Moreover, after the first episode's "poor people" comment Charlotte had learned to be clever about it. Her comments, and the timings thereof, were evidence of long nights spent at home planning impromptu asides. The average watching moron would not recognise these for what they were, but Genevieve did. Genevieve also realised, happily in this respect, that had it not been for that early warning, Charlotte might already have plunged into even deeper water, water in which even she would have sunk without trace. As it was she was being clever, astute.

All the signs were there. Genevieve had caught her answering the telephone with authority; giving her name with undisguised relish, listening for the recognition at the end of the line. Then her appearance had started to change. Not overnight, but gradually, like the coming of spring, and before you knew it, spring it was. Charlotte had, in the space of three short episodes, become a sort of sexy twin sister to herself. Gone were the days when she wore clothes that covered her bulk.

Now she seemed to have a wardrobe that emphasised her body, capturing every massive curve. Frankly, it repulsed Genevieve in the extreme. Still, come the end of the project Genevieve knew that Charlotte would be out into the everyday world, free to ride her little donkey of fame for as far along the beach as it could manage.

'Having secured London Zoo as the setting for the party, we must now set about ensuring that it operates as a safe, secure and enjoyable venue.'

Where once Charlotte would have spluttered her way through such occasions with all the self-regard of a pig on the spit, now she could been seen bouncing enthusiastically in her seat as the presentation grew nearer. The voice had changed too, aided, Genevieve suspected, by some form of elocution exercises. Listen to her, the tubby minx.

'What was that Genevieve?'

Johnny was asking her a question, and Genevieve immediately regretted the stiff gin and tonic she'd had before coming over. Intended to calm the ire that she knew would be rising during Charlotte's presentation, it had clearly loosened her lips too.

'Nothing Johnny; just making a mental note about fencing. Do go on Charlotte.'

Charlotte paused in the manner of one brushing over an unwelcome interruption and set off again.

'Our key factor must be the safety and security of our guests.'

What made it worse was that Genevieve had written all of this. She had had to. Charlotte's own compositional skills ended at the framing of a postal address. It would never do for Charlotte to reveal her true colours on television. Let whoever employs her afterwards enjoy the surprise, Genevieve smirked inwardly. In the meantime she would make sure that everything looked good for the Rutherfords and the cameras.

'Excellent! Well done, Charlotte . . . and Genevieve.'

Genevieve good-naturedly accepted Johnny's incidental congratulations.

'Yes, well done you two. This is all looking excellent,' Ginny chipped in.

'Now then, what's the story on the cost of all this?' Johnny asked in his best hardnosed voice.

'Yes, well. To be frank, it's going to be incredibly expensive,' Genevieve said softly.

'In the aid of a good cause, of course!' Ginny thumped out loudly, for the benefit of the sound recordist.

'Yes, absolutely. In the aid of a good cause,' Genevieve agreed with dutiful gusto. In the corner of her eye she saw Johnny giving Steve the guillotine motion. Steve dutifully called 'Cut.'

By prior arrangement, it had been decided that, while terms like "expensive", "costly" and so forth might be captured on film, actual cost-related discussions would not be open to the cameras. The compromise was that the narrator might refer, in suitably salacious tones, to what the costs might be, provided these were not too low. As it happened, the absence of cameras two minutes later was indeed a pity, as they would have been able to capture the shocked expressions on Johnny and Ginny's faces as Genevieve revealed the true cost of doing something truly different.

forty-three

A quarter-page advertisement, nothing too flamboyant, in the financial pages of all of the newspapers invited shareholders to apply for a copy of *Setting The Tiger Free*, a booklet which would explain the Exodus strategy for "realising the full potential of your investment in Belston Corporation". Lawson had embarked on a series of meetings with institutional shareholders. These affairs were all equally – fastidiously – dowdy in appearance. Muted-suited Lawson would take the back seat as his management team passed the baton in a smooth-not-showy relay presentation.

'In summary, we see a magnificent opportunity with Belston Corporation. To take our empowering management systems and apply them to, and for, their resources. We do not see this as a takeover. We are the natural next stage in the development of Belston Corporation.' Jennings himself now, rounding the whole thing off.

There were questions of course, which allowed him to demonstrate how well the structure and operations of Belston Corporation had been analysed, broken down and re-structured.

'Have you had a chance to talk with Freiberg about this directly?'

The question, from a senior analyst, momentarily froze the room, as all eyes, especially his own people's, turned to Jennings. He smiled, widely: 'Mr Freiberg and I were most fortunate in being able to agree at a very early stage of the bid that our individual visions did not enjoy a coincidence of objective.'

A gap, and then laughter. The documentation was passed round and Lawson and his group departed for a debrief at their own offices. In the lift on the way down he was pleased. 'Things seem to be proceeding well enough,' he said, as his executives exchanged comments about how their presentations could be made smoother without becoming smug.

Jennings had correctly anticipated that he might be seen as the less substantial, showier, figure; thus his emphasis on the downbeat when it came to fighting the battle for the heads. He knew that he may already have won the much softer battle for the hearts.

As for Pommy, he felt it necessary to focus on the new methodologies, to show that he was just as capable of being "new" as anybody else. He was not ill-equipped to do so. For all his platform speech had talked up Jenning's interest in the less concrete side of business, Pommy was no less interested in that area. In some respects he was more alert than most to the subtleties of the modern.

The Internet served as a case in point. What seemed like a lifetime before, Pommy had recognised the potential of 'this fucking Internet thingy' quickly. As he generally did whenever anything buzzy appeared on the business horizon, anything that the City Boys might see fit to ask some stupid question on. For such developments he immediately put in place a number of 'initiatives' to point at, to serve as a shield behind which he might get on with the real work. Should the questions get more aggressive, well, buy somebody else or import a bunch of people. Over the years this policy had stood Pommy in good stead.

'What are you doing about China?' A pokey office in Tianjin had covered that for a long time while others discovered the lie of the land, expensively.

'What are you doing about the Euro?'

A couple of new people in Accounts had held that one at bay long enough.

When it came to business smarts, Pommy knew he took some beating.

'You'd better be playing with two sets of cards if you're going to try and trump me!'

And so it had been with the Internet. The formation of an E-Business Group at Belston Corporation had been cause for a little party at Disneyworld, Paris for the City Boys. Since then it had bubbled along, doing nothing spectacular, keeping pace as Pommy realised that this was more than one of those 'buzzy' trends that served to occupy the minds of those whose affairs were about watching business rather than doing it.

What mattered when it came to doing the walk round the shareholders was this: although Pommy had nothing approaching Jennings' level of depth on the new media side of affairs, he wasn't a virgin either. And since he wasn't a virgin, he could afford to talk dirty.

'I am struck by Mr Jennings' fixation with technology. It strikes me sometimes as being all a bit for its own sake, rather than for a definite purpose,' Pommy said over lunch with an important City Boy.

'As you know, we have been running a strong Internet programme for several years. You will recall that we were first in no less than three industries to understand the opportunities that the Internet might bring. But we insist on profitable developments – maybe not jam today. Perhaps jam tomorrow. But certainly not jam on cloud nine.'

And to another he made his point, and the inherent comparison with Jennings, more forcefully. 'What all this media stuff does is take your mind off the knitting, the basics. A sound business using all appropriate means, including everything Seattle, Palo Alto and Cambridge can throw at us, is what we want, what we have built. Not running around with a shiny new saddle trying to find some fucking mule to throw it on!'

forty-four

'But you're keeping well, though?'

Roger Williamson's friendliness sat uneasily on the border-line between effusion and nervousness. Jonathan nodded, again. Roger had already asked the question twice; in the manner familiar to anyone who has ever had to make conversation with someone they're embarrassed to see.

Jonathan had insisted, when given time off to get his life sorted, that he be allowed to come in for a couple of hours once a week. It was a pride thing. He did not want to be seen to be shirking or falling by the wayside. So once a week since his (compulsory) compassionate leave had started, Jonathan had driven into work, sat at his desk and looked at things. He had noticed after the third visit that the office seemed to be unusually quiet when he came in and had realised that this must be some form of sympathy absence, people preferring to leave him alone for fear of saying the wrong thing.

Jonathan was thankful of having such good companions and entirely ignorant of the dash for the cafeteria that his visits occasioned, or the furious flurry of meetings that materialised at twelve-hour notice as people realised what day tomorrow was. This reaction was entirely understandable. People don't want to go to work and deal with emotional or mental crip-ples. By and large they want to go in, work, go home, get paid. Encounters of such a nature did not fit into the acceptable, let alone ideal, profile of a good job.

Jonathan did not like the idea of putting his colleagues out on account of their sympathy and had therefore explained to a fraught Human Resources Manager that although he would always come in on a Friday, the hours might vary from week to week depending on how things were. Jonathan cut the connection to forestall any needless discussion of the point. He knew what was best.

Strolling through reception he felt strangely buoyant, not at all like someone who wasn't wanted in the building. Had he looked over his shoulder after signing in – 'Just a security thing, Jonathan, as you're officially on leave' – he would have seen the receptionist hammering various numbers in frantic succession. Walking along the corridor to his work area he encountered a number of people who said 'Hi. How's it going?' although not as a question, an action emphasised by their not stopping. Jonathan waved to their backs and walked cheerily on.

'Oh boy, a tough week,' he said, sitting down at his desk, although there was no one at the surrounding desks to hear him. All the incoming mail had been stacked for him to see, although any issues therein were being dealt with elsewhere. Jonathan skimmed through the assorted sheets anyway, along with those printed-out e-mails relevant to him. Access to the system itself was "not compatible with his status", something he understood entirely. There had been a noise behind him and he'd turned abruptly to find Roger scampering up the stairs from the men's toilet.

'Roger!' Jonathan had called, 'How are you?'

'Fine thanks, Jonathan,' Roger said without stopping, his voice coming through the slats in the stairway, 'How are you keeping?'

'Good. Listen, can I have a word?'

Before Roger could think of a reply he heard the sound of other footsteps on the stair and looking down saw Jonathan approaching. Roger stopped and a hasty smile appeared: 'Of course Jonathan, come into the office.'

They sat down. Jonathan asked how things were. Roger explained they were great. Then he asked how Jonathan was, and the children. Five non-informative minutes later Jonathan found himself shaking hands with Roger, who was expecting someone and needed to get things ready. Jonathan understood and said he'd see him next week. Roger nodded slowly. Walking down the stairs again, Jonathan couldn't remember what it was he had wanted to see Roger about in the first place. Never mind, it would come to him. He admonished himself for this memory lapse.

Downstairs all was quiet. There were a few people he didn't recognise sitting at desks but their stern demeanour before the screens gave a strong signal that they did not wish to be disturbed. As he approached his own desk, a telephone began to ring nearby. That's Mike's phone, Jonathan thought. He looked around – no sign of Mike. Jonathan walked round and answered the call, pulling the receiver to his mouth with a hesitant, quiet, 'Hello?' still looking around for Mike.

'Has he gone yet?' a male voice asked firmly.

'Has who gone yet?' Jonathan asked, curiously.

The line went dead. Uninterestedly, Jonathan replaced the handset and gathered the stuff from his desk.

'See you next week,' Jonathan said to a nervous, smiling receptionist as he handed her his visitor's pass. Through the revolving glass door Jonathan could see the figure of Roger Williamson, waving good-naturedly to someone in the car park. This made Jonathan pause because part of him had suspected that Roger might not have had a visitor and might have just said so to get rid of Jonathan. Now Jonathan felt little guilt pangs.

He popped out on the other side of the glass just as two gentlemen arrived, one in an off-grey suit, the other in a sports jacket and slacks. Jonathan was sure he recognised the man in the suit as Roger made them both welcome, shaking their hands and gesturing as to the weather of the day. Then the man in the suit caught Jonathan's eye and announced, 'Jonathan, how the devil you doing?' putting his hand out and making Jonathan smile.

Roger looked to the ground and then, indicating the vehicle the two had arrived in, sought to engage the other man in car-based conversation. The man in a suit was pumping Jonathan's hand and Jonathan was most embarrassed to realise that he could not recall his name.

'So how are you, Jonathan?'

'Fine, thanks . . .,' Jonathan was caught red-faced.

'Lawrence, Lawrence Dexter – not surprised you don't remember. It's been a couple of years. How's . . . Alison, is it?'

'Alison is . . . fine, she's fine too,' Jonathan said, and would have been aware of Roger having stopped his conversation and now watching him intently, had he been his normal self.

'Great! I saw her in London the other day, getting . . .'

Not being his normal self, it took Jonathan less than one second to react to Lawrence's words, drop his briefcase, pick Lawrence up by the lapels and ram him against the building's walls.

'What did you say?' Jonathan screamed.

Roger and the other man began pulling at Jonathan.

'Uuuh,' managed a winded Lawrence.

'You said you saw my wife. Where did you see her? Where?' Jonathan pressed Lawrence tightly to the wall, oblivious to and undeterred by the tugging of two good-sized men on either side of him.

'Waterloo,' Lawrence gasped. 'Getting on a train. To Brussels.'

Jonathan paused and thought, still holding Lawrence as the other two now pounded on his back.

'What was she carrying?'

'What?' Lawrence replied, unable to understand anything about his situation. He was here to have a meeting. He was a customer. This wasn't right.

'What was she carrying?' Jonathan shouted angrily.

'Nothing. Just one weekend bag, I think.'

Jonathan released his grip and stepped back, and Roger and the other man directed their attention to the fallen, wheezing pile that was Lawrence. Jonathan picked up his briefcase and walked calmly to his car. No need to rush. Not now. She had only taken a weekend bag. That meant she was coming back. Coming back to London. In his mind it was searchlight clear. Armed with the right answer, albeit for the wrong reasons, Jonathan hopped smartly behind the wheel of the MG and drove with full care and attention out of his company car park, never to return.

forty-five

Nick looked down at the kitchen table, a carton of orange juice in hand. Laid out before him was every fact he had been able to assemble about Pommy Freiberg, his history, and those of the companies he had worked for. Every newspaper article, profile or interview was there. Each and every web reference had been checked. Nick picked up the photocopied sheet from *Who's Who*, scanning the hard facts once more:

Peter "Pommy" Freiberg, md. Katherine, dv. , md. Lynette, two daughters, Hannah and Lynette, dv., md. Genevieve, two sons, George and Justin. CEO, Belston Corporation, Non-Exec Chairman, Regal Insurance, Director, Tempus Investments, Non-Exec Director KFB Holdings, Chairman, London Heritage Group, Vice-Chairman, Business in Arts. Hobbies: Not Suffering Fools Gladly; yacht Schadenfreude.

That was what Pommy Freiberg boiled down to.

Nick felt rather silly. He had expected more. Compared to the corporate analysis to which he was so accustomed, this was an unfamiliar situation. One could look up and down the balance sheets and across the activities of any company and come up with a strong understanding of what they were about. But this was different. He knew Pommy Freiberg and nothing on this kitchen table gave any indication of what the man was like. Nick was learning one of life's fundamentals: how it is possible to know all the facts about someone, and still know nothing about the person.

He had all but given up hope of finding anything worthwhile on the business side. Nick was a severely tainted source even if he could find something worth sniping about to the media. The resources of Belston Corporation would have little trouble in dealing with the bitter nit-picking of a grudge-bearing ex-employee. Those secrets he did know did not amount to much anyway. As such he felt no more empowered than the average citizen.

What made it worse was the burning of Martin's Mobility Centre. That had made him feel fantastic, as Alison had told him it would. Now it was doubly crippling to be unable to find an appropriate course of action, let alone get on with it

'What is it exactly we're trying to do?' Alison had asked the previous evening over lasagne and wine.

'I need to make him feel something of what I felt.'

'Like what?'

Nick smiled. Two months ago these thoughts would not have troubled him. If anything he might have said, if pushed, 'Forget it – walk away. By spending valuable time on Freiberg you are simply compounding the damage already done.'

But now, alive to the glory of action, Nick felt differently. He knew that he needed to address the issue. Indeed, that phrase had now entered his mind as the new fulcrum of his thinking. Not the old, 'What is the issue?' but 'How do we address it?'

Nick knew he had Alison to thank. Not for anything she had said, but for how she went about things. Her simplistic 'it's either on or off' approach to things had worked a powerful magic on Nick and he felt all the better, more than recovered, for it.

'He humiliated, no, in some way, *emasculated* me. I need to do the same to him,' he sighed.

There was nothing to be seen in all this documentation. Despite everything that Nick knew or suspected it was hardly going to put a dent in the old battleship, let alone blow it out of the water. Rumours or innuendo were hardly sufficient. It needed to be harder, something in black and white. What made it worse was that his period of separation from corporate life had only fired Nick's appetite. Each scanning of the business pages only confirmed his love for that life. Indeed, that was his life. A new sadness had formed around him, as he recognized that he would never be happy outside of that world and if he was not happy he would never be much use to Alison. What could he say?

'Where have you got to?' Alison was standing in the kitchen doorway.

'Same as before,' he said unhappily, hating the thought that he was disappointing her.

'Are women really his only weakness?' Alison said, sitting down, flicking idly through the assorted papers.

'Yes,' Nick sighed, lowering his head onto the table, 'He's tried to cut down but it never works'.

'Let's go for a walk,' Alison said, getting up.

They walked for the rest of the afternoon, and on until it was dusk. For the most part Nick's mood would not lift, although he did make the effort.

'You do understand, don't you Alison?' he asked as they stood waiting to cross a road.

'You know I do. I still don't understand why we don't just kill him or something. You know, something nice and direct.'

'Whatever we do has to be right, in the sense of appropriate.'

'Appropriate for what?'

'For me. And for him.'

Alison stopped Nick.

'What is it you want? After all this?'

'I . . . I'm not sure now. But I think I know something.'

Nick paused.

'I'm a company man.'

Turning into their street, Nick doubled back to get an evening paper. The business pages were starting to join the dots in the Belston story – Pommy was going to lose. Nick hated the fact that he would not be the one to bring him down. It wasn't even as if he could join in. He had nothing to offer Lawson Jennings.

'All behind the scenes now, I suppose,' he said, as he cast the newspaper down on the sofa next to Alison. He flicked on the television and Alison began looking through the paper. Ten minutes passed in silence, with only the turning of pages and the switching of channels as a sign of life.

'Have you met her then?' Alison asked.

'Met who?' Nick said, still watching the news.

'Her. Pommy's wife. Genevieve Marsden.'

'No,' replied Nick, curious that her name should arise, yet not sufficiently so to distract him from his viewing.

'Says she's organising some massive party. That's what she does apparently.'

Nick nodded absently.

'Wife of business tycoon Pommy Freiberg and party organiser to the swank set of London. There was a programme on about her last night. Starred some fat thing called Charlotte.'

Nick grabbed the paper from Alison. How had he forgotten? *Genevieve*. Those parties, where Pommy liked to preen and strut. Nick read the piece feverishly, his focus poring over this new chasm of opportunity. Maybe there was a way. Surely he had enough to work with.

forty-six

Sponsorship. There would be sponsorship. For this one event the Rutherfords would have sponsorship. Normally they abhorred any form of corporate involvement. That was part of what made them the Rutherfords. While most of social London was happy to slut its way to making their party happen, the Rutherfords held out, an isolated bastion of dignity. This made them both hated and loved in equal measure. 'How do they do it? It makes me sick!'

No invitation was as valuable as the small, plain, barely italicised piece of card that always began 'Johnny and Ginny Rutherford are pleased . . .' And regardless of the what, where and when of it, the meaning of 'pleased' was clear. Pleased to be who they were, pleased to be doing what they're doing, pleased to be above you and have you know it.

Yet for this bash, this one bash, there would be a corporate involvement. Genevieve got the gossip flowing, got the phrases going round the people that mattered. A word here, a simple line here. Costs, you see, costs. So the stories gathered pace. Not just costs but unprecedented costs. Costs that no other social gathering had ever taken on.

London Zoo, you see. London Zoo, once secure, is not cheap. It's all for charity too. 'Save the . . . you know, that thing, save it,' you see. London Zoo necessitates a great many provisions in order to make it work. A lot of it is outdoors. Walkways must be covered against the rain, the wind, the potential for circling helicopters eager for an eyeful of the happening few. Wind blocks must be put up across perimeter fencing to prevent the unnecessary ruffling of that happening few and coincidentally shut out the telescopic intrusion of the spies from the ordinary world. For they would undermine the whole thing. They would take liberties. They cannot be expected to understand and so they must be barred, neutered. Everyone knew how much damage they could do – a touch of the nose told it all. They would not get in. There would be no unauthorised imaging. Another trademark of the Rutherfords, for no cameras at all were allowed. Everyone understood. So rigid was the rule that it wasn't even mentioned on the invitations. Everyone knew. Together they would gather and no subjective record would remain of their being there. Only the one true record, the authorised photography of the Rutherfords' own photographer, who would wander the party, carefully compiling the basis for an album of photographs that all present would receive two weeks later.

Genevieve laid precautions down in detail: don't look at what people are holding, look at how they are standing, how they are looking at something. That's the giveaway in terms of whether or not someone is taking a photograph. And just to be sure all phones and similar equipment were lovingly taken into care as each guest was happily frisked on the way in.

The invitations, the absence of cameras, the lack of sponsorship – this wilful preservation of social anachronism made the Rutherfords who they were. And the guests wanted to be part of that, to feel their inclusion in the most distinguished of company. Company so elite, so above it all, that it surpassed mere membership. It was organic; a knowing, pulsing sludge of the finest few.

Some transgressed, of course they did. Pictures appeared. Tittle-tattle appeared. As a result, people disappeared, were never heard of again, save in disparaging tones over coffee on private premises. For who would ever associate with the likes of them? Who would dare to be seen in conversation with such persons? Genevieve made sure of that both before and especially after. Lifetimes of social elevation were flushed away for want of containing one's excitement at being at an event of the

Rutherfords. Oh the humanity! To throw so much away through the aperture of a camera.

So, the fear of exclusion restricted the intrusion of the modern. By and large. That which it did not restrict was Genevieve's to control. The covered walkways and social areas did their bit. The convenient all-round windcheaters played their part. The string of security guards circling the grounds made their presence known. They were all individually selected by Genevieve; a private army of occupation that brooked no complaint in maintaining the integrity of the event. The inclusion of several off-duty police officers within this dedicated pool ensured that the right contacts were made before and during. People who attempted entry were clearly using threatening behaviour. Any photographers were undoubtedly breaching the peace. Bystanders were clearly loitering with intent.The party was able to relax and the guests kick off behind a well-trained string of well-paid loyalty to the cause; uncompromising, unquestioning, untouchable.

Ordinarily, anything corporate would be a breach of all this, a bridgehead over which the real world might march. So nothing corporate – keep that at bay. But not this time. This time it would be necessary to let the sticky, unpleasant world of the corporate in. The cost, you see, the cost. The whole zoo thing. It's for charity, you see. So there is a one-off business arrangement. A little something. What could it be? Well, it might be the champagne, or the cars, or the jewellery. Nothing else. They are allowed to come along and be discreet. Discreet branding, discreet logos, discreet representation. They are made to feel lucky to be there. After all, they have been selected to be given access to the most discerning, most assured, most worthy public in the world.

Costs. Animals are problems, regardless of how thematically correct they might be. Shielding is needed; a pre-requisite of using the zoo. An entire system of expensive sound deadening, one-way glass placed around each and every cage in order that the sensitive animals are not exposed to the elite drunken buffoonery. The elite can see the animals, can stand making faces at them, tucking their hands into their armpits before the monkeys, roar at the lions, pull faces and generally behave like schoolchildren, but from all of this the animals are safely screened, seeing no more than a dull, black reflection of themselves. A battalion of technicians and workmen will descend on the zoo for four hours to put this fortification in place. And that costs.

'Rutherfords . . . the zoo . . . charity . . . fantastic!' Genevieve took note of the responses

So the word was passed, communicated from parlour to parlour like a war-time secret. Those in the centre, who were comfortable about their positions, waited with conspicuous grace; not concerned, merely curious. Where would it be? What would it be?

Yet for others, this was a time of furious waiting. Of consideration of the potential dates, likely venues and necessary excuses. Excuses would be necessary. If you were not invited, then you would need a good excuse as to why you couldn't be there.

'A weekend in Venice, booked ages ago.'

'Parents' anniversary, Madrid. Can't be helped.'

'Festival, outside Lisbon, what's the place called . . .?'

And they would vanish, to trudge round ill-fitting European towns and cities in order to make their excuses. Suitably validated, coloured and cultured, they could return and carry it all off. Woe betide those who lied, who explained at length the Berlin gallery opening and were then seen sloping along the shelves of some all-night delicatessen, scarf around face, in pursuit of wines and spirits.

So the invitations descended and those they settled on took jocund note and the others quickly make their travel arrangements and, safely inoculated, were then able to go out again. What joy the invitations brought – what wonder!

'Keepers and Beasts! Magnificent! Hooray!'

What will everyone wear? What will we wear? What will I

wear? The telephones rang off the hook in every fancy dress and costume shop. Bookings were made and altered. Ridiculous requests refused; fantastic demands costed and charged.

And the forgotten victims wept. Those who had so long ago made their own party arrangements for the same date found themselves excused upon from every angle, from every height, by their closest friends, and left only with those guests that the Rutherfords did not require. No amount of brazen smiling could hide the darkness of their souls.

forty-seven

Pommy knew he was losing. Doing the rounds, he sensed it in the handshakes he received, in the small silences after his presentations concluded. He sensed it in the time they spent with him and in the directionless, almost uninterested questions that were asked. Pommy knew what going through the motions was all about.

In the newspaper analyses Pommy had the rare pleasure of seeing his virtues turned into vices. His at-one-time laudable "firm leadership" was now "egoistic indulgence"; "instinctive know-how" became "antiquated methodology"; for "corporate determination" read "dogmatic whim".

He knew he was losing. Knowing this did not frighten him. Rather, it pleased him. Not knowing, well, that would have been a sure sign of the end. Instead Pommy took comfort from his position of calm understanding: I'm losing, but I've not lost. Most people never know where they fucking are. Better to be somewhere on a map than nowhere. At least I've got a fucking map. Most people spend a lot of time looking around without one. Always know where you are. When you're fucked, you'd better fucking know it. Or you're finished. Fucked and finished – two business terms often confused.

Pommy leaned back in his chair. Across from him sat two advisers from the investment bank which was being paid ludicrous chunks of money to assist his defence. Pommy could see the chunks of money sliding down their greasy throats with every word they uttered.

'So what are my options?' he growled.

Neither of them flinched, despite this being the third time

that the options had been explained. On each occasion they had noticed Pommy slide off into his own thoughts within a few sentences.

'The first option,' the bald, fidgety one began patiently, 'The first option, as we see it, is simply to continue as is. Continue doing the rounds. Continue strengthening existing relationships. Continue trying to get our message through.'

Pommy knew this option. It was his favourite, his instinctive preference. He also knew what the second option was.

'The second option,' began the black-haired, puffy-cheeked one, 'Is to initiate some form of defensive action. Without acknowledging the merits, sorry, possible merits,' he corrected himself rapidly, as Pommy snapped out of his apparent daydream with a glare of pursed-lip reprimand.

'. . . possible merits, however unlikely these might be . . .'

Fucking crawler.

'. . . the second option is to take on board some appropriate changes. Significant restructuring. Show the world that we are not frightened of change.'

Pommy knew what all this meant. Didn't like it one bit. Man feeds ducks in park every now and then, everything fine. No problem with feeding ducks every now and then. But, man starts feeding ducks in pond suddenly, turns up suddenly at pond with loaves and loaves, fucking weird. People don't like sudden things. Man now under suspicion by people. Not good for man. Not good for people. Only good for fucking ducks. Fuckers. No. Can't start changing things. As good as admitting change at the top needed. Stupid advice.

'The third option . . . '

Pommy heard the sound shift from one end of the desk to the other. Disconcerting, should have asked them to sit closer together. Third option, not an option at all. It was almost as bad as the fourth option. Had already told them straight that the third option was not up for discussion; he would not be seeking aid from a third party.

'Forget any fucking alliances, white knights or chocolate

teddy bears. I will not be going cap in hand to any fucker.'

So they only had two options to go over. Of course, the fourth option was what Lawson Jennings wanted: Surrender. Oh, yes – ask for more, of course. Say something like 'Offer does not fully realise asset worth.' Gave the fucker the nod, though. Stick a few more logs on the fire and its all yours. All get together for a chummy barbecue afterwards. I get to walk with dignity into sunset, with a sack of fucking loot for being nice about everything. Walk with dignity. Not real dignity though. Only made-up dignity. Actor's dignity. Real dignity chucked on fire with logs. I'm not an actor. I'm the fucking real thing. Not like that fucker Jennings. No dent in mattress when he gets out of bed in the morning. No trace on a beach after he's been for a walk in the sand. Not like me – footprints fucking everywhere. Big ones; deep. Like puddles. All over the fucking beach.

It's not about money either. Don't care about money. Making it about money means you're a whore. I am not a whore. Don't want to become one either.

Pommy looked up and saw the two expensive advisors looking at him expectantly. What did they want? It was their job to talk, to advise, wasn't it?

'So, there are three options?' Pommy said, looking at them with unrequited disdain. Fucking money gobblers.

One hour later Pommy was alone in his office. He had finally told the two advisers that it would be option one, the other two not being options at all, in his opinion. Yet even as they left Pommy knew that option one – getting the message across – was about to crawl behind a bush and die. He needed more than that to win. Special tactics were required now. Special tactics and special people. Pommy went to his door and looked out across the dark and mostly deserted office. Cleaners were beginning to make their way along the floors, emptying baskets, wiping desks and screens. But it wasn't them he was thinking of.

forty-eight

There was a knock at the door. A slight, hesitant knock. The type of knock that nagged rather than urged. Jonathan turned over, pulling the duvet around his shoulder, nuzzling closer into the pillow. A huge block of tiredness still weighed down on top of his shoulders, pinning him to the bed. For a fortnight now, since finding out that Alison was in London, he had driven back and forth to the city every day, driving round and round and round, looking, searching. This was after he had dropped the children off and he always raced back to make sure he was there for them in the evenings, just as normal. But it was all beginning to take its toll. Today he had come back to the house after seeing Samuel through the school gate, ostensibly to make a packed lunch for the car, and instead collapsed on the bed, his body exhausted from the pounding grind of twelve-hour driving days.

The knock at the door came again, this time more demanding. Jonathan's eyes opened as he realised that somebody was there. Somebody was trying to get into the house. The knock came again. It seemed soft, sensitive; somehow feminine. Someone who didn't want just to come in. Perhaps someone who wanted to come home. The duvet exploded off the bed, settling like a fog on the floor as Jonathan burst into the bathroom to grab his white towelling robe, not realising he was still fully dressed from the previous day.

The wooden stairs beat out the sharp tattoo of his approach to the front door as Jonathan's deliberately playful 'Coming! Coming!' resonated around the hall. Of course she would come back and, being shy, embarrassed, repentant, would not simply walk in. No, she would want to be asked in, greeted on the threshold of their home, perhaps even carried over it as she had been so joyfully on that first night not so many years ago.

'Coming!' Jonathan managed one last jubilant cry, bereft of alarm or fear, before slipping the lock and tugging the door open. Now he was entirely unable to contain his smile. She was back!

A small woman stood in front of a tall man, her head obscuring her colleague's body, so that they appeared as two heads, one balanced atop the other. The woman held a notepad. Jonathan's smile vanished.

'Mr Greenmeadow?'

The woman seemed disturbingly confident, used to official business, used to dealing with relatives.

'Oh my God,' Jonathan heard himself say, raising hand to mouth in horror. Why did it have to be this? Where had she been found? A canal, a rubbish tip, a foreign embassy's car park? What could he tell the children? Mummy's holiday has been extended. Mummy isn't coming back. Mummy's gone away, far, far away. So far we can never go there.

'Mr Greenmeadow? Jonathan Greenmeadow?'

Jonathan nodded, as the woman looked again at her notepad, then flashed up a card with a newspaper name on it and her photograph.

'Mr Greenmeadow, my name is Judy Hamilton. I'd like to ask you about Spontaneous Sex. Apparently you're a bit of an expert.'

Jonathan looked at her in a stupor. What was going on? He felt his mouth open and then freeze.

'So then, Jonathan, tell us all about it. How good is Spontaneous Sex? Can anyone do it?'

Poom! The man had stepped out from behind the woman and swiftly raised and fired a large camera and flash at the bewildered Jonathan. Poom! Poom! Poom!

Jonathan juddered back in the doorway, a smile of terror beginning to spread across his bed-hungry, unshaven face.

'Jonathan? It is Jonathan Greenmeadow, isn't it? Is your wife in, by the way . . ., ' the woman shuffled through her notes, '. . . Alison, is it?'

Jonathan saw the cover of a magazine sticking out from Judy's sheaf of paper. The same magazine that he had written to what seemed – was – a lifetime before. He jumped back and slammed the door.

'Mr Greenmeadow?' Judy's voice was accompanied by a fervent, excited rapping on the door.

'Mr Greenmeadow? You did write this letter didn't you? Have we interrupted something?'

Slowly, squeakily, the hinge of the letterbox raised itself and with a sad *thunk* the magazine dropped onto the carpet. Jonathan stepped forward and picked it up, while Judy's voice and hand continued to demand answers. Jonathan raked through the magazine in search of the letters page.

There, in beefy bold, was his letter, the "Star Letter", with his name and town printed underneath it. Above this in red felt tip pen was written, 'Find this guy. Get photos, details, wife's story.' Jonathan's heart banged against his chest. He had asked for his name and address to be withheld, hadn't he?

Judy could be heard moving round the outside of the house now, calling loudly at the windows. Jonathan ran into the study, snapped the computer on and called up messages sent. Where is it? There! He scrolled down to the bottom of his e-mail, nauseous as he caught the occasional phrase of trumpeting testosterone. Nothing. There was no "please withhold my name and address". Jonathan tried to force the mouse further down the page, but there was no more page. That was it.

'Mr Greenmeadow! We might be able to come to some arrangement on this.'

Judy was approaching the study window. Jonathan slid off the seat and through the door, slamming it behind him, then dropped to the floor, shameful and breathless at his stupidity.

By and by, Judy's voice trailed off and Jonathan heard retreating footsteps. Maybe it was a ruse. Slowly, stealthily, he lowered himself to the ground and crept into the living room. Crossing the carpet on all fours, he raised his eyes over the window's edge, staring past the jungle of family snapshots scattered along the frame. Judy and the photographer were gone. Good. Then he found them, standing on Laura and Robert's doorstep, talking to Laura, pointing over at his house. Jonathan ducked from view and crawled back into the hallway. There was post. Sitting against the front door he opened an electricity bill and a long legalese letter from work, with a large cheque attached, explaining something or other. He placed these indifferently to one side and opened a small packet, a posh pen; the magazine's prize for being Star Letter writer. Then he picked up the magazine and read and re-read the vain, boastful words of a man who felt it only his duty to inform the world of his triumph. Someone else entirely from the man now reading about it.

forty-nine

'I am in total control. I am in TOTAL control.'

Genevieve breathed deeply in, and then told Charlotte to say it again. She herself was in no doubt about her state of control but would often ask members of her team to do this drill in the run-up to an event. They would be stopped whilst running down a corridor, or tapped on the shoulder while going through a sheaf of papers. After the tenth repetition Genevieve would let them be. No need to labour the point needlessly.

Things were shaping up. TipTop McGee had completed the recruitment of a great foundation crew, all of whom Genevieve would meet, approve and congratulate in about five minutes time. These were the builders; the organisers, who would put in place the necessary infrastructure for the party to take place.

More importantly, Genevieve had just returned from a meeting with the Rutherfords, where she had finally managed to get Johnny and Ginny to make their choice.

'I like cars,' Jonny had said wistfully.

'I like jewellery,' Ginny had said mournfully.

Genevieve had then sat in silence while they had padded with coarse logic through the merits of having an upmarket car or jewellery presence at London Zoo. She had already tried to force the issue in one direction and then the other only to be reminded that in this, as in so many matters, Johnny and Ginny had hearts that outweighed their heads and were thus prone to unseen forces, forces which could not be reasoned with. So Genevieve waited until she could wait no longer and the cameras were not there.

'You must decide on this matter today.'

Johnny and Ginny had been upset by this sudden resolution.

'But, why, why?' Ginny had implored, as if enquiring as to the reason for the presence in the world of suffering when God was omniscient, omnipresent and good. 'Why must we decide today, Genevieve?'

'Because today is the last possible date from which I can accommodate the requirements of any corporate affiliate at the event,' Genevieve said slowly, carefully avoiding the cheap "sponsor".

Johnny placed his hand manfully on Ginny's thigh: 'Come on now girl; it's time to make a choice. We have to. And you can make it. I don't care. It's up to you. You choose.'

Ginny dabbed her face gently. She was not made for the world of decisions. Johnny looked to Genevieve, who smiled understandingly. As she did so Ginny pulled herself together in the abrupt, firm manner of one who was doing their duty for king and country.

'We're going to have the . . . the . . . car!' Ginny winced, and then turning, collapsed into Johnny's waiting arms. He looked over at Genevieve and nodded. Genevieve picked up her papers and silently departed the room, Johnny's 'there, theres' masking her footsteps.

'I am in total control.' Charlotte's voice never wavered in its eerie sense of calm. Genevieve patted her gently on the head. Despite her increasing disgust with this particular previously Dependable Ugly she was absolutely resolved that she would do everything in her power to ensure that her clients got what they wanted out of the programme. There was no point in letting Charlotte fail in public. No good would come of it. This was the way. Deliver the project and then, and only then, take care of things.

Genevieve turned, pleased with herself and discovered that Steve and his cameraman had captured the entire scene. Genevieve walked calmly over to them.

'Top stuff,' Steve enthused. 'Very natural.'

'It was natural,' Genevieve said firmly. This was not the first time that she had suddenly realised that filming was taking place. They were clearly skilled in the arts of stealth.

'Yes, but it was very . . . natural, all the same,' Steve continued, eyes panning the room like a man expecting a shot to ring out. Genevieve smiled, in control, and left Steve staring out at the passing traffic while the cameraman reviewed the footage.

fifty

Nick had been right in his inclination to get every last scintilla of information on Pommy Freiberg, despite lacking the wherewithal to do so. Yet even if he had had the resources to spend and the contacts to get it, Nick's searches would have come to nothing, or next to nothing. Pommy had made sure of that.

Nearly ten years before, when Pommy had first begun to feel his star was in the public ascendant, not from anything he was doing, but from the attention paid to him by others, he had engaged a firm, a special firm, to look into his own history. In order to get what he wanted – an independent opinion of himself – Pommy had hired a lawyer from outside his usual legal circle to brief the special firm, thus masking the true client. A couple of weeks later, they had returned a slender dossier on Peter "Pommy" Freiberg that pulled no punches in its description. He was, the file informed, an egotistical, overbearing corporate thug, albeit one with an instinctive business mind and an engaging, competitively charismatic personality. On a personal level it noted his two failed marriages. Both ex-wives, Pommy had been delighted to note, were tight-lipped about him, largely because they were both tied fearsomely into generous settlement packages. Although identified as a ladies' man, very little could be discovered about his private life. For all his faults, the report concluded, Pommy seemed to generate an enviable degree of loyalty, even among those who might have wished him ill. There was nothing of real squalor; no illegitimate children, unaccountable funds or curious passports.

Pommy did not feel safe as a result of this report. He knew better than that. But he did feel pleased with himself, that all of the precautions he had taken were able, it seemed, to act as a barrier to genuine revelations. The most important precautions he took were with people. As the report noted, loyalty was his primary asset.

Pommy often fancied that he could actually scent disloyalty coming from those he had dealings with, as others might identify a perfume. And even allowing for that, he was careful. Those who passed into his innermost circle were a rare breed indeed. Those who knew everything numbered only one: Pommy. Divide and conquer is never more important than when it comes to those closest to you. Of that, Pommy was in no doubt. He was also in no doubt that not everyone was as careful as he. Not everyone thought about how things might look with the degree of constancy that Pommy exerted. He did not feel the need to make himself a public figure. People in business knew who he was. That was enough for Pommy, because they were all that mattered. Others might feel the need to make an exhibition of themselves, become well-known. Not Pommy. What had Durning called it? "Improvident displaying" or something. Hostages to fortune, Pommy called it. Get in the public eye too much and the public want to know more. Only fucking natural. Best stay away. If you're in the public eye, people tend to recognise you. Remember things. Look for things. Suddenly everything is noteworthy, memorable, and significant.

Pommy felt that an investigation of Lawson Jennings was worth a quid or two. Instinct told him to forget the business side. Jennings would be pathetically scrupulous on those counts. No, go for the personal. Let's see the man up close. Then let's see what we can show everyone else. Let's pray there's something there, otherwise we're fucked . . .

'Get the picture?' Pommy asked. There was a knock at the door and Pommy slipped deftly into the bathroom. When he came back twenty seconds later, Grant Mullaby was pouring the just-delivered coffee. Grant was Managing Partner of Laston Burley, the special firm. Time did not allow the concomitant

225

delay in the otherwise desirable use of a third-party channel on this occasion. The fucking heat was on now.

'Yes, Mr Freiberg, I get the picture. The personal – that's what we're after,' he'd said quietly, in an Australian accent so pronounced that "picture" came out as "picha". This foreign tang and his quiet voice enhanced the already furtive air in the room.

'And fucking fast too,' Pommy whispered angrily.

Grant winked and was gone, leaving Pommy staring at the two cups of coffee. Didn't even want one fucking coffee.

fifty-one

A din. Genevieve walked quietly, unnoticed into the hubbub. For her this was always a moment of great joy. What naught but a few weeks before had been a near-tranquil office space was now a throbbing mass of organisation. Here her people sat, forging chaos and disorder into a definition of event excellence. Layer upon layer of staff had been added. Team Genevieve was almost complete. Its matriarch stood in the doorway and sucked in the thrill.

Genevieve's policy was to arrive later than usual in these key days. She had noticed that staff seemed eager to have things to complete and show her on arrival, in a way that they didn't if she simply sat there with them from the off. Not that she was lagging. No, she would be with some supplier or retailer, engaged in careful consideration of one of the infinite variables for which she was justly renowned.

Coming hotfoot into such a powerhouse of activity was a soothing balm of unparalleled depth. Around the building, well into her corridor, and out onto the patio they sat, stood, knelt and crouched; each little station devoted to some aspect of the party. Invitation list correlation, menu selection and refinement, table-setting management, music acquisition and supervision, entertainment coordination. Everything that could be identified and separated as a deliverable party package had been.

Just as rewarding for Genevieve was the sting of tension that her own arrival gave everyone in the room. She caught the eyes flashing up, the almost imperceptible intakes of breath, the sitting-up in chairs. All these cues served to tell her that things were going well.

'Has anybody seen Charlotte?' she asked loudly, dispensing with any form of greeting – didn't want them to think she'd just started work.

'In the kitchen,' came the word. Genevieve walked down the short corridor, passing two girls measuring the circumference of assorted helium balloons.

Charlotte was kneeling in front of three apparently identical chocolate desserts.

'How's it going there?' Genevieve asked brightly.

Charlotte spoke as she scrutinised the plates side-on, one eye closed: 'I'm just going to run these over to the Rutherfords. Mr Rutherford wanted to get a quick taste of the final three options before selection.'

'He's not meddling is he?'

Genevieve was always wary of hosts becoming involved with detailed preparations. Interest was one thing, involvement was quite another.

'No, I think he just wants to make sure. The cameras will probably be there, I imagine,' Charlotte said with as much nonchalance as she could manage.

'Good, excellent,' Genevieve said without feeling, picturing the scene of Charlotte explaining the composition of the desserts and the differences in the cocoa content and quality of each.

'Don't forget to let them know how many we started out with,' Genevieve cautioned, getting down to examine the desserts.

'Oh, of course. One hundred and fifteen, selected from the best that Europe has to offer. Don't worry, I'll let it slip properly.'

Charlotte got up, seemingly satisfied, and began putting plastic covers over the dishes, oblivious to the mild anger rising in Genevieve as she digested Charlotte's words. Let it slip, indeed! Only the other day Genevieve had felt compelled to give Charlotte a bit of a master class in Letting It Slip, having watched her struggle to do so with some fact or other about the napkin linen. Let it slip, indeed.

'Genevieve – interview time.'

Genevieve took TipTop's arrival gratefully, leaving Charlotte carefully placing the plates in a bespoke carrier. TipTop handed Genevieve a stack of ten résumés, then indicated the back office.

'First one's in there, waiting. Came fifteen minutes early, so we're OK there. Next one in twenty, yes?'

Genevieve gave a succinct nod and TipTop vanished. Excellent lieutenant, TipTop. No need for constant "please" and "thank you". Still looking over the first résumé, Genevieve opened the back office door and, without acknowledging the person seated there, proceeded directly to the only other chair in the room, aware and impressed nevertheless that whoever it was had got up when she entered, and remained standing even when Genevieve sat.

These were the crucial moments. Fall down now and no interview technique would save you. Genevieve generally left interviewees standing for a full minute while she ignored them with ostentatious rudeness, sniffing deliberately at a random part of their life described on the paper she had before her.

Genevieve knew what most of them did not: that it was highly possible, likely even, that in the course of the actual evening's event, all staff would be treated to displays of demanding, self-satisfied, drunken bad manners the like of which few of them would ever have experienced. If they couldn't stomach some woman in a back office giving them a bit of an attitude, then it was highly unlikely that they were the right person for the night. Abruptly, Genevieve looked up. An effortless smile looked back at her. Excellent. Genevieve motioned, pleasantly now, for the young lady to sit.

'It's Katherine, with a K, isn't it?'

'Yes, that's right. Like Hepburn.'

Nice girl; good chat.

Three hours later, Genevieve was tired but more or less satis-fied. She held twenty-minute only interviews, having worked out long before that this was all that was needed to ascertain the individual's fitness for the simple yet important tasks ahead. These were far from the weighty organisational jobs currently being accomplished. No, these were the footsoldiers of the event, the greeters, pointers, carriers and sweepers. (Not waiters, of course. Waiting staff was an entirely different matter, one that would account for the absence of many individuals from a certain standard of restaurant, across the land, on the evening of the event itself.)

These people, the last layer, were required to be on hand to do whatever was required and so ensure that the brilliance of the event flowed as envisioned. As such they had to be polite, articulate and mannered. Clean, clear, anonymous advertisements in the appropriate media were the acknowledged best tool for filling up with such crew.

From this final recruiting session they had hoped for four and Genevieve felt that five were good enough; three men and two females. She was pleased.

'How did it go?' TipTop asked, head poking around the door frame as Genevieve stretched her neck.

'Fine. Five, I think. See anything out there?'

Genevieve and TipTop had developed a routine of having applicants wait together in a rather uncomfortable line in the corridor, thus forcing them to socialise and endure collectively for a short but important period of time. During this time TipTop would keep an eye on them. Watch for things.

'Well, that last chap . . . Fernando.'

'The Spanish mature student?'

'Yes,' TipTop said thoughtfully.

'Excellent English,' Genevieve remarked, looking for his details. 'He's one of my five.'

TipTop nodded. 'Out there, he got a bit impatient, seemed to get bored standing around. Asked someone for a seat. Nothing much, but, you know . . .'

'Yes,' Genevieve concurred, 'If they don't like standing around . . .'

'Quite.'

'Fine,' Genevieve said, standing up, flicking through the papers. 'These four it is then: Katherine, David, Hilary and Andrew.'

'Think we should just go round and tell them in the café?'

There was a tendency for interviewees to meet afterwards in the café next to the station, having in some way bonded through the shared interview experience. Genevieve laughed impishly at the suggestion.

'Best be formal, TipTop. Don't want to see any disgruntled faces on the bloody documentary.'

TipTop nodded, took the documentation from Genevieve and set off briskly to get the letters done. The boss smiled to herself, before marching through to the big room to see how Charlotte had got on with the desserts.

Around the corner, four of the interviewees were indeed enjoying a coffee together. Katherine was explaining about her recent holiday in Spain, while David and Hilary listened and Fernando waited to come in with a favourite observation on the origins of the siesta and its relevance to Latin American economies. As it turned out, Fernando got neither the job nor the opportunity to come in with his observation as Hilary excused herself and the others followed suit. Fernando stayed, toying glumly with his half-full individual cafetiere. Making their goodbyes at the underground ticket barrier, Hilary wished the other two well.

'Hopefully, you know, we'll all be working together.'

'Yes, who knows?' shouted David. Together with Katherine he watched Hilary head down the stairs to the platform. Once she was out of sight Nick and Alison became themselves again and walked up to the end of the road to hail a taxi.

fifty-two

The red car bustled merrily up the side of the green field. This was driving. Driving was meant to be like this. The car swerved gently, avoiding a rabbit that appeared and sat nonchalantly at the side of the road. Jonathan knew there was one thing missing but also knew better than to reflect on it now. The sun on his head and the warm smell of the countryside was enough to let him know that he was on the right path. He had the irrepressible feeling of putting things into position, of constructing a huge jigsaw.

This was, he reflected, delicate work, and the awareness of this pleased him. Such a delicate assembly was his life, or it had been until not too long ago. The transition from Engineering to Engineering Management was something that, at the time, had been of enormous value to Jonathan. It had been a big and nervously anticipated step. Not everyone made it. Not everyone was able to move from the toolbox to the flipchart. He had done it, and done it well. Yet now, driving along these back roads and byways, Jonathan felt the call of the craftsman, remembered viscerally why he had wanted to be an engineer in the first place. To put things together; to make things whole; to make things better for people.

He opened and closed his hands around the steering wheel, feeling the restful throb of the engine flowing up his arms. This was how it worked, and it made him smile. Strip everything down to the bare essentials then start the structure afresh. The car, he knew, was undoubtedly part of the rebuilding process. Jonathan breathed out and honked his horn, the sound disappearing into the empty fields. He wanted to shout 'Whoopee!' but didn't. No point in tempting fate.

As ever, Joe and Philippa were expecting him at three-thirty. Jonathan's face darkened slightly at the realisation that he was in some ways imitating the life now gone. The whole family used to go over to Joe and Philippa's every Sunday. Now Jonathan would go over on his own; the children were already there.

'Joe and Philippa are being magnificent,' he thought, picturing the day when they would sit round together and Jonathan would lay his arm on the arm of an untroubled Alison, and he would say 'Joe and Philippa were magnificent, you know.'

Three-thirty. 'In time for Sunday lunch. We'll get the children cleaned up.'

Joe and Philippa, great guys.

A small cloud sat over the hill behind the house as Jonathan arrived. Carefully he eased the MG past the silver estate, U-turning it perfectly into prime side-on viewing position. Walking slowly away from his car, Jonathan turned to consider its appeal once more and realised that he had got it wrong. The children would see it from the house first, not the road. Smiling at his failure to anticipate their viewing perspective he went back to the car and with three quick thrusts switched it round. Getting out, he saw Joe and Philippa standing on the doorstep, their faces lit with happiness. Jonathan broke into a broad grin, gave a small wave. From inside could be heard the commotion of children at play and there was at once a reassuring warmth in his chest, something he took as confirmation of the correctness of his course.

'Isn't it grand?' Joe called from the doorway, stepping forward slightly, arms apart.

Jonathan turned and looked at the car again. A sparkling beauty indeed, he thought.

'It sure is,' he said happily, jauntily, striding up to his father- and mother-in-law.

'Who would have thought it?' Philippa, hands wiping down on her apron, the smell of cooking beef floating down and around her.

'I suppose the children still aren't ready to eat yet though?' Jonathan asked, looking down over the landscape of English countryside with sports car. They never were. Always wanting more time for some sort of play. He turned, still beaming, to Joe and Philippa.

But they did not beam down at him from the step above. The beam was one way only. What came from both their faces was mild incomprehension. And while an inappropriate response to a remark or question can be caused by a mishearing or a misunderstanding, there could be no doubt that the cause of this one was much more serious and soon the look of mild incomprehension tremored and collapsed into baffled horror.

Jonathan looked at their strange, strange faces and in one enormous thump felt something unrecognisable hit his stomach. Philippa gave a short yelp and Jonathan moved past her into the house to see his children, to find them playing somewhere, to be with them, but they were not there.

They were not in the lounge as he swept through it; they were not in the kitchen playing with educational plasticine and they were not in the garden, running around in the country air. He turned and looked at the television and its presentation of a classic film about children who stop a train crashing with their clothes. The only thing to see in the garden was the electric lawnmower, its yellow coil snaking in through the kitchen door, the grass uncut. Jonathan took in the back garden emptiness. He heard a step behind him.

'Where are they?' he asked, still facing the garden.

'Jonathan,' Joe's voice, apologetic, 'We thought that . . .'

'Where are they?' Jonathan demanded, turning round now, his face a malevolent red.

'Alison came . . . she took them,' Philippa blurted out, stepping back as Jonathan turned his fiery gaze on her.

'Jonathan, we're as confused as you . . .' Joe struggled through his incomprehension. 'She turned up and said that, that . . . everything was OK. Fine again.'

'She said you'd be round to pick up their things later,' Philippa's voice, keen for their position to be understood.

Jonathan said nothing, his mouth open. He turned and looked at the lawnmower again. There was a mumble of conference behind him.

'I'll . . . I'll make some tea,' said Philippa.

Jonathan became sentient again once he was seated at the pine trestle table. Joe was sitting opposite him, earnest, while Philippa stood by the sideboard, the steam of a recently boiled kettle appearing to rise from her crown. Jonathan looked at Joe, who was now speaking.

'We are as shocked as you, Jonathan. She just turned up, looking happy and bright. She said everything was fine, that you were at work. That you'd be round later to collect the things.'

Joe gestured lamely towards a large cardboard box packed with toys. Philippa stirred the teapot, taking sustenance from the normality of the routine, dovetailing with Joe's last words.

'That's right. We were pleased to see her. We thought everything was fine. She said everything was fine, didn't she, Joe?'

Joe nodded.

'We didn't know, Jonathan,' Philippa continued, advancing confidently towards the table with a tray of mugs, sugar, milk, biscuits and spoons, by which to anchor their rocking ship.

'I mean, she just turned up in that car and –'

'Which car?' Jonathan demanded from Philippa, saying it quickly enough for him to turn and catch Joe trying to pull some sort of face signal to his wife. Philippa set the tray down.

'The car –,' she managed, nervous, before Joe cut in.

'Jonathan, we had no idea that – '

'Which car? What type of car?'

'A green one,' Philippa said softly, eager to give something, mechanically placing a full mug of tea in front of each of them.

'Jonathan. We don't . . .we don't know. What is going on?' Joe pleaded, trying to gain something to balance his discomfort.

Jonathan looked dispassionately at the two of them, then out through the still-open kitchen door to the lawnmower.

'She's our daughter, you know,' Philippa, said so very quietly, dropping one lump into Joe's mug. Jonathan stared out the door.

'You – ,' he fought for breath and description.

'Jonathan, you must understand. We don't know what is going on.'

Joe was reaching over to Jonathan for his hand but the gentle touch triggered Jonathan to stand up abruptly, knocking the table edge, and making Philippa watch the mugs for signs of spillage.

'You ... family of cunts,' Jonathan said, looking down at them both.

'Oh!' said Philippa, staring down.

Jonathan walked over to the box of toys, picked it up and walked out to the MG, closing the door quietly behind him.

Joe sat silent.

'She's our daughter, you know,' said Philippa, stirring his tea for her husband.

After the tea had been taken Joe went out to the garden to pack away the lawnmower. He did not feel like cutting the grass any more. Tomorrow would be soon enough. Distracted, he hung the device back on its wall-bracket, looking absently around the tool-shed. Something seemed different. He lingered on this briefly and then went back into the kitchen to have another cup of tea and wait for a sign from somewhere that things would indeed be fine.

On a road not too far away, with a box of toys nestling in the passenger seat, Jonathan had got himself under control. The situation had changed but the mission had not, not really. There was more at stake now. Joe and Philippa's misguided betrayal was only to be expected. They could not possibly understand what this was all about. Now he would have to rescue his entire family from a terrible fate. Jonathan turned slightly and patted the head of a non-specific furry creature sticking out of the box. Yes, now he had to rescue them all.

fifty-three

'So let's have it then.' Pommy sat, motionless, a dignified statue of desperate hope, in exactly the same seat in exactly the same hotel room where he had sat not two weeks previously. Opposite him was Grant Mullaby. Unlike the room, Grant had lost some of his lustre, had had it rubbed off in a frenzy of frantic filth-finding.

When cases like this came up, everything went by the board. For fourteen days most of the resources of Laston Burley, and one or two extra ones, had been focused on examining Lawson Jennings. Lawson Jennings, the person. By any means necessary. If, during this time, Jennings had woken in the middle of the night, as if pricked by means of a voodoo doll, it would surely not have been surprising. In many ways, what Laston Burley did was a form of black magic. They produced items that had disappeared. They found things never imagined. More importantly, they had the gift of resurrection; they were able to bring things back to life. They could take something long buried and forgotten and make it walk like Lazarus through the world. Of course, theirs was not a healthy, rejuvenated Lazarus. Theirs was always a fetid, rotting corpse, thanklessly reanimated and forced to trudge among the living so that all who saw it cowered and held their noses at the reek of its disclosure. Truly, they were sorcerers. In dealing with such people all but the most steely-nerved could sense the touch of the unnatural. Pommy rather liked them.

'Come on man, what have you got?'

Pommy was eager to see. His mood was not helped by Grant's appearance. Eyes red from scraping through all manner of documents and goodness knows what else, face unshaven, hair unkempt. A bit scrawny-looking too. This annoyed Pommy. Pommy knew that appearances matter. There were no dress-down days at Belston. 'People like to know that they're dealing with people in suits,' Pommy explained on a yearly basis to staff representatives. 'We're not here to be comfortable – we're here to make money.'

'Well,' Grant began hesitantly, 'Lawson . . . Jennings.' He paused and looked up. 'Bit of a flatty.'

Pommy grimaced. Grant continued, opening the brown file in front of him. Pommy could make out the unmistakably manu-ally-typed pages. Nothing at Laston Burley was printed out from, committed to, or held on, computer or any other form of electronic device. They had no address; only a telephone number. All briefings and de-briefings were done in person.

'We started at his birth and then worked forward, at each step going two or three levels sideways, as far as felt . . . fertile, so to speak. Good performance at school, nothing spectacular. Nothing remarkable on the school record either. No real disci-plinary problems, although, interestingly, he was once cautioned for bullying. Still, nothing earth-shattering. School years basi-cally non-descript. Nothing really. No one remembers anything remarkable at all. Certainly nothing bad.'

Pommy kept his gaze down, somewhat engaged by the thought of Jennings as a school bully. 'What went wrong?' he wondered inwardly.

'University. More of the same. Sure, there were the usual high jinks involving this that or the other. Nothing much, you know, excessive drinking on occasion. Minor drug use. Nothing really.'

A despondent Pommy shook his head. Those were the type of things that Jennings would use to enhance rather than dimin-ish his reputation.

'Good basic degree. Nothing special. As you know he'd started Exodus back then and it seemed to consume most of his time. Heartbreak over some girl he loved a lot, Monica. She went off with one of his friends. Jennings was done for speeding in the ice-cream van . . .'

Pommy looked up, momentarily enthused.

'. . . on the way to a charity function,' Grant continued.

Pommy looked down again.

'University seems to have used up whatever little wild fire there was in Jennings. Since then he's been clean, if not squeaky clean.'

Pommy said nothing.

'Family. Father died while Jennings was at university. Mother still going – he's kind to her, of course. Three sisters, all married, or as near as damn, you know. Nieces and nephews, that sort of thing. Sees them often enough. Married to Elisabeth, ex-company employee. Three children. Normal little angels. Two dogs. Never bitten anyone. Gives adequate if not generous tips in bars and restaurants. Only drinks decaffeinated. Favours the missionary position. Doesn't speak dirty on the telephone.'

Pommy puzzled briefly over the last two items, before writing them off as interesting but not worthwhile. How Grant got this strange assortment of information was of no concern.

Although most Laston Burley employees were ex-journalists, they didn't bother with what little exists by way of journalistic ethics. Their job was to get information, end of story. Pommy knew that going through the rubbish bins was just the start of it. Besides, people in the know were careful what they put in their rubbish bins. He was.

'Nothing much at all,' Grant concluded.

'So he's fucking clean then?' Pommy asked, after several moments' moody reflection.

'Yes, depending on your viewpoint. There is something, though,' Grant said with sufficient care and attention to make Pommy sit bolt upright, like a dog hearing its bowl being rattled.

'What?'

Grant almost smiled: 'Jennings was brought up a Roman Catholic. Nothing severe but a left-footer none the less.'

Pommy was lost, although his face was careful not to show

it. Any mention of religion always made him feel a bit strange; a combination of knowing he must be missing something, together with utter contempt for a concept so very removed from the here and now. One day he intended to look into it further. Maybe ask one of the fucking boffins to do a paper.

'The death of his father – minor heart attack with complications – seems to have been a bit of a kick in the holy pants for Lawson,' Grant went on at a leisurely pace. 'Since then he's been pretty devout. So have the whole Jennings family, to tell the truth. Mother extremely devout. Nothing too ostentatious, mind you. Generous donations to affiliated overseas aid organisations, that sort of thing. He did have an audience with the Pope a year ago though.'

That was right. Pommy remembered the photographs well. Jennings smiling. Pope smiling. Every fucker smiling.

'Thing is, it seems that Jennings has broken one of the biggies in the Roman Catholic book of dos and don'ts. Been a bit morally naughty.'

Grant looked to Pommy for confirmation that this might be good stuff and Pommy nodded.

'About one month after meeting the Pope, Jennings paid for one of his sisters to have an abortion. All private, of course. Very hushy-hushy.'

Pommy began to grin.

'The fetus was hydrocephalic, you know, the big head thing, otherwise healthy. She didn't want it.'

'She?' Pommy asked.

'Patricia, the sister,' Grant said, smiling now. 'So Lawson had it all taken care of. Backwoods private hospital. No one knows. Pretty sure no-one else in the family knows. It's difficult to be 100% sure without asking. But we think we know.'

'Are you absolutely positive on this?' Pommy asked precisely, mind whirring, not sure what he'd got, but knowing it was something.

'Oh absolutely. There was nothing wrong with the fetus other than the hydrocephaly. It would have lived. Just a big head thing, that's all.'

'How can you be so sure about the details?' Pommy asked quickly.

Grant glowed with pride.

'Oh, we've seen the baby, the fetus, whatever. Had it examined. Not easy, of course. There was some sort of faux-Roman Catholic burial ceremony. Pseudonym on grave, "John Kennedy". That sort of thing. No, we've had it all checked, first-hand. It would have lived. It's all here, photos too, and independent doctor's stuff.'

'Really?' Pommy purred. Grant handed over a file that Pommy opened and glanced at briefly before handing it straight back.

'Don't give that to me. I don't want it.'

'What do you want us to do?' Grant asked, pleased with Pommy's satisfaction.

'Don't know yet. Give me a few hours to think.'

'OK. One more thing, which the report makes clear: we think there might have been a bit of jiggery-pokery involving the dates.'

'Meaning?' Pommy asked, standing up to leave.

'It's by no means clear that the abortion took place within the appointed legal time. If it didn't, well . . .'

Pommy smiled, and sat down again. He was still sitting and smiling when he came to, about thirty seconds later, as the door closed behind Grant. He blinked and was himself again, noting immediately the two coffees, untouched on the table. Didn't want fucking coffee. But he knew what he did want. A couple of whores. This was something to celebrate.

fifty-four

'Hey, bonehead, what do you think you're doing?'

There was a honk as the larger car that had narrowly escaped running into the back of the emergency-stopped MG spurted past. Jonathan wasn't listening. After what seemed endless days and was immeasurable distances, the odometer having now rounded on itself, he had become used to the abuse and insults. He wore them well. They were part of the process, part of the sacrifice involved in putting his family back together again. He liked cruising the streets. On the road by 5.30 a.m. in order to catch the flow into work, he searched the crowds, day-in, day-out.

Jonathan felt righteous; this was his duty. In years to come Alison and the children would thank him for having found them, for bringing them back. Once into central London he would drive against the flow along the pedestrian rush hour thoroughfares, never doubting that he would find her. Doubt was not permissible. Setting out each morning, he had in his car all the sandwiches, chocolate bars and water he needed to make it through the day and well into the night. So far, he had got it wrong twice. On the first occasion he had screeched to a halt outside a pub on Gloucester Road, as Alison's precise hairstyle walked in as part of a group of office workers. With cars piling up behind him he had ignored the blistering cacophony of horns and shouts, and dived through the pub doors, knocking aside an elderly Japanese couple intent on traditional British fare. The busy room froze at their Asiatic yelps of terror and Jonathan was able to walk undisturbed through the staring throng to a table where Alison turned around and revealed herself to be someone else. The second occasion had been more troublesome.

He'd spotted her slipping into a large supermarket, near The Angel, Islington. Jonathan had remembered that she preferred to shop mid-afternoon and had thus taken to skulking around supermarket car parks between two and four. Three times the police had been called by vigilant security, as this daffy-looking man in a sports car hung around near the entrance, watching everyone go by. Each time Jonathan had been politely moved on.

Again, he took it as a mark of courage that he had to deal with the police every now and then. It was a tribute to his determination. Soon enough all four of them would be driving around the English countryside, popping into children-friendly country inns, enjoying bitter and orange juice, and the piddling police could go fuck themselves.

That hadn't helped him however when he'd been arrested in the supermarket. He had only just arrived, just finished parking the car, when he saw her walk in that sprightly fashion he knew and loved through the automatic doors, her bag swinging slightly as the cool outdraught caught it. He began to run but then thought of how he might look and slowed himself deliberately. No, he should be calm, in control; sensitive and respectful: 'Hello, Alison, how are you?'

That was how he should be. He got himself a trolley and went in. For 2.15 p.m. the place was crowded. Jonathan whistled happily to himself as he overtly breezed along, picking up random fresh vegetables, turning into the sauce and condiments lane. No sign. But not to worry; she'd still be there.

'Hello, Alison, how are you?' Nice and calm.

She had been pushing one of the biggest trolleys. Obviously getting food for the children. And someone else. He dismissed this latter thought as he had realised that such thinking made him too angry to move. Jonathan forced himself to think of only Alison and the children. Trundling on, arriving at the delicatessen, scanning left and right. No sign. Less comfortably too. Where had she gone?

Jonathan marched along the top of all the aisles, looking down each in turn, raising himself on tiptoe to see to the end. Nothing. Where was she? Back along the aisles again. Try to stay cool. It had been a big trolley. She must have been after lots. Was that her? Yes, it was! Jonathan hurled himself down the tinned soup lane, trolley in front, ramming other shoppers out of the way, leaving a wake of overturned baskets.

'Alison! Wait!' he hollered without restraint. Upstairs in the Store Control Room a panic button was hammered as the mayhem below became apparent. Reaching the tills he saw her outside, nonchalantly wheeling a trolley stacked mostly with toilet rolls into the car park. With venomous anger he threw his own trolley to one side, skittling both of the approaching assistant managers, before jumping onto a conveyor belt and running over the checkout area, crushing everything below his desperate feet. There she was!

'Alison!'

Jonathan ran full steam into the revolving door going the wrong way and flew backwards with the force, momentarily concussing himself. Sitting up, he breathed deeply, felt blood flowing over his lips, down his chin. He mumbled Alison's name again and moved to stand up, only to find himself unable to do so. Looking around he saw that he was being held at each shoulder by a security guard. Still, through the bottom pane of the door, he could see Alison loading the toilet rolls into the back of a small blue car. Only it wasn't Alison after all.

'Alison,' he said meekly, and then saw the flashing blue light pull up in front of the entrance.

'Please stay away from supermarkets, in the meantime, Mr Greenmeadow'.

This was the constable's advice. Jonathan promised he would and was allowed to leave, with an impending charge of "Causing An Affray" hanging over him. The police processing had taken less than one hour. They had worse things to be getting on with and he was treated as a formality to be got rid of. Indeed, considering the scene of grocery carnage that Jonathan had caused, the consequences were far from severe. All that Jonathan cared about was that he was still on the street. Promising to stay away from supermarkets was an easy swap for his freedom. By the time he hit the open air again Jonathan had distilled the whole episode down to yet more fiery fuel for his tank of chivalrous duty.

He got out of the taxi to find that the MG had been clamped. Sitting on the bonnet, waiting to be released for the second time that day, he was able to reflect on a job well done. Of course, that hadn't been Alison at the supermarket. But if it had been, he would have had her. Now was not the time for hesitation or lack of resolve. Rescue would be his.

Unbeknown to him, Jonathan had had a visitor at the police station. She'd arrived shortly after he left, disgusted that she had missed him. Judy Hamilton had heard of his arrest on the police scanner that she kept in her car and had disengaged as quickly as she could from covering the minor pop star shoplifting trial she had been on her way to. The police station gave her the basics. Then she headed down to the supermarket to speak to the staff there. This had all the feel of a top-notch slow burner. Driving into the car park, she completely missed Jonathan driving out. Two highly focused minds seeking glorious ends.

fifty-five

A conspiracy of two is a wonderful thing. Every thought and action is powered by a simple notion: it's you and me against the world! Craft plans on your own and, well, you might be deluded, sad, desperate. Together, you have backing and demonstrable evidence that you are not alone in your beliefs. And again, more than two and it's a different feel altogether: the one-on-oneness is gone, as is the absolute cohesion. Three more easily becomes four, then five, then six, then . . . . Two holds itself strongly against intrusion. The bond cuts a swathe through any crowd so that, even in the most tightly-packed room, there can be no doubt of the strength of the link. Indeed, the greater the depth, the greater the pressure, the more intense the compact becomes; bending, flexing, stretching but never breaking.

'Let me repeat that. Do not leave your post under any circumstances. All guidance must be sought and received on the spot. You will always have another blue sweatshirt in line of sight in whatever direction you look. There is no need to leave your post. Those guests who appear unsure – drink combined with an unfamiliar environment guarantees there will be many such guests – and ask you to escort them somewhere must be directed on to the next blue sweatshirt, and so on down the line. If you leave your post you will break the chain and the entire system will collapse. Remember also that Genevieve, TipTop, Jill and I will be on patrol throughout the event. We can be contacted at all times. Do not leave your post.'

Olly Hampton paused and looked out over the jammed room

of 120 Team Genevieve staff. There was no murmur of dissent, simply the soft, pleasurable sound of the basic rules of the Team Genevieve organisation and standards being reinforced in compliant minds. Olly looked over to Genevieve, who was sitting, with unobtrusive authority, to one side. She gave a tiny nod.

'Now,' Olly continued, 'We are going to consider the layout of the zoo. Everyone in this room must be able to walk around it blindfold. Not that we're going to make you.'

Titters of tension relief.

'David, could you hand these out please?'

Olly stepped down and handed 'David' a pile of A4 maps, as a much larger one was wheeled onto the church hall stage. Halfway along the first row of helpers, Nick handed a sheet to Alison. His heart leaped slightly, and there was a momentary weakness in his legs, as the unmistakable feeling of being back in school waylaid a mind entirely focused on the here and now. Stopping for a second, ostensibly to reposition the papers in his hand, he gathered himself and proceeded without further pause.

At the back Spiggy, Steve and the cameraman stopped filming as the mundane nature of the scene became clear. Spiggy walked over to Genevieve.

'Is this basically all that is going to happen?'

Genevieve stood up, swallowing her gut response. "Is this basically all that is going to happen?" Yes, media chump, this is basically all that is going to happen. We are only going to put in place the vital human resources that are going to make the entire event a success. That is *all* that is going to happen.

Asked to isolate any one area of activity upon which the whole almighty party would stand or fall, Genevieve would point to these training sessions. Their dull efficacy determined the power of the event mechanism. But Genevieve knew that, through the shallow lens of a camera, these scenes and the reasoning behind them were just a bunch of people sitting in an old church hall. There was no glamour, no character, no action.

'Yes, Spiggy, this is, regretfully, all that is going to happen. For the rest of the day most likely.'

'Right,' Spiggy said thoughtfully, nodding her head, trying to give the impression that she was mulling over a weighty decision. 'In that case,' looking up after a few more nods, 'I think we'll head back to the offices. Charlotte is getting some champagne chilled for testing. We're going shopping for shoes with her at lunchtime anyway.'

Now it was Genevieve's turn to nod and nod and nod, 'Excellent, Spiggy. You'd best run along then, eh?'

Spiggy needed no further invitation to exit. Indeed, Genevieve noticed, Steve and the cameraman were already halfway through the door. She sighed and wrinkled her nose in signal to Olly, who announced, 'Right everyone, eyes front.'

Genevieve watched as David moved back into his seat. She had not noticed his minor limp before, and was struck by this. Normally such aspects of a person's physique were the sorts of thing she picked up on immediately. She gave a thought to sacking him. All staff were required to note any disabilities on their application forms. Then again, this far down the line and no trouble . . . . Perhaps she would let it go, this once.

'Know your position at all times.'

Olly's commanding voice boomed out over the helpers and Genevieve sank back into the comfort of close quarters drill instruction.

Seven wearing hours later, Nick and Alison were able to meet back at their rented house in a non-chic Zone 3 suburb. The effect of being in such close proximity all day without speaking or even acknowledging one another was magnified by the secret power of conspiracy, and the return home saw them collapse into a single heap of giggling incoherence. This turned rapidly into an impassioned fury of sex at such intensity that in its aftermath the state of being alive was as much activity as either could muster. After one hour of catatonic recovery, Alison forced herself up for water, quenching herself directly from the tap before bringing a glass for Nick. Then they cuddled and whispered, thus preserving and relishing the excitement of their secret status. The eventual drift off to sleep came as unnoticed as the darkness. Waking in the dead of night, wrapped warmly together on the sofa, they scurried like nocturnal forest creatures to their bed and were soon asleep again, together and complete in a way few could imagine and fewer still will ever know.

fifty-six

Rumours of a meeting tiptoed around the City among the chosen few, before a leap in the share price of Belston caused a stampede of calls. Finally, a meeting! Who would have believed it? Well, even Pommy Freiberg would know when it's time to raise the white flag.

Not surprisingly, the meeting would be at Belston HQ. Everyone could see that Pommy would insist on that. A mark of due respect from Jennings. Nothing more. They expected an announcement about two days later: Jennings had a thing about getting it right internally before getting it out externally. No rush anyway. Give everyone time to get the statements fine-tuned. Besides, don't really need statements. Bit of cosmetics. As long as the meeting has taken place, everything is in order. Excellent. Right, what's next?

'Someone like me, going up against someone like him, and winning too. . .'

Lawson Jennings could not stop this thought going through his head as the company car shuffled forward in the mid-morning traffic. My oh my.

Faith Barclay caught him grinning from ear to ear and chided him as if he was a naughty schoolboy.

'I can't help it,' he protested, laughing, loving the tease. Pommy had turned out to be more of a realist than he'd expected. All that stuff about no further discussions had only been a bit of puffy pride. No harm in that, I suppose, Jennings thought. Still, nobody had been more surprised than he was to get the call from the bank.

'Apparently he'll meet. Eleven o'clock. His place. You and him. No, just you and him.'

Jennings hadn't believed it at first but his advisors were adamant.

'Its over. He's not asking you round to talk about the weather.'

'Why alone then?'

'Dunno. Who cares? One of his things. You know what he's like, all macho posturing. This way it looks a bit more gladiatorial, you know. Roman. His sort of thing, one Emperor handing over to another.'

The car dropped Lawson and Faith at the front door, and they walked together, calmly, into the Belston foyer, where Jenny was waiting for them.

'Hello, Mr Jennings, lovely to meet you. And Ms Barclay. Do come this way.'

A motionless security guard was holding a lift for them. Lawson felt the buildings' eyes upon him. Was there not, in fact, a mild euphoria in the air? The floors went by, the doors opened and suddenly, he was there, walking across to shake the hand of Pommy Freiberg, who was saying, 'Good to meet you, Lawson. Sorry it's taken so long.'

'Yes, you too, Pommy. Still these things happen, you know.'

'Yes, of course. Spot of dandruff, is that?'

Pommy, unable to refrain from one of his oldest unsettling tricks was wiping at something on Lawson's shoulder. All the time they were moving; moving from the corridor, past Jenny's desk and into Pommy's office, Faith being politely channelled by the gentle Jenny into a side office on the way.

'Oh, I don't . . . maybe . . . yes,' Lawson mumbled.

Pommy stepped back and called for Jenny.

'Coffee, Mr Jennings?' she asked from the doorway, interrupting Lawson's self-examination, causing him to turn round to answer.

'Yes, lovely. Decaffeinated, if you have it.'

Jenny nodded.

'Lawson, come over here. Take a seat.'

Jennings jerked around, finding that Pommy wasn't where he had been and was now sitting at a coffee table near the window, indicating for Jennings to join him. Pommy was pleased to see that this obtrusive friendliness, coupled with the distraction of movement since he entered the office, had left Jennings a bit out of sorts.

'Things will get even better when we sit down and get on with it,' he thought.

Gratefully, Lawson took the easy seat next to Pommy, who leaned over and slapped his thigh warmly.

'Excellent!' Pommy announced.

Lawson waited, like he knew he had to. It would not be correct for him to just up and say 'Thanks for accepting', or 'How much more is it you want?'

He had to wait for Pommy to make the admission. So he waited. Pommy looked at Jennings again, raised his eyebrows as if waiting himself for some word, then said 'Excellent!' again, this time more loudly. He slapped Lawson's thigh again. Then again.

Jenny came into the room with a tray and set a fat mug before each of them. Pommy breathed out, a sense of relief unquestionably filling the air. Jennings smiled.

'See, Lawson: mugs. Don't use cups now. Moved on from cups. Use mugs. Modern, effective. Cups? History.'

Jennings prolonged his smile, allowing politeness to mask confusion.

'Know where these are from, Lawson?' Pommy asked, keeping the younger man in his gaze while indicating the coffee table. Lawson swivelled his eyes and considered the mugs of coffee, and decided to wait for further illumination.

'Down the road, Lawson. At the newsagents.'

Jennings smile dropped slightly.

'Newspapers, Lawson, tabloids to be specific. As opposed to broadsheets, you know, the big ones.' Pommy framed the size of a broadsheet with his hands in the air. Lawson looked again to the table. He had been aware that it had some publications on it but had presumed them to be the usual glossy boardroom matter.

'Some of the big ones are small ones now, but you get my point,' Pommy noted. Lawson realised that they were not magazines but newspapers; a copy of every one of that day's populist tabloids neatly laid out, edges pressed crisply to a sharp crease.

'They come out on Sunday too,' Pommy's voice came in.

Lawson tried very hard not to appear confused.

'Puzzled, eh?' Pommy asked philosophically. 'So am I sometimes, so am I. So much trouble in the world. Trouble, trouble . . .' and his words trailed slowly off.

Lawson maintained his silence. He had known, been warned, that Pommy might be a bit difficult, but this was not what he had been expecting. In his briefcase was a fistful of offers to deal with what he, and numerous advisors, had been expecting: a range of improved offers, pension deals, share options, places on boards, retirement plans, golden goodbyes – an almost exhaustive list of contingency outlines. Pommy only had to ask. But Pommy wasn't asking. No, Pommy was advising:

'Best to avoid trouble. That's what I've found. Especially trouble with a capital T. That's what I've found.'

Pommy moved forward onto the edge of his seat, now hunching inwards to Lawson, speaking softly, so that Lawson too had to move forward, giving the impression of some form of sporting camaraderie.

'Trouble can creep up on you. Destroy you. Everything you've built. Like that,' Pommy snapped his fingers in Lawson's face, before smiling obliquely and saying, 'Have some coffee.'

Lawson took up his mug and Pommy followed suit, making an appreciative "Mmm" noise after each of not one but two leisurely mouthfuls. Then Pommy set his mug down and sat back slightly in his chair, as if considering something. He looked around the office, gestured with an empty hand at nothing in particular. Lawson looked around him. It was more Spartan than he had been expecting. No vainglorious trophies.

'This whole takeover thing has made you even more

high-profile than before, hasn't it Lawson? Of course,' Pommy reflected, 'you were pretty high-profile before, you know, with the ice-cream van and the other . . . stuff. But this takeover has really got your beacon flashing, hasn't it?'

Lawson realised that he had said nothing since sitting down, yet this realisation seemed to even more effectively seal his lips. What was going on?

'Thing is,' Pommy was continuing, 'if you've got a beacon flashing away, people are going to want to come over to your place and have a look round. See what's what. You know, maybe hang about on the porch, look through the letterbox, see what's hanging out to dry in the back garden.'

Pommy indicated with a quick head movement for Lawson to attend his coffee, which Lawson dutifully did, for want of anything more positive to do.

'Some of these people, and I think you might guess which people,' Pommy paused to stare wide-eyed at the tabloids, 'might not be content with having a look around from the outside. They might want to see if there's a window open. Maybe climb in, have a peek in the fridge, open a few wardrobes, maybe the odd cupboard. And this,' Pommy said quietly, moving forward again, 'can only mean trouble with a capital T.'

Then he sat back and rested his hands on his thighs, in the manner of somebody wishing to brace themselves. He sat this way in silence for about fifteen seconds, before letting a quiet voice rise up. Jennings, a mesmerised man, said nothing.

'I have been approached,' Pommy began, with regret, 'and I cannot say with any certainty by whom, by an individual who knows something about you and your family Lawson. I believe that this individual works for one of these publications.'

Lawson sat motionless. Pommy looked at him, every inch the doctor not knowing how to break some terrible news. With great care he gathered himself: 'How can I put this? It's the fucking baby, Lawson. It's your sister's baby and the fucking big head thing. They have everything, including fucking photographic evidence and medical tests and dates and locations and

all sorts of fuck. It's the works and fucking more and . . . and
. . . when the fuck did the act take place exactly, if you know
what I mean?'

Pommy stopped, sipped at his coffee and considered the
liquefying presence of Lawson Jennings, who sat with a fat mug
frozen midway to his lips.

'By the way, Lawson, that's not decaffeinated. We don't have
any.'

fifty-seven

Jonathan drove slowly along the road, his right hand trailing outside the car, his attempt at casualness given away by the tightly clenched fist drumming gently against the metalwork. For how many days and nights he had done this he did not know, not now. Earlier he had. Earlier he had marked down each minute that he spent on the street. The A-Z had rapidly become a frazzled inch-thick pile of disjointed maps as Jonathan tried to be methodical about his search. He knew that if he thought about it even for a minute he would be lost. That if for one moment he was to be fully conscious of trying to find one person in a city of millions, some part of him would know the game was up the pole, finished, and he would crumble. Jonathan would not crumble. He would be strong. He would get her back. They would be happy.

Two hours later, Jonathan got out the day's last sandwich and pulled his baseball cap down against the cold. That was the problem with an MG. Although with the top down you had better street survey visibility than with an ordinary car, you did tend to notice the chill as night came on. Jonathan checked the fuel gauge. He'd need to fill up before morning. It was always best to fill up at night. Far more queues in the morning. He looked around to remind himself where he was. NW somewhere. He'd sat across from the underground station and watched the rush hour come out, before driving round the area for an hour or so. It was quiet now. The occasional person carrying a bottle of wine or a bag of groceries. Going home to their loved ones. So would he, soon. There'd be no more of this. People would remember though. It would become a family legend, like the Crusades: Jonathan's Crusade, Granddad Greenmeadow's Crusade. Alison knew all about that stuff. He'd seen one of her books on it, with King Richard kicking butt down in Palestine or something. Jonathan wondered if he'd have to kick any butts. Probably; hopefully, not. A simple rescue would be enough. That was what was needed. A rescue. People always liked to be rescued. Jonathan unscrewed his flask and poured out the last of the coffee. Still hot. Clever things, flasks. Good engineering. Can't fault that. Keep hot things hot and cold things cold. Functional engineering at its best. Making the world better for people. Just like him.

Looking across the road he saw the flickering screens inside a rental shop, almost invisible an hour or so ago but now broadcasting through the dusk to an empty pavement. Taking the car keys he walked across, holding his plastic mug of coffee, liking the comfort of its warmth in the cool evening air. He hadn't seen much television recently. Missing all these good nature programmes was a nuisance but he knew it would be worth it. Maybe he'd catch a bit of one now. That would be ni – . . . Jonathan choked and sprayed coffee out. She was there! On the television. Sitting in an office with a bunch of people. Yet it wasn't her in some way. There was something different. Damn! Where did she go? Jonathan hammered pointlessly on the window as the camera panned around the group, doing close-ups of individual faces. There she was again, but wearing a wig of some sort. What the . . . what *was* this programme? He hammered on the glass, pressed his ear against it. 'Jesus Christ, let me in!' he hollered. On the other side of the street a group of people looked at him and hurried on.

Jonathan peered through the glass, pressing his ears to the glass alternately, trying desperately to hear something, anything. What the hell was going on? Where was she? Abruptly he peeled himself from the window and ran across the street to the MG. In one fluid movement he rammed the keys in, started the car, turned the steering wheel to full lock and accelerated across the road, jumping onto the pavement and through the shop window, stopping expertly a mere inch from a television screen, entirely ignorant of the razor sharp sheet of jagged glass which sliced the air behind his head. Then he climbed down the bonnet and turned the volume up above the screeching alarm. Jonathan listened and watched. Alison didn't reappear but he knew that it had been her. Peoples' ticks and movements are as sure an indication of identity as any larger aspect of their person. Thirty seconds letter Jonathan had heard all he needed to, his mind tuned to the television, cutting out entirely the sounds of rupture he had caused.

'With the party at London Zoo only a week away, event supremo Genevieve Marsden has gathered her team for the day itself to go over what their responsibilities will be. Charlotte is once again on hand to go through the details . . .'

The screen filled with a ponderous fat female face, trying to look coquettish. Jonathan leaped back into the driving seat, reversed out of the shop and tore off down the street.

By noon the next day, Jonathan was beginning to sweat with agitation. It was more difficult to find than he had imagined it would be. A simple Yellow Pages enquiry hadn't worked. 'What type of business doesn't get itself a listing in the obvious places?' Jonathan pondered with compounding infuriation, as he looked again under "Events – Organisers", "Party Suppliers" and "Entertainments", and every "See also" category suggested, none of which had anything remotely like "Genevieve Marsden" listed. This must be, Jonathan worked out, because although Genevieve is the owner and boss, it is actually called something else. So he had called all the generically titled companies, the "Party Party's", "Entertainment Business's", the "Fun Time Factory's", asking each of them if Genevieve was there. All answered in the negative. Even the internet café threw up her name without attaching itself to a company or number. Didn't she want people to call her?

In truth the answer was no, not really. Genevieve did not want anybody inconsequential to be able to bother her with trivial enquiries about celebrations of the norm. She found it more profitable to be, like her favoured clients, almost unknown in the real world, only part of it by legend. People passed on her number, but only within certain circles. In this way, every time the telephone rang, she knew it meant business. All of which was no use to Jonathan. His luck changed with London Zoo.

'I'm calling about the Genevieve Marsden party,' he said to numerous people before someone twigged and a connection was made to someone who 'deals with all that'. Then, by feigning delivery of a refrigeration unit for the event, Jonathan was able to get the details he wanted. He simply noted the information he had received – some random dates and times – 'just to confirm, you know', and was happy to be connected with the real dates and times. Jonathan pretended annoyance at having been given the wrong information: 'This is really bad. I'd better double-check all of this with Ms Marsden. You don't happen to have a number there, do you?'

Of course, the obliging departmental secretary did. Two minutes later Jonathan was on that number explaining that he had a delivery of flowers for a "Ms Geraldine 'I think' Marsden" and could they confirm the address please?

'That would be Genevieve, I imagine,' the curt female voice said, against a bustle of activity in the background. Nevertheless the address followed and Jonathan was soon on his way.

fifty-eight

'Lots and lots of places.'

Samuel looked up at his mother, then back again at the huge atlas of the world that sat across his lap like a duvet.

'Is it near China?' Samuel asked. He had done a school project on China and, as it was the only country he knew, any question of travel had to include China. Alison smiled, delighted by her son's questions.

'Yes, it's near China. And not just China, lots and lots of other places too.'

All this in response to explaining what going round the world meant.

'When will we see Daddy?'

'Daddy is off on a long journey too, so I'm not sure when we'll see him next.'

'Oh. Has he taken his new car with him?'

Alison paused momentarily. What new car? Oh, yes. Her parents had mentioned some sports car or other. Her mother said it was the first time she had had "serious misgivings". 'Yes, he's taken his new car with him. Go to sleep now, Samuel.'

Alison rose softly from the bed and looked over at the other one, where Kimberley was already lightly snoring, her young mouth wide open against the pillow. As Alison tipped quietly down the stairs, she thought of how wonderful the innocence of children is. That Samuel and Kimberley should accept so readily the explanations offered to them; that they should be so unaware of all the movement around them and be so happy to give their trust. Alison's arrival at their grandparents' had prompted only delight, none of the suspicions or scrutinizing that adults would have succumbed to.

Nick was watching television, making sure that neither he nor Alison was appearing too much in the documentary. They had taken much care to ensure that they turned from the camera as soon as possible, without appearing downright devious. Inevitably their faces popped up from time to time. This was why the hair colouring and wig were so important. Nick turned and picked up the newspaper clippings at his side. Although he had been singularly unable to inflict any business damage on Pommy, he was pleased to see that the other man was nevertheless on the brink. He looked at the picture of Pommy going through some revolving doors, captioned "End of the Merry-Go-Round?" What had Pommy once said about when best to strike? 'Don't get in the fucking ring until it's halfway through the fight. No point wasting energy when there's someone else there to do the punching. Wise man gets in the ring when no-one is looking, delivers a couple of punches in the interval. No one expects that. Fight over, wise man the winner.'

Nick found it difficult to believe but he was nevertheless delighted that Pommy had been beaten. What made it better was that while someone else might have fought the fight, it would be Nick who would finish it off and it would be Nick that Pommy saw as he tumbled down the gaping chasm of his doom. Alison came up behind him and tousled his hair lightly. His hand reached up and took hers. 'Everyone asleep?' he asked gently.

'Yes, more or less,' she said, sitting down on the arm of the chair, 'We're almost done, aren't we?'

Nick nodded. They had been very busy. Just the two of them, but so very busy. Nick had worked it all out and then they had agreed on what to do.

'The babysitter is all set up for tomorrow. Taxis booked.' Nick said, circling her waist with his arm as they both absently considered the screen.

'Did you make the call?' Alison asked, trying not to sound sceptical of Nick's ability to do it.

261

'Yes,' Nick said, grabbing her hand, 'I made the call. Everything is set.'

'Good,' Alison replied, releasing herself. They paused as the advertisements appeared.

'I'm just going to check the kit again.' she said, and bounced out of the room, leaving him ensconced in consideration of his approaching victory. Tomorrow it is. Getting out of the chair, Nick stood at the window, staring off into the dusk where London waited.

fifty-nine

There is no night like London's. Streets shake off the cloak of business as the city's fervent occupants head out to stake their claims. For this is their business – the business of being in London. To have been in this pool, this quickening slurry of humanity, is to know that, for whatever a period of time, you existed. 'Ah yes', they will acknowledge in later times in other places, 'Yes, I remember that time well – London,' and all around will nod with sanguine equanimity. The dull thump of the underground trains is bearable; the filth of air-conditioned air is breathable; the biting rudeness of strangers forgivable, if only I can stay here and be a part of it. If only I can write notes headed "London"; if only I can dilly and dally on those streets of folklore; if only I can pass as one of the herd as we whoosh out of the stations that stand for London. If only London, London, London.

Getting to the end of the day is the balancing act. Set aside the dirt until then, and you are safe. The night is comfort. Only seeing as deep as the lights will allow, as far as the nearest crowd; happily blinkered from the unconvincing sky of an outside world.

Reasons do not prevail. There are better places to be. One is part of an unspoken conspiracy with all those around you. We don't need to be here, do we? We could be somewhere else, couldn't we? But we're not, are we? We're here. Wink, wink, wink; out of my way! London.

Jonathan looked up at the pressing night sky. This was not where he wanted to be. He wanted to be home, with his family, in his family house. He had been forced into this. It was not of his making. But he would not be found wanting. Not now. Not when everything was laid out before him so clearly. Already much had been done. He had been abandoned, left without a clue by Alison. And he had found her. Against every conceivable chance he had found her. Was this not evidence enough of the truth of his course? Others would have collapsed long before now. Others might not have been willing to make the sacrifices. Besides, at the end of life, what is the real worth of this job or that job? He would get another job. Losing one was nothing. Once the family status had been reaffirmed, then the build would begin again. Only better, this time.

And what was the house without a family? It mattered not that access had been denied Jonathan on his last visit there. He had had his suspicions, and had arrived carefully, unseen and on foot. An anonymous but unmistakable police car sat across from the neat house. Jonathan had almost smirked at their transparency. As if that was going to either catch or forestall a man such as himself! He had got in through the back, taking what needed, not bothering now to check the telephone for messages. Then into the garage, and the toolbox and the old, patched overalls, and away through the suburban mist. Becoming a criminal meant nothing either. That was no real sacrifice. Was it not the mark of the true hero that he must become a criminal, an outcast, a renegade for the sake of his family? Of course it was. Thus, when Jonathan had found himself approaching the offices of Genevieve Marsden and had seen the soft recognition in the faces of the police car going the other way as they caught his licence plate, he had known then that he had achieved the ultimate distinction. Now he was a fugitive from justice – what justice? The justice of a world where a man can provide for his family and have it torn from him and hidden? And even as he saw the police car beginning a hasty U-turn in the tree- and car-lined street, Jonathan was pressing the pedals and making himself gone and safe.

Even as the little red car tight-turned its way to shelter,

Jonathan could see now where and how the rescue would have to take place. He cursed his wayward mind for not recognising earlier so obvious a happening as an arena for reclamation. Now, with the sheeted stars so faint above him, Jonathan felt the fit of the occasion and knew that this was the place.

In a small office elsewhere at London Zoo, checklist sat on checklist sat on checklist. Genevieve's routine on the afternoon of any event was always the same. All of the morning was spent with her people, on the ground, moving around, letting her presence be felt. That was, she knew, sufficient to ensure that things moved in a manner that was more than merely efficient. Throughout these hours everyone was immaculately focused on what they were working towards, and it wasn't the event itself. It was Genevieve's Check.

Five hours before the final briefing, Genevieve would lock herself away in whatever space was available and go through the returned set of checklists that she had issued to all team leaders that morning. Until that moment they had never seen these checklists. The team leaders had, over the weeks, been encouraged and guided to set up their own checklists, and so had taken complete ownership of their particular areas of responsibility. But they all knew that in the end Genevieve's checklists would be issued.

Of course, those able lieutenants, TipTop, Olly and Jill knew what would be on Genevieve's checklists. So their advice was pointed and guidance astute. But the pretence was maintained that they did not know and so the pressure was unrelenting – what would be on the checklists? Genevieve always put one or two unexpected items in, which would cause a moment or two of frenetic searching, before TipTop or Olly stepped in with an appropriate solution. Other than that, the checklists generally left the team leaders and their teams in a state of semi-bliss. Genevieve knew that the act of completion itself bestowed on the teams the beginnings of a sense of control that would grow throughout the crucial few hours before the event itself.

Attain this too early, say a few days before the event, and a crippling sense of smugness would be the result. No, this sense of control could only come about at the right time, when it would result in confident command, not blasé arrogance.

Genevieve sat, having gone through the checklists to her own, completely unsurprised, satisfaction. She experienced that state of sublime achievement that she reached just before each of her events. From this moment on she would stand or fall on the plans that had been formed, the training that had been given, the provisions that had been made. In some respects the event was already in the past. In its execution Genevieve would merely be completing an act whose outcome was already decided. She looked again, happily but without a smile, at the checklists. The game is done, she thought, London is waiting, and began to gather herself for the final briefing.

Alison brushed her hair and looked for the kirby grips to keep it in place. This was, she realised, the second change she had undergone in a short period of time. And although this one was in many ways more radical – the hair colour, the mascara, the lipstick – it was the other that made her feel so very different. Looking back on her old life was like watching a doppelganger, an impostor, someone she hated walking around in her body. Not "someone" either; "some*thing*". She shuddered with disgust.

The children were playing downstairs with the babysitter, a young Filipino woman with an interest in Dickens and all the right certificates. Mummy had promised to tell them all about her big secret mission later. When they went away together, round the world. The aberration that had been her marriage was not, she concluded, an entirely worthless time. She had two beautiful children whom she loved very much

Alison looked up at herself. She liked the way she looked; different but still herself. Just enough of a difference around the eyes to suggest a total revision in the depths. She pulled the seat closer to the mirror, looking into herself. She liked what she saw: purpose, resolve, determination. On the bed behind her she caught the blurred outline of her holdall. All Team Genevieve staff had been issued with a complete, fitted uniform and instructed only to put it on before the final briefing. They were to look "continually pristine". A large supply of spare sweatshirts would ensure that any staining would be on show for only as long as it took to get a replacement.

Alison was not thinking of replacement sweatshirts though. She was considering the bag. Unlike Nick, who had absolute confidence in their plan, Alison had concerns. Not over the plan itself: that seemed sound enough. Her concern was over making the plan work. They would be dealing directly with Pommy Freiberg. Who knew what might happen? Perhaps Nick would buckle under the pressure of the personal. Perhaps there would be resistance. Alison would not brook such resistance. Things were going to happen exactly as she and Nick wanted them to. There was a need for action. Alison would make sure of it.

No analysis he had ever completed, however good it might have been, had left Nick in the state of euphoric tension he now felt. There was an overwhelming feeling of completion, like that of a young man having lost his virginity, or a soldier having made his first kill. Indeed, as he went through the packing and repacking of his Team Genevieve bag, he imagined himself as an infantryman, off for a tour at the front.

Nick looked down at his naked legs, still damp, sticking out from the towel. Would he have been a different person had they been exactly the same length? Would different feet have taken him down different roads? He had for so long avoided such thoughts, and now he knew why – because he had no answers for them. Now he knew. He knew that the questions could be asked because they did not matter. He liked who he was, what he had become. With Alison he had found something of balance and even, he reflected cruelly, if Alison were not to be with him at some point in the future, there was no

267

going back to what he had been. Thoughts of a life without her made him wince, but the ability to think such thoughts was a part of himself he would never lose, part of what he liked about himself. Wherever and whatever this night took him to, whatever paths were chosen from now on, Nick was pleased to have arrived at this present state. In that respect he had come as far as the few who can see their lives from outside, and consider themselves from afar. He could look and himself and like what he saw. Nick looked down again at his uneven legs and wiggled his toes in non-parallel glee.

sixty

Anybody can do an indoor event; indoor is easy. Bit of spot lighting there, some colour spreads here, the odd decorative display – bread and butter stuff. Fairy lights and fancy, Genevieve called it. But outdoor . . . well, outdoor is different. Winds blow, rain falls, temperatures swing. You could go to somewhere like, yes, somewhere like the Natural History Museum and set things up with two blind aunts and a ball of twine, day-in, day-out. But outdoor? No draught was exactly the same, no downpour, no mist, no unexpected heat. Everything was variable. Outdoors, without a doubt, 'you're in the arena of God, now,' as Genevieve would often say as part of an attempt to put off those who didn't know what they might be dealing with, but were nonetheless aware of the prestige attached to a gathering conducted under open skies. Indoors or outdoors: the true decider between mere givers of parties and masters of events.

London Zoo was a shrine to mastery of the outdoors. Every conceivable elemental intrusion has been factored into the plans. The marquees, ten in all, so fine in appearance, so meticulously outfitted, could withstand both a force 10 gale and a 7.2 on the Richter scale. Small animals could be swimming outside them and still no water would slip between the reinforced walls. Connecting these various centres of celebration, each major walkway was covered with an awning of infinite flexibility. Walls could be dropped from either side of the bevelled, guttered roof, allowing immediate protection from whatever gusts or drizzles might occur. The walkways themselves were raised paths of English oak, certifiably varnished to non-slip, non-stain gorgeous practicality. A glow of light on either side of the wooden paths betrayed the existence of underside-mounted deep-sea diving lights, safely circuited to guide, no, caress, the guests as they weaved their way from one stressless stop to another. An elaborate, tested system of vents and anchors ensured that Genevieve need fear only the unlikely appearance of a metropolitan hurricane to render the structure inoperable.

That was Genevieve's word: inoperable. While others might consider a room or a venue as something static, Genevieve had long understood that every venue is a device that needs to be operated: 'Leave a venue unmanned and you're turning your back on a monster,' she counselled any who might question why such and such a small area required someone to be there at all times. So when it came to giving the OK to the set-up, Genevieve wanted to know one thing only, 'Is it operable?'

London Zoo was operable. No area remained unconsidered. The dynamic had been nailed early on. Over the course of the years Genevieve had built up an enviable understanding of the dynamic of venues. She could arrive in any hall, restaurant, lobby or shop and within minutes be able to pinpoint the likely trouble spots 'And there are always trouble spots,' she would explain to whoever was with her on the way to the venue. It might be a corner, or a walkway, or a step. Once identified it could be, as far as possible, in some way, neutralised. Genevieve's particular talent was in understanding that the trouble spot could shift within venues. Maybe it was the nature of the event, the time of day, a certain new painting. Any of these might radically alter the dynamic of the venue and so change the trouble spot. When it came to identifying the trouble spots, Genevieve had no equals. All trouble spots were trouble because they disrupted the flow. The flow was all-important.

'Without flow the event is dead,' was another Genevieve maxim, often linked with 'Flow makes it happen.' Everyone knows what "it" is. The one student – new, eager, bubbly – who had once asked what was being referred to was dismissed on the spot, shepherded from the office like a bad-smelling dog, to stand outside for two hours thinking this was some sort of test, before realising it wasn't. Everyone knows what "it" is. "It" is what the party is about.

On her first walk around the zoo Genevieve had been less than jubilant. She knew that this would not be easy. The range of guests and their egocentric look-at-me needs expanded the number of areas that might be trouble. Furthermore, the random architecture and layout of the zoo, established in 1828 according to the wishes of Sir Stanford Raffles, did not lend itself to easy marshalling. Yet Genevieve knew it could be done. She had walked and walked and walked, pacing out the distances which invitees would be willing to wander without a drink, estimating where throngs might occur, feeling where assorted loud-mouths would consider suitably expansive to hold court. All of this and innumerable other facets of socialisation had been factored into the final plan, the aim of which was to create a living host body for the guests to feast on.

No thought would be necessary. Guests had only to arrive and be sucked into the Team Genevieve's elaborate, silky, machinations. Oh that everyone might one day enjoy a world so meticulously fashioned to remove the burden of real decision-making while preserving the illusion of personal choice.

The final briefing was at 1830 hrs. Perimeter security, who had had their own briefing at 1630 hrs, had been in position since 1730 hrs. The zoo cafeteria buzzed with the thrill of those on the inside of something big. No party they would ever attend would be as exclusive as the one they were about to produce. Over 250 staff were gathered when Genevieve finally began to work her way through them. Outside, a secondary crew of providers were still putting things in place. They would be, right up until the start of the party. But it was all on schedule. There was not even a scent of panic.

Through, through, effortlessly, calmly, through. A pat there, a tap here and the crowd began to shift as Genevieve passed by on her way to the small stage that had been pushed into place in front of a mural of exotic birds. Genevieve hopped up and turned to face her people. She took the microphone. The hubbub diminished to nothing.

'Good evening, everybody,' she began, followed by the traditional, 'is this thing working?' Everyone laughed. Of course it was working. Just one of Genevieve's much-loved event jokes. Woe betide somebody if the microphone wasn't working. Everyone knew that.

'Now listen, team. We're more or less ready to go. Right, TipTop?'

To the left, against the window, TipTop McGee gave a confident thumbs-up. TipTop had, of course, known this was coming. But not everyone did, and in that brief exchange between Commander and Lieutenant everyone felt the spark of organisation.

'You all know your duties tonight, and the principle one which we must never ever forget, is that we are only here so that others may enjoy themselves. We are here to allow their enjoyment to happen. Above all else – and there is much, I know – do not forget this. You all know your duties. You all know the drills. I know all your names.' Laughter. 'So. Here we are and here we go. And remember to enjoy yourselves too. Have fun doing what you're doing. Fine. Debrief at . . .' Genevieve paused for the briefest of moments.

'. . . 0330 hrs!' thundered TipTop, making everyone start; the threatening edge to Genevieve's camaraderie.

'Good. See you then. To your positions.'

And now the room jumped as, from behind TipTop's curtain, out stepped a bugler in full regalia, stridently sounding the US Cavalry charge. At this one piece of theatrical grandstanding Team Genevieve collected itself and departed, each member dedicated to fulfilling their appointed role. On stage Genevieve winked at TipTop, then looked back at her people leaving the building. Genevieve had, on occasion, been known to cry at this point. And who would not, seeing this troop of good people setting out to help others. Sure enough, as the last young man strode proudly through the doors, Genevieve felt a single tear gliding down her cheek. Unseen by anyone else, she saluted their backs, wiped her face, and walked out in their wake.

sixty-one

Everyone came on time. There was none of the usual polite minutes after or stylish hour late. This was the Rutherfords and they welcomed you personally at the door. Up to a point. Once they felt that the event was underway and had started, the door was closed and that was that. Don't try being fashionably delayed for the Rutherfords, not unless you fancied a cold evening spent grovelling to security guards followed by a bitter drive home.

So the guests arrived on time, shrieking and cackling with merriment. Here they were, at the Rutherfords's zoo bash, all in aid of save the . . . thingy. More media than usual had turned up, far more than the usual straggle of snappers and snippers. This was one of the unfortunate by-products of the documentary series. Yet, because of that, everyone knew they were playing a role, that they were cast in the thrilling conclusion to something popular. How ironic! The guests chortled at the thought of it and all the while they looked around and took in the spectacle of which they were a part. Wizard of Oz lions, Paddington bears, Jungle Book monkeys, Animal Farm pigs, as well as some costumes that were eerily realistic – one or two of the gorillas were quite remarkable. A festival of expensive costuming and make-up made the scene almost biblical in appearance, as two by two they went through the subtly lit gates.

'Oh my word, is that, is that . . .? Yes, it is! Look at him!'
'Baa!'
'Oink!'
'Eek! Eek! Eek!'
What a noise they made, let loose from the confines of conformity. How wild they went!

'Down boy, down.' Here and there strode a keeper of sorts, mostly in safari outfits with pith helmets, generally male: the senior members of each group, happy to be able to maintain some form of status while still being part of the throng. What a bloody good idea, the Rutherfords, you know. And London Zoo too. Save the . . . that animal job, you know.

As the guests entered they heard the distant beat of drums, played over a sound system outside the perimeter, and in such a way as to always appear tropically distant. Throughout the park, secondary units gave out the constant chirp of cicadas, while random animal noises – real ones of course – thanks to the amazingly precise overhead acoustics, sounded around each pathway and social area.

Here and there, so informal as to seem almost unnecessary, yet formal enough to exude the correct tone of comfort and control, stood the greeters and pointers in their immaculate sky-blue sweatshirts. Guests of this calibre don't like to ask, you see. Yet they need to be told, helped along, shown the way. So the team are there, pointing and shepherding. They do not mind the gruff one-word demands – 'Bar?!', 'Gents?!' – because they are expecting them. Genevieve has made it quite clear how to deal with it: invert your pride. The ruder it gets, the more pleasant you become, without being condescending of course. So they are ready, spiritually prepared for use and abuse. Looking forward to it. Some are looking forward to it more than others. Nick and Alison are looking forward to it immensely.

'This way, sir'

Nick, spotless in his Team Genevieve outfit and friendly "David" badge, indicated the route to the toilet for a fat badger, who nodded and moved off, without thanks of course. Nick waited. Alison had wanted an absolutely clear plan but Nick had known better.

'There is no point in having too clear, too inflexible a plan. We have no idea how everything will play out once we're inside.

What we must do is use the first few hours to understand the possibilities and from that we formulate the when and where. We already know the what and the how.'

Alison had nodded, accepting his reasoning with a degree of mild discomfort. As long as they got it done, she didn't care. Everything they needed for the plan was in Alison's holdall, brought in much earlier, before the security screening was set-up.

Genevieve wandered up to one of her ground team.

'Right . . . Christopher,' she said, reading his badge, 'How is it going?'

'Fine thanks. Everyone seems quite happy.'

'Good. Let's keep it that way.'

And so on around as many of her people as she could find. TipTop and Olly were doing much the same, only in a more hands-on way, asking specific questions about the flow and density of traffic. Ground staff were required to say approximately how many people had passed them moving in either direction in the previous five minutes. TipTop and Olly would radio these figures back to Jill in the Control Room. Genevieve was in touch with all three on her own radio.

Team Genevieve staff worn unobtrusive radio pieces, allowing them to listen and communicate if need be. They were under strict instructions not to speak unless spoken to, not to tune in to any frequency other than their own. Genevieve knew it was better to keep them in relative isolation and thus focused on their own particular areas, feeling the responsibility, rather than distract them with the ongoing overall control of the event. She wandered around acknowledging the occasional nod from a known client or contact, ignoring all others and always making it quite clear that tonight, for her, meant business. The Patagonian Buffet had just opened and was shovelling out delightful little fistfuls of tropical treats, all elegantly wrapped in a beautifully tied coconut frond. Genevieve popped her head behind the counter, sniffed the air decisively, and gave a commanding thumbs-up to the Head Chef, who nodded graciously.

Coming out of this large marquee, Genevieve stopped dead. With a recognisable feeling of cold prescience, she turned and looked over her left shoulder. Of course; there he was: her husband, holding court alongside – what? A bird of some sort, was it? An ostrich? Abruptly aware of her own mortified countenance, Genevieve bent her head to the ground and, with a quick tug with the left index finger, pulled down her rigidly curled lip. Coming up with a smile of efficient good nature, she turned back to her course and walked briskly towards the gleaming outline of an upmarket car, the star prize in tonight's Rangoon Raffle.

The performance of the greeters and pointers was, from the start, the perfect model of patient understanding, polite guidance and admirable self-control. In this respect, the work of David and Katherine did not stand out. Indeed, they had spent much time discussing and resolving how not to stand out in any respect. Their hair – Alison's wig, Nick's packet dye – was unexceptional, their gaze uninspiring. They stood with practised anonymity, speaking with voices bereft of discernable accent or tone. They became, in as far as it is possible to be, utterly unremarkable and unmemorable.

The only activities in which they excelled were watching and waiting. As the night progressed an observer might have noticed how they moved slightly, this way and that from their ordained positions, taking in what was happening around, understanding which places were full, which empty, which might be available for use at the right moment. Both of them watched for the key people, correcting and presenting themselves with meticulous care whenever Genevieve or TipTop or Olly came into view. They watched and waited.

And Nick in particular watched and waited for Pommy Freiberg. Behind his heavy-rimmed spectacles, underneath his newly black hair, beneath the best bottled tan available, his faint limp giving nothing away, a largely unrecognisable Nick Durning looked for Pommy.

'Excuse me, may I have a word.'

Genevieve was looking along the polished marble of the imported bar, checking for empty glasses, when she felt the tap on her shoulder. She turned round to find Charlotte looking at her plaintively, yet in a manner that conveyed somehow a previously unknown level of boldness.

'Charlotte. Shouldn't you be in the catering tent?' Charlotte nodded without apologising,

'Everything is going well. This will only take a couple of minutes'.

Genevieve looked around mistrustfully.

'Where are Steve and Spiggy?' she asked, eyeing Charlotte closely.

'They're getting some establishment shots . . .'

'Establish*ing* shots,' Genevieve corrected. Charlotte looked down and Genevieve took her by the arm.

'Very well. Over here.'

They walked in silence to the side of the building. Before Genevieve had even gathered herself properly Charlotte spoke.

'I've decided to leave. To start up on my own.'

Genevieve surveyed Charlotte with undisguised incredulity.

'The thing is,' Charlotte continued, unperturbed, her eyes dancing around as if seeing opportunities popping in the air, 'This television programme got me thinking. And I've got backing. So, I've decided.'

She looked directly at her boss, expecting some form of rage, but instead met with a look of unabashed joy.

'Well, Charlotte,' Genevieve gushed. 'What can I can say? Good luck!' And praise the heavens, she thought, turning on her heels and walked back into the mass of gleeful, heaving fauna. She could hardly believe her good fortune. No uncomfortable post-party conversation, no pay-off and, most importantly, no messy explanation to the Rutherfords. What could be better? Without thinking, she caught the eye of the barman and demanded a glass of champagne. Genevieve never drank, as a rule, not at an event. This however was something special. As the glass touched her lips, her mind was filled with the vision of Charlotte sitting proudly on her pathetic beach donkey, as the waves crashed all around and ultimately swallowed her and the braying mount entirely.

sixty-two

'Sorry chaps. Lips are sealed,' Pommy said, laughing off another attempt by a couple of foreign exchange traders, both in ornate parrot outfits, their faces sticking out from a hole in the neck beneath a magnificent head of real feathers. This is glorious, Pommy thought. He had half a mind to tell, but knew there would be hell to pay if anything hit the market before it opened in the morning. No, let them wait for the statement. Take all the fuckers by surprise. Look at them all, looking at me. Thinking, no doubt. Thinking this is my little swan song. Wait until tomorrow. That will show the fixed-up fuckers what's what. What's what *and* who's who. Fuckers. Whole party full of them.

Pommy chortled companionably as the two birds stumbled off. He looked around, his eyes sucking the night scene down, down, down into a gut of fathomless disdain. A gentle tinkle of laughter caused a flicker of relief to pass across his face and he turned his head like a hawk. Mmh. Lot of women here tonight, mind you. Difficult to tell what they're like though, all dressed up and painted like they are. That's the problem with fancy dress. Have to judge a lot from the face. God knows what might be waiting underneath the outfit.

For his own outfit, Pommy had chosen the quintessential circus animal trainer, with a bright red coat, white shirt, crisp fawn cotton trousers tucked into sharp black boots. In his left hand he carried a large whip with which he had been practising all afternoon in his office, remembering the dismissal of Lawson Jennings.

Odd thing that. Expected shock, but not that much. Jennings completely overboard. All sorts of splashing. Wailing. Moaning.

Uncontrolled chatter. Flying off at mouth about protecting mother. Maybe it was the coffee. It had taken about an hour to get Jennings into some form of presentable form, during which time he had to send Jenny to fetch something from the drinks cabinet.

'Bottle of champagne'll do,' Pommy had said, envisaging the newspaper reports. Sure enough the late edition of the evening paper had carried a story entitled 'Bubbly at Belston.' These things always got out.

Once the alcohol was fizzing around his system, Jennings had proven a bit more manageable. Pommy had everything ready. Jennings would announce that he had – in the light of a frank and wide-ranging conversation with Pommy – decided to withdraw his takeover bid for Belston. The two companies, Belston and Exodus, would instead embark on a joint venture "to explore areas of mutual interest" and "would look forward to increased co-operation in the future". Good news all round, that sort of thing. Shares don't tumble too much, as everyone thinks that a takeover is still on the cards in the long run. But we know, Lawson and I, we know . . . it's going nowhere.

As part of the agreement, Jennings would be joining the board of Belston, with immediate effect. Likewise Pommy at Exodus. Happily, Andrew Midgely had ready the appropriate legal documentation, which Pommy was pleased for Lawson to take away with him for the lawyers to check before signing. And, most importantly, Pommy, using his influence, would ensure that the material Jennings was so worried about . . . disappeared.

'You see, Lawson, it's all very well to be, you know, laying new roads, stretching the horizons and . . . and that sort of thing. But there will be times when you need the personal know-how of how to dig deep holes. Never underestimate the importance of a hole.'

Disappeared, buried . . . but not destroyed. A few months down the line, maybe six, they'd probably pop back up again. By which time Pommy would have put the necessary resources

281

and power lines in place to take advantage of Lawson's public destruction.

As Jenny had held the door open for Jennings to exit, Pommy had reached over and patted Lawson's wrist sympathetically. Jennings had stared at him bitterly, his eyes less red now, more knowing that they had ever been. The younger man had collected what remained of his dignity, and slid off with Faith Barclay, who had been waiting in an otherwise empty meeting room for over two and a half hours.

Pommy had noticed Barne, Humphreys and McClintock hovering on the floor as the two departed, eager no doubt for the relief of the Exodus' owner's enlightening management. Or for a lucrative sacking. Pommy waved gaily to them, in a way that all three found transparently unsettling. Then he'd gone back into his office and got the whip out of the hire box, spending what hours the day had left snatching coffee cups off tables and snapping pens and pencils across the floor, in a carefree manner that was entirely consistent with someone who had decided to jack it all in. He'd had half a mind for another session with the two whores but thought better of it, reasoning that he might pick something up at the zoo anyway.

Pommy smiled to himself, then turned on his heels and began one of his walkabouts, the social mechanism whereby he could survey the available crop of females. So much fun. So much joy. So much to distract, entice and amuse. Everywhere Pommy looked there was something going on, from wandering magicians, to gamekeeper jugglers, to cuddly monkey clowns. So very, very much.

So very much that it is entirely understandable how no one would recall seeing a man in overalls emerge from a bush near the gibbon enclosure. Jonathan had been lying on top of the brick hut since midday, clutching his box, nibbling at sandwiches, sucking down the odd bit of water, a plastic bag attached to his penis to collect urine. He had lain there through closing time, he had lain there while school groups were hustled out, and he had lain there while preparations were made. Once he fancied that he heard Alison's voice, but he did not move. His was the resolve of champions. He did not move.

Once out, once moving among the party people, Jonathan experienced a new level of invisibility. On top of the hut, there might have been a chance of being accidentally revealed. Now, openly going about the place, there was no possibility of such discovery.

While Genevieve's team might be a necessary presence for the partygoers, albeit fit only to provide answers to gruff enquiries, a workman on his way to make something work was of no consequence whatsoever. Jonathan felt himself being looked through in a way that would, in subsequent newspaper reporting, defy belief. No one stopped him when he went down back passages. No one questioned him when he bent down in front of displays. No one bothered to think twice when grates were removed from vents or generators apparently examined. All the time Jonathan worked with a single vision in mind : the rescue of Alison from an apocalypse and the rising from its ashes of the phoenix of their family life. So empowered, Jonathan worked dutifully and with no fuss, bearing all the hallmarks of the trusty labourer who was helping to make things perform correctly for this wonderful, wonderful occasion.

Thinking all this out had not been too difficult. For all that Jonathan might be losing his mind, he was an intelligent person, more than capable, still, of thinking "out of the box". So he had thought about the requirements of the event, his own profile, and decided that he would simply be himself: an engineer of some sort. That was the straightforward bit. No one ever questioned a man in overalls who looked like he was on his way to fix something. Jonathan had seen it himself at work often enough. How often had someone come in with a battered briefcase and simply said, 'Photocopier', before being led to the machine and thereafter immediately forgotten?

For a uniform he had obtained a boiler suit and scruffed it up suitably. His own toolbox from home was ideal; in addition to having most of the equipment he wanted, it was stickered. People liked to see stickers on toolboxes. Then Jonathan had gone round a few electrical and industrial suppliers remembered from his university days: shops, stores and outlets that had been sources of much fun when he and his rugby friends had wanted to play practical jokes. Funny that; he couldn't remember the last time he'd seen any of those guys. They'd gone to a few international matches for a couple of years and then, well . . . he didn't know. Job, kid, money, kid, job, kids, money. His own life had been pumped dry to give life to his family. He had no life. His life had been taken from him already, used up and accounted for, before Alison even left. With her gone, and now the children, there really was nothing left. He missed rugby. He missed his rugby friends.

All it takes to kill the President is a man who is willing to trade his life for the President's – the truth, according to John F. Kennedy and history. If your aim is less than the death of a President, then you need not, necessarily, trade your own life. But if you were willing to trade your life, then there was almost nothing you could not perform. Everyone knows that. Trading your life is the joker in the pack of the common man. No one can trump it.

All that Jonathan wanted was to see Alison, speak to her, tell her . . . things. That would be enough, he was sure, to get the rescue underway. In order to achieve this he was willing to do anything. And if at the end of it, things were not going to be as he wished them to be then, yes, he would make sure that she and whoever else would suffer for it.

Jonathan had turned up at the zoo at lunchtime, having worked out on his previous visits the exact time at which the shifts changed. He had approached the ticket gate and explained to the volunteer behind the counter that he'd been called to fix a fault in the cooling system, without being specific as to which one. Presumably, Jonathan told the volunteer, they had been told about this.

'Nobody tells us anything,' was the predictable reply and in a few minutes he was inside and roaming at will. As he'd expected, preparations were already under way for the night-time event. Supplies were being brought in by side entrances, being stored in tents, stacked to one side, inside and outside buildings, much to the annoyance of the regular zoo staff, most of whom had not been invited along for the event and had no idea what it was. 'Nobody tells us anything,' was the spiteful phrase on everyone's lips, as Jonathan passed through kitchens, offices, storerooms and cages. At the rear entrance was a massed convoy of lorries bearing sheets of one-way Plexiglas. The drivers were milling around the gate, smoking and bitching. Nobody told them anything either. Jonathan enquired when they expected to start putting things up. Nobody knew.

'Are you Stephen?' asked one of them urgently. 'I've to find Stephen.'

Jonathan demurred and was on his way. As he moved he picked up more and more pieces of information, gradually piecing together a technical picture of how the event would be fitting into place once the zoo closed. At one point he even sat down to have a coffee with one of the keepers, a large chap who worked with the camels but who wanted to get the elephants.

'Thing is, of course, everyone wants the elephants,' the keeper said, sipping his coffee philosophically.

'Of course,' said Jonathan sympathetically.

'Camels are good, but, you know, they can be a bit temperamental, and it's just not the same as an elephant. People respect elephants. They can be quite scary sometimes.'

Jonathan nodded. The man had a point.

sixty-three

'TipTop, where are the replacement sweatshirts?' Genevieve surveyed the party's frantically milling beasts as she waited for a response. A certain sadness was falling on her. This often occurred when the halfway point in the event had passed, as the motivational motors began to stop firing quite as quickly, choked by the success of plans well-made and executed. On this occasion Genevieve had a few glasses of champagne to thank for a further dulling of her attitude.

She shook her head from side to side, trying to throw off what she knew was an unacceptable disposition. Little incidents like this kept you on the right side of complacency. Someone, some sort of furry mammal apparently, had been unhappy that one of the pointers – Jurgen, foreign exchange student – was unwilling to go and get them a drink, and had thrown what remained of their old one over him. Genevieve had come across Jurgen, stained but still in position, and, having ascertained that the incident had ended there, was now intent on restoring presentation values. Her earpiece hissed.

'In the storage tent behind the disco. All sizes. In yellow bags. Over.'

Genevieve confirmed receipt of the information, told Jurgen well done, and set off to get him a new top. Always good the Germans, she thought, keep to their positions no matter what.

The disco looked to be going well as she passed it for the umpteenth time, although she predicted a few pass-outs before the night was over, a result of costume fatigue. Consequently the private medical service was stationed, inconspicuously of course, not too far from here.

What size did Jurgen say he was? Genevieve thought as she pushed open the flap, tripped over something and fell head long into a pile of Team Genevieve clothing.

'Bugger!'

How often did she need to tell people about keeping storage spaces clear? Anything might be needed. She snapped on her torch and caught the screwed up face of Charlotte, who was sitting astride the heavily panting Johnny Rutherford, now bereft of his racoon outfit.

'Oh dear,' Genevieve sighed.

Neither of the two said anything. Genevieve played the light over their sweaty bodies: 'No need to enquire who is giving you the backing then, is there Charlotte?'

She picked herself up and began raking through the pile of sweatshirts for an XL. Finding it, Genevieve stepped past the still silent coupling, looking down, flicking the accusatory beam on them as she passed.

'There's always one that likes the fat hump, eh Johnny?' she muttered.

Pommy was being avoided. He could tell. By now, even on a bad night, he would have expected to encounter a couple of lookers standing provocatively across his path, wanting to sample his brusque, wolfish charm. They always did. No fucking wolves left, that's why. All fucking extinct, killed off or on something. He was one of the last, possibly the last wolf around. Vast fucking appeal. But not tonight.

Tonight he sensed a reticence in the otherwise fun-time air. And he knew why. Everybody, women included, was avoiding the spectre of a fallen man walking among them, one who, if he'd had the good grace, would surely have spared them his apparitional presence. Wasn't fair, was it, to be hanging around after you're dead but before the burial. After the burial fine. People know how to talk to someone who has crossed to the other side. But a corpse? Corpses throw people. Leave them wondering. Don't know what to say, so best avoid. Oh yes, he was being avoided.

The only side-benefit to this was that Pommy was able to saunter around completely uninterrupted. Every now and then he gave a crack of his whip near some group of animals, cackling loudly in the manner of one who has lost it, knowing that this would upset them all the more. Wait until they get the news tomorrow, he thought. Crack! Ha Ha!

Nothing is as dull as the wait. All journalists know this. Despite what non-journalists might think, there is no sense of apprehension or tension, just the enduring absence of reason. Why am I here? What are my friends up to? What do I really want to do with my life? These questions never arise during a one-on-one interview or in the buzz of the late night office or when actually writing the piece. But they do on the wait. Starting out, a young reporter, eager to experience all the fabled clichés of the newshound life, might enjoy the buzz of the street. This was quickly replaced by the chill of the empty pavement, the discomfort of the folding chair, the rank tongue of too much nasty coffee. Doorstepping someone might be unpleasant, but at least it was quick and soon over with. Not like the wait.

Judy tried again to walk it off but after twenty-five minutes of going up and down the gutter realised she was only making it worse. Besides, this might go on all night, particularly as the party inside the zoo could well last until dawn, although her information was for three at the latest.

'Juicy pictures of top, top figure,' the message had said, noting only that they would be delivered, outside the entrance to London Zoo before the party ended. There was also a list of four excellent names and a guarantee that this concerned one of them. No money was required either, which had sounded too good to be true then and was feeling increasingly suspicious as the hours went by.

What was she doing here anyway? Trying to make up for

Jonathan Greenmeadow and his amazing vanishing act, that's what. His appearance on the police wanted list was good, but it had opened the door for one or two others, and then he had just disappeared. So far as she knew, she had got closest, and no one else had made the Spontaneous Sex link, of that she was confident. Still, she should have known better. Never get an editor excited unless you can deliver. How many times had she heard that? Judy sighed and took out another stick of chewing gum. What do I really want to do with my life?

Genevieve stood at the Elephant House Bar, watching the animals go by. She raised the bottle of beer to her lips and chugged down as much as she could. Before and all around her was the last Rutherford's party she would ever run. Charlotte would have the next.

'Ooh, ooh, ooh!'

Genevieve turned dispassionately to find the prancing form of Ginny Rutherford doing her best monkey impression. She smiled appreciatively.

'Genevieve!' Ginny shouted, her mouth visible below the half-mask. 'This is fabulous. Everyone says they've never been to anything like it. It's so . . . different!'

At that moment, Genevieve wanted nothing more than to punch Ginny full in the face. Ginny was right. This was a fabulous, different party. People would be talking about it for years. But Genevieve knew that fat Charlotte and her new company would be taking away her most important contract, and with it a lot of her aura. Everything she had worked for gone.

Genevieve gave Ginny a mock bow, turned, reached over the bar, and pulled a bottle of beer up. Might as well enjoy herself.

'So you're pleased, are you Ginny? Pleased with the party?' Genevieve asked in a tone which Ginny might one day come to recognise as facetious.

'Oh, yes! Totally!' and Ginny did another little monkey dance and waved a plastic banana at Genevieve.

'I'm so glad,' Genevieve replied, taking a long slug at the

bottle. 'Johnny is very happy too, by the way. He asked me to tell you. Although apparently something has come up and he'd like a word. He asked me to tell you that too.' Genevieve inclined her bottle towards Ginny to emphasise her point.

'Oh, really?' Ginny asked, stopping her performance to think. 'Better find him then. Know where he is?' she asked.

'Mmh, try behind the disco. He was sorting something out in the storage shed, I think,' Genevieve said thoughtfully, between gulps.

'Great!' exclaimed Ginny, 'Tell me Genevieve, do you think I could make it all the way over there while doing the whole monkey thing?' she asked excitedly, arms beginning to lope, body moving up and down in the ludicrous impersonation often used by those whose principle understanding of primate physiology has not changed since childhood.

'Oh, I am absolutely positive that if anyone could, you could Ginny!'

Genevieve laughed uproariously. As did Ginny, before setting off with a huge screech through the crowds. Genevieve reached for another beer, catching the eye of one of her best barmen who looked at her questioningly.

'Mind your own business!' she spat, storming off into the decadence.

sixty-four

There was a hand on his shoulder, female too, judging by the weight. Pommy stared straight ahead of him, happy that his star had not fallen totally. He sneaked a side-glance and saw a gentle, young set of fingers. Excellent. Just his luck if it had been the fucking wife. No, the snare had worked. Lots of men talk about snaring women. Don't understand snare, though. Snare means they come to you. Need fucking patience. Patience is the bait in the snare.

Pommy was standing at the spider monkey enclosure, watching them swing from branch to branch, and enjoying their vigour. Haven't seen the wife yet, come to think of it, must be here somewhere, checking some mincey details or other.

'Do you like animals, Mr Freiberg?'

Don't turn round. Make them demand your attention. 'Don't mind them. Like these ones. Frisky.'

One of the spider monkeys was swinging by its tail from a steel upright, while another tried to rob it of a bunch of leaves.

'Those tails are clever, aren't they? Like an extra arm or something,' noted his unseen companion, Pommy feeling her being drawn closer into his orbit.

'Yes. The tail. Prehensile. Means "with muscle",' Pommy explained, having just read the nearby plaque. 'Just like an extra arm,' he went on, 'Very handy thing to have. Wonder why we don't have one?' This latter thought with genuine concern. Why don't we have one? Must be a reason. Fucking clever thing these prehensile tails. Particularly useful on the yacht. Always short-handed at sea. One of those would be fucking ideal. Pommy felt his companion drawing closer.

'My name's Linda.'

291

Little devices. You don't need a lot of size to make a big splash, not really, Jonathan thought, as he dusted himself down outside the Small Mammals area. He looked at the window he was standing in front of. Cotton-Head Tamarind. Jonathan watched the delicate, monkey-like creature skip across its sandy enclosure. There was a sign. Apparently the tamarind was from South America.

'Inquisitive group-based mammals. Monogamous and family-orientated. Extremely aggressive when defending territory.'

A bit like him really. Such a little thing too. Like his own little things; highly effective in their own little way.

A dog was watching him, a large comical Bassett hound, with enormous floppy ears, an amusingly miserable face and a red and yellow cocktail.

'Hey, you!' it said angrily.

Jonathan turned and smiled, 'Yes, eh, sir, please don't mind me. I was just checking the security on the temporary screens.'

'Humph,' the dog snorted, 'Why didn't you do that earlier? There's a party going on, you know. And it's "Ms", by the way.'

Jonathan dropped his pliers into the toolbox and bent down to close the lid.

'We weren't able to,' he apologized. 'Not enough time to get round the whole site before kick-off. Anyway, I'm off now. Enjoy the party.'

'Where's the magician going to be on next?' the dog demanded, walking up to Jonathan, slurping its drink messily through the mouth hole.

'I'm afraid I don't know Ms. Why don't you – ?'

The dog pushed past him and moved off unsteadily. 'Fat load of use you are,' it said unappreciatively. Jonathan turned back to the cotton-head tamarind.

They walked in style through the mêlée, a serene, almost regal presence in the incessant celebrations. That was Pommy's influence, of course. He knew better than most how not to be part of the mass, how to be a rhythm apart from the crowd. It was like walking with a Roman senator, or so he believed. Women love that. Don't want to be part of the hoi polloi. Want to be part of the high polloi. This girl, Linda, sexy as hell in a tasty fox suit, was definitely up for it. No doubt about it. Interested in everything, all sorts of questions. Lots to expand on for me. Knows quality this one. Wouldn't mind seeing her face a bit more. Looks good but difficult to tell for sure through that fox mask.

Alison smiled as Pommy explained how he negotiated with the Italians, a subject which he always enjoyed re-visiting.

'Don't let them sit down for half an hour after lunch – that's the trick, you see.'

As Alison and Pommy continued their circumnavigation of the zoo, only one of them was aware of someone following them. And neither of them was aware of a second presence that even as they chatted was preparing an end to the whole charade.

Genevieve swung round to find herself being filmed by the documentary crew. She smiled elegantly, and served herself from a champagne bottle, raising a glass with good nature to the camera. Then she gestured at the jolly scenes to be seen on all sides, as Spiggy and Steve smiled, pleased to have found her in such welcoming good humour.

'Look at this. Isn't it fantastic?'

Steve and Spiggy nodded vociferously, eager to capture some form of on-camera success talk from Genevieve.

'All thanks, I suppose, to that fat chump Charlotte, wouldn't you agree, oh nation of the Isles of Britain?' Genevieve leered into the camera, giving her immediate audience the first understanding of a mind let loose by drink.

'I did this you know. Me, Genevieve Marsden, of Genevieve Marsden Associates. Dog, desk, telephone, maybe but it's all mine nonetheless.'

Steve gave a look to Spiggy, who nodded tersely without looking at him. The cameraman never wavered.

'They never see,' Genevieve was saying with a wave of her hand, 'Never see. Have no idea what is done to get all this ... for them to enjoy. It is the detail!' she said, rounding on the camera, looking into it, enraged, 'the detail. That is what matters, what I do. This lot of Hand Wank Harry's would never know that.'

She slowed now, seemed to drift in and out of consciousness slightly. Then to the camera again.

'It's our secret. They will never know. Details ... desserts ... napkins.'

Genevieve stopped and looked at Steve and Spiggy, who were both trying to disguise their glee.

'Come with me,' she barked, and stomped off at speed.

'The Turks are good too. Robust. Historical people. Lots of ... history'

Pommy could feel himself moving along nicely. He had decided that Linda wasn't the brightest. The fact that she was talking to him at all showed that she had not heard any of the rumours about his imminent demise. She seemed to be in complete awe of him. On other occasions, at other non-wife events, this might have made Pommy suspicious. He was always on the lookout for the type of tabloid set-up that would have him on the front page for non-business reasons. Which is why he enjoyed Genevieve's get-togethers. If there was one thing his wife knew it was how to set-up and protect events. Always difficult for the media. And none more difficult than the fucking Rutherfords. No, any girlie here was a safe fuck. Including you, he thought, turning to smile.

'Shall we saunter on?' Pommy asked.

'Oh yes!' Alison gushed, 'And can we get a drink too?'

She looked up at him pleadingly, begging with her eyes, shoulders dropped in supplication. Not long now, thought Pommy, and cast his head magisterially around for someone with a tray.

*

Genevieve stopped abruptly at a gathering of fun-makers on a corner near the Reptile House. This wasn't right. Why were they standing here? Should have been moved on. This is a flow-through. She turned to Spiggy and Steve, both almost out of breath, the cameraman thick with perspiration, after their subject had given it some speed on the way over.

'Look at this!' Genevieve exclaimed, indignant, 'No bloody pointer. No pointer to move these people on. This is what I plan for. This is what we do not, repeat NOT, want. Where the hell are they?'

She spun round twice, like a cat hearing noise, unable to locate the source.

'What the fuck is going on?' she demanded, thumbing the radio on, 'TipTop, who the fuck is meant to be on ...,' she paused and assessed her position, '. . . on Reptile Four . . . no, Five; Reptile Five.'

TipTop checked and responded.

'Well, David is nowhere to be seen,' Genevieve explained, 'Get one of the replacements in immediately. I'll deal with it personally until they arrive.'

'Personally,' Genevieve repeated for the camera, then speaking to Spiggy, 'Can't have this,' indicating the group of eagerly guffawing animals behind her with the end of her bottle, 'Blocks the flow ... it's a dynamic thing, you know.'

She turned to the blocking animals. 'Excuse me; you'll have to move along from here. This is a key thoroughfare. A key path through. Move along please.'

The menagerie ignored her, were not even aware they were being addressed. Why should they be? It wasn't one of them. Somebody official maybe, but not one of them.

Genevieve turned to Spiggy again, 'We have to move this. It's not dynamic.' And she repeated her request, this time more loudly, but with the same absence of effect.

Genevieve set her champagne bottle down on the ground. Then, with the swift agility common to those who have been drinking, she ran up to a large black bear figure in the group and kicked it viciously in the back of its leg, causing it to collapse on the ground, where she delivered two more kicks to its stomach.

'I said, "Move, please!"' she shouted, before jumping slightly back and adopting a fighting posture that indicated she was quite ready and able to take on all the animals if necessary. The bear lay on the ground, spluttering and clutching its belly, while a penguin and a lion comforted it.

'Move, now!' Genevieve shouted, and the group gathered itself meekly, no longer so sure of their position, and wandered fearfully off down the path. Steve and Spiggy were clapping their hands without making any noise, almost unable to control themselves. Genevieve wandered over and waved them to stillness.

'It's the path, you see. Got to keep it clear. Dynamically speaking.'

David had, some time earlier, become Nick, changing in the undergrowth, pulling on a black and white cat suit, completed by a lovely velvet cat mask with spindly whiskers which bounced gracefully with each step the wearer took. Nick and Alison were now linked through one of the strictly prohibited alternative channels on their headsets, Alison having disposed of the microphone element altogether, the tiny earpiece almost invisible beneath the straggles of her wig.

As Nick stalked the couple, guiding Alison away from the crowded areas, patiently identifying the likely spots, it was impossible not to feel excited. Nick too had heard about the morning meeting between Pommy Freiberg and Lawson Jennings and his pleasure at the news of what must have meant Pommy's fall was muted by a desire to have somehow been involved in it. This will suffice though, Nick thought, as he packed his clothes into the bag. It will be enough that I can provide the shit to rub his face in. This will do. Nick knew that his old boss would have worked out some kind of dignified exit, some way of leaving the stage to appreciative applause with his dignity intact. Well, I'm here to take your dignity, Pommy Freiberg, he thought.

sixty-five

No, not her. Or her.

That it would be difficult to find Alison within the confines of the party had never occurred to Jonathan. Quite the opposite. He had imagined that there was a strong risk of her spotting him and fleeing before he could rescue her. Consequently, although he had been open in movement, he had been closed of face, keeping his gaze to the ground, avoiding eye contact with anyone. Now, searching wildly through the morass of costumed glee and extravagance, Jonathan understood that he had got something wrong. Alison was not on show. He had been round the entire area twice now and was convinced of it. Where was she? Jonathan looked down at his watch. Goddamn it! Everything was in place. There wasn't long to go.

'There. The smaller of the two tents. It's empty. Just storage boxes for cutlery and things. Get in quickly.'

Alison struggled to maintain her look of engrossment as Nick's words erupted in her ear.

'. . . not that the Russians are any better. No. Russians – too much heritage. Lots of czars and things. Monarchy in the genes but not in the palaces. Insecure people – all very wary. Think everyone is out to fu– . . . to screw them.'

Pommy's arm was wrapped lightly around Alison's waist as they walked gently round the outskirts of the party. Alison, at a loss as to how to respond to this observation, pushed herself closer into him, at the same time edging Pommy towards the smaller tent.

'This is the idea,' Pommy thought, 'Out to the perimeters.

298

Nobody around.' Apart from the occasional scampering pair of animals – the last had been a velveteen wolf chasing a polypropylene otter – the outlying paths and walkways were relatively empty.

'Go on,' Nick's voice hissed in Alison's ear.

Alison looked around. She slowed and then stopped altogether. Pommy put his arms fully round her, drawing her in. Alison resisted, holding back but not withdrawing. She leaned her head up to the side of Pommy's, mouth so close to his ear that light flecks of warm saliva struck his lobe as she whispered, 'Pommy, I'm cold out here. Let's go inside.'

Pommy looked around and saw the ideal place. As they walked towards the small tent, almost hidden behind a much larger one, Pommy realised that there was something about this lovely girl that reminded him of Henrietta. Henrietta who, earlier that day had received notification of a promotion to her law firm's Shanghai office, courtesy of a thirty-second telephone call from Pommy to the firm's Managing Partner. There had always been something about Henrietta, and there was something about this Linda too. Nothing in the looks – completely different in that respect. No, something in the attitude.

'I am worthful. I provide ... worth. But most of this lot ... they're worthless. That is to say, they're worth less than me.'

Genevieve smiled broadly as she indicated the thronging animals behind her. She had been standing for about five minutes on an empty orange crate – 'all the way from buggery Florida for this bunch' – giving her opinion on the quality of the hosts. In her ear TipTop's voice crackled and Genevieve said 'OK' in response, although she was not entirely sure what to.

'Are you sure you lot don't want a drink?'

Spiggy, Steve and the camera shoogled their gaze back and forth to indicate "no".

Genevieve shrugged and hopped off the box, kicking it into the undergrowth, before reaching behind her and removing an open bottle of beer from the waist of her trousers.

'Right, where to next?' she asked, looking for guidance to Spiggy.

'Wait, Ginny, wait!'

All four turned to look as Johnny Racoon Rutherford sped past in pursuit of Ginny who, in running shocked, distraught and drunken, was achieving a level of chimpanzee impersonation that few who attempted it would ever come close to.

Genevieve turned to Spiggy and winked ostentatiously 'Something special that . . .Different.'

Not in the open. Nor round the edges. Open and edges were done. Had to be somewhere else. Inside. Unless she's gone entirely. No, definitely not. Cannot have gone entirely. Must be inside somewhere. Take a breath. Inside one of the tents. All the tents have been checked. Correct. No! All the OPEN tents have been checked. All the tents for the guests. But not the other tents. Not the ones you can't see into. The ones behind. Right. Check them all. Start at the middle. What time is it? Hurry.

In terms of seduction, few men ever get The Drop. Mention it and most will think you are talking about being hanged, about an execution. It is a worthy namesake. The Drop has about it a degree of guarantee that makes it a winner without match when it comes to hitting men where it counts. Alison gave Pommy The Drop. She had remembered it from one of those magazines Jonathan had wanted her to read, something to do with an exciting way to welcome your husband home, particularly on those long, dark winter nights in.

Entering the marquee both had checked that they were alone, Alison with a quick eye here and there, Pommy by sensory osmosis, as was his gift. Alison had then swiftly, and unexpectedly, handed Pommy her drink, which he took automatically. In one fluid movement – and only she and Nick knew just how much practice, re-seaming and exfoliant had gone into this manoeuvre – Alison cast off her slinky fox outfit, letting it glide with syrupy ease down her golden body. Only the mask remained.

Had this been an ordinary item of clothing, say, a dress or the like, the effect would have been intense and, without a doubt, successful. This, however, was more. For any heterosexual man to see the female figure emerge from something animal in form represents a union of extraordinary base instincts; the sexual with the hunting. Given this, given Alison's generous build-up, given Pommy's own character, his reaction was inevitable. His lips parted slightly, his mind slipped out of its chains, and he snarled. Not a big, nasty snarl, but an involuntary, haunted, wooing, snarl. Pommy threw one, then the other drink to his side, the glass breaking on the floor like the very tension of the moment. Then he approached Alison with huge restraint, each step wanting to be quicker than the last. 'Ah-ah!' the minx in the fox mask chided, turning her naked back to him, 'Now you.'

Pommy kept coming. Alison scampered with provocative baby steps away, and she bent as if to pull her outfit on again. Pommy stopped and began to undress with slow, manly consideration.

'Giving these buffoons a good time isn't particularly difficult. They all think the same, so once you've got their measure it's all over, really,' Genevieve barked as she walked brazenly through a large bunch of said buffoons, cavorting along in a bestial conga formation. Spiggy, Steve and the cameraman hemmed in around her.

'They never grow up – don't need to. They don't actually need to learn. Why should they? Money is not dependent on it. Maybe for one or two. Take a look.'

The conga had now wheeled round on itself, creating an arm-linked dancing circle that whirled with gusto round the smaller group, whooping with frenzied delight. The cameraman spun counter to this movement, envisioning the edit suite wonder. 'Come on,' Genevieve said, almost wearily, 'Plenty more where they came from,' and she broke her way through the link of a squirrel and a leopard for the others to follow, the circle closing behind them with amorphous self-satisfaction.

Pommy stood naked. Pommy Freiberg, he thought, reminding himself of who he was, making sure that his lack of clothing had not diminished him. Pommy Freiberg. Wait a minute – that's not my fucking voice.

'Pommy Freiberg,' Nick whispered again, walking out of the shadows behind Alison, now bending to pull her costume back on. Pommy stood without motion. While this was a new and different situation, he knew better than to show panic.

'Hello, Durning.'

Pommy stayed resolutely still, but neutrally so, as if being addressed by an ex-employee holding a large shotgun and woman dressed as a fox was a common situation in his life.

'I think you've met Linda before,' Nick announced, as Alison slipped off her fox mask. Pommy looked at her. There was something familiar right enough.

'No?' Alison asked. Pommy stared, trying to remember. Nick gestured to the back of the tent and Alison retrieved her holdall, and removed a blonde wig, jamming it on with no great precision. Pommy gasped. It was one of the whores from the other night. The one that said she felt queasy and wouldn't do anything. Kept herself to herself.

'And now, Pommy, I think I would like you to explain a bit about why I was spat out,' Nick said. Pommy reached down for his clothes but Nick waved the shotgun. 'No, I think naked is fine,' Nick pulled up a storage crate to sit on, 'and if you think I might not be willing to use this,' he continued, passing her father's gun to Alison, 'I can assure you she will not hesitate.' Alison nodded, 'I want to use it now, Pommy, to be frank.'

Nick sat and listened to Pommy's story about Argentina. As it unfolded he felt the pain of his removal once more, and the anger rose within him at having been treated as nothing more than a bit of cannon fodder for the City. At the conclusion,

302

which with Pommy's clipped explanations took less than five minutes and forty 'fuckings', Nick got up and was still.

'Do you know what you did to me?' he asked, reaching into the holdall. Pommy said nothing. He had no idea. As it was his 'Don't suppose you're very fucking happy' didn't help. Nick smiled.

'You know what, Pommy? I don't need to get you to think about what you did to me. Because now we are going to do the same to you. You do remember the other night don't you? With –' Nick hesitated as he found the right name, 'Linda, here'. Nick nodded towards Alison and Pommy without shifting his gaze nodded towards Nick. He had been wondering when the whore story was going to come into it.

'I knew that sooner or later you would decide to have one of your little threesomes. Although you did have us worried at how long it took you to get round to it. What was it in the end? A bit of comfort after losing the battle?'

'Listen, Durning –' Pommy tried to break in.

'You will wait!' Nick commanded, 'I've had to wait.'

Composing himself, he resumed. 'You might remember how you gave me the number, told me that I might find it useful at some point. Turns out, I did. Turns out, some of your generous redundancy package was useful too.'

All the while Alison kept the shotgun raised, patrolling back and forth between Nick and Pommy and the door.

'On that last little visit you arranged – what was that anyway? To cheer you up after Lawson had been in to see you? – we'd already been in touch with your service provider. Made an arrangement. Not as complex or admirable as Argentina, I'll grant you, but an arrangement nevertheless.'

Nick bent down and pulled out a cardboard folder.

'Take a seat, Pommy. It'll be easier for you to flick through this.'

Alison waved the gun and Pommy moved over and sat down on the crate. Nick handed him the folder.

'You'd better get ready,' he told Alison, 'Judy will be there now.' Alison turned but as she did so she thought she heard something, like a ball being kicked hard against a wall, a sort of hard, loud slap somewhere in the distance.

To others, it did not sound like a football being kicked against a wall. Most thought it the beginning of some airborne celebrations.

'Goody!' cried a tiger, its elaborately painted face smiling merrily, 'Firework time!'

'Yay!' said the tiger's companion, a marvellous, spongy kangaroo, jumping up and down. Together they scrambled off to see the show.

Yet, as for others, the show was not easy to find. All over the area people stopped and looked to the skies for guidance, for a sign among the stars. Some bright whoosh or sparkling whizz. They did not know that it was a condition of hire of the Zoo that no fireworks of any sort were permitted. So strain their eyes as they might, there was never any prospect of a performance on high.

Team Genevieve was not fooled for a moment. Team Genevieve knew all about the prohibition on fireworks. It was one of the questions they were programmed to respond to.

'No, regrettably, because of London Zoo regulations, it has not been possible to build a firework component into the evening.' Then smile, genuinely.

Team Genevieve immediately knew something was up. At least, TipTop McGee did.

'TipTop to Genevieve, Over'

Pause. Nothing.

'TipTop to Genevieve, Over.' Nothing. 'TipTop to all stations: what are those noises? Over'

Some people were better placed to say what the noises were. A scruffy lion – 'outfit's been in the family for years' – was trying to remember where he had left his drinking buddy. He turned and looked at the Egyptian Tortoise, tried to wave to it through the double-glazing. He was waving at it still when a small, almost delicate, explosion removed most of his left leg, sending a fine spray of blood over another group of African mammals. As his blood volleyed from the spout of his severed limb, the lion was still wondering where old whatsisname was. On a picnic table next to the rhinoceros compound, a happy looking pig maintained its plastic-faced good nature, even when its companion happy pig – 'Only two in the country and we got them both!' – abruptly ruptured outwards, splattering guts over their tray of nibbles. In the Small Mammals section a glum looking Bassett hound, freshly returned to give that lippy work-man a hard time, bent down to inspect the workman's handi-work and found itself decapitated.

The initial deaths and maimings were not actually part of Jonathan's grand design. They were a side effect of the series of minor incendiary explosions that he had calculated would be necessary to create a suitably impressive inferno from which Alison might be rescued. Those little boxes only exploded at all in order to set fire to the various chemical compounds within: extremely high-temperature burning compounds which could themselves set fire instantly to any material whatsoever. Everything in short to which Jonathan had attached them. He could not count on a fire gradually spreading. No, he needed an instant result.

Pommy looked down at the images of him and two whores in a series of photographs. Mostly it was the other one, but Linda was in frame enough, clearly recognizable with the blonde wig. 'And?' he asked, looking over to Nick.

'Don't worry, Pommy, it's not just the photographs. Linda will be giving a detailed account of your performance, or lack thereof. Extensive note will be made of how you weren't up to it, how you were an old man. That will be about it for you, I imagine, Pommy Freiberg. Humiliating ejection from Belston followed by exposure as a sad, limp user of prostitutes. Let's see how you feel after all that.'

Pommy laughed loudly.

'Must admit, Durning. Were it the case that I had been fucked out of Belston, I think you'd have something. Thing is, I fucking haven't been.'

Nick looked to Alison, and then back to Pommy. This couldn't be true. He had analysed every report, read every scrap of information there was on the takeover. Pommy was finished. He had to be.

'Lawson Jennings has got you. It's all over the place,' Nick blurted. Alison came closer, concerned.

'You don't imagine for a moment that I'd let that fuckhead get his hands on Belston, do you Durning? You don't really think that people like him can beat people like me, even if I am the only people like me left?'

'So, what –?' Nick was incapable of forming the sentence.

'For your information, Lawson Jennings and I have agreed on a mutually beneficial way out. There will be no fucking takeover of Belston Corporation and there will never be someone like him on the fucking bridge of Belston Corporation. Fuck – the very thought of it!'

Nick shook his head, and Alison, letting the shotgun swing down by her side, took his hand. Each of these physical capitulations added to Pommy's strident recovery.

'No, takeover is dead. It'll all be out tomorrow for the market. New partners and all that fucking guff. Nice try, Durning. Have to fucking give you that. If I was about to walk the plank that impotent stuff would certainly have been like concrete round the fucking feet. As it is, anything to do with sex is just going to make me look good right now. City likes men who are still up for it.'

Pommy threw the folder across to Nick, the photos spilling out on the floor like spent dreams. Alison bent to pick them up, laying the shotgun down. Pommy couldn't move that fast.

'Fact is,' Pommy said, standing up, 'it wouldn't make a flying fuck of a difference if it was me with the Pope's wife. No, you'll have to do better than that to make an impact on me, Durning, something a bit more fucking . . . substantial.'

306

'Alison? Is that you, Alison?' asked a voice Alison recognised. She slowed, and then turned, already in a state of disbelief. It couldn't be, not here! But it was. Pommy, Nick and Alison turned to the tent entrance.

Jonathan had trouble understanding what he was seeing. There was his wife, dressed as a fox, with a large naked man and another man dressed as a cat.

'What a time I've had,' Jonathan said, walking fully into the tent, as arriving home, clutching his briefcase, from a difficult day at work. But he had no briefcase, only a satchel of sorts, from which he pulled a nail gun. At this point Pommy moved ever so little and Jonathan planted a six-inch nail about two inches from his foot.

'Don't move; please don't.'

'It's not a matter of brains, you see, not like in my game. In my game, you need to be able to think many, many moves ahead,' Genevieve explained to Spiggy, again. Spiggy indulging her, nodding, eager not to interrupt the flow but wishing Genevieve would move on.

Puh.

'So, Genevieve, what type of people are these, who are here tonight?'

To hell with entrapment, thought Spiggy.

Puh!

Genevieve snorted derisively, 'For starters, they're not people. They're animals.'

Enormous laughter at own joke.

Puh!!

Spiggy looked up at Steve, who shrugged his shoulders. They were sitting inside Genevieve's tiny office.

'Nice and quiet,' Spiggy had said, which was true, although Spiggy's interest in finding somewhere nice and quiet was to get Genevieve's increasingly vitriolic outbursts captured with unambiguous clarity.

PUH!

Now Genevieve started, 'What the hell was that?'

'It's fireworks, isn't it?' Steve said coyly, desperate not to interrupt Genevieve's flow.

'Fireworks?' Genevieve exclaimed, 'There aren't any bloody fireworks!'

She snatched up the headset, which Spiggy had asked her to lay down to avoid interruptions.

'What?' Genevieve screamed, as TipTop launched a frantic explanation down the earpiece.

'I'm' – out of the seat – 'on' – hand on the door – 'my way' – the words barely caught by Spiggy and Steve as Genevieve rocketed to save the day.

Civilisation goes into reverse when human beings are panicked. Which is why watching scenes of panic are so troubling, so upsetting that only an ability to raise contempt for those involved allows you to continue watching. Not me, everyone thinks;

I would be one of the sensible ones. I'd know what to do – I'd follow the drill. I would be clever and resourceful. But we wouldn't be. Minds, reasons and dignity desert us more quickly than it is comfortable to realise when it is felt – and it is felt, not thought – that death is coming. Drink and drugs amplify such debasement further still.

As the crowd became aware that this was an ongoing situation, that it was not a one-off, that they were under attack, the flight to safety was ignited. Mammal fought with mammal as they shouldered their way this way and that to get out. Those who had fallen, struck down by either one of Jonathan's devices or panicked fellow revellers became mere obstacles to overcome. The showy camaraderie of celebration vanished beneath a desperate rush for survival.

Pity those who did not know what to do, who suddenly found themselves surrounded by a screaming, bloodied mass. Pity the animals. For Jonathan's devices had been very cleverly placed, with the trained eye of an engineer who knew how to make buildings open. While many animals chose to stay within, aware that to cower in the shadows of their cages was by far the best option, some ventured out. The fearless and the dumb and the territorial came out and did what they could by way of instinct. The lions and tigers chased and mauled and the gorillas defended their territory and the snakes bit and suffocated.

'Everyone stay calm. We are in control!'

Genevieve shouted vainly across the mêlée. Then she thumbed on her radio.

'Jill, TipTop! Come in! Over'

No response.

'Everyone stay calm!' she shouted again, and ran towards the nearest fire she could see, getting three steps towards it before a guy rope from one of the marquees caught her across the knee, slamming Genevieve into the ground like a mousetrap closing. She lay still and unremarked as Spiggy, Steve and the cameraman flew past.

Jonathan was still struggling with the fact of being in a tent with a naked man and his wife in a fox suit and some other guy. What had been going on? What horror had his wife been subjected to? Good job he was here for the rescue.

'I mean, Alison, what was it?'

And he thumped another nail into the ground near Pommy, who had now been joined in statue-like immobility by everyone else. For while all watching Jonathan's entrance knew they were in some way different from the average person, they also knew they were not mad, insane, or altogether removed from reason, whereas the person before them with the nail gun certainly seemed to be. And in such a presence, immobility seems as good a default as any.

'What wasn't enough?'

Jonathan circled Alison and Nick, sizing them up, his eyes flicking back and forth between them and Pommy. For good measure he continued to punctuate his chat with nails into the floor.

'Everything we needed, I worked to get. There was very little of modern life that we didn't have. Or could not have got if we had stayed together as a family. As a happy family.'

PUH!

And there was no doubting that noise.

'What the –'

Pommy's words were interrupted by a nail impacting right next to his big toe. There was now screaming outside.

'Anyway, I've decided to that I'm going to rescue you from the mistake you have made.'

Jonathan would not be interrupted.

'I'm going to rescue you from all of this. I mean, Alison, what on earth were you thinking?'

Then he gathered himself, as the mayhem outside became louder.

'Don't mind that, its part of the rescue,' Jonathan smiled at his wife. 'It's part of the demonstration of my love for you, and our family. I set it all up. Have a look.'

Jonathan indicated with his nail gun for Alison to go to the tent entrance, which she did, pulling back the flap to reveal a scene of medieval chaos: animals staggering under the weight of injury, fires all around, smoke, mayhem and general non-specific entropy.

Alison took all this in, as did Pommy and Nick, leaning over to see through the parted doorway.

'I did all of this for you, Alison. For you! Come on, its rescue time!' Nick shifted his weight and Jonathan let another nail off. As he did so he noticed the photographs on the floor. Reaching down, he lifted one up, looking at in horror. It is one thing to suspect something, it is quite another to see it. There was his wife, Alison, on a bed sitting next to another woman having sex with . . .

Jonathan turned and raised the nail gun, placing it in line with Pommy's forehead.

'That's my wife!' he screamed, placing both hands on the trigger.

Boom! Boom!

Jonathan tumbled forward as Alison released both barrels of the shotgun into his back.

As the smoke cleared, and the rising cacophony outside became audible again, Pommy looked down at Jonathan's body, then up at Alison.

'See what you mean about using the gun, Durning.'

Then he stood and walked over to his pile of clothes.

'Right, best be off then,' Pommy concluded, looking round just in time for the downswing of the gun-butt to catch him on the side of the head.Nick handed the gun back to Alison. 'Right, let's get to work. Judy's going to be disappointed.'

About one hour later, Pommy's head hurt. He picked a way through the destruction, as the sirens and others sounds of civilised salvation began to overpower those of rampant destruction. A figure appeared to the left, causing Pommy to stop. Face filthy, hair tangled, nose trailing a mixture of blood and mucus, it was Genevieve. Pommy offered his arm. 'Hello, my dear, I was wandering when we might meet.'

Without speaking, Genevieve put her arm through his, and together they strode from the zoo.

sixty-six

Pommy slammed down the telephone. This was not what he had wanted. In the hour or so since the joint statement to the markets from himself and Jennings there had been no end of reporters on the line. The first Pommy had considered an aberration. Yet by the time he got the last one off the line it became clear that they were only interested in one thing: the fucking party.

'Jenny! This is fucking ridiculous. Few high-enders get crispy and everything goes to the fucking mango hut.'

Pommy got up and wandered round the room as his secretary awaited further instruction. She could always tell when further instruction was coming, one of the reasons Pommy held her in such high regard. Not like some of them.

'Where's that lot?' Pommy demanded. Jenny thought for a minute.

'Mr Humphreys is in a meeting, Mr McClintock . . . eh, I don't know where he is. And Mr Barne went . . . home . . . sick, I think. That's what Deborah, his secretary told me.'

Pommy stopped pacing.

'When did Barne go home sick?'

'I think, shortly after news came in of the announcement. About the takeover not happening anymore,' Jenny said, without a hint of judgement.

'Right. Well, find the other two. Get Midgely to call Barne. He'll know what to say, don't worry.'

Over the next two days Pommy did receive much of the coverage he had envisioned and desired. That first morning news of the party proved a distraction for many, there being a

312

fair number of those in attendance who did something or other in The City. And while the market is more than willing to crush countries or annihilate companies, it is also capable of being distracted with concern over the fate of its own. The market does have feelings. Yet it cannot halt forever and within appropriate hours the whirr is on again and business is business is business.

Pommy Freiberg and Lawson Jennings appeared at a series of suitably public events, visibly enjoying each other company, scotching rumours that beneath the surface all manner of tensions and fissures were forming. At each of these events Pommy dealt with the odd question about his role at the infamous London Zoo party and how he rescued his wife from the jaws of death. Poor, poor Genevieve, for whom the shock of the party was exacerbated by the possibility of criminal prosecution for breaches of safety regulations. Poor Genevieve, who lost so much in that single night. TipTop McGee, trampled in the attempt to guide the stampeding guests to an alternative exit. Jill Prestwick, burned alive in the radio control room, last seen against a wall of flame, fingers still jabbing wildly at the switches in front of her. Olly Hampton, a mental and physical wreck, bones broken and mind run amok, left behind somewhere in the carnage. Three other staff, dead, found among the wreckage, including Jurgen, still in position. And no one could ever forget the image of Genevieve at the funeral of her indispensable assistant Charlotte, asphyxiated in a storage marquee where she had gone to ... to ... who knows? There was so very much to consider. Twenty-four fatalities in all, not including the animals that had to be shot or put down. Poor, poor Lionel Partridge, limp body found hanging in his bijou apartment, a note of immense regret and a bequest of all funds for the restoration of the insect house: 'the least appreciated and most misunderstood of creatures'.

Through this time Pommy was a rock, standing by his wife in a variety of poses; at the bedside, in the church, outside the coroner's office. And although he would have been there if need be, Pommy did not need to stand outside the court. There was no prosecution, criminal or private. Nor was there ever going to be, once the true culprit was identified and his story told. So entered Jonathan Greenmeadow into folklore. Such a nice name, such a nice English name. Such lovely children, and such a lovely wife. How could he have treated her like that? Forcing them to flee to her parents. And then this obsession with sex and sports cars and the fast life; the need to destroy it all. He had everything, an intelligent man with a beautiful family. But the signs were there, on the front pages: the testimony of colleagues and kitchen staff, the assaulting of workmates, and the doctor's notes. And the arrest. Why did the police let him go? Helmets rolled for that. The burnt corpse found at the zoo. Evil man.

No-one ever saw the photographs of Jonathan entwined with Pommy Freiberg, their bodies a writhing mass on the ground, as posed by Nick and Alison once Pommy was unconscious. Pommy had seen them, of course. Rather admired them. It showed that Durning had been listening, showed that he had learnt about the successful combination of analysis and action. Yes, fucking Durning had seen that the resources before him offered a new, improved opportunity, one that Pommy would find more difficult to shake off than mere photos of hanky-panky. No, it certainly wouldn't do for Pommy to have been connected in any way, let alone a sexual way, to the deranged killer responsible for the "Atrocity at London Zoo!" headlines. No, had to hand it to fucking Durning; clever stuff, clever chap. As such it was far better to have him around again, rather than away. Ideal replacement for Jennings once he walks the plank.

On a beach, Nick and Alison waited, far, far away. Having lived the wrong life for so long, it was time to live the right one. They were happy to travel for quite a while yet, knowing it was all worked out. Knowing that when everything had quietened down, Nick, Alison and the children would return. Nick in particular was looking forward to going back to work.

314